To Oscar,
with [...]

Jas ma [...]
November 2003

# THE SCROLLS

Merry Christmas!
Love Nick & Lowell
12-23-03

This book is dedicated
with love and appreciation
to my dear wife Elizabeth whose help
and encouragement made all this possible.

# THE SCROLLS

*John's Voice in the Wilderness*

**George Truett Moore**

Copyright © 2003 by George Truett Moore.
Library of Congress Number: 2003093153
ISBN: Hardcover 1-4134-0938-5
Softcover 1-4134-0937-7

All rights reserved. No part of this book may be reproduced or transmitted in any form or by any means, electronic or mechanical, including photocopying, recording, or by any information storage and retrieval system, without permission in writing from the copyright owner.

This is a work of fiction. Names, characters, places and incidents either are the product of the author's imagination or are used fictitiously, and any resemblance to any actual persons, living or dead, events, or locales is entirely coincidental.

This book was printed in the United States of America.

**To order additional copies of this book, contact:**
Xlibris Corporation
1-888-795-4274
www.Xlibris.com
Orders@Xlibris.com
19084

# PROLOGUE

It was the last thing he would see, the reflection of the blazing torch moving rapidly along the edge of the descending blade. He lay on his back, forcefully held down by two guards. He could have closed his eyes, but he would not. He faced his death; eyes wide open.

There was hardly time to feel any pain. The cut was swift and true, the work of a skilled executioner. The cleanly severed head fell to one side as the blood spurted across the rough stone floor. The headless body jerked violently, but was quickly stilled, lifeless. Darkness, powerful darkness; and then the light, the awesome light, which only he could see, even without his eyes!

He didn't see the rest, the young guard on his left stumbling out into the passageway as he threw up. The older guard on the other side did not move. It was deep inside he felt sick, painfully sick. Fighting and killings had been a major part of his adult life and should have hardened him to this, but he still felt sick. This one was wrong, so terribly wrong! Here was no criminal, no thief, no rebel. This was a simple man, a man of the desert. Some had called him a holy man.

However, there was something more disturbing. He was certain; somehow he knew it would not end here. This death would bear fruit, bitter fruit for those above. It would not be his doing. He simply obeyed orders. Their fate would be in other hands, the hands of the gods. Of course there was Yahweh, but you had to wonder. He had failed to save this one!

His thoughts were interrupted by a loud, impatient voice. The executioner, the soldier sent to do what was commanded, was on his way immediately, carrying the head a large platter. He gripped tightly the burden with bloodstained fingers, also wishing it had never happened, that he had not been the one to carry out the order. Moving carefully up the sloping corridor to the steps, painfully aware of the noisey sound of his heavy sandals on the stones, his whole body was drenched with sweat. Adding to his discomfort were the cries of anguish from those chained to the dungeon walls far below. They knew what he had done!

More riveting were the reactions of the host and guests. As the soldier of the guard entered, carrying the head, a spoken sentence was never finished. A laugh caught in the throat and ended in a cough. There was silence, total silence. Minutes went by before anyone dared speak.

The daughter, who had expressed her mother's wishes for the head, quickly forgot the applause and praise for her senseous dance. She paled at the sight, as did all the others. What had seemed so right in silencing criticism of royalty had now turned sour. What had started out on such a light, even frivolous, note, was no longer laughable. The drama had turned to tragedy, a tragedy filled with ominous overtones.

They were afraid, even the mother whose fury and pent-up anger had demanded this. Her evil, resentful wishes had been realized, but no one was sharing her satisfaction. Death was visible, pushing its cold, clammy face into every mind and soul present. Some shivered, as though the heat of the summer night had suddenly been swept away. They were gripped by the horrible thought of their own future fate. They were afraid!

And the host? Both regret and fear; regret for having made such a foolish promise and a fear he had never known before. He, too, knew this was wrong, something that would haunt him as long as he lived.

Under other circumstances no one would have wakened

the next morning until the sun had risen high above the eastern hills. Too much eating and drinking, too many dancing girls stirring passions out of control, did not make for early risers.

Not this morning! The sun was barely up when the exodus began. First, the guests with their servants, guards and carriers, quickly saying their goodbyes, anxious to be on their way down the winding road. They would not return.

The host and family were not far behind. Servants, slaves and guards moved rapidly to assist. Sharp commands demanded immediate action. All were quite ready to leave the fortress.

Overhead, in the clear, cloudless sky, the eagles soared silently, far above the human tragedy played out below. Their slow and effortless gliding on the westward winds seemed to reflect the sadness of Yahweh's world, a world burdened with its grief!

# BOOK ONE
## *The Promise*

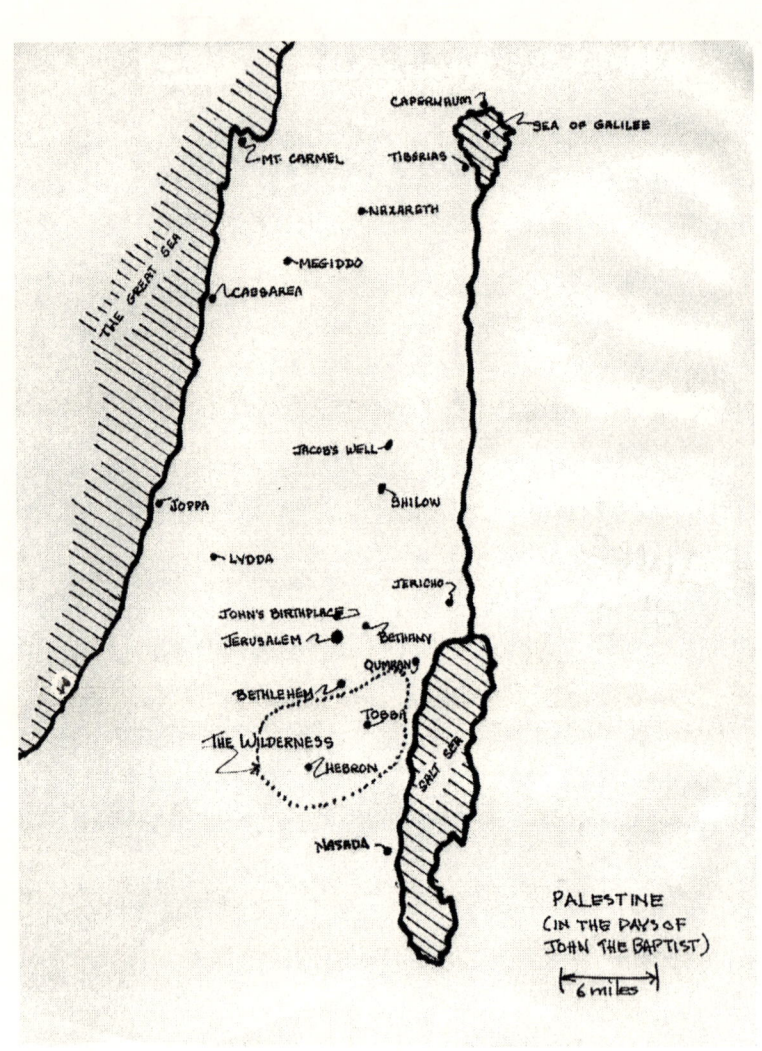

# CHAPTER 1

*There was a priest named Zechariah, of the division
of Abijah; and he had a wife of the daughters
of Aaron, and her name was Elizabeth . . .
but they had no child, because Elizabeth was barren,
and both were advanced in years.*

Luke 1:5b-7

Zechariah, eyesight going bad, wasn't sure. He questioned what he was seeing and couldn't believe what he was hearing! Sometimes the sweet odor and billowing smoke of the burning incense made him dizzy. He had to wonder. Perhaps his wife Elizabeth was right, that it was time to give up his duties in the Temple. His good friend Jonathan, leader of his Division, had hinted the same. It wasn't an order, only a subtle suggestion.

"Zechariah," he had said more than once and in a variety of ways, "old age is catching up with us and we both have to think about retiring. You have been a faithful servant of Yahweh for many years and you deserve more time with your dear Elizabeth. Think about that, seriously."

As for his unexpected visitor who called himself Gabriel, if he was sent from Yahweh, he was in the wrong place talking to the wrong person.

The High Priest, standing alone in the Holy of holies, should be the one receiving messages from Yahweh, not old Zechariah. Why would divine messengers speak to ordinary priests? Sure, he was one of Yahweh's chosen. He thought of himself as a good priest. At the same time, he was well aware of his status. No question about it. Yahweh should go to the top, not the bottom!

Yet, here he was, right at Zechariah's elbow, suggesting his wife was going to have a baby. That was crazy! Any talk about Elizabeth being pregnant at her age was ridiculous. They found that out long ago. Some women were destined to be barren, just as the writings of Moses described it. There was that passage from Job. It was about another matter, but it sure seemed to fit their situation. "The Lord gave and the Lord has taken away. Blessed be the name of the Lord."

It wasn't that they hadn't tried. Over the years they had enjoyed their marriage relationship. Their long-ago wedding was not an arranged affair. It was a love affair! As a young priest he had made his own choice. Beautiful Elizabeth, daughter of Elkanah the Levite, had caught his eye when she was 16, and he was determined to marry her.

Admiring her from a distance, he kept looking for a chance to express his feelings, and it finally came. What a picture, a scene he would never forget! She had been walking with her father in the Court of Women, just as he was leaving the Court of Priests.

Elkanah was on his way to offer the Evening Sacrifice. Being acquainted with the older priest, he joined them, bowed properly before the renowned Levite and offered to escort Elizabeth to her waiting servants. To his delight Elkanah agreed. They were alone!

As they walked side by side, and before they arrived at Solomon's Porch and the stairs leading down from the Temple Mount, Zechariah poured out both his compliments and feelings.

"Elizabeth," he almost shouted, "you might not believe this

and I know it sounds crazy, but I'm in love! I knew the moment I first saw you I wanted to marry you. This has to be Yahweh's doings. How else can I explain it? You have to say yes! And I'll do it properly. I'll talk to your parents!"

His words, as he remembered, were spilled out in tumbled profusion, looking for some response in her lovely eyes. Somewhere in their conversation he noted their heritage. Both were descended from ancient Aaron, brother to Moses. It would be a marriage made in heaven! Neither Elkanah nor her mother could object to that. He was a priest and she was the daughter of a priest!

Amazing! Miracle of miracles! There was, indeed, a response. The smile on her lips and the sparkle in her eyes were enough. He knew their wedding would become a reality! Little did he know at the time, she had been admiring him from a distance, long before. The meeting at the Court of Women was no accident. Elizabeth knew the one she wanted, a young priest by the name of Zechariah!

He was right. In less than a year they were man and wife. It was a simple, but beautiful wedding, first celebrated in the home of Elkanah and, later, in his own humble home just north of Jerusalem.

He loved his wife Elizabeth and their shared experiences were delightful. After each time away from her, taking his turn in the Temple, he wanted nothing more than to rush home. The many wonderful times of intimacy, of intercourse, were natural expressions of that love. He couldn't have asked for more. He had been richly blessed!

As to the matter of Elizabeth having babies, not having a child around kept them closer to each other without any distractions. He was quite content with both home life and Temple duties.

However, he knew that was selfish. Elizabeth really wanted a child. Not having one was a disgrace in the eyes of her friends, especially those with children. She had prayed to Yahweh many times, and complained to Zechariah, always asking the same questions:

"My friends have children, lots of children. Why doesn't Yahweh answer my prayers, give me at least one child? Why should I be put to shame, with everyone calling me barren, wondering what's wrong with me? Anyway, aren't you supposed to have some influence with Yahweh, you or Jonathan or someone doing all that praying in the Temple?"

As the years went by, knowing now the impossibility of her bearing a child, he tried to avoid any confrontation over the subject. He would listen patiently to his wife's complaints; nod his head, then make some excuse to slip away to other duties.

Yet, she was right. Zechariah knew it and was distressed over her hurt. He, truly, shared her concerns, and her questions. He had done his best to console her, and he, too, had prayed about it! But, for whatever reason, Yahweh had seen fit to deny them that joy.

So, in response to this strange but eloquent speaker, he gave the only rejoinder possible, expressing his frustration over what had not happened in their earlier years.

"Now you come, but it's too late. I am an old man and so is my wife. Her periods stopped long ago. What you are suggesting is impossible! You ought to know that. You are talking to the wrong person, if you are from Yahweh."

Zechariah was hardly prepared for what was to come, the angry, blistering response from this unwelcome intruder.

"I am Gabriel and I have come from Yahweh himself! You two have always wanted a child. Your wife Elizabeth has prayed for one, over and over again. You have tried to comfort her, help her. Now your prayers are being answered and you don't believe it.

"Are you refusing to accept what I am telling you, simply because of your age? Don't you know that with Yahweh all things are possible? He does things when he wants to do things. He has chosen this time for your child to be conceived, a child he will use for his purpose.

"I told you that in the beginning. Elizabeth will have that

child. As for you, because you won't believe what I'm saying, you will not be able to speak, not until the child is born!"

Zechariah had to lean against the altar, reaching for the supports near the edge of the stone. Now he did feel faint and dizzy. Was he losing his mind? This was more than he could handle. Had this visitor, now disappeared, really come from Yahweh? And what he had said, could it be true? It can't be true!

Outside, the people were beginning to wonder. Pretty soon they were voicing their own complaints.

"Why is this Evening Sacrifice taking so long? Surely he has said the prayers, all the prayers. What's keeping him?"

"It's time for our final blessing before the sun goes down!"

"Old Zechariah must have forgotten his lines," one laughed. "He's getting senile."

"The sun will be setting soon. It is time for him to come out and bless us before we have to leave, before the Sabbath begins."

The questions came from more than one worshipper. They were not only wondering what was going on inside, but becoming more impatient by the minute. Religion was fine, but there was a limit. Daylight would be gone soon, and they would have to hurry home in the dark. The shadow-filled, darkening, narrow streets of old Jerusalem were not safe. It was time to depart!

All that ended as Zechariah came out, visibly shaken, pale and speechless! It was impossible for him to do more than raise both arms in blessing.

The crowd drew back. The old priest had seen something; something frightening, perhaps a heavenly vision, and they weren't about to get involved. Zechariah's face was as white as the High Priest's linen shawl and he could not speak!

However, as they began to leave the Temple area, homeward bound, the murmuring, the talk, began again, intensified the farther they walked. All this would be shared with their friends and neighbors for days to come.

"Old Zechariah had a vision . . . perhaps it was an angel, or a spirit. Something has left him speechless!"

"We were there!"

"We saw it with our own eyes!"

Others chose to think that sort of speculation was nonsense.

"Old Zechariah probably had an upset stomach. He is just too old for Temple duties!"

As for Zechariah, he turned his back on the people and moved slowly toward the priest's quarters. Most days he looked forward to the evening meal with his fellow workers. They could relax, share their stories of the day, and tell the latest jokes. Nowadays, the new High Priest, Joseph of Sepphoris, was not exempt from their light-hearted jests. He was a natural for all their suggestive stories about priests, coming as he did from Galilee, and from the house of Boethus. To them he was an outsider, a stranger. On top of that, he was hard to get along with, never very friendly.

Tonight Zechariah was in no mood for companionship or funny stories. He wasn't hungry and wanted to be left alone. His head was spinning. That mysterious encounter at the altar had shaken his life and he needed time to think. To the others he made excuses, pointing to his neck as though a sore throat prevented him from speaking. He desperately needed time to sort everything out before tomorrow's part of the Sabbath and his final day of duty. Then he would have to go home to Elizabeth and see what she might think. He would have to tell her!

His self-imposed isolation didn't last long. His Division leader, Jonathan, rushed in; questions tumbling out in rapid succession.

"Zechariah, what happened at the altar? I'm told you had a vision! Was it a messenger from Yahweh? If so, what did he say? Why can't you speak now? Tell me if any of this is true! All the other priests on duty are upset, excited, and even afraid. Everyone is talking about it and I need some answers!"

Question after question after question, and Zechariah unable to respond! However, as Jonathan paused to catch his breath,

Zechariah held up his hand to get his attention. With a mixture of sign language and writing, he told him the whole story. As best he could, he described what he had seen and heard. Finally, writing in big letters, he asked his friend what he thought about this strange and frightening episode. Then there was one more question, which Zechariah knew both were thinking,

"What do I do now, and what do I tell Elizabeth?"

Jonathan, faced with something beyond his ability to comprehend, had only one answer.

"This is a matter you cannot hide. However, we must keep the story simple, but tell the truth. You had a vision and only time will tell what it all means. The vision was real and you are unable to speak, not now. And don't try to write out an explanation. No details! We will leave it at that.

"After your regular period of rest, you will be back, doing those things which will require no speaking. Surely your voice will return soon, in spite of what your visitor said. Perhaps then we will understand. That's the best we can do.

"On the other hand, we will say absolutely nothing about the prophecy concerning a child. That will stir up too many other questions and you and Elizabeth don't need that. Who knows, it may never happen!

"Zechariah, you might be quite a man, but I doubt you can pull this off! Let's wait and see. Yet, remember this, if Yahweh really has his hand in all this, it will happen, just as you were told."

After their talk together, almost a one-sided conversation, Zechariah felt better. He rejoined his fellow priests, nibbled at the food and shared a glass of wine. Jonathan did his best to explain the vision, enough reason for anyone to lose his voice. Apparently it was Yahweh's way of letting his faithful priests know the Temple sacrifices were acceptable. At the same time he did his best to play it down, reminding all present that Yahweh works in mysterious ways. He was sure all their questions would be answered in Yahweh's own good time. This called for patience on their part. The less said the better.

Trying to divert their attention, he laid out a revised schedule of Temple duties for tomorrow's Sabbath and for their return on their next tour of duty. Not a thing was said about the promise of a child. Jonathan knew his priests, their inability to keep a secret, especially like this one. That would have to wait.

Zechariah didn't sleep well that night. Restless and upset he tossed and turned until the dark hours before dawn. Finally he dozed off, only to dream. Above him the heavens opened and he heard voices, deep thundering voices calling his name. Suddenly the voices changed, coming not from the heavens, but from his little village. Now it was Elizabeth's voice calling for help.

"Zechariah, help me! I'm having a baby, not just one baby, but three babies. Come! Help me! I can't do this by myself! Where are you, Zechariah? You must come home, now!"

Zechariah sat up, perspiring and shaken. He realized it was only a dream, but one far too real. Tomorrow he would have to go home and tell Elizabeth about his vision, but how could he tell her with no way of using his voice? He had hoped that, too, was a part of the dream, but it was not. Several times during the night he had tried to talk, but couldn't. He had lost his voice! That part of Gabriel's prediction was true.

Rising earlier than the others and after washing, taking care of his personal needs, Zechariah began preparing the morning meal, water from the Temple cistern, bread from the oven and some leftover meat from yesterday's sacrifice. It was still good, but what was left from the morning meal would have to be given away. Meat spoiled quickly in the heat of the day. He wanted a cup of wine to clear his head, but thought better of that. Such would not be fitting this early.

As the others began to gather, they moved into the inner part of the Temple, dressed for prayer. They would thank Yahweh that they were his people, true sons of Abraham. That was important and they did that every day. They were Yahweh's chosen and they would come into his presence with singing! Only Zechariah's voice would be muted. He would pray and sing from the heart, silently.

Early morning was their favorite time of the day. It was quiet, with only the priests on duty present. It might be called Herod's Temple, but it belonged to Yahweh! It was a beautiful work of art, the crowning jewel of the Jewish nation. The very best in stone, cedar, sandalwood, gold and silver had gone into the construction, evidence of a national treasure. The Temple was a thing of beauty, indeed! The tall marble columns above them added to that beauty. The stonemasons, some of them priests, had spent years on the carvings. There was a lot more work to be done, but one could appreciate the design, the planning that attracted visitors from all over the world. This was an awesome structure. This was Yahweh's dwelling place! They, of all people, were most richly blessed. They were standing on holy ground!

After prayers, and after sharing a modest meal, they began to gather the morning sacrifices for those who would come from the city and the surrounding villages. Some would be coming from distant lands, speaking-other-languages people, but they, too, were sons and daughters of Abraham. It would be an exciting day!

All that would give the priests plenty to do. Today, being the Sabbath, many more would come, some bringing their own sacrificial animals and birds, some bringing their tithes. The animals and birds would have to be examined for blemishes and foreign coins would have to be exchanged.

Seldom did the animals and birds measure up to demanded standards. Most would have to be replaced with those provided by the priests, animals and birds that must be purchased. The same was true for the coins; only the official Temple money was permitted inside the Temple area. In Yahweh's holy Temple everything had to be perfect!

Again, such rules and requirements meant additional revenue. After all, it was an expensive operation and building costs were rising. Between reverence for Yahweh's dwelling place and the desire for additional income, everything had a price. Although few would admit it, the revenue factor sometimes outweighed the matter of perfection in the Temple area. As long as it benefited the Temple hierarchy, Sabbath rules on work and travel were usually ignored. Only the Pharisees objected.

Jonathan assigned Zechariah to the table for exchanging money. He was sure he could handle that easily enough with a sort of sign language, especially for those who came from other countries and who spoke no Hebrew or Aramaic.

Zechariah was grateful. At least he had enough seniority to escape the worst duty, handling the sacrificial animals and birds, and then cleaning up at the end of the day. No matter how much worshippers were reminded this was Yahweh's dwelling place, there was always trash. Some people might not be permitted to work on the Sabbath, but priests and helpers had their duties, no matter the day of the week. It would be a busy schedule and he would leave little time for worrying about yesterday. Such would have to wait until sunset and the trip home.

As the day's end approached, Zechariah wished the hour for departure would come sooner. He was glad to see the sun going down. The whole day had been frustrating. The moneychanger duty was far more difficult than he could have imagined. With the inability to use his voice, a lot of the pilgrims thought he was handicapped in more ways than one. They made their complaints to anyone who would listen.

"Isn't the Temple the place for 'perfect' things, and 'perfect' people?"

Of greater concern was his trip home. He kept wondering how he could handle the many questions he knew would be asked. It was a terrible distraction! Those thoughts were constantly creeping into his mind. He simply could not concentrate fully on the task before him.

What would be Elizabeth's reaction to the news he knew he must share with her? How would she deal with the predictions of what was to come, what Zechariah was told would happen? You don't just rush in and say, or write, "You're going to have a baby because a stranger told me so in a vision!"

That wouldn't make sense. He knew she wasn't pregnant! She knew that and she would think he had lost his mind, bringing a story about a mysterious visitor who suddenly appeared and, just as abruptly, disappeared. How would he be able to handle that?

Finally, both silence and shadows began to fall across the arches, the latticework, the columns, and the pavement. The Sabbath was over! The people had departed and there was nothing more to do, except to gather his belongings for the trip home.

As he walked along the streets and out into the countryside, those traveling with him began to drop off, one by one. They said little, knowing Zechariah could not respond by voice. Also, they were hesitant to speak to one who had seen a vision! To them he was a special person now, almost an oddity. How do you relate to one who gets a visit from a heavenly messenger? Most still felt apprehensive and somewhat afraid. There was the mystery of it all. Jonathan had talked in riddles, never having fully explained the vision.

However, once they arrived home it would be different. There they would try to impress their neighbors with what they had seen and heard. Zechariah was in their Division, the Division of Abijah! Their group would have a special niche in the history of the nation. They were sure of that!

As he approached his own village Zechariah caught his first glimpse of Elizabeth. Even in the fading light he could see her, waiting, standing alone by the old olive tree just above their home. With no word of greeting she came forward, embraced him, smiled, kissed him, took his two hands in hers and looked deep into his eyes. They stood still for the longest time and then Elizabeth took his hand and gently led him down the hill into the house. She had heard!

The house wasn't much as you looked at it from the outside. There was a woven branch shelter over the cooking and eating areas. Walls were almost non-existent. There was an enclosed area inside, inside the cave, or grotto. Here there was real shelter and privacy. It was not typical of the homes in their little village, but it was theirs! A stonewall which Zechariah had built years ago separated this area from the outside and was lighted at night by a small oil lamp. Their bed, set on a raised clay base, was made of feathers sewn into a woven cloth bag. It was laid on top of fresh branches from the palm trees, something that had to be changed and refreshed often.

Their meager possessions and keepsakes were set along the vertical side of the cave. Nothing was locked away for there were no locks. Anyway, no one would have dared enter the home of another without an invitation. "You shall not steal" was Yahweh's word of law and you did not disobey Yahweh!

Elizabeth hurried to prepare the evening meal, some cereal, a piece of meat and, tonight, a glass of wine, good wine. They ate slowly and quietly. Zechariah thanked Yahweh for the gifts and asked his blessing upon the food, themselves, their home and their village. He thanked Yahweh for the deliverance of their ancestors out of Egypt. Of course, Zechariah could not speak, but the prayer was made, the same prayer he had offered day after day. As such, Elizabeth knew precisely what Zechariah was saying, even without the hearing.

It was completely dark now. Elizabeth cleared away and cleaned the bowls and cups as quickly as possible. It was time to talk! Both knew there was much to share. The neighbors made sure Elizabeth had heard about Zechariah's experience, and now she wanted some answers. She needed to hear from her own husband the details of this reported vision. Was it for real or was Zechariah beginning to see things that didn't exist? To say the least, she was deeply disturbed. Beyond that, there was a fearful anxiety that refused to go away! She believed there was more, much more than what the friends and neighbors had shared.

The little oil lamp did not help much, but at least they could see each other. Elizabeth spoke:

"My dear husband," she began, "I was told by our neighbor Sarah, and by many others, you had a vision yesterday at the time of the Evening Sacrifice. I've heard nothing else since. Some have said it was a vision of a man, a messenger from Yahweh. After he departed you came out from the altar area, speechless.

"Zechariah, is that true? If it was a man, who was he? What did he say to you? Why was he talking to you? If he was from Yahweh he should have been talking to the High Priest, not you! It's not that you are unimportant, but Joseph of Sepphoris is the High Priest, not you! He is Yahweh's leader of Israel. Even I know that!

"But, if he had a message for you, it had to be something very special, something for both of us. My husband, I am almost afraid to ask."

As she paused and looked intently into Zechariah's face, tears filled his eyes. How could he answer her, communicate what he longed to share with her? How would she receive the news, the prediction about a child?

He stood up, wiped his eyes, searching for a piece of an old scroll. Finding it and a writing pen, he began to put down the story. His emotions didn't help; neither did the rough paper he had turned over to find a place to pour out those momentous events of the night before. Nevertheless, slowly, carefully, he began to write:

"Standing at the altar, I was almost through with the Evening Sacrifice. Then it happened! As the smoke began to clear I saw a man standing on my right. He said his name was Gabriel and that he was a messenger sent from Yahweh. He began with a strange story about a child to be born, that he would be very special, filled with the Holy Spirit. He would turn people to Yahweh, and would prepare for the coming of Yahweh's promised Messiah.

"That child would be ours, born to us, Elizabeth! He said you were going to have a baby boy!"

It was Elizabeth's turn to lose her voice, pale and grasp for support. Finally she responded, choking on every word.

"Zechariah, you cannot be serious. That's impossible! After all these years we can't have a baby. You know that and I know that! This Gabriel was, indeed, talking to the wrong one!"

There was a long silence, Elizabeth looking at her husband, still unable to speak, and Zechariah looking at her. Both knew, without any need for voice, Yahweh had touched their lives and nothing would ever be the same again. Both knew, deep inside, this messenger from Yahweh was not a dream, the figment of their imagination. Surprisingly, suddenly, Elizabeth laughed, almost hysterically.

"Just think! After all these years, after all these years of wanting, praying for a child, I'm promised a baby boy! Now, I can't believe it! I'm saying, we're both saying, it's impossible. We both know that. Yet Yahweh says we are wrong! I will give birth to a child, a baby boy!"

Her last sentence was almost a shout, but as Zechariah reached out to hold her close and calm her outburst, she had one more question.

"If all this is so, if we will have a child, why can't you talk about it? Surely Yahweh would not keep you from speaking concerning the prophecy. I sure don't want the word to get around, not now, but why can't you talk? Is that what happens when Yahweh comes near?"

Zechariah had to write again, confessing his own words of disbelief to Yahweh's messenger. He gave her Gabriel's response and the verdict of silence, which would last until the child was born. He then reassured her. No one, other than Jonathan, knew anything about the promise of a child.

For a long time they sat in silence, individual thoughts tumbling back and forth until they were mentally exhausted. The questions were almost too much to handle. It was time to let them rest. Deeply concerned for her husband's traumatic experience and his inability to speak, Elizabeth helped him up, extinguished the little oil lamp, and led him to their bed. Holding him close, the warmth of her body stirred an almost forgotten response from Zechariah, and it happened! That night a child was conceived, a child promised by Yahweh's own special messenger, Gabriel. Both were right. Their lives would never be the same again!

# CHAPTER 2

*After these days his wife Elizabeth conceived,
and for five months she hid herself . . . .*
                                        Luke 1:24

Obviously, Elizabeth knew it first. It wasn't a matter of losing a period. Those had stopped years before. It started with the nausea that came early one morning. She had never felt that way before. It was far more than an upset stomach, most disturbing in its intensity. Something was happening to her, something different. It couldn't be, but it had to be. She was going to have that baby. This wasn't a dream, or her imagination. She was pregnant!

No one had any idea just how much Zechariah and Elizabeth had wrestled with the possibilities. Both knew the prediction of Yahweh's messenger, Gabriel, was something utterly impossible. Yet, both knew they had to take Yahweh seriously. They could not escape the awareness that the unbelievable was believable. It couldn't happen, but it would happen!

That raised another concern, Elizabeth's health. Would she be able to survive the ordeal of carrying and delivering a baby? Would they actually become parents of a child at their age?

Sometimes, in the middle of the night, Elizabeth would get up. Without disturbing Zechariah, she would step outside and sit on the low wall, adjacent to their home. Resting next to the myrtle tree in full bloom, watching the stars moving overhead, she would ask a lot of questions, silently.

"From the first day we were married, I have wanted a baby. That's natural, isn't it? Every woman wants to have a baby. For years we have tried, but now that we have been told we will have a child, a special child, we are worried. Is this right for us? Are we too old? It does not make any sense!"

Thinking how nice it would be if it were as simple as the myrtle tree bearing its fragrant berries, she would return to her bed. Back inside, she would nudge her husband to stop his snoring, and try to sleep. As far as she could tell nothing had changed. Perhaps the whole thing was an impossible dream. However, with that first wave of intense nausea, Elizabeth's questions were answered, her doubts erased. It was no dream. She would have that baby!

Zechariah was on duty at the Temple. It wasn't his Division's turn to serve, the Division of Abijah, but he was there. The High Priest and the other leaders depended on the older priests. They were needed to help train and direct the activities of the young men just entering the priesthood. Altogether, there were twenty-four divisions, involving hundreds of priests. Some survived, while others didn't. It was a rigious and demanding life. With new men coming in each year, there was much for the experienced men to do.

Above all, the routine was most important. Nothing was left to chance. Perfection was the goal in the worship of Yahweh. Such demanded a rigid schedule. Each division served only one week every six months. It was a problem, both the scheduling and the training! Priests like Zechariah were called upon frequently. All Division priests served in the liturgies of worship, the singing, the preparation and the offering of the sacrifices. For the more experienced ones, administrative and teaching duties were added.

It had been a rare privilege for Zechariah to burn the twice-daily incense in the Temple, but he was one of the best. It was also most unusual for one priest to be called on for special, ongoing duties, but Zechariah was special! He would not return home until the close of the next Sabbath.

Zechariah did have other work, as most priests did. Oil was his business, olive oil. He had inherited the property from his grandfather. This would have been handed down from his father, but he, also a priest, had died young. The business came directly to Zechariah.

His olive tree grove was large, and the trees were very old. However, the oil that came from his olive press was the finest. His was the only oil used in the Temple lamps! There were times he wished he could rid himself of the business, but he would not. It was his tie to family, generations of family. Also, it was a good source of income, even though hired help did all the labor. As a priest, his zeal for Temple affairs, for the worship of Yahweh, he kept holding on. His oil was top quality!

What bothered Elizabeth most was the need for secrecy, something Jonathan believed to be best. Anyway, how could she face her neighbors? What would they think of her, an old woman expecting a baby? She would be the laughing stock of the village. Some would even wonder about the father. She could hear them now.

"Surely, old Zechariah couldn't father a child at his age!"

"If you ask me, there are some strange things going on in that house."

She wanted to go up to the top of the nearest hill and shout to any and all her astounding news; not only was she going to have a baby, but this baby's birth was being determined by Yahweh himself! Yahweh's own messenger had come to her husband and told him so. Even their son's name had already been chosen.

Yet, she dare not. Soon enough they would be the talk of

the village, with a lot of unkind remarks and suggestions. Many would laugh at them, two old people going to be parents for the first time. Besides, and this was the more critical point, they had been assured there was more to it than just another birth. With Yahweh's hand involved, this child was going to be Yahweh's child! That's precisely what Gabrial had told Zechariah: "He will turn many to Yahweh."

Zechariah had remembered, written down Gabriel's words of promise, but neither he nor she had been able to reach any satisfactory understanding of the divine prediction. To them it made little sense, this talk about the Holy Spirit and ancient Elijah.

Was their son really going to grow up to be a prophet for Yahweh? It was all the more disturbing because they knew they would never live to see how it turned out. They were too old!

Almost every day Elizabeth or Zechariah, or both, would go over the litany of questions.

"Why does Yahweh want us to have this child? What does He want to do with him? What will happen to him if he isn't able or is unwilling to do what Yahweh wants? Will he be able to marry and raise a family, to have a son to carry on our family name?"

The one thing they did know at the moment was the promise becoming a reality. She was pregnant! Yet, they couldn't talk about it or tell what they could not understand. They, like everyone else, would have to wait.

It wasn't long until Elizabeth began to make excuses to her village friends.

"I just don't feel well these days . . . it must be the weather . . . I think I have some sort of fever . . . my bones ache and I have to rest a lot . . . . no, I really don't feel like talking, or having company . . . if you don't mind I would rather be alone . . . really, I can manage by myself . . . I'll get back out and talk to you when I'm feeling better."

With those responses, with Elizabeth acting anti-social, with her apparent standoffish attitude, most of her neighbors stopped coming by.

"If Elizabeth wants to be like that, I'm not going to put myself out for her; if she doesn't want us around we'll just stay away."

One woman of the village voiced another explanation. Milcah and her husband Jamin lived farther out, but she was always dropping by to visit. Actually, she had the reputation of being the village gossip. Her explanation was very simple.

"Zechariah had a vision in the Temple. Now the two of them think they are better than the rest of us and want to ignore us. The only thing to do is to let them alone! Maybe they would do better to move away, move in with the High Priest!"

Her listeners laughed at the suggestion, but Elizabeth's closest friends were disturbed and upset. They weren't mad, just perplexed. Something strange was taking place and they wished they knew what. Ever since the day Zechariah came home speechless an obvious, subtle change was evident in both Elizabeth and Zechariah. There was far more to the situation than Elizabeth wanting to be alone!

Her best friend and neighbor, Deborah, sensed that and went to see her.

"Elizabeth, I hear what you are saying, and I don't want to upset you. And, if that is what you really want, I won't disturb you. But, please, let me know if there is anything I can do. We've known you and Zechariah a long time and we love you very much. We want the best for both of you! I know it is most difficult since the day of the vision and Zechariah losing his voice, but it is not the end of the world."

Tears welled up in Elizabeth's eyes and she reached out and hugged Deborah.

"I wish I could tell you, but I can't, not now! Please trust me! You will know soon enough."

With that she took Deborah's hand, kissed it, and releasing it, gently closed the curtain that separated the outer area of their home from their little room of privacy. Inside, alone, she lay down and cried, sobbing quietly!

As the days and weeks passed, Elizabeth began to go into Jerusalem with Zechariah. Whenever he was home and his services were needed, they would leave home quite early in the morning, before their neighbors were up. It was a way to minimize contact with their friends, especially those who were merely curious, looking for any tidbit of gossip.

The Division leader, Jonathan, was quite excited for them. It wasn't a matter of understanding, but one of accepting as true what the messenger Gabriel had promised. Now, sure of that, Jonathan saw Zechariah in a different light. He was far more than an old and experienced priest who could be of special assistance when needed. He was more than a good friend. He was one to whom Yahweh had spoken! Yahweh had chosen Zechariah and Elizabeth for something very special. This baby was going to be special! Jonathan was proud of the relationship!

So, each time she traveled in with her husband, Elizabeth stayed in Jonathan's home. His wife, Miriam, was most understanding, concerned for Elizabeth's health. It was a strain on their facilities and provisions, but helping Elizabeth was important. The secret would be protected in Jonathan's home, and the two women could share their experiences as wives of priests.

Miriam wasn't much help in dealing with a pregnant woman. She and Jonathan had no children. However, she did her best to make Elizabeth comfortable, preparing and serving dishes the expectant mother could enjoy. They did their best to be of help to their close friends facing parenthood.

It was unfortunate Zechariah had to be away so much, but the situation demanded it. With the change in the High priesthood and the coming of a new governor, a Caesar-appointed procurator, Jerusalem was in turmoil. The Temple didn't escape the upheaval or the excitement. No one knew just how much the political might affect the religious. It was critical and most important that all the priests, both old and young, carry out their assigned duties without any incident that might disturb the ruling authorities.

Also, the Temple had always been a refuge for anyone in trouble or at odds with their foreign rulers. Few knew about that and it was imperative to keep the secrets. For a number of years they had been able to get along with the Romans without any major problems, and the new High Priest, Joseph, wanted that to continue. Zechariah was most helpful, both as a stabilizing influence and as an instructor. Even though he had the present limitation of being voiceless, he was able to communicate his expertise quite well.

For Elizabeth, those trips became more infrequent. It was a long walk and she began to have trouble getting about. Miriam did her best to make Elizabeth comfortable, but she talked about the pregnancy over and over. If she wasn't talking about Elizabeth's condition, she was sharing all the news she knew concerning the city and the Temple. At this stage Elizabeth had no interest in Jerusalem matters and Miriam's chatter about Temple problems didn't help. She could care less! She wanted the quietness and security of her own simple home.

Finally, she resigned herself to staying home, inviting her best friend Deborah in to help. Once Deborah learned about the baby, she pitched in, doing all she could to make things easy for Elizabeth. She couldn't believe what was happening, and she wondered about the pregnancy, how it might tie in to Zechariah's vision. Could Yahweh have a hand in this? She could only guess because Elizabeth would not respond to such questions. She said absolutely nothing about the prophecy, but Deborah was excited. She was happy for her dear friend who had prayed so many times for a child. Also, you had to do a lot of planning and a lot of sewing for a new baby and she wanted to help!

"Elizabeth," she said, "You keep talking about a baby boy. How can you be so certain? I think you're simply guessing, or else it's wishful thinking. I'm sure it would really please Zechariah. All fathers want a son, a son to carry on his father's name. If it is true, if it is a boy, you will name him for his father, won't you?"

Elizabeth could only repeat what she had already said. She believed the baby would be a boy. It was just a feeling, intuition if you please, but she believed she was right. As to the suggestion about the name she said nothing. That would have to wait.

"It has to be a boy!" she would say.

After a time the rest of the village knew Elizabeth was expecting, but for the most part, still stayed away. Along with a priest of Yahweh not being able to talk and an expectant woman far too old to have children, it was too much to accept. They had never encountered anything so disturbing. The best thing was to keep their distance, and wait. There was the usual gossip about the father of the baby, but those stories finally faded away. Even Milcah had to admit there was nothing of substance in what was being said by others.

As the weeks went by it was only natural that other interests would consume the greater time and attention of the neighbors. Jerusalem was not that far away and they wanted to see what was taking place in the coming of a new Roman governor. Also, there was more to their village life than an old woman expecting a child. Daily work and duties were the more important things. Making it possible to survive under Roman rule demanded hard work and concentration. These were the things they could see, touch and handle, without any mystery involved. Trees, fields, sheep and shops needed their constant attention. Those with goods or produce to sell were kept busy traveling to Jerusalem and back. The best markets were in the city. Anyway, gossip was for the lazy, or for the rich.

After all, you couldn't talk to Zechariah and Elizabeth that much, even when Zechariah was home. They stayed inside most of the time, or else, Zechariah was up the valley, checking on his ripening olives. Even when they did talk, they told very little about all the strange events that had touched and changed them. Elizabeth had to do the talking for both and her responses were always quite brief. Any questions about the Temple event involving Zechariah were simply ignored.

That raised another question, and more speculation. Why

was Zechariah away so much of the time? Most priests, whether young or old, served only once every six months. What was so special about him? Did his frequent absences have anything to do with the greater mystery, his loss of voice and an old woman expecting a child?

However, if Zechariah and Elizabeth and their neighbors thought they had seen it all, they were wrong. They were totally unprepared for what was to come next, unexpected guests, strangers, coming all the way down from distant Galilee. For Zechariah and Elizabeth it would be more news, startling news from Yahweh's messenger, Gabriel! He was not going to leave them alone. There was much more to come! Yahweh did move in mysterious ways. For them, husband, wife and neighbors, the mystery intensified.

# CHAPTER 3

*.In the sixth month the angel Gabriel was sent
from God to a city of Galilee named Nazareth,
to a virgin betrothed to a man whose name was
Joseph, of the house of David;
and the virgin's name was Mary.*

*Luke 1:26,27*

Mary was a dreamer. It wasn't that she didn't have enough to do. Her father, Joachim, was stern and demanding. Mary knew he loved her and her two brothers, Levi and Nathaniel, but he expected them to be diligent, never lazy. The two sons had to work much harder than their sister, but her mother, Anna, kept Mary busy with household things; the cleaning, the washing, the sewing, the mending and the cooking. When needed at harvest time she, too, went to the fields and helped gather the grain.

Yet, there were times to relax and think of other things, something she enjoyed sharing with her closest friend. As young girls will do, both loved to dream. The two of them did that whenever they could get away from their daily tasks. Girl talk provided their own little world, away from daily chores and demanding parents.

The best time was late in the afternoon, just before the sun dropped toward the western sea. Sometimes they would talk of events and people of long ago, the heroes and heroines of their people. Then, there was the future. Someday their own heroes would come, marry them, and take them away to a new and exciting life. Their dreams were shared over and over again, spoken with the assurance these were their secrets.

Their vantage point was the ridge just above the village, the little town of Nazareth. It was quite a climb, but it was worth the effort. From there they could look to the northeast and on a clear day make out the blue of The Lake, the Sea of Gennesaret. Some called it the Sea of Tiberius, but that was a Roman name. Some called it the Sea of Galilee.

To the southeast was Mount Tabor. No one could miss that rounded hill standing apart from all the others, the juncture of the ancient territories of Issachar, Zebulan and Naphtali. Farther down to the southwest was Megiddo, Solomon's ancient fortress and the fertile Esdraelon valley. To the west was Elijah's mountain, Carmel, the "vineyard" of the Lord, overlooking the big sea. You couldn't quite see the neighboring village of Cana, but it was there, nestled in the next valley, a half-days walk to the north. They had friends there.

Mary's best friend was also named Mary, but she preferred to be called Miriam. Even though the names meant the same, her heroine was the sister of Moses and Aaron. They had been taught that Miriam was the first woman to be called a prophetess, and that appealed to the young girl and her dreams. That Miriam helped change the course of their nation's history in caring for her brother, the baby Moses. Friend Mary wanted to be called Miriam. One day everyone would remember her name! She was confident of that.

Mary's interests went in a different direction; the life of her people as the chosen ones, Yahweh's blessed. From her mother, first, and then from her father, Mary was instilled with a deep, burning desire for freedom in the land Yahweh had given their ancestors. Someday Yahweh would send the Anointed One promised by the prophets. He would come and drive out those terrible Romans and Israel would be restored, not only to serve

Yahweh, but also to be, as the prophet said, "a light to the nations."

Her people were a chosen people, a great people, going all the way back to David and Solomon. Sure, Moses was a part of that story, but King David was the greatest! He had fought for their nation and land. Yahweh would, someday, set things straight under the leadership of a new king like David!

That history was a part of their heritage and even though the girls had to be separated from the boys in the synagogue, they, too, learned about the prophets and the kings, how they led their ancestors under the guidance of Yahweh. They studied the divine prophecies of things to come. In those lay their hopes for the future.

Mary, above all the other girls in the village, took that seriously. She offered her own daily prayers for deliverance. She knew Yahweh would provide the way. Somehow He would come and set them free! Mary was a dreamer, but, above all, a believer!

Their dreams of the future had been stimulated recently by the passage of a camel caravan going down from Damascus to Egypt.

"Miriam, Miriam!" Mary called to her friend as she ran down the village street.

"Strangers are here, in our town, strangers riding on camels. We've never seen anything like this! Hurry!"

Quickly they joined families and friends, excited over that late afternoon arrival of tired and dusty travelers.

It was all the more exciting in that no caravan of any sort had ever stopped or come by way of Nazareth. Their town was small, an agricultural village with few shops, just an out-of-the-way town of little significance. There was a synagogue, but that had no appeal to travelers from distant lands. The main trade routes were to the east and west.

The visitors did not linger long, staying only two nights, They pitched their tents in the open pasture below the village, beautiful tents, large tents of a dark woven material, quite different from the local ones of goat's-hair. The rich, pungent odor of animals and hay permeated the air, adding to the excitement of the visit.

The men wore strange-looking clothes and colorful boots of soft leather. There were no women present; at least the girls saw none. But the men were so handsome, those who came to greet the village elders, asking permission to stop over, rest and water their animals.

That was quite a chore, carrying water from the town's one well, but there seemed to be lots of servants for that. It was an event to be remembered, the glow from the evening fires outside the tents, the soft sounds of music drifting up into the village. None could understand their language, but they managed to communicate the essentials.

No one really knew why they were traveling by way of Nazareth, but that didn't matter to Mary and Miriam. They made sure they were at the town well when the leaders of the caravan came to thank the elders for their hospitality. When they saw Mary and Miriam they stopped, smiled and bowed low to the ground.

Then, as they turned away, the tallest of the three men, obviously the leader, turned back again, looked deep into Mary's eyes, dropped to the ground and bowed his head before her! Dreams! They had more, much more, for days to come.

After the caravan moved on down the valley that was all the girls could talk about; traveling to distant places like Damascus, or even Jerusalem, David's city! Thinking about those handsome Egyptians they whispered to each other their thoughts on betrothal and marriage. They talked of meeting future husbands like those strangers, caring and wealthy husbands. The simple life style of their village would be replaced by travel and adventure! They would live in distant cities and wear beautiful clothing, with servants to care for their daily needs.

The burning question for Mary centered on the tall stranger. Why did he turn back and bow his head before her? What prompted him to do that? What did he see in her, a young girl living in a remote village? He didn't even know her name. She was quite sure she would never see him again! Yet she had an uneasy feeling, a strange sense of anticipation!

As the days went by, their dreams of travel and adventure were replaced by the realities of growing up. Then, there was something else, not quite what Mary expected. Her parents began to talk of arrangements.

"Mary," said her mother, "you are a young woman now. It is time for you and Miriam to put away your childhood dreams. Your father and I are getting older and we need to plan for your future. It will be some years before Levi and Nathaniel will be able to marry, but we must begin to look for a good husband for you."

"But, mother, I'm not ready for that. Besides, there is no one here I want to marry. All the eligible men in Nazareth are farmers, masons or carpenters. There are a few shepherds, but no one would want to marry them. There aren't even any young priests. I want a handsome man, a wealthy man, someone who will really love me, someone to take me away from this little village. I want to travel, visit cities, big cities!"

"Mary," her mother responded, "don't be silly! Anyway, love is something that comes with the years together. The main thing is a good home, a secure home, with a good, devout man. My parents arranged my marriage and that worked out fine! We will do the very same thing for you, and now is the time!"

Mary wanted to say "No!" She wanted to give voice to her strong protest, but she did not. She bowed in submission. She knew there was little she could do to change her parents' minds. At times they could be very stubborn and this seemed to be one of those situations. The only thing she could do was to share with Miriam what they both knew. Girls and their opinions didn't count!

Little did they know that others were thinking about the same, betrothal and marriage. Mary's future had already been discussed. Joseph, son of Jacob, had talked to his parents about her.

"The young girl Mary, daughter of Joachim and Anna, is my choice. I think she is a good girl. I know she is a devout girl, deeply concerned that our people remain faithful to Yahweh. Besides that, she works hard and gets along well with the other girls in the village. We have talked some, just a little bit at some of the festivals. I was impressed! I'm confident we have the same desire to serve the Most High and that is important to me."

Joseph hesitated, blushed, and then smiled.

"She is pretty, the prettiest girl in our town. Will you speak to her parents for me?"

Jacob and his wife, Zeruah, nodded in agreement.

Zeruah spoke for both.

"Yes, it is time for you to take a wife. You have spent years building your own home, preparing for the day you would marry.

"We are happy over your choice. We know her parents well, good friends of ours, and we like Mary! She will make you a good wife. Hopefully, she will bless us with many grandchildren. We will talk to them right away!"

They wasted no time. In response to Joseph's request, they called on Mary's parents the next evening. Son Joseph was getting on in years and they wanted to see him married, blessing them with grandchildren. Not only that, this was the first time he had shown any interest in any girl! It was time to act!

As expected, their visit started out with talk about many things, things other than the real purpose of their visit. Mary's parents knew why they had come, but courtesy and custom dictated the conversation. First things would come last!

"Welcome my good friends. We welcome you in the name of Yahweh. Jacob and Zeruah, you look well. Yahweh has truly blessed you!"

In his formal greeting, Joachim saluted both Jacob and his wife. After all, they had been neighbors for years, and good friends.

Jacob's response was a grateful thank you.

"Yes, we are well, and it is good to see you. We stay so busy these days, and hardly have time to visit. We trust you two are fine. How are your two sons and your daughter Mary? Your sheep! How many sheep do you have? Are they providing you with a good supply of wool? You know your reputation. Your wool is the finest around."

One had to include all the important things; both children and sheep were important!

Finally, after discussing home and village life, Jacob spoke concerning his son, Joseph, and his desire to marry Joachim's daughter, Mary. They would provide the best they could. Neither Joseph nor his parents were wealthy, but Joseph would bring the bride price, the *mohar*, according to custom. It would be a bracelet, 5 silver coins and a staff, or crook, of silver, something which had been handed down from generation to generation. It was small and well worn, but it did reflect their heritage, a shepherd's staff. They were descendents of David, the Shepherd King! The bride's dowry would be a set of treasured bronze vessels for their new home.

Jacob spoke the joy they all felt.

"We will be blessed in this marriage. Surely Yahweh's hand is in the choice that has been made. In the giving and sharing of gifts, our children will be betrothed! Let us call them in from their tasks, now. Together we will share a cup of our best wine."

It was a strange betrothal, even with the expected exchange of gifts. Mary came in with head bowed in submission, unwilling to look up at this tall man, almost a stranger. Yet, when Joseph took her hand, reached down and lifted up her chin and smiled, she smiled shyly in return.

"Mary," he said softly, "I ask you to marry me. I will care for you and I will love you. I will give you the best home possible. I know it is the custom for parents to make marriage arrangements for their sons and daughters, but I ask you to accept me as your husband! I would hope it would be your choice, too.

"Also, there is something else, not only our relationships with each other, but our relationship with Yahweh! My faith in Yahweh is important to me and I believe that is so for you. If you are willing, we will serve Yahweh together, as husband and wife!"

"Joseph," she answered, "I know you are a good man, a man from the house of David. That is our heritage. And I must trust the wisdom of my parents. It is the custom. But, I hardly know you. I do accept your offer and the betrothal and I thank you for talking about your faith, your devotion to our Lord. However, I ask for a little time, three months, before we come to the wedding. Will that be acceptable to you?"

Mary surprised herself with the request, but she knew it was right. Preparations would have to be made before she was ready to move into Joseph's home and arms. Not only that, she felt that something stood between the two of them, and she had to know what. Somehow it related to the traveler from Egypt, the one who had turned back and bowed low before her. Hopefully, she would find the right answers before the three months were spent.

Joseph agreed. He was willing to wait. He, too, faced a new life and the coming responsibilities made him nervous. How would he act as husband and lover to this beautiful young girl? He needed time to think, now that betrothal was a reality!

The answer for Mary came sooner than expected. As the betrothal became public knowledge, the two girls, Mary and Miriam, began to drift apart. Mary was busy with wedding plans and Miriam felt pushed aside. Their dreaming had been interrupted and their relationship had changed.

Quickly, the preparations for what was to come demanded Mary's constant attention. Even for a young woman, hardly more than a girl, the preparations for a wedding were almost too much. Also, there were the daily chores and, at times, wedding plans had to take second place in a family preparing for the upcoming harvest. Mary worked early and late, trying to get ready for what was to come, her wedding to Joseph.

It was quite different now, her attitude toward her future husband. To her surprise and delight she was looking forward to becoming the wife of this village carpenter. She believed him to be in love with her and now she was quite sure he was the most handsome bachelor in Nazareth. She was impressed by Joseph's concern for her. Also, she was relieved and happy he believed as she did. Yahweh would not only bless their marriage, but he would use them in their new relationship. Joseph would be a good, caring husband.

Knowing she might not have the opportunity to get away any time soon, Mary excused herself at the end of a very stressful day and climbed to the top of the ridge above the village. Her mother sensed her need to be alone and encouraged Mary to go. It was time for a moment of rest! Anyway, the sun would be setting soon and she couldn't linger long. She would have to return in time for the evening meal. Even so, it would be a break in the demanding schedule.

Then it happened, high above the town! Mary realized she was not alone. There was a man standing before her and almost before she could react or draw back he spoke:

"Greetings, Mary! You have received Yahweh's blessings. I want you to know he is with you!"

What in the world was this stranger saying to her? She had never seen him before. Surely, Yahweh was always with his people. What was so special about that? Anyway, who was this stranger? The man was talking in riddles.

Then, he spoke again.

"Please do not be afraid of me. I am Gabriel and I am Yahweh's messenger, sent to tell you that Yahweh is going to bless you in a most wonderful way. You are going to have a baby boy and you will name him Jesus because he will deliver you and your people from bondage.

"He will be great and will be called the son of the Most High. He will be given the throne of David, and he will be ruler over his people forever!"

That made absolutely no sense to Mary and she said so.

"I'm not married and I certainly have not had any man lie with me. You can't have babies without that. It will be three months before Joseph and I will be married and who knows when a child will be born! I don't know and you certainly don't know! The first child, if we have children, could just as well be a girl. Not only that, a king like David would not be born in a little town like Nazareth! We are not royalty, only common, ordinary village people. What you are saying cannot be! I refuse to believe what you are saying!"

Patiently, Gabriel responded. He had to make clear Yahweh's intentions for this young girl. She would be the mother of Yahweh's own son!

"This birth will be the work of the Spirit of Yahweh himself and not a conception with Joseph as father. Yahweh's power will enter into your life, and you will carry his Son! You will be the mother of the son of Yahweh!

"I know this is almost too much to believe but you will find the proof of what I am telling you in the news about your cousin Elizabeth. Yahweh has chosen her to have a son, even in her old age. Yahweh will use him in a very special manner. He will enter into your son's life when they are grown.

"She who was barren all these years is now expecting that child. It will happen soon, in a few months. I gave that news to her husband Zechariah before any of that happened and he wouldn't believe me either. I had to leave him without a voice in order to help convince him that what I was saying was true. He will not be able to speak again until his son is born. When you see your cousin and her husband Zechariah, whom you should visit soon, that should convince you Yahweh can and will do what he says!"

Mary was dumbfounded and now she was afraid. If what this Gabriel was saying would come to pass, Joseph would divorce her and her own people would reject her. Births don't happen like that. There had never been a birth like that, not without a man. It was impossible!

Yet, she had prayed so many times for the deliverance of her people. She had asked Yahweh over and over again for his help! If Yahweh was as powerful as she had been taught to believe, could this be his answer? Could Yahweh be using her to accomplish his purpose? Was this the answer to what had disturbed and upset her life, a stranger from Egypt bowing down before her on the dusty streets of Nazareth?

Why Yahweh would choose her for this special honor was beyond her, difficult to see and accept. It really made no sense. However, she would have to see for herself. She would have to make that long journey south, to the home of Elizabeth and Zechariah in order to see if this one, this messenger Gabriel, was telling the truth.

If she found Elizabeth as Gabriel had said, she would have to believe. She would be a part of what she had prayed for so many times, the freedom of her own people. Would that be worth the price, the sacrifice?

Mary bowed her head before the one called Gabriel, and before he disappeared, responded softly.

"Yahweh is my Lord! If what you say is true, I will agree to his choosing me! However, there is one more question. What about my betrothed, Joseph? What will he do when he finds out? He is truly a devout man, but this may be too much for him."

"Do not concern yourself about your husband-to-be. I will tell him and he will support you and love you all the more. Joseph will be blessed, used of Yahweh to raise your son. I only ask you to trust me and believe."

As the sun dropped into the western sea, Mary made her way back down to the village, knowing her life would be changed, forever. Perhaps she would lose all she had, her dreams, her hopes, her family and Joseph! Only Yahweh could answer that.

# CHAPTER 4

*When his mother Mary had been betrothed
to Joseph, before they came together she was
found
to be with child of the Holy Spirit*

Matthew 1:18b

Joseph was the first to notice and he wished with all his heart he was mistaken. Mary was pregnant! He was sure of it. Her mother, Anna, had gone over to see relatives in Cana and would not be back until after the Sabbath. He was thankful for that, but what would happen when she returned? What would she say? He was certain she would see what he was seeing.

If it were true, he had a decision to make. He felt he could not and would not wed an unmarried woman expecting a child. If true, should he send Mary away until he could deal quietly with the proper procedures for divorce? If he did that, no matter where she might go, her life would be destroyed. She would be shamed for the rest of her life. In the old days she would have been stoned to death. What made it worse were his feelings toward Mary. He loved her! He wanted Mary to be his wife!

He first noticed the difference a few days following her afternoon break from the daily routine. He had stopped by that day, but couldn't find her. After a busy week of trying to complete a small table he was constructing for Mary's mother, he wanted her to see the results.

"Joseph, Mary is not here. She's climbing up the ridge to her favorite spot overlooking the town and valley. She and Miriam did that often, whenever they could get away. Mary really needed some rest and I encouraged her to go. She should be back soon, before dark."

"I can't wait for her now," replied Joseph. "Tell her I'll see her tomorrow. If she is late, let me know and I'll go meet her."

He didn't get by the next afternoon, but when they did meet, walking together in Joachim's fields below the town, Joseph sensed a difference in Mary's eyes and speech. To be sure, it was a subtle thing, a glow, almost an aurora about her face. At first he saw it as her growing and responding love for him, but then he wasn't so sure. This was different. Something had happened to Mary, something disturbing! She was different! It was difficult to be sure about her eyes. She avoided looking directly into his; her's downcast.

And now she wanted to move up their wedding date! Was she trying to cover up something? That wouldn't work, if she really were pregnant. He knew that was a part of the wedding celebration, the women checking her virginity. No, it wasn't always done, but the bride could never be sure.

"Joseph," she said, "let's go ahead with our wedding. We are betrothed and there's really no reason to wait. All our friends and neighbors think of us as being married, now that we have had our betrothal. Anyway, my life is getting so hectic these days. I have to help with all the work at home, as well as make our plans. What do you think?"

"Are you sure, Mary? You asked for three months, less than a month ago. How soon can we have everything ready? What will our families think? They will want to know why we have changed our plans."

"My dear husband-to-be, they will be happy for us. You

remember how reluctant I was at first. This will please them, that I was the one to suggest an earlier date. I know they will be pleased, and we can be ready! I will make sure of that."

Not being able to put his finger on what was happening, and not quite sure of himself, he kept quiet while Mary rambled on about other things, the details of the wedding, which friends would be invited, who would be the main guest of honor, what they would be able to serve.

After awhile Joseph excused himself.

"Mary, I need to get back to my shop. I have some work I promised a friend who lives in Sepphoris. He is pushing me to finish and get it to him. I'll come by as soon as I can and help you with our plans. Let me sleep on the matter; think about it while I am away. Then we can decide about our going ahead with the wedding."

With that he left, wanting to be alone with his thoughts. Could his love for her overcome what seemed so obvious, or was he imagining things? If his suspicions were true, did he love her enough to take her as his wife?

For several days Joseph stayed away; spent two days in nearby Sepphoris, about a half-day's journey up the valley. That had been Herod Antipas' capitol where there was always work for carpenters and masons. From time to time he made that journey, helping friends with their houses and furniture repairs. Anyway, there was more work and money in Sepphoris than in Nazareth and he needed that now. Besides, he could think about his problems without any distractions.

Back home he ate little for supper and went to bed early. He needed time to think carefully about his next step, just how he would deal with his dilemma. His love for this young woman was being torn apart by what he feared was happening. With all his heart he wanted to go ahead with their plans, regardless. On the other hand, he knew he must deal with the Law.

Finally, that night, he learned the truth. After several restless hours, he fell asleep, only to be awakened and confronted by Mary's messenger, Gabriel.

"Joseph, Joseph," he called. "Mary is pregnant, but do not be afraid to take her as your wife. She has done nothing wrong. She has been with no man. What is taking place is the work of Yahweh himself. He has chosen your betrothed, Mary, to be the mother of Yahweh's son. What is conceived in her is by Yahweh's Spirit. She will give birth to a baby boy, one you shall name Jesus, for he will be the Savior for you and your people!

"I know this is hard for you to believe and accept, but you were taught long ago that Yahweh moves in mysterious ways. He has selected you and Mary to fulfill the promise he made many years ago. Trust me when I say you two devout people are special in the sight of Yahweh! He is answering your prayers for your people.

"Mary knows this and has accepted Yahweh's plan. Her greatest concern is for you, the one she loves. Hear me Joseph! Mary loves you! However, you must proceed with the marriage as soon as possible because Mary needs to visit her cousin Elizabeth in Judea. She, even in her old age, is going to deliver a son very soon. He, too, will be used of Yahweh. He will be named John! Also, you will find her husband Zechariah speechless because he wouldn't believe me. Talk to Mary about this, today! She will share the conversation we had, when she climbed the hill above the town. All that will help convince you!

"Remember, others may begin to notice what is happening to Mary. We do not want people talking about her carrying a child. So, make your wedding plans now! Do not delay."

Suddenly, he disappeared!

Was it a dream or a vision? Was it his own wishful thinking, or was this, in fact, a messenger from Yahweh? How could he be sure? He had to know! As soon as daylight came he would go looking for Mary, to hear what she had to say!

He found her as she was returning from the village well,

carrying her jar of water. Lifting it to his shoulder, something most of the village men would never do, they continued up the dusty, but well-worn path.

"Mary," Joseph began, "I had a visitor last night, a stranger who called himself Gabriel. At first I thought it was only a dream, a very disturbing dream. Now I'm not so sure. Please help me understand what is going on in our lives! I need some answers!

"He told me what I suspected, that you are pregnant. He told me you are carrying the Son of Yahweh, the promised Messiah! Tell me, Mary, is this true? I have trouble accepting that. Such a thing has never happened before. We are plain, ordinary people, living in a small, unimportant, village far from the center of things. Why would Yahweh choose us for such a miracle? I want to believe, but I am only human, a man wanting a wife and children of his own!"

Mary stopped, put her arms around Joseph, hid her face against his cloak and began to cry.

"Oh, Joseph," she sobbed. "I do love you, and would never, never do anything to hurt you. I want to be your wife and bear your children. I hope you will say yes to that and that we will be married as soon as possible!

"Yes, I am pregnant, not by another man, but as this messenger Gabriel said, by Yahweh himself. I can't believe it! I cannot explain how it happened. It is, in my eyes, impossible, but it is true!

"Gabriel came to me to tell me that, asking for my acceptance. He told me not to worry about you, that he would tell you how Yahweh had chosen us for this marvelous event.

"Also, he told me about my cousin Elizabeth, that she would soon give birth to a son. Can you imagine that! She is far too old to be having children. He wants me to visit her as soon as we are married. That visit would be positive proof of Yahweh's intent, the truth of what we have been told. I would find Zechariah speechless, just as he told me, and told you.

"My dear Joseph! What are we to do? If this is what Yahweh wants of us, what are we to do? How can we do this and, at the same time, live with family and friends who would never believe what is happening? They will think we have committed adultery and condemn us for that! Oh Joseph! What are we to do?"

It took Joseph a long time to answer. He did so, finally, but with much difficulty.

"I knew you were a devout woman, Mary. You have shared your faith and your concerns for our people a number of times. As you told me early on, you prayed often for some sign from Yahweh, some sign of deliverance. I, too, have had those concerns. My prayers have been for our people. We are Yahweh's chosen, chosen to do his will, whatever that might be.

"If that is so, why wouldn't Yahweh hear our prayers and use us to do what He wants for his people? Yes, I know it seems impossible, but there are far too many things that have happened for us to doubt this messenger Gabriel. I have to believe and you have to believe. We might be little people in an out-of-the-way village, but our psalms say it over and over, that Yahweh has done and will do marvelous things.

"If you believe all this, and if I believe all this, we have to be practical. We need to be married right away and we need to send you to see your cousin Elizabeth. Do you agree?"

"Yes, I do believe," responded Mary. "Knowing you love me and knowing you are accepting what Yahweh is doing, my heart is filled with joy! We do not know what the future will bring, but we will face it together, trusting in our Lord Yahweh."

Only a few moments earlier, Joseph would have never dared do what came next. He laughed! He sat down the water jug, grabbed Mary around her waist, lifted her high, swung her around, and laughed!

"Yahweh gave you to me, and I will never let you go!"

With that they hurried on to Mary's home, carrying the news of their plans. The wedding would take place as soon as possible!


A bride never looked lovelier! Mary was radiant, a beautiful young lady adorned for her husband-to-be. Nervous? Yes, so very nervous! After all, she was so young, and this was her one and only wedding. Not only that, she was pregnant!

In preparing for the wedding, Mary was very careful in making sure there was no visible evidence of what was happening to her. Wearing tight fitting under garments, she was able to convince herself no one would notice. And she was happy, happy for Joseph and for herself. Yahweh had chosen them to carry and care for Yahweh's own son. No matter what might happen, or what people might think, she had not been unfaithful. She had "known no man." This was Yahweh's doing and he would watch over and care for them! After all, weddings were, in the eyes of many, metaphors of the relationship between Yahweh and Israel. She was going to be married!

Their wedding lasted three nights and three days. The wedding procession began the first evening on the northern edge of the town, near his parents' home, the home of Jacob and Zeruah. Gathered about Joseph were a number of his friends. Most of the men had grown up with him, gone to the synagogue with him, learning those hard lessons taught by Rabbi Ashael. Now they would be his escort along the dusty streets of Nazareth. With torches, bells, horns and harps, they shouted to all who would come out to hear:

"Come to the wedding of our stupid friend Joseph! He has lost his mind, but we will go with him to his doom!"

Although some of the villagers kept their doors closed, grumbling about the noise, most laughed and joined in the procession. They would go, join in the celebration and, just as important, enjoy the food and wine. Such events were rare and one had to make the most of such occasions. Also, these were nice people, both families well liked.

Pretty soon the elders of the town and the rabbi joined them. They, together, would be in charge. All took their time, wandering here and there along the open areas between the houses, several times crossing the main road, which ran from the Esdraelon valley northeast toward Tiberius. The son of Jacob and Zerauh and the daughter of Joachim and Anna deserved the best!

When they arrived at Mary's home, her friends, the bridesmaids of her choosing, joined them. The one nearest to her was her dear friend Mary, the one who insisted on being called Miriam. They laughed and giggled and waved both branches and torches. By now the sun had set and darkness was fast approaching. It was time to gather around the several small tables and enjoy both food and drink. This they did, long into the night. Finally, all said their good-byes and went home to sleep. The festivities would resume the next day.

On the third evening, all the parents gathered around Joseph and Mary to give their blessings. This would be the religious part, including the words of the rabbi, his prayers and readings from the Psalms and the Song of Solomon. The town elders dealt more with the marriage contract and the giving of the *mohar*. Bride and groom of the House of David were now man and wife! The contract was sealed!

They now moved on to Joseph's house, where they would live as husband and wife. Meats, bread, cheeses, nuts, fruits and wine were shared and consumed, until there was little left. Joseph and Mary were grateful it was enough and lasted until all the guests had departed, just as the morning star was rising in the eastern sky. They were alone, but with one limitation. Their marriage as husband and wife would not be consummated until Yahweh's son was born! Mary wept tears of both joy and sorrow as Joseph held her tightly in his arms, until she fell asleep.

Neither family questioned their decision to travel south for a visit with Mary's cousin Elizabeth. No one in Nazareth had heard from Zechariah or Elizabeth in quite some time. It would be good to hear. Was Zechariah still carrying out his duties as priest, or had he retired? He was old enough. How was Elizabeth's health? She had never been able to have a child and her relatives wondered about that. They hoped the news would be good, that Joseph and Mary would find them well. Also, who could blame Joseph and Mary wanting to be alone as newlyweds?

Wouldn't they be surprised! Little Mary was now married, married to a descendent of David, a prosperous carpenter. The other news was only suspected; perhaps wishful thinking. Was Mary pregnant, already? If so, that would be something special to share with their Judean relatives!

The original plan was to have Mary's brother, Nathaniel, travel with her. Joseph would stay home and work. They would need the money. At the last moment plans were changed. Joseph was far too concerned for Mary's health and safety. He would go with her. The work could wait. Also, he wanted verification of Gabriel's statements.

It would not be an easy journey. They knew it would be long and tiresome. With just the two of them going they were reluctant to go south through Samaria. They knew no one along that road, and the Samaritans were never very friendly. They traveled east, skirting the mountain called Tabor, following a small stream until they came to the Jordan River. There they turned south. At times they were on the eastern side of the Jordan, crossing at the fords, which made that possible.

Finally, on the third day, they crossed back over and came to the ancient city of Jericho. They spent the night, staying with an elderly couple, friends of Joseph's parents. The man, Eliphaz, and his wife Ruth were originally from Bethlehem, but now lived in Jericho. Eliphaz had worked for years in mining, extracting minerals from the Salt Sea. They had known Jacob when both families lived in Bethlehem. Catching up on the news from old friends, they talked long into the night.

Joseph and Mary left early the next morning, tired from walking, but wanting to be on their way. They wanted to make that long climb toward Jerusalem before the sun was high. It would be difficult enough. The winding road was long and steep. Mingling with a larger group of travelers for safety, they began the last leg of their journey.

At Bethany they paused for a brief rest, sharing some delicious grapes given them by their friends in Jericho. Then they crossed the Mount of Olives, and on the other side turned north, skirting the city of Jerusalem. They had no need or desire to enter one of the gates, anxious to reach the home of Zechariah and Elizabeth. They were tired!

No, Zechariah had not retired. In fact, he was not at home but in Jerusalem, at the Temple! He would return home in a few days, at the end of the Sabbath. Elizabeth was alone, napping in the early afternoon heat.

That came to an abrupt end! Her cousin Mary had come to see her! With cries and shouts of joy they greeted each other. Laughing and crying, they hugged each other. Then it was that Elizabeth felt the strongest kick ever, the baby who would be called John. It would be so recorded: "The baby leaped in her womb!" He was alive and well!

And, wonder of wonders, she sensed what was difficult to put into words. Her cousin Mary was also pregnant, bearing a child, Yahweh's child! How this could be was beyond her, but she knew they, together, were caught up in a divine plan greater than they could ever imagine. Gabriel's message was right. Her son-to-be-born would, someday, be bound up in the life of Mary's son. From the day of Gabriel's visit to Zechariah in the Temple, miracle after miracle kept pointing to marvelous things yet to come. To say the least, they were staggered by Gabriel's promise to both!

Mary helped verify that, as she responded to Elizabeth's outburst with her own:

> *My soul magnifies the Lord, and my spirit rejoices in Yahweh my Savior, for he has regarded the low estate of his handmaiden.*
> *For behold, henceforth all generations will call me blessed;*
> *For he who is mighty has done great things for me, and holy is his name.*

> *And his mercy is on those who fear him from generation to generation.*
> *He has shown strength with his arm,*
> *He has scattered the proud in the imagination of their hearts,*
> *He has put down the mighty from their thrones, and exalted those of low degree;*
> *He has filled the hungry with good things, and the rich he has sent empty away.*
> *He has helped his servant Israel, in remembrance of his mercy, as he spoke to our fathers, to Abraham and to his posterity together.*

Tears ran down their cheeks, tears of joy, wonder and hope. They were in this together, soul mates bound to what Yahweh had in store for them!

Through it all, Joseph stood speechless. He knew he was witnessing something far beyond his comprehension. However, the one thing he did know was the confirmation of what he had agonized over, even to this very moment. Mary was carrying a divine child, the son of Yahweh! All doubts were gone! Questions remained, questions about their future together, but that would have to wait. For the present he had to be content with the miracles already evident. Yahweh did move in wondrous ways and they had to live in faith, trusting in the divine plan.

Joseph agreed to the arrangements for Mary to stay with Elizabeth as long as possible. She would be of tremendous help in the final months of her pregnancy. He also knew they would be good company for each other, supporting each other and catching up on family news.

He would return to Nazareth and share the good news about Elizabeth. Also, it was imperative for him to earn what he could. Caring for and feeding a wife and child would call for more income. That, too, would be welcome news for both families, the news that Mary was expecting!

He did wait past the Sabbath, in order to meet and speak

with Zechariah. With Zechariah's inability to talk, that was not easy, but they could at least get acquainted. Both agreed, what was most difficult to accept, they were only instruments in Yahweh's hands. As men, they would have preferred an in-charge role, but both knew that it was through their wives the promised plan of redemption and salvation for their people would come. That much was clear. The full unfolding of the plan was still a mystery, but they knew that in Yahweh's own good time, sons John and Jesus would stand on center stage, long after Zechariah and Joseph were dead. In the meantime, they were to care for Elizabeth and Mary and their sons in the best way possible. This they promised to do before Joseph left to go north.

For the return journey Joseph went up the ridge that led through Samaria. Joining a larger group of travelers he knew he would be safe going though what he had always considered to be "enemy" territory. The Samaritans were not true sons and daughters of Abraham and he wanted to minimize contact with them. As a group they could camp along the way, avoiding stopping in the Samaritan villages. The larger group made for slower travel, but it provided safety and company.

It would be a difficult journey, but he was anxious to be on his way. Saying his good-byes to his beloved wife Mary, he headed north; quite unaware of the fact he would be retracing his steps in less than a year. He and Mary would be required to return south to his ancestral home, Bethlehem! The Roman decree had already arrived in Nazareth. All citizens would be counted and taxed in their hometown. That, too, was amazing! Even Caesar Augustas was a part of the divine plan, along with Zechariah, Elizabeth, Joseph and Mary. Yahweh would use them all!

# CHAPTER 5

*Now the time came for Elizabeth to be
delivered,
And she gave birth to a son.*

Luke 1:57

The baby's birth was one to remember; both the boy's lusty cry and Elizabeth's scream, impossible to stifle. It was a difficult delivery, with the midwife Miriam voicing her opinion on old people having babies. It was her opportunity to be seen and heard, sharing her skills and knowledge with those willing to listen. Miriam was the best midwife around and she wanted everyone to know it! She not only "knew" it was going to be a boy, but she also "knew" he would be a problem child. People who have babies late in life always have problem children and this one would be no exception! Zachariah and Elizabeth were asking for trouble. The very idea of people having sex at their age!

Finally it was over and the congratulations came from far and near, from friends and neighbors, even from strangers. Zechariah's fellow priests were ecstatic. Their old friend was special! The prayed-for baby had finally arrived! Old Zechariah and aging wife Elizabeth were now the proud parents of a healthy baby boy! It had to be a miracle, one that must have been predicted at the time of Zechariah's vision. No wonder he was left speechless!

Zechariah was beside himself! There would be no more questioning his virility, not now. He, even at his age, was the father of a strong, healthy son! The only problem was his speech. He could only smile, hold Elizabeth's hand and accept the congratulations in silence. However, vindication was nice!

"I'm content, my husband," whispered Elizabeth. "I'm overwhelmed by all this, something I believed would never happen, but now it has come to pass and I am relieved. Yahweh's messenger was right! He said I would bear a son and it happened, just as he told you. Wherever he is now he has to be smiling.

"Yet, so many things have touched and changed our lives. I find it difficult to make sense of what Yahweh has done to us. Our concern now, dear Zechariah, is the future, the future of this little baby. What will happen to him when we are gone? We are old and our remaining years are few! Perhaps it is the exhaustion and the difficulty of his birth, but I can't help but be afraid. Please, Yahweh let nothing bad happen to him!"

"Yes, my lovely wife," he was thinking, as he patted her hand. "You are exhausted and you must rest. I'm confident your fears will not be realized. Yahweh's prediction, given by Gabriel, promises good things for our son! Let's be happy in his birth."

Zechariah did his best to console her, to assure her all was well, now that the baby had come.

Elizabeth couldn't hear what Zechariah's was thinking, but she was happy to see his smiling response to those who came. Finally, as the visitors left and went on their various ways, she drifted off to sleep, a rarity in those final hours before delivery. She was exhausted!

With Elizabeth doing fairly well, slowly recovering from the ordeal, it was time to circumcise the boy according to custom, and to give him his father's name. They were determined to follow the Mosaic Law. This would be done in the Temple, in Yahweh's Temple! Invitations were delivered to friends and neighbors. Many more planned to be present. This birth was unique, and everyone was curious to see what would happen.

The eighth day came quickly. The trip into Jerusalem and the Temple was difficult for Elizabeth, but a neighbor's donkey provided the needed transportation. As friends and Zechariah's fellow priests gathered for the ceremony of circumcision, the first surprise came at the moment of giving the baby his father's name. Zechariah could not speak so Elizabeth announced the choice. He would be named John!

"Elizabeth," her friend Deborah protested, "that makes no sense at all. No one in your family has ever been given the name of John. Zechariah deserves better than that!"

Turning to the father she demanded: "Zechariah, you need to give your name to your son!"

More than one said so, emphatically, asking for his help in setting things straight.

Then came the second surprise. Zechariah reached for a writing sheet and spelled it out in large letters. "His name is John!"

The real shocker followed that! He not only opened his mouth and talked, but talked of holy things, calling the baby a prophet of Yahweh!

> *Blessed be the Lord Yahweh of Israel, for he has visited and redeemed His people, and has raised up a horn of salvation for us in the house of his servant David, as he has spoken by the mouth of his holy prophets from of old, that we should be saved from our enemies, and from the hand of all that hate us; to perform the mercy promised to our fathers, and to remember his holy covenant, the oath which he swore to our father Abraham, to grant us, that we, being delivered from the hand of our enemies, might serve him without fear, in holiness and righteousness before him all the days of our life.*

> *And you, child, shall be called the prophet of the Most high; for you shall go before the lord to prepare his ways, to give knowledge of salvation to his people in the forgiveness of their sins, through the tender mercy of our Yahweh, when the day shall dawn upon us from high, to give light to those who sit in darkness and in the shadow of death, to guide our feet in the way of peace.*

The crowd was incredulous! No one had ever heard the like. They were staggered by Zechariah's words. This was too much, beginning with Zechariah's vision in the Temple months before. At the hour of the Evening Sacrifice nine months earlier, Zechariah had come out speechless. Now he talks in riddles. The very idea that this little baby is destined to be Yahweh's prophet! He is the son of an old, soon-to-be-retired priest and his aging wife, Elizabeth; just common, ordinary people like us. Yet, at the same time, they were disturbed. There were too many events, too many surprises, no one could explain. It would be recorded:

> *Fear came on all their neighbors, and all these things were talked through all the hill country of Judea.*

It wasn't difficult to tell what Zechariah's fellow priests thought about his outburst. It sounded proper, coming from one they knew and respected. It reinforced their certainty that Yahweh was involved. It was a mystery, but one with the assurance of a divine presence. Their Zechariah was truly a man of Yahweh!

Those who were neighbors of Zechariah and Elizabeth wondered about the lengthy visit of Elizabeth's cousin Mary. She had come all the way down from Nazareth in Galilee. Her older husband had come with her, but didn't stay. He left his wife for almost three months while he went back north. No one in the village could get much information from her. She was shy, talking very little to those dropping by. The general opinion related all that to the fact she was from Galilee, foreign territory to them.

Also, before she left to return to Galilee, it was rather obvious. She, too, was pregnant! What was going on with those two? What did all that have to do with this miracle of baby John's birth, the one who should have been named for his father?

Sure, Elizabeth needed help during that period, but her good friends and neighbors could have cared for her! They could have done as well or better than her young cousin expecting her first child. What did she know about such things? That, too, added to the mystery concerning Zechariah, Elizabeth and their son, John.

Mystery or not, the house of Zechariah was changed drastically. The baby boy turned their home upside down in more ways than one. Feeding was the first problem, with Elizabeth not very helpful. Fortunately, they were able to find a neighbor to serve as a wet nurse. She had just lost a child at birth and the nursing helped her, as well as providing milk for John. He was breast fed for the first weeks of his life, quite adequately. After that there was a plentiful supply of goat's milk. He was well fed and it showed.

*And the child grew and became strong in spirit.*

That, too, became part of the record. Most misunderstood the "spirit" thing, but all took note of his growth and strength. He was a strong, healthy boy, almost too much for his elderly parents. It wasn't long until Elizabeth could not lift her son to her lap.

He did have spirit! As soon as he could crawl he was into everything. If he could not pick it up or move it, he would chew on it. Soon he was able to climb up on his mother's lap by himself. At times it seemed he had more strength than Elizabeth.

The problems multiplied by the time he was able to walk. Their little home could not hold him. Before long he had learned where to go for treats, and which homes to avoid. He also learned where he could hide and who would speak up for him when he had done something forbidden.

He was into everything, seemingly thinking up things to do which would disturb both his parents and the neighbors. As a result there was a steady line bringing their complaints about little John. A few close friends, including Deborah, were brave enough to speak for the villagers.

"Elizabeth, you simply have to do something about John. We know Zechariah is at the Temple more than he is at home, but he needs to deal with this problem, bringing up the child in the right way. He really needs more discipline. If he doesn't teach John what is right and wrong this child of yours will become a serious problem!"

Each time, tears would come to her eyes. As the days and weeks passed she realized more and more her limitations. Those who had said it were probably right. They were too old to be having children! Her health was failing and something drastic was needed. She could not keep track of everything John was doing, especially in his wanderings around the town.

When Zechariah returned home from Jerusalem, she tried to get him to see the problem, but he was not much help.

"John is just a growing boy and growing boys his age get into things. That's the way they learn. Sure, I'll talk to him, but you'll see. He will outgrow his childish ways before long. Very soon he should be of help, helpful with what you need done. He is a fine boy and we should be proud of him. You know as well as I, some of our neighbors are jealous. We have a son and they don't! Anyway, this son is special!"

Both Zechariah and Elizabeth remembered what Gabriel had said about their son-to-be and kept their hopes strong, hoping things would improve. They kept expecting more miracles in their lives. If John was to give them joy and happiness, it was time for Yahweh to start. They were getting older and couldn't take much more.

It came to a head when a neighbor, Jonathan, came with the latest complaint. His best milk goat was at the point of giving birth to a pair of fine kids, but lost both. John had chased her down the valley. In the long run and the heat, the kids were dead upon delivery. The mother goat survived, but the loss of the kids was the loss of money. Both could have been sold for a good price!

Zechariah paid his neighbor for the two kids. That was the least he could do. Beyond that he could only explain to John what he had done wrong.

"Father, I'm sorry! I will try to do better."

It sounded good, but Zechariah knew such promises had been given before. What was he to do?

The other Jonathan, his Division leader, came up with a good suggestion.

"Zechariah, why don't you bring John with you to the Temple? We'll help watch out for him. Anyway, he needs to begin to learn about such things. If he is going to follow in your steps, he is not too young to start. Don't you remember the story about young Samuel? His mother Hannah brought him to the Tabernacle right after he was weaned. That was early in Samuel's life, probably younger than John. If I remember John is 7 now . . . correct?

"Young Samuel's home was the Tabernacle. His father wasn't a priest, but Eli took care of the young boy! The next time you return to Jerusalem, bring John with you."

The records never reflected it, but the Temple in Jerusalem would never be the same either. Little John was hard to control. He was into everything! He had to be kept away from the animals and the birds waiting to be sacrificed. More than once he let some of the pigeons go free. He knew keeping birds and animals cooped up was wrong and he made it his goal to free as many as he could!

Where the meat and vegetables were prepared and cooked, he would add much more salt and pepper, especially the pepper. He loved to see the priests gasp for water. For those on duty, he would hide some of their clothes, tying coats and cloaks in knots. Personal belongings were taken and either hidden, given away or sold. On more than one occasion he interrupted the evening worship! That was the most serious prank of all and Jonathan was compelled to act.

For a long time, for more than a year, everyone tried to ignore the pranks. Understanding the situation, Elizabeth and Zechariah's ages, as well as the divine intervention in the promise and birth of John, all wanted a success story. However, it went from bad to worse. Something had to be done!

At a gathering of the priests in his Division, Jonathan asked for suggestions. How could they be of help in training a young boy who refused to do what he was told? Sure, he was young, but with all the scolding he should have learned by now what not to do!

One of the younger priests, named Eljah, offered to help.

"As I was growing up in my village, I was known as a 'bad' boy."

He laughed and continued: "Just like young John, I was into everything. My parents didn't know what to do with me; neither did our neighbors. They hated to see me coming. I was awful! It was my rabbi who helped me. He kept me with him most of each day. Patiently, he taught me what was right and what not to do, and why! It took a long time, but it worked. Now, here I am, a priest in the Temple of Yahweh . . . not the best priest, but I'm learning. Let me work with John. If you will let me have more time with him, I'll see what I can do."

No one had a better suggestion. All agreed to give Eljah the time and needed assistance in dealing with a real problem. That night Zechariah raised his voice in thanksgiving. Maybe this was Yahweh's answer to their heartache! Hopefully, Gabriel's first prediction would come true.

Eljah tried. As the weeks and months went by he kept John with him, making sure he was busy with his assigned tasks. Each day he made sure John did what he was told. He punished him when he disobeyed. The punishment was not terribly severe, only additional duties in order to get John's attention.

He tried a more positive approach. From time to time he would, with Zechariah's approval, take John to his own home when he was not on duty in the Temple. Eljah's family tried to help, but nothing seemed to turn John in the right direction. The family took John with them on a journey to the big sea, all the way to Caesarea. Very few boys had ever traveled that far from Jerusalem, but that didn't impress John. He was "trouble" every step of the way.

Back at the Temple it was the same, more problems and more punishments. John took it all in stride. He laughed when Eljah fussed. He laughed when Eljah added to his duties as punishment. Before long Eljah began to suspect John saw everything as a big joke, and that disaster was just waiting to happen. It did, sooner than expected!

John was 12 years old when Eljah had his scheduled meeting with the High Priest. It was his turn for another evaluation, something all novices had to endure. It wasn't so difficult if you were doing well with your assignments, but it was tedious. The High Priest was not very popular. He made a point of trying to impress everyone with his importance! The interviews were long and boring, but one had to be polite and gracious. Eljah knew he had a difficult hour ahead.

Before going to meet the High Priest, Eljah made sure John would be kept busy. Today he would work in the kitchen, assisting those in charge. The big task would be sweeping out the trash, the husks, the trimmings, the debris brought in with the vegetables and fruits.

Meats were prepared elsewhere and were brought in ready for cooking; the parts not placed on the altar. This was for the priests on duty, food for the table. For John, after the area was clean, the pots and dishes had to be washed and scrubbed. Cleanliness was not only a virtue; it was essential for good health. Yahweh's people had learned that long before.

"John," admonished Eljah, "you are growing up and anyone your age needs to be more responsible. You have been doing better, but that last trick you pulled on old Nathan was not very nice. Respect for older people like your parents is a virtue you must learn! While I am with the High Priest I want you to help clean up this mess, wash all the pots and dishes. When I get back I want to see this kitchen area spotless!

John laughed, nodded his head and headed for the kitchen. He never arrived. Before anyone could miss him, he was off the Temple Mount and into the city. The day was too nice for cleaning and scrubbing. It was a day for adventure!

Dashing through the Gate Beautiful, he almost tripped over a blind beggar. Making his apologies, he took time to remove a small copper coin from his belt and drop it in the man's cup. It wasn't much, only a natural concern for one so unfortunate. John did care for the weak and helpless, just as he cared for cooped-up birds and animals.

As it turned out, that was a mistake. Some older boys had seen the bag tucked in his belt and started toward him. He would be easy prey for them. Sensing their intent, he began to run. He might be young and small, but he could run. He dashed through the Court of Gentiles, the Royal Porch and out the nearest gate. A Temple guard tried to stop him, but John easily escaped his grasp. Finally, the older boys gave up in disgust. They decided chasing a young boy wasn't worth the effort. At his age he could not have had much in that purse.

Almost before he knew it, John was in the lower city, where he had never been before. It was a different and fascinating world. All around him were markets and bazaars filled with delightful smells and sounds. There were the fruit markets with baskets of olives and grapes, figs and beans, limes and oranges. There was the strong odor of spices and meat. People! He had never seen so many. Merchants were shouting their prices. There were soldiers, Roman soldiers making sure there were no problems requiring their attention. It was their assignment to keep the peace. On their own, they took what they wanted, both food and trinkets.

There were the residents of Jerusalem, as well as visitors from all parts of the world, looking for bargains. There were slaves, carrying loads bought and sold. He had never seen anything like it, even on his trip to Cesarea.

Fascinated by it all, John lost track of time and place. He could not see where he had entered the lower city. He suddenly realized he didn't have any idea of direction. He was lost!

How could he find his way back to the Temple? If he had been taller he might have caught some glimpse of the Temple Mount, but for him that was impossible. He could only keep moving, hopefully in the right direction.

Now he was in a part of the city occupied mostly by strangers. Their dress was different and their speech was different. Trying to listen to some of their conversations, he could not make out a single word. How could he ask directions from them? Wandering here and there he hoped to come across a recognizable face. Surely, someone there could speak his language, but he heard no familiar voice!

The sun was beginning to drop into the west. It would soon be dark. For the first time in his life, John was afraid. It was a new emotion for him. Alone, with no one to watch over him, no one to guide him, he did not know what to do. Even Eljah would have been a welcome sight. He would have welcomed his punishment! He had never felt so alone!

There was a chill in the air and he was not ready for that. His loincloth and tunic were not enough to keep him warm. His cloak was in his quarters back at the Temple. Shivering, he was attracted to the warmth of a nearby fire. Just under the canopy of a large tent there was a brazier filled with hot coals. Moving slowly, trying not to attract attention, he crept closer to the fire and began to warm his hands.

For a time no one noticed John. He was short, just another body standing in the semi-darkness. Then one of the adults spotted the little stranger and spoke in Aramaic, something John could understand.

"Well, what do we have here? Maybe this is a gift from the gods, a nice, well-dressed little boy with no place to live! Why don't we keep him, fatten him up and sell him to the highest bidder? He ought to bring a good price in the slave market!"

All the other men laughed, coming closer to examine their new find. Yes, he would be worth something. They would keep him!

"Let's throw the dice," one suggested. "The one with the lowest number wins!"

John wasn't sure whether these strangers were joking or not. Looking intently into their faces he could not tell, but he wasn't taking any chances. Believing they were serious, he broke loose from the grasp of the speaker and dashed away into the darkness. Behind him he could hear bursts of laughter, but was unable to tell whether there was any pursuit. Taking care to avoid that possibility, he ran as fast as he could, until he was out of breath. He ran until he had left the buildings and lights of the lower city behind.

Apparently no one had given chase. There was only darkness and silence. Now he was really alone! Yet, as his eyes adjusted to the darkness, he realized he was not so alone after all. There were few permanent buildings, but there were tents all around him, as well as animals. Donkeys and goats and camels were tethered to short lines. In the distance there were the sounds of sheep settling down for the night. There was the glow of open fires, warmth for the shepherds. As he listened he could hear voices and music coming from the tents. Inside there must be shelter and warmth, but he dared not enter.

Worn out, exhausted from running, the best he could do was to curl up by one of tents, away from the wind coming up from the valley below. Perhaps he could sleep there, unnoticed by those inside. Tomorrow, once the sun was up, he would have to find his way back to his Temple home, to Eljah and his father Zechariah.

He was awakened by the sound of voices. Opening his eyes he realized he was the center of attention. It was still quite dark, but a torch gave light to the scene. Several men dressed in strange, colorful clothing were peering down at him. Somehow he realized they were no threat to him, only curious.

At first he could not grasp what they were saying. Each time one would ask a question, he simply shook his head, holding out his hands palms up. Finally, he did try to answer in Aramaic.

"My name is John. My father is a priest in the Temple of Yahweh. Please help me! I am lost."

With that, there came another new experience for him. Tears welled up in his eyes and rolled down his cheeks.

There was no response from those gathered around him. They, too, shook their heads. The words of John were different from theirs. In a few minutes, after talking among themselves, one disappeared in the darkness, but returned shortly, bringing with him another man. This one began to talk in Aramaic.

"Son, what is your name? Are you from Jerusalem? Where is your family, or do you have a family? Dry your tears, young man. We are not going to harm you. We want to help you."

With that John ran to him, grasped him around his legs, and began to pour out his story of the events of the day.

"My name is John. My father's name is Zechariah. He is one of Yahweh's priests, in the Temple, in Jerusalem. I live there under the care of a young priest named Eljah.

"I disobeyed him and ran away. Now I am lost! Please, sir, I want to go home."

That prompted a lot of conversation between those gathered

around. Obviously, the one understanding John, was explaining to the others what he had said. Finally, he turned to John.

"Our leader is inside the tent. We are going to take you to him and let him decide on our course of action. Be assured, we will not harm you, but you must be most respectful to our exalted one. We are sure he will help you."

Immediately, they took John inside, into a world he had never encountered before. The ground was covered with the softest, the most beautiful rugs he had ever seen. Large cushions were scattered from one wall of the tent to the other. Two silver lamps hung from overhead ropes. In the middle of the tent was a bronze brazier, holding glowing coals, heating the entire area. Just beyond was a man, a tall, handsome man, seated on a cushion. His face and darkened skin seemed to glow in the soft light. On his left was a small table holding bread and a chalice. In a dish there was some meat, which John thought to be some sort of bird. The smells were overwhelming, especially for one who had not eaten all day.

John, remembering the instruction to be respectful, bowed down before the one seated, then stood and waited.

For the longest time, or so it seemed to John, no one spoke. There was an awkward moment of silence as the man peered intently into John's eyes. At last the man stood up, came closer and, without a word, knelt down and bowed his head. Reaching out he took John's hands in his, kissed them and placed them for a moment on his own head!

By this time John was trembling, wondering. He turned to the one person with whom he had spoken. He dared not break the silence, but simply raised his eyes in question. Who was this stranger, and why did he kneel down before John?

Finally, following a long conversation and a nod of approval from their leader, the speaker responded.

"Our exalted leader is a very wise man. He not only understands the past, but he can, at times, envision the future. He knows much we do not know. He sees in you a holy person, one through whom great events will take place. He does not know precisely what that might be, but he is confident it will be so.

"He does not understand what he sees and he is perplexed over that. One other person in your land has touched his life, as you have, a young girl far to the north of Jerusalem.

"You see, we are from another land, far to the south. We are from Egypt, the land of the flooding river and the monuments of stone rising toward the heavens. Our leaders are students of the heavens. They study the stars as they come and go above us. Some hold their positions year after year, while others move, wander rapidly. It is in these our leader finds paths of knowledge and understanding; and, we suspect, the gods also speak to him. We dare not ask!

"We are also traders, traveling year after year to cities both north and south. At the moment we are resting here, outside the walls of your city, preparing for the long journey south, across the deserted wasteland.

"Now, he wants you to eat and rest. Tomorrow we will take you to your Temple and find your father. He wants me to assure you of his protective care and concern. You will not be harmed. You are safe here."

Their leader disappeared into the dark recesses of the tent and the others gathered about John, bringing warm water for washing, food and drink. The bread and the meat were delicious and John ate without any prompting. The drink was milk, but with a different and rather strong taste. Back home he would have spit it out and made a face. Here, he remembered to be polite and drank it all. Hungry and thirsty, he ate and drank until there was nothing left.

Soon, tired and exhausted, he was sound asleep. This time no one wakened him, and he slept soundly until the sun had risen, sending a ray of light through the tent's opening.

Refreshed and renewed in strength, John was ready to go, even before anyone entered the tent. He was ready to leave and return home, to find Eljah and, above all, his father and mother. All would be welcome sights. Along with that, he sensed his life would be different. This leader of these Egyptian travelers had touched him, and made a deep impression on him. It was something he could not fathom or understand, but perhaps the stories of his miraculous birth were really true! Somehow he knew it was time to grow up! There had to be a purpose for his life and, if Yahweh had plans for him, it was time to let Yahweh have his way. From now on his parents, and Eljah, would be proud of him!

With these thoughts running through his head, he turned to see a slave girl enter, bearing a basin with hot water and towel. Over his protests she washed his face and hands. Then, she unfastened his tunic, leaving him standing naked, except for his loincloth. Again, with water and cloth she washed his back, chest and stomach. Smiling at him, she rubbed his genitals through the loincloth. Embarrassed and squirming, he tried to avoid the procedure, but she was stronger. It did feel good, a rising warmth in his groin, something he had never experienced before. Her hands were gentle, but firm, and he began to relax.

Suddenly, hearing the sound of approaching voices, she stopped, dried him with another towel, refastened his tunic and led him to the tent's opening. Pointing toward his loincloth, she laughed and headed him in the direction of what turned out to be the public toilets.

When he returned, food was set before him, a small, flat loaf of sweet bread, some dried figs and a hot drink. It was something he had never tasted before. He guessed that it might be tea, strong tea. It took no persuasion for him to devour the food and drink. All was good and filling!

Once he was through, another girl took the plate and cup and disappeared. It was not long before the spokesman entered and identified himself as Makir, assuring John he would be his guide.

"Our esteemed leader wants to know if you slept well, if all your needs have been met. He will not see you, but wishes you well on your return to the walled city and the Temple. Perhaps you will remember him as you come to the fulfillment of your life's journey!"

John could not fathom that last, but did remember to respond properly. He could be well behaved.

"Please thank him for caring for me. I will not forget him!"

With that he went outside and, led by the spokesman, re-entered the lower city. They continued through the shop-lined streets and bazaars, but this time John had no desire to linger. Once he spotted the Temple he began to run. For a moment he forgot his Egyptian guide, but when he turned to wait for him, Makir had disappeared in the crowd. He was on his own.

Climbing the stairs to the Temple Mount, he entered and passed through all the courts, beginning with the Court of the Gentiles. He was home!

Yet, it was not quite the same. There was an eerie silence wherever he went. There were people in the outer courts, but their conversations seemed muted, almost whispers. Something was wrong. Where were the priests? Where was Eljah? Where was his father Zechariah?

He began to run, something one was not supposed to do in the Temple area. He could not help it. Something was wrong! Just as he reached the quarters occupied by the priests on duty, he ran into Eljah, almost knocking him down.

"What's wrong?" he demanded. "Where is my father? Has he returned home? Is he looking for me?

"I know I did something bad in running away, but I'm back. Boy, do I have a story to tell! You won't believe it! Anyway, I'll never do that again. I've changed . . . you'll see! Tell me, why is everything so quiet? Where is our Division leader, Jonathan?"

Eljah began to cry, hardly knowing what to say. He reached down and grabbed John in a big hug, sobbing.

"Your mother! She died last night, in her sleep. Your father was there with her when she died. It was all so peaceful, but she's gone, John. She's gone!

"We never told her about your not being here. She thought you were with me, here in the Temple, and that made her happy. She said, again, that Yahweh had something special for you, something she knew would happen, even though she would not see it. She said to tell you she loved you, very much!"

John choked up, tears ran down his cheeks, but he was silent. For a long time he was quiet, looking into the far distance. Finally he asked Eljah:

"Will you go with me? I want to see my mother before she is buried. I want to tell her I have changed, that she will be proud of me. And you, Eljah, you will be proud of me, too!"

With Jonathan's permission and blessing, they left the Temple. Zechariah's Division leader and friend assured them he would follow as soon as he could, after turning his duties over to his Assistant. He would be present for the funeral.

Eljah and John left Jerusalem and began that long journey home. John would comfort his father and give his promises to his mother. He had changed and he wanted both to understand. Even in death and with Yahweh's help, his mother would know!

# CHAPTER 6

*And the child grew . . .*

Luke 1:50a

John had no trouble finding his father. Zechariah was home, sitting by his bed. Elizabeth's body was still there, washed, clothed and wrapped in a shroud. Deborah and the other women close to Elizabeth had prepared the body according to custom. Outside, other neighbors had gathered to mourn the death of their dear friend. The burial would have to be that day. The sprinkling of aromatic herbs would not suffice for long.

This was a new experience for young John. He had seen dead bodies before and had watched funeral processions going to the tombs, but this was different. His own mother was dead! For a long time he stood speechless, not knowing what to do or say. He had cried with Eljah as they were walking home. Now, his tears were flowing again.

He wanted to comfort his father and he needed that from him, but Zechariah didn't help. He sat there, a blank stare on his face. When John ran to him and hugged him, he gave no response. It was as though no one else was present, only he and his dear Elizabeth.

"Father," shouted John, "look at me. I'm home!"

There was no response. It was as though he was in another world, far away. If he heard his son's outburst he gave no sign.

He seemed deaf to all except the one fact. His Elizabeth was dead!

Not knowing what else to do, Eljah went over to Zechariah and helped him to his feet. He had to force him toward the door, leading him out. It was time for the burial! Outside, his eyes finally focused on the crowd and on John. It was only then he took note of his son, stooped down and embraced him.

As they stood, clinging to each other, those nearby began to wail, singing the traditional, familiar, funeral dirges. Their voices penetrated the whole village and beyond. At that moment Zechariah's Division leader, Jonathan, arrived. He took charge immediately. After embracing Zechariah and John he led the long, slow walk to the tombs. Those who followed, friends and neighbors, continued to pay their respect through their songs of grief. These were mournful funeral songs they all knew so well. Death was no stranger to them. They had traveled this path many times!

These were not hired mourners, crying because thay had been paid. These were friends, touched by the death of a dear friend. As Jeremiah had written concerning the nation,

*let them make haste and raise a wailing over us.*

Arriving at the place of the family tomb, Jonathan read a few of the Psalms and offered prayers. Those carrying the bier stepped through the opening and placed Elizabeth's body on the prepared platform. It would remain there until the next family member was buried. Then the remains would be placed in the back of the tomb, along with those ancestors of long ago. Elizabeth was now in Yahweh's hands.

One by one, those close to the family stepped inside to say their farewells. The others remained outside and waited. When Zechariah's turn came, he would not budge.

"I will not enter, not until I join her in death. For now we are apart, but soon we will be together again. Yahweh gives and Yahweh takes away!"

Choked with grief, he began a slow walk home, alone. Head bowed, he looked neither to the right nor the left. He was leaving the joy of his life behind him.

Then it was John's turn. Entering the dark and cool interior he moved slowly toward the bier. Looking down on his mother's body, he began to speak, hesitantly, slowly.

"Mother, I know I caused you and father a lot of trouble. I thought life was nothing but fun. Even when I went to stay at Yahweh's Temple, I kept playing games.

"Now I know better. Mother, I'm growing up! In my running away, and being away, even if it was just one night, I see my life differently. You and father were right. I believe Yahweh does have a purpose for me. I don't know what it is, but I will try to be patient and wait until he shows me the way.

"I promise, mother, I will! You will be proud of me! And I promise I will take good care of your Zechariah!"

With that, the longest serious speech he had ever made, he leaned over, kissed his mother's forehead, wiped his eyes and stepped outside.

In the manliest voice he could muster he commanded, "Roll the stone in place!"

The next morning John could not find his father. He was neither in the house nor in the village. At first, John thought he had gone to the tomb, but he was wrong. Thinking of all the other possibilities, he walked up the valley to the olive tree grove. He was not there. Finally, he decided to make the long walk into Jerusalem and to the Temple, hoping his father would be there. It was not his turn to serve, but John could think of no other place where his father might be found. Other than his love for Elizabeth, the Temple was his life!

John was right. His father was in the Temple, making work where there was no work. He was polishing the bronze jars that held water for Temple use. That was the work of servants or the young novice priests, not for the elders of the priesthood, but Zechariah was doing it.

When John questioned him, he became rather angry.

"No one in all this holy place polishes these vessels properly. I'm doing it because I want to make sure everyone understands. This is Yahweh's Temple, Yahweh's perfect Temple, and everything here must be perfect! Can't you see that? Everyone working here needs to see how it is done!"

With every word his voice grew louder, until those some distance away turned, wondering about the commotion. It was not right to make that sort of noise here. Surely, old Zechariah, of all people, should know that!

When he finally paused to rest, John suggested his father stop and turn that duty over to someone else.

"After all, father, you are too important to be doing this. You do set a good example, but there are other important duties needing your attention. Let's go find Jonathan. You know how much he depends on you! He wants you to help him with other responsibilities, not just the polishing. Yes, you are right. This is Yahweh's holy Temple."

With some difficulty, John moved his father toward the priest's quarters. He would do his best to divert his attention. Suddenly, John realized his father was an old man. His mind was failing!

Later that morning, after John had persuaded his father to rest, he went to find Jonathan. He needed his advice. He knew, first of all, his father would not be happy away from the Temple. With Elizabeth's death, their home would create too much heartache, and bring back too many memories. At the same time, because of his age and condition, he would be of little help to his Division leader. What could he do for his father? Where could his father stay and be happy?

"Sir, may I share my concerns with you?" he asked Jonathan. He laughed as he began to respond to Jonathan's "Yes."

"I'm still quite young, just a boy, but I am almost 13 years old. Before this year is out I will begin my religious training under Rabbi Justin. I am growing up.

"I know how much trouble I've been these past years. You must have been terribly upset over the way I acted when I came with my father to the Temple. You should have sent me back home long ago, but you didn't. You not only showed a lot of patience, but you gave me a good friend, Eljah, to work with me.

"The day I ran away was no accident. I believe Yahweh had his hand in that. In those few hours I learned so very much. I met a stranger who touched my life in a most unusual way. I do not understand it, but my life was changed. You remember what my father said at my naming, that Yahweh had something in store for me? I've heard that story many times, and now I am convinced!

"However, the first and most important matter is my father. It is time to do what is best for him. I realize his age and his grief have made a big difference in his life. I believe you understand that and will want to help him."

"Yes, John," responded Jonathan, "I, too, believe Yahweh has a special task for you. Having been on duty when his messenger Gabriel spoke to your father at that Evening Sacrifice long ago, I know there is something unique ahead for you. As to what that might be, I have no idea.

"However, as you say, our main concern is your father. He is old, too old to be serving here. Yet, at the same time, we dare not tell him so, not now. On the other hand, we will not be able to convince him to return home and retire. That would kill him!

"For the present we will find simple tasks, things he can do. We want to convince him these are important! In the meantime I will talk with some of our elders. We need to find a better solution for him and for you."

John felt better, once he knew his father would be cared for and protected by close friends and co-workers. He didn't feel so good about himself. What could he do? Where would he stay? Would Jonathan permit him to be a part of the Temple life at his age? Things were different now. He was no longer a problem child, needing Eljah's oversight and direction. Yet, he was sure if he were permitted to stay, he would do little more than run errands, work in the kitchen area; probably feed birds and animals. If Yahweh had something in mind for him, it must be more than those duties!

For the next several days he stayed close to his father. He made sure he was eating properly, dressing properly, staying out of the way of the priests on duty. For himself, he, too, enjoyed the early morning prayers.

*Yahweh is in his holy Temple!*
*Let all the earth keep silent!*

It was only right and proper they come into his holy House with praise and thanksgiving and he needed to do just that! However, John knew he stood out like a sore thumb. He was not a priest and those who were from the other divisions raised questions from time to time.

"What is he doing here?"

"What right does he have to join us in worship and prayer?"

"He should be kept outside the Priest's Court. Ever since he has been here he has been nothing but trouble."

It was only through the word and influence of Jonathan, and the reluctant approval of the High Priest, he was permitted to stay and share in some of the Temple duties. Eljah, of course, was delighted. Whenever he was on duty he did his best to be of help to both John and his father Zechariah, watching over both in their assigned duties, making room for them in his own sleeping space.

When his Division was not serving, he would invite John to his own quarters. He had secured rooms as close as possible to the Temple Mount, sharing expenses with two other young priests. There was always room for one more, and John was welcome.

For those times Jonathan would take Zechariah home with him. It made life difficult for Jonathan's wife, Miriam, but Zechariah was a dear friend. Both agreed Zechariah desperately needed both supervision and care.

As the weeks went by, John's life around the Temple became somewhat easier. He passed his 13th birthday and was now a taller young man. Because of his size many though he was older, perhaps a novice priest. In height he stood above Eljah's shoulder. Growing stronger he could handle most every task. A local rabbi helped him with his education, and in accordance with Jewish tradition, prepared him for acceptance into the next level of his life. He was taught the responsibilities of approaching manhood. The elders were impressed and Jonathan, representing his father Zechariah, took John into the Temple for the ceremony. For John it was confirmation of Yahweh's lordship over his life!

Occasionally, John would make the journey to their village, checking on the house, making sure all was in order. He made no attempt to encourage his father's company. Zechariah never offered to talk about his village life or his dear Elizabeth. Any questions were answered briefly or ignored.

The first time John walked home, he almost turned around before reaching the little village. He was ready to hurry back to Jerusalem, dreading the sight of an empty house. How could he go back and why should he? Neither his father nor his mother would be there to greet him. There was nothing awaiting him, only an unoccupied space! It took him a long time to move from the edge of the village, down the slope to their home.

He did go, but the first night he had trouble sleeping. The silence was frightening! Remembering, he could envision his mother preparing the meals and his father resting or talking to the neighbors. Those were pleasant memories, but also disturbing.

His mother was dead and his father's health was failing. This was no longer home, not as he had known it during those early childhood years. He had no family! He was alone!

He did recall his mother talking about a relative far to the north, up in the territory called Galilee. Her name was Mary and her husband's name, he thought, was Joseph. Long ago, when his mother was expecting his birth, this Mary had visited her and she, too, was expecting a baby. However, before John was born, and before this cousin Mary's baby was born, she returned to Galilee. To his knowledge, they never saw each other again. There were stories about the other baby being born south of Jerusalem, in Bethlehem, but John was quite young when those events were discussed, too young to remember the details. It had something to do with a Roman census that required every male to go back to his place of birth. Apparently, Mary's husband Joseph was a native of Bethlehem and their baby had been born there.

That first night, trying to dispel his fear and frustration, his imagination was aroused. Perhaps, someday, when he was older, he would travel north and find this family, his mother's relatives. The parents might not be living, but the baby would be. He should be just about John's age. John really wasn't sure as to whether the baby was a boy or a girl, but he seemed to remember his parents talking about a boy. Just think, he might find a cousin, a boy cousin! Before he fell asleep he promised himself he would try to get some information from his father. His father had trouble remembering a lot of things, but might remember that.

With the help of Jonathan, he made plans to sell the family property. However, his mother's best friend, Deborah, protested, insisting it should remain in Zechariah's family.

"Who knows?" she asked John. "You might come back here to live someday. I believe your mother would want that. If you don't object, we will look out for the land and the house while you are away. We will be happy to protect what is yours.

"Anyway, your father's health is failing and before long you will come back for his burial. I know we should not talk about that, but you are growing up John and I'm sure you understand. Your mother would be so proud of you. You are becoming a fine young man."

John agreed. He would wait.

Concerning the information about his mother's relatives in Galilee, his father was of no help. John approached the question in a number of different ways, but to no avail. Zechariah did remember someone named Mary, but the circumstances escaped him. He did know it was long ago, when they were expecting John's birth, with that being the focal point of their concern. Worry about his dear Elizabeth had blocked out everything else. There was a husband, he thought, a big man, a carpenter. Beyond that there was nothing.

Hoping the Division leader, Jonathan, might be of some help, John went to him with his questions. He, too, remembered the visitors coming, but little more. Zechariah did not attempt to share any such information since he was still speechless at the time. Anyway, Elizabeth's condition was of far greater concern back then, far greater than visiting relatives. Not being of any help, Jonathan laughed.

"With all that was going on then, John, you took center stage. Your parents had little time for anything else. If there is a cousin in the north I have no knowledge of that."

John tried to forget, but could not. There was a connection! He was sure of that. Someday he would find the answer. Someday, he hoped, their paths would cross. If Yahweh was working out something for him, it just might happen!

Late one afternoon, a few days before the annual Festival of the Passover, Jonathan sent for John. He wanted to discuss plans for his father Zechariah.

"John, I have talked with a number of the elders and they agree your father cannot continue here. With the passing of each day his condition worsens. I'm sure you are quite aware of our problem. He is interfering with too many of our activities.

"At the same time, they want you to know how much they appreciate his ministry. He has been a faithful servant of Yahweh, much longer than anyone else. We all hold him in high regard. We want to do what is best for him.

"Here is our consensus, that you move with him to a community located on this side of the Salt Sea. In distance that is not too far away, a little more than a day's journey. Actually, there are several communities located in the area, and all are occupied by groups of devout men we know as the pious ones or Essenes. Many of these men were priests or descendents of priests. Some were Pharisees, living and working here in Jerusalem. For the most part they think the priesthood and the Temple worship has strayed too far from the strict laws of Moses. They believe the Temple itself has been desecrated by what we do here. They say we worry too much about earthly possessions. You will see they worship Yahweh very intently!"

John interrupted.

"Why should we go there? From what I have heard and from what you tell me, we wouldn't fit in. Those people live a very dull and strict life; do a lot of ritual washing. Do you really think that would help my father?"

"No, John, they are not all like that. There are several communities, some not as strict as others. I have a friend living near Qumran, one who is a part of a more open group. At Qumran there are only men, males of all ages. They do have daily rituals of bathing and they frown on any sort of levity and fun. Their main concern centers on their teachings about the forces of Light and the forces of Darkness. They have many scribes copying the books of Moses, the psalms, the prophets, but mostly other writings that spell out their beliefs. You would not fit in there and that sort of life would not help your father.

"In my friend's village, the community of Tobba, they are permitted to marry and have their families with them. They grow their own food; prepare the animal skins for the scrolls used by the scribes at Qumran. That means many of the men are hunters, skilled in stalking the deer. The deer meat provides food for the community and most of the skins provide leather for the scribes of Qumran. Because of that, the residents of Tobba have much more freedom than some others. They can travel, visit outside the community.

"At Qumran and at another village being rebuilt, they need lots of skins for their writings. So they tolerate the others and permit them greater freedom, as long as they help the scribes. I believe you will like it. You are 13 years old now, and I think you will enjoy the outdoor life with those your age.

"Two things enter into our recommendation. First of all, the climate is mild, especially at this time of the year. We think that might help your father regain some strength. The other reason for our suggestion has to do with their simple life style, away from the busyness and confusion of Jerusalem. We believe that, too, will help your father.

"Also, I'm having difficulty getting approval to keep your father here any longer. Some of our priests with more influence than I have, want your father to retire to his village as soon as possible. I'm afraid they have the ear of the High Priest and will force the decision. That could come at any moment."

"I really don't like the idea," John answered. "Yet, I understand. It's sad to see, but I do know my father has reached the point of not being able to serve. He simply cannot remember what he is supposed to do. However, I know that retiring to our village would bring on my father's death sooner than necessary. We cannot do that!"

Thinking of his parents and the death of his mother, tears welled up in his eyes.

"We will miss you. You and your wife have done so much for my father. You were of much help with my mother, and I will certainly miss Eljah. He has meant so much to me, from the very first day I came to the Temple! We can never repay you!

"I will need your help! How soon do we have to leave and how will we travel? Who will go with us, to make sure we are safe? Who will help me get our possessions from home?"

"John, we will give you all the assistance we can. You can depend upon that. We love you and want the best for you and your father! I will hire some men to move your belongings. Eljah will have to stay here, preparing for the Passover. You really don't need to take much, only your personal things and extra clothing.

"My friend, Tobiah, will see that you have what you need in the way of furnishings. I have already contacted him and he is expecting you. He has assured me you will be in good hands, both you and your father. In a few days, right after the Passover, there will be a number of travelers going down to Jericho. There is safety in numbers and they will be with you until the road divides just above the Salt Sea. Tobiah and his friends will be waiting there. Your father will be provided a donkey. He will not have to walk!"

John, realizing the need to act, began to make plans for this new adventure. He would have to convince his father this was something exciting, a chance to see a different part of their land, an area traveled by their ancestor and leader, Moses! Also, he would be able to share his priesthood experiences with others!

It took a couple of days to take care of essentials in Jerusalem, putting his father's affairs in order. He left just as the Passover was beginning. He wanted to stay for the celebration, but time would not permit. For the present his greater concern was his father. They must be ready to leave Jerusalem when most of the travelers would be departing. It would be too dangerous for them to travel alone.

It was with a heavy heart John headed home, perhaps for the last time. The thought of leaving home was scary. Would he ever come back? What would happen to his father, facing a new way of life? Would it be better to bring him back to his village, or would Jonathan's plan be best? Those were nagging questions and the answers were difficult to find. Yet, he knew he must trust the advice of his elders and, above all, put his trust in Yahweh!

Arriving in late afternoon, his mother's friend, Deborah,

insisted he have the evening meal with her. She lived alone. Her husband, Jeriel, had died when John was just a small boy. They had one child, a son, who had married and moved away several years earlier. He lived in a small village near the shore of the Great Sea.

After supper they talked long into the night. John had forgotten that Deborah might know something concerning his mother's cousin; so he questioned her.

"Yes," responded Deborah. "At the time we thought her cousin would be of little help. She was so young! Her husband came with her, a tall, strong, handsome man. His name was Joseph. He didn't stay long, leaving your mother's cousin, Mary, here. His concern was his carpenter's work in Galilee, being able to earn enough money to care for his wife. Before she left we knew he had greater responsibilities. She, too, was expecting a child.

"Your mother knew, somehow, it would be a boy. I do remember that! And this young Mary insisted it would be a boy, just as your mother insisted you would be a boy.

"If your mother ever heard from her cousin again, I don't know. No one else came for a visit. Also, our immediate concerns were for your mother. At her age she was having a very difficult time carrying you!"

"That is strange," John responded. "If my mother had so few relatives. you would think they would have kept in touch, sharing news about their little boys."

"No," answered Deborah, "it is a long distance to Galilee and the route is difficult. Going directly north from Jerusalem, the shortest route takes you through Samaria. Most of our people have always tried to avoid contact with the Samaritans. So, they go down to the Jordan River at Jericho and cross over to the other side before heading north. It is a longer and slower route, but it is safe and it avoids any contact with those people."

"I'm not familiar with any of that," John responded. "I can't make that journey now, but I will someday! Now I must put things in order here. My father's Division leader, Jonathan, is sending some men to help me with the packing. As soon as the Passover is over we will be leaving for that community near the Salt Sea. If you will look out for our home here I will feel much better about leaving. We are very grateful for your offer to do so.

"Also, with Jonathan's help, I have made arrangement to turn my father's olive oil business over to the Temple. That way they can still make use of the oil for the Temple lamps. Any income will be held in trust for my father."

Deborah assured John again she would care for their home, making sure no one would disturb the house or contents.

Where were the men Jonathan had promised to send? John had gone through every corner of the house and property; packing up what he felt would be needed for the move. He had stored some things in Deborah's home, items she could use. Now, he was ready to leave, anxious to return to Jerusalem. Knowing the Passover was over, John was impatient to be on his way. If the promised help did not come soon, he would have to return to Jerusalem alone, carrying what he could. That meant he would have to make one more trip back.

Finally, late the next day, after the sun had set, two men arrived. Busy with the affairs of the Passover, Jonathan had forgotten. It was only after the Festival he remembered what he had promised. Along with the men came his apologies and the assurance there was plenty of time. The largest group going to Jericho would not leave for two more days.

Again, Deborah came to the rescue. She had three guests for dinner that night. The hour was late, too late to be walking back to Jerusalem. The two workers sent by Jonathan slept in Zechariah's empty house, using their cloaks as cover. The air was cool, but they were protected by the enclosure Zechariah had built years before. John slept at Deborah's, his last night in his home village. Although he had no way of knowing, he would never return!

Early the next morning John said his thankful but tearful goodbyes to Deborah. Several other early risers came by to wish him well. They reminded John their town would never be the same. He and his father Zechariah would be missed! It was a difficult morning.

Returning to Jerusalem, John and the two workers headed for the priest's quarters. As the Morning Prayers were over John went looking for Eljah. However, Eljah was nowhere to be found. He had completed his tour of duty with the ending of the Passover and the Sabbath and had returned to his own quarters in the city.

Finding Jonathan, John was assured the carriers had been paid and the loads would be safe at Jonathan's house. Tomorrow they would be leaving for their new home! In the meantime, Jonathan suggested that John find Eljah. He would share with John some rather exciting news concerning the Passover. He could do so better than Jonathan, sharing firsthand news, something he had seen with his own eyes. Zechariah was resting at Jonathan's home, with Miriam keeping him busy, away from the Temple!

Immediately, John left the Temple Mount and headed for the city streets and Eljah's residence. He hadn't gone too far until he spotted his friend. Eljah, seeing John coming, rushed to meet him in the busy street. Thinking of things to come, their separation, they embraced each other, mindless of the people walking by. It would not be easy to say goodbye!

Eljah lived near one of the larger markets in the city, a convenience for shopping, but seldom ever quiet during the day. He had just finished purchasing bread and fruit and was on his way to his own quarters. As they walked along, he began to tell the news of the Passover

"John, we've missed you! I only wish Jonathan had let you stay here for the Passover. We really had some excitement! A young boy, just about your age, sure made an impact on those who heard him. Everyone said they had never seen or heard such a thing."

"What do you mean 'heard him'? What was he saying," asked John.

"No one seems to know because no one expected a young boy like that to talk so seriously about Yahweh and Yahweh's Temple. It all started with the rabbis gathering for their daily teaching on the Torah as it related to the Festival. You know how some of them love to talk, especially the younger ones just out of rabbinical school.

"As usual, they were surrounded by quite a crowd, especially those from other territories. It was then this young boy, obviously from the north, I think from Galilee, began to ask questions, questions about the Torah. You could tell by his tunic and cloak he was not from Judea.

"Several times he asked, "Was this Yahweh's Law or man's law?" They were hard pushed to come up with the answers. Some, particularly the younger ones, tried to bluster their way through, as though he was just an ignorant child wanting to make trouble.

"That's when the crowd began to chuckle and even laugh. They were enjoying the embarrassment of those who tried to show they knew so much. Rabbis are supposed to be learned men, teachers of the Law, and this boy seemed to know more than they knew. It was something to see! As we watched we were not only amazed at his questions, but we sensed this was so very different from anything we had ever seen or heard! You should have been here!

"And, would you believe it! The next day he was back again. This time he was doing most of the talking, describing the importance of Yahweh in their lives. Not only that, he kept referring to Yahweh as his father! That really caused quite a stir, most disturbing to those teachers of the Law. They just didn't know what to make of this young boy. Even the older priests were impressed.

"I'm not sure what would have happened, if it had gone on much longer, but it didn't. It came to an abrupt end when his parents came, looking for him. They were quite upset. From what they said, they had been looking for him for three days. You know what he said?"

"No," said John, "I don't know, but hurry and tell me. I can't believe what I'm hearing!"

"He said, 'Didn't you know I would be in my father's Temple?' Can you believe that? What do you think, John, what do you think he meant?"

"Eljah, I have no idea, but I have a strange feeling this is more than a boy full of curiosity. This disturbs me! Tell me about his parents. Describe them!"

"As best I can remember, the mother was quite beautiful, not too tall. Surprisingly, she was the one speaking first. She rushed up, hugged the boy and asked: 'Son, why have you treated us like this? Your father and I have been so worried. We thought you were with our friends, but you weren't. It has been three days of searching before we found you!'

"That's when he talked about his father's Temple, as though they should have known where to find him."

"Eljah, was the man tall, broad-shouldered, bearded? Did he have the hands of a farmer or carpenter? Did he have very little to say?"

"How did you know that, John? That's a perfect picture, a man fitting precisely your description. He was quiet, saying very little. The mother did most of the talking."

"Eljah, I can't explain it, but I truly believe this boy, as you call him, just might be my cousin on my mother's side. His mother's name would be Mary, and his father's name would be Joseph. Did you hear their names mentioned?"

"No, I didn't hear any names, and they left right away with nothing more being said. The boy took his mother's hand, smiled at her and walked away, the father following behind. They simply disappeared."

"Eljah, I must find out if this boy might be my cousin. Not only that, I can't help but believe there is more, that this cousin has been called of Yahweh, just as my parents have always said Yahweh planned my birth.

"You remember the day I ran away! Since coming back, I've never had the chance to tell you all that happened. With my mother's death, my father's failing health and our concerns for the future, there were just too many things going on.

"That night, after leaving the Temple Mount, I ended up far beyond the lower city. Tired and cold I went to sleep against the wall of one of the tents erected in a large open space, surrounded by sheep and camels. Those occupying the tent woke me up during the night, took me in to warmth and food.

"That's when it happened, standing before those strangers, Egyptians they were. They introduced me to their leader, the person they called the exalted one. He looked at me a long time, and then bowed down, placing my hands on his head. The one man understanding our language explained:

"Our leader who studies the stars sees you as a holy person. He cannot see your future, but he knows great events will be a part of your life. He has seen only one other person like you, a young girl he met some years ago, a girl living in a small village far north of Jerusalem.

"Eljah, that has to be that young boy's mother, the one we think is from Galilee. I have to know! I have to find out if all this is true, that this one is truly related to me. I'm frightened, Eljah!"

"John, that is frightening and I sure don't have the answers, but I do know your immediate concern is your father. I think your best move is to go through with Jonathan's plans, moving your father down near the Salt Sea. The group going to Jericho is leaving in the morning and you need to be with them.

"As to the family from Galilee, if that is their home, I will ask Jonathan's permission to travel north, as far as the sea located there. You will not be too far away and I will be able to let you know what I learn. Trust me, we will find them!"

Early next morning the small group of travelers gathered near Jonathan's home. Jonathan, Miriam, Eljah and a number of Zechariah's fellow priests were there to see them off. An early start was essential. Although it was pleasant weather in Jerusalem, it would be hot in the wilderness below. The road to Jericho, winding south below the Temple Mount, would go through a dry and desolate land. There would be little vegetation and few trees.

All were concerned about marauders, the ones many called the "wild ones." They were always a danger to travelers, robbing and killing. No one dared travel that road alone, and even groups like theirs could be attacked. It was time to be on their way, arriving in the area of Jericho before dark. Most of the Passover pilgrims had departed the day before and there would be few others on the road.

They were all walking, except for John's father. Jonathan had made arrangements for a saddle placed on a donkey. It was not the most comfortable ride, but better than walking! It would be a tiring journey for everyone.

The appointed leader of the group was Ephlal, a man from Jericho. John was amazed to hear his father comment on the name, after introductions were made.

"You should be the leader! One of our ancestors named Ephlal was a tribal leader, a descendant of Judah."

Perhaps, John thought, this move south might be good for his father after all. He had hopes it would be so and a silent prayer to Yahweh expressed his wishes.

Near the middle of the day, with the sun rising high in the clear sky, they stopped to rest at a place well known to those who had made that journey. There was one tree and a house, a shelter of mud and stonewalls. Overhead was a flat roof of sticks and palm branches. Some called it an inn, but there was little to offer, other than shade from the sun. A man and his wife lived there, alone. She pointed to a large jar of water, water from the only spring in the area, but no one wanted to drink from it. A few washed faces and hands. They had brought their own water for the trip, water from the pools of Solomon; carried in goatskins.

Very soon Ephlal insisted they should be on their way, even though some wanted rest longer. He was anxious to reach Jericho as soon as possible.

"We need to be very careful now. The road is steeper, with many turns and there are caves where the wild ones can hide. Hopefully, we will have no trouble, but you can never be sure."

Leaving the so-called inn, they followed Ephlal's instructions. They began to move a little faster as the winding road sloped downward. Zechariah wanted to get off his donkey and walk with the others, but John managed to prevent that.

"Father, you will help us more if you ride. We can move more rapidly that way. Besides, Jonathan was nice to provide the animal and you wouldn't want to hurt his feelings, would you?"

Those who had never traveled the road down to Jericho began to experience the reality of a wilderness for the first time. It was desolate! In the distance the rolling hills, now rising steeper as they descended, were dark and foreboding. There was hardly any grass and the plants along the way were scrubby and dry. Sometimes in the late Spring there were a few showers, but not this year. It was dry, and hot!

By now, the sun was beginning to drop into the western sky. With the hills rising higher and steeper toward the southwest, shadows began to stretch across the descending road. Early in the afternoon they had met a few people going upward to Jerusalem, but for the last hour they had seen no others.

John, concerned for his father, caught up with Ephlal.

"How much farther is it to the road which turns west to the Salt Sea? It is getting late and my father is very tired. Friends living near Qumran are to meet us where the road forks. From there we still have some distance to travel."

Ephlal's response was heartening: "Do you see that ridge over to the right, the one just beyond that one on the left side?

I remember that beyond that hill the road forks. We should be there very soon!"

Knowing they were nearing the place of the two roads, their pace quickened. It would be nice to see other people again. Even though the hills on either side were higher, blocking out most of the afternoon sun, the journey was coming to an end. They understood that from the fork in the road one could see the houses of Jericho. In the other direction Qumran was nearby.

Almost without any warning, it happened! They were attacked, surrounded by marauders, robbers, the wild ones. There was little time to defend themselves, even if they had carried any weapons. John tried his best to use his fists, swinging arms toward those who came. He would protect his father at any cost!

John was almost the only one resisting and he drew the immediate attention of the attackers. Surrounded by two men, he had little chance. A blow to his head ended his attempted resistance. The last thing he saw was his father being dragged off the donkey. There was a brilliant, shattering light and then, darkness!

# CHAPTER 7

*... the hand of the Lord was with him*
                              Luke 1:66b

He was awakened by the sound of voices, sometimes loud, but most times soft and muted. He thought they were voices. He was sure they were voices! The disturbing thing for John was his inability to make sense of what was being said, or respond. Also, there was another sound, a scraping sound. He didn't know it, but he was being rocked back and forth, and it was not comfortable. In fact, it was a bumpy swing, sometimes more up and down than from side to side. He hurt, at every sudden jolt!

He tried to open his eyes, but with little success. He sensed only noise and movement and neither helped explain what was happening. Where was he and why couldn't he see? Sure! It was only a dream. It must be! Once he awakened, all this would disappear and he would find himself in his own bed in the priest's quarters. After a time, what seemed to be an eternity, the sounds and the noises were gone. He drifted off into the darkness, again.

Each time he tried to open his eyes he could not focus them on anything. The light would return and then disappear. Yet, even when there was light, he could not distinguish any shape or form. Also, the sounds of voices and the bumpy swing returned, but gave no clue as to what was taking place. He felt he was in a thick cloud, cut off from the real world and very much alone! He did remember there was darkness, then the light, then the darkness returning, followed by more light, a different light. One other thing was different. There was no movement, no bumpy swinging up and down. All was still and quiet.

Then the voices returned, close voices, now hovering right above him. However there was no comprehension. Nothing made sense! Was he dead or alive?

After a time, and he wasn't sure when, he felt pressure on his face. The pressure was that of a rough but warm, wet cloth. This time his effort to open his eyes was successful. Above him was a form, the shape of a figure. At first the figure was just a dark object out of focus. Then, as the cloth was rubbed across his face again, wiping his eyes, the figure took shape. It was a girl, a young girl with the longest, darkest hair he had ever seen!

This time he tried to lift his head. He wanted to sit up. He tried to push down with his arms so that he could sit up, but that was a mistake, a big mistake! Pain! He had never experienced such pain. This was in his right arm, his strongest arm. He passed out, again. He didn't know it, but his arm was broken, badly broken!

Drifting in and out of darkness and trying, desperately to clear his throat, he managed, finally, a brief "Where am I?" He wanted to ask another question, but the words would not come. He wanted to know who was this pretty girl, a girl he had never seen before. Why was she wiping that warm cloth across his face?

A flood of memories raced through his brain. Somewhere in the past another girl had washed his face, and more. Could this be the same girl? Was he back in the warmth of a nomad's tent, waiting for something to eat? It was too confusing!

The response didn't help John at all. At the sound of his voice the girl turned away, calling to someone else. She said, "Father, he's awake! He's awake!" With that outburst, she ran from the room, leaving John without answering his "Where am I?"

Watching her exit, staring at the door, John saw a man enter, a tall, thin man. Coming over to John he looked down, smiled, and spoke.

"I am Tobiah, the one your Jonathan said would meet you at the fork in the Jericho road. We met you, but you didn't know it. You were bleeding, unconscious and almost dead. Two others were dead, one being your father Zechariah. I am sorry I have to be the bearer of bad news, but it is only right you should know. There were no signs of injuries. Apparently his heart had given out. When we arrived he was lying beside the road. There was nothing we could do to revive him."

John fainted, again. In no condition to deal with such tragic information, he blacked out. Hurriedly, Tobiah called for help. He did not believe John's condition was critical, but he could not be sure. Upon the return of his daughter, he sent her to fetch Japhia, the village elder skilled in medicine. He would know what to do!

Japhia was nowhere to be found, but by the time his daughter came back, John was conscious, trying to ask more questions.

"Tell me, where am I! What happened to my father? What happened to those traveling with us? My mind is blank! I can't remember a thing! One minute we were approaching our destination, and now I'm here, wherever here might be. You are telling me my father Zechariah is dead? Why did Yahweh let that happen?"

Exhausted, he closed his eyes, eyes filled with tears, too many tears for one so young. What would happen next, and where was Yahweh in all this?

Tobiah kept silent, letting John cry. There was little he could do, other than wait.

Finally, after the sobs had subsided, after John opened his eyes again, Tobiah went on telling him what had happened.

"Let me go back and tell the whole story, as I know it. We were at the arranged spot early, waiting for your party to arrive. It was a pleasant afternoon and the sun was still shining above the hills. Thinking we had plenty of time we walked on into

Jericho, picking up some needed supplies. Meeting friends who had just returned from the festival of the Passover in Jerusalem, we left Jericho later than we intended. We hurried back as fast as we could, but when we reached the fork in the road, you had not arrived. At first we weren't worried, but that changed quickly.

"It was then we heard the commotion up the road, around the bend, in the direction of Jerusalem. Fearing the worst, we ran as fast as we could, but not in time to prevent the attack by the wild ones. We did have reason to thank Yahweh for what followed. Our arrival and our shouting drove off the robbers. Left alone they would have taken everything, even your clothes. We arrived before that happened.

"We though you were dead, along with your father and one other man. Apparently, two of you put up some resistance. It was quite evident they attacked you first, with much force.

"Our first duty was to bind up your wounds and the wounds of others. By that time some men had come out from Jericho, and they were kind enough to see the others in your party safely home. Also, at my request, a friend from Jericho brought his oxen and threshing sled. We placed you and your father's body on that and started home to our village.

"By then it was dark, and we had to move slowly. We wanted to make sure the ride would not do more damage to your wounds. We could tell one arm was broken. The worst wound was a deep gash on the back of your head. You had lost a lot of blood.

"Before we arrived here, the waning moon was rising in the east, giving better light to our travels. You stirred several times, but never really awakened. I suppose the moonlight and the light from our torches did that, made you react. There was very little light as we passed Qumran. By that time of the night most of the residents were asleep. Only the scribes work late at their tables, writing by oil lamps.

"Once we arrived, our elder skilled in medicine took charge, setting your arm, cleaning your cuts and applying salve. The worst was the cut on your head, but he assured us you would be fine. So, here you are, where Jonathan wanted you to live, you and your father. Welcome to Tobba!"

As the days and weeks went by, John's wounds and fracture healed. His right arm was still weaker than the left, but daily exercise prescribed by the elder, Japhia, made for improvement. He knew he would be strong and healthy again!

There was little healing for his spirit. Both mother and father were dead, his father's tomb nearby. Most every day, as he regained his strength, he would walk to the burial place. Although he avoided the daily rituals of the village, unwilling to be involved in the cleansing baths prescribed for the worship of Yahweh, he prayed. He prayed the prayers learned in the Temple, those taught him by his father and by the rabbis, but he went beyond that. He questioned Yahweh, something he had heard no one else dare do. He argued with Yahweh, although that was one-sided. He asked Yahweh for a sign, something to show him Yahweh was listening. He reminded Yahweh of the promise made long ago, the promise that he, John, was destined to be an instrument of Yahweh.

Now that he had passed his 13th birthday, he felt it was time for some answers, some call or instruction, but no answers came! Yahweh, as far as John could tell, was either deaf to what he had to say, or did not want to respond. There was little healing for his spirit.

Frustrated by what was not happening, John tried a different approach. He would forget about Yahweh! He would take part in the village activities. He would fill his mind with other things. He would shut out all thoughts of Yahweh. If Yahweh wanted something of him he, Yahweh would have to be the one to speak, or ask!

He went to Tobiah, asking for permission to go with the hunters looking for deer. That should take his mind off his problems! He knew it would involve a lot of work, but be good for him. He would have to learn the use of the bow, but that shouldn't be too difficult.

Tobias asked and the hunters agreed to teach John, but with a warning. If he were not serious about learning their skills, he would not be accepted. If he could not keep up with them in the hunt, he would be rejected. They took their talents seriously, a work both helpful and essential to those preparing the scrolls at Qumran. The deerskins would have to be dried, softened and scraped thin. Their work would not be complete until the skins were ready for the scribes' pens.

For the first few weeks, they assigned one of the younger hunters as John's teacher, a sixteen-year-old named Mered. He would teach John in the use of the bow. However, bows and arrows required wood. They would go hunting, not for deer, but for wood. Mered knew where to go and which woods were most desirable for making strong bows and straight arrows. The bows would be strung with deer gut. The arrows would be tipped with bone or flint.

John had not anticipated this, but knowing the rules set by the hunters, he agreed. He would go with Mered and look for wood. Actually, there was wood on hand, already drying, some ready to be used, but for each bow bent and each arrow tipped, additional wood must be gathered for future use. You dare not run out of the proper materials.

Early one morning John met Mered in the courtyard of the villa, the farm estate. Some years before, a wealthy Roman had tried to develop farming near the Salt Sea. Conscripted labor and slaves had built a complex centered around the living quarters of the owner and his family. The rather elaborate and extensive villa had a central hall, a reception hall, a library, a dining area for both indoor and outdoor eating, and bedrooms for sleeping. Trellises had been built over all the exterior spaces, with plants providing shade from the hot sun. Date palms had been carted in and planted in profusion.

There was a bathing pool, a kitchen, a bake house, a wine-storing yard and a threshing floor. There were walled areas for the farm animals, oxen and donkeys. There were barracks for the slaves and farm workers.

However, the attempts at farming were unsuccessful. The estate had been abandoned. Also, King Herod had built a fortress on a nearby mountaintop and the Romans wanted no part of this eccentric half-Jew. Neither the Jews nor the Romans thought much of this Idumean. If he wanted to live in that desolate part of Judea, actually a part of ancient Idumea, let him. He could have it!

With no protest or opposition, the Essenes moved in, expanding the villa into a whole village. Tobiah, with his wife and children, occupied the main house and the rest of the villagers built their homes around the Roman villa. It was ideal! The bathing pools provided water for their baptismal and ritual baths. All were pleased with the results.

It was to this villa and house they had brought John the night of the attack. He was cared for and nursed back to health in Tobiah's son's room. After he was well, able to care for himself, he was given space in the old barracks. No one else lived there. It was reserved for guests like himself. His meals were served in the large open dining room in good weather, which meant most of the time. The community, which was not a large one, took their meals together. Mothers with very small children ate in their own living quarters.

Supplied with dried fruit and skins of water Mered and John left the village and headed east, away from the direction of Herod's fortress. Skirting the Qumran community they turned toward the cliffs.

"Mered," asked John, "why are we going up against those high cliffs? We surely can't climb up there!"

Mered laughed. "No, we aren't climbing, not today. Just over that next rise you will see where we are headed. You will be pleasantly surprised. There is a narrow opening, a small wadi that cuts into the cliff and leads to a waterfall and lots of surrounding trees. It is a beautiful place! Most strangers walking on this side of the Salt Sea can't see the opening, and don't know about the waterfall. It is so out of place in this desolate country, and no one wants to wander far off the road. The thorns and spiny thistles don't make for easy walking. Their blossoms are pretty in the Spring. Most of the year they are hard and dry.

"Also, the water from the falls, for the most part, goes underground as it runs toward the sea. The rest is absorbed in the rocky sand. If you want to use that water you have to dig a well."

Mered was right! It was a surprise, an unexpected and beautiful setting. High overhead, the water tumbled down a worn recess in the cliff. After years of flowing, the water had cut deeply into the rocky face. With the passage of time the cut had widened, providing space for several kinds of trees, large trees. There were cypress, oak, sycamore, birch, ash and cedar. Here, the oaks were not very tall, not useful for their needs. It was from the young ash trees they would get wood for their bows. The birch would provide wood for arrows. Arrow tips were made of bone taken from the deer. Stone tips were available, but had to be purchased from traders coming down from the far north. Very few could afford the cost.

Mered knew just where to swing the short axe he had carried across his shoulder. It was sharp and they soon had a supply of wood. He stood the birch pieces on end and, with John holding the wood upright, began to split the wood. This was best done while the wood was still green. The final trimming would come later. Others would trim the ash into the bow shapes, bending the ends before drying.

Tired from their long walk and the cutting and splitting, Mered and John sat down to rest in the shade of the largest sycamore tree, sharing dried fruit and water. The water tumbling down the cliff had a rather unpleasant taste. One could drink it, but the better water was drawn from wells. Those living at Qumran had water from a similar source, but, according to

Mered, the water from their waterfall was of much better quality. This they used for drinking, cooking and their ritual baths.

Lying back, watching the sea birds, the small woods birds and the large hawks overhead, John closed his eyes. The rest was good for him, just recovering from his wounds and fractures. For a time it was very quiet and peaceful.

He was awakened by Mered's voice and questions.

"Tell me, John, about the Temple. I understand you lived there with your father. I thought the Temple was for old men, the priests serving in the Temple. What did you do?"

"Yes, Mered, I did live there with my father, at least part of the time. My parents were quite old when I was born and my mother couldn't keep up with a little boy running all over the place. Our village was some distance from Jerusalem and when my father was on duty at the Temple, mother tried to keep up with me, but that was a problem. From all indications I was not only overactive, I was into everything, at home and everywhere. The neighbors made their complaints, so much so that my father decided to keep me in Jerusalem when he was on duty.

"They put me under a young priest, hoping he could get me to settle down, grow up and be a good boy. Eljah, the young priest, did his best, but with not much success. It was not until my mother died that I began to act like I should."

John said nothing about the prediction of Yahweh's messenger, or about his encounter with the stranger from Egypt.

"The Temple is an awesome place. It is beautiful! You must see it someday. Maybe you and I could make that trip together. I could introduce you to some special people; get you into areas forbidden to most people. You would be impressed! When the priests on duty come together for worship, singing the psalms, offering the prayers and sacrificies, you feel close to Yahweh himself!

"As to what I did, it wasn't much. I ran errands for the priests, cleaned out the cages for the sacrificial birds and animals. That part I did not like. Sometimes I would let some go, and that made the priests angry. Then, I worked in the kitchen, helping clean and prepare the food for cooking. That was the one job I really didn't like. I took every chance to be absent when I was called."

Mered didn't think too much of what John was describing.

"My father says the Temple is not being used properly, that there is too much interest in power and wealth, that too many priests think more of themselves than they think of Yahweh. That's why they moved here, before I was born. This is our home and here I want to stay! Maybe, just maybe, I'll go with you for a visit. From what you tell me, I'm curious to see Jerusalem, and the Temple.

"But, tell me, what about the girls? Were there any pretty girls around the Temple? Did you know any girls from Jerusalem?"

John thought for a moment, puzzled by Mered's question. "There were no girls within the Temple, only those who came with their parents to worship in the outer courts. Girls didn't have anything to do with the Temple! Why do you ask?"

"Have you ever kissed a girl?" Mered responded, "gotten close to a girl so that you get excited down here," pointing to his loincloth.

Seeing John's puzzled expression over his unexpected question, Mered went on.

"John, you are old enough, and big enough to know about such things. Didn't you ever hear men talk about making babies? If you don't know, it's time you learned!"

"Sure," said John, "I've heard the priests, when they didn't know I was listening, telling jokes and laughing about such things. However, they always shut up when they saw me coming. Growing up, all that made little sense to me, and didn't interest me. No one, neither my father nor my mother ever told me about babies. The rabbi tried to explain, especially about what you were not to do, something about adultery. We had to study the laws of Moses and that was included. However, when we wanted to know more, asking a lot of questions, the rabbi put us off. He said we would learn all that when we grew up. I guess

I learned more from other boys my age, but we weren't old enough to do more than giggle over all that.

"What about you? How do you know all this? Have you gotten excited as you say? Surely, you haven't made any babies, have you? That's not supposed to happen before you're married. That's what the rabbi taught us."

"No, I haven't made any babies, but I have been excited . . . but enough of that! Let's get our things together and go home. We don't want to be late for the evening meal."

Back at Tobba, John's days were filled with bows and arrows. Sometimes, at night, he would try to think through what Mered had said about girls. The only time he had attention called to his groin, he had been sent off to the public toilets by the Egyptian's slave girl. He did remember in the washing, as she held him around the waist and touched his genitils, he had a flushed feeling and a sudden erection, but that was very brief. At his age, he had thought no more about it. There were too many traumatic things happening in his life.

More recently, brought wounded to Tobba, he first opened his eyes to Tobiah's daughter washing his face. He couldn't get that out of his mind, the warm touch of a pretty girl with long, black hair. It was a nice feeling! Was that what Mered was talking about, the excitement of being close to girls? He would have to find out!

For John, the bows were hard to handle. It took a lot of strength to pull back the string of deer gut. Then there was the problem of the arrow, aiming it accurrately and hitting the target. John had learned well the art of bow and arrow construction. His skill at heading and feathering the arrows was unique, especially for one who had never made arrows. Using the leg bone of the deer, he could fashion a point able to cut through the toughest hide used as a target. The feathers of the hawk were used to send the arrow straight and true. The men were pleased with his developing skills of construction, but not of action.

John's problem, failing to develop the hunter's accurracy with the bow, was irritating to say the least. For his first, feeble attempts, they all laughed at him, but before long the laughter stopped. There was no great improvement. It wasn't that his arms were not strong enough. His healing was complete. It was a matter of coordination, understanding the dynamics of flight; the smooth movement of both arms working together. Some of the arrows reached the distance, but fell wide of the target. All wanted him to succed, but they knew he would not be able to join them if he could not handle the bow. On the next hunt he was left behind, and the next, and the next.

John's daily routine became boring. Confined to the area around the village, there was little or no contact with the outside world. He and Mered did make another trip to the waterfalls, looking for a special wood for arrows, as well as flint for the arrowheads. There was the report of a passing stranger, saying he had seen flint stone protruding from the base of a particular cliff. They searched, but never found any.

One trip was to Qumran, carrying a supply of deerskins ready for the scrolls. Tobiah took John with him, wanting to introduce him to the elders. To John's surprise they were well received, invited to walk through the village and observe the scribes at work. In one of the largest buildings, in a long narrow room called the Scriptorium, a number of men were bent over tall desks, copying from one scroll to another. They neither looked up nor spoke as John and Tobiah entered. They were intent upon their writing! With fine brushes and ink cups of baked clay they continued to write, as John noted, in Hebrew. He could not see what was being written or copied, not daring to peer too closely over a man's shoulder.

At that time of the day, sunlight poured through several

open windows. He was told that many worked late at night after the sun went down and after the windows were closed. Oil lamps provided the necessary light. There seemed to be a sense of urgency in their writing. Time was a factor!

Other members of the community were busy with a grove of fruit trees and a small area for planting grain. These were located some distance away. Bread was prepared in a mill and bakery. There was a long arbor of grape vines and a wine press. The Qumran community was noted for its fine wine. Throughout the area there were a number of small pools for the daily ritual bathing required of all. Their water source was a broad aqueduct, bringing a good supply from a distant waterfall, as Mered had explained.

There were a few young men around, but most of the villagers were much older. John took note of the quietness. There was no loud talk. There was no laughter of children. It was depressing!

The elder in charge, Kemuel, seemed quite interested in John and the events that brought him to Tobba. Years before, he had lived in Jerusalem and served in the Temple as a young priest. Although he did not work with or under John's father, Zechariah, he remembered meeting him. Even back then, Zechariah the priest was well known and respected.

"John," he promised, "if you are ever in need, or if we can help you in any way, we will be here. We pray Yahwah's blessings on you and your life. May he use you for his work!"

In thanking him, John wondered. Why did Kemuel say that about Yahweh, and about him? Was his understanding of Yahweh that different from John's? Did he know something concerning the wrestling of John's heart and mind? He was sure he would never know!

John reached and passed his 14th birthday. Some days he was ready to leave, filled with anger and resentment. He was, it seemed, a prisoner in a life entirely foreign to him. Why should he stay? Why doesn't Yahweh speak to him? How long do I have to wait? Why do I have to put up with this village and these people?

On other days he was content to be lazy, to participate in the daily routine of the people of Tobba. He did learn to know the families, what they did each day, who cared for the few sheep they had raised, who did the farming and who cared for the fruit trees and the grape arbors. Those who did the tanning of the deer hides were a special group with a perculiar smell to their clothes and bodies. That was one trade that held little attraction! The one thing he wanted, more than anything else, was to go hunting for deer. He wanted to make use of his acquired skills!

Determined to perfect his shooting, he asked Tobiah's help in suggesting an out-of-the-way place where he could practice in private. He believed he would do much better without an audience watching him.

"There is an area west of here," responded Tobiah. We seldom go in that direction. For whatever reason, the deer never graze there. It could be they are avoiding the wildcats. Some think these are really lions, but we are not sure. I've never seen one, but we simply stay away. It is too desolate. I really wouldn't recommend it, but if you are determined to practice alone, that is the best place.

"Do you see that large outcropping of rock? No, not in that direction. Get behind me and look to where my arm is pointing. Do you see it?"

With John nodding his head he went on.

"It's a long walk, but not too far; if you need to call. On the other side the ground drops off into a narrow ravine. No one can see you there. It is the best place nearby. However, let me warn you! Don't go beyond the ravine. As you go around the next bend in the road, beyond the next high cliff, you can see King Herod's mountaintop fortress. If you get too close, you can really be in trouble. His soldiers and guards would not like that, and could arrest you.

On an afternoon, cooler than most days, even with a clear sky and the sun shining, the hunters were preparing to leave. John saw them off, gathered his gear of bow and arrows and headed west. He didn't know how long he would be gone so he went by the kitchen for a skin of water and a piece of hard sweet cake. He would be back in time for the evening meal.

The trip took longer than expected. There was no path in that direction. There was a road, but it was closer to the Salt Sea, in the direction of Herod's mountaintop fortress. He had to keep skirting around low bushes and thorn trees, trying to keep the rock in view.

Finally, arriving at the tall outcropping, John had to agree the place was ideal. There was the ravine, well hidden from the road. It would be perfect for his purpose. There were a lot of huge boulders around, and some scrubby bushes, thistles, but these would not interfere with his practice. If there were any wild animals about, he did have his weapon, the bow and arrows. He also carried a knife in his belt.

Stringing the bow, he began his practice. Using a distant small bush as a target, he shot every arrow. None came close! Disgusted, he retrieved the arrows and started over. Trying to remember Mered's instructions, he tried again. This time two arrows hit nearer to the target, but that was little satisfaction. He had to do better. He had to succeed!

The first arrow on his third try was the poorest shot yet, worse than all his other attempts. What was he doing wrong? If they could do it, he could do it! Putting the next arrow against the bow, he was determined to do better, but stopped. He thought he heard a noise, a strange sound. Was it a wild animal? Clutching his knife, he waited.

There it was, again, coming from a large clump of bushes. Trying to keep up his courage, he walked in that direction, until he heard the noise the third time. This time he relaxed. It was the sound of laughter. Someone was watching him!

Somewhat embarressed because of his poor performance, he called out.

"Who's there? Come on out!"

It was Tobiah's daughter, Debra, the one who had washed his face the night of his arrival. She had followed him from the village, had come to watch him practice.

"What are you doing here," John demanded. "Don't you know that's dangerous? I could have hit you with an arrow."

Debra laughed and said, "I don't think so, not the way you handle the bow. I can shoot better than that! It isn't hard to do, once you get the knack of it. He won't admit it, but I can shoot as well as Mered. Would you let me help?"

"What do you know about hunting, and where did you learn? You are just a girl, not a hunter!"

Debra, face flushed, shot back.

"Do you want to learn to shoot arrows, or not? I think you better learn, if you expect to go with those who kill deer."

John wasn't quite sure how to handle this. He did need to learn, and he wasn't getting anywhere on his own. Maybe, just maybe, this girl does know something. She was a part of a village and people whose lives centered in on hunting and preparing leather for the scribes of Qumran.

"Very well, if you know so much, tell me what to do."

"I can't tell you! I have to show you!"

Coming close, she had John put the notch of the arrow in the bowstring, pulling the string back until the head of the arrow was firmly against the center of the bow. Then she moved in closer, reaching her right arm around his. Her closeness, unexpected, felt good, but he tried to concentrate on her instructions.

"Hold the arrow with only two fingers," she said, "like this. Now look along your line of sight toward the target. At this distance you will have to elevate the bow this much. Use your forearm for sighting direction. Yes! That's it! Now! Release the arrow!"

Miracle of miracles! The arrow cut neatly into the distant

target bush. John couldn't believe his eyes. Now, it seemed so easy, so simple. He laughed, and Debra laughed.

"Once more, try it again."

This time she pushed her body closer against his, fixed his fingers, helped elevate the bow to the proper angle, reminding him to sight along his arm.

Again, it was distracting, most distracting, making it harder to think about accurate arrows.

"How can I shoot," he thought, "with you so close to me?"

What he said out loud was more to the point.

"You know you make it hard for me to practice, but I'm glad you're my teacher."

"Nonsense," Debra responded. "Just pay attention to what I say. Now! Let it fly!"

The second shot was as good as the first! Success!

"See there! You needed me, a girl, to teach you. That's the way it's done. Now, you have to pay me!"

"What do you mean, I have to pay you? I would, but I have nothing. The wild ones stole my money. What sort of pay do you want?"

"This is what I want. Kiss me!"

Before John could react, Debra took the bow out of his hands, put her arms tightly around him and raised her face to his, waiting.

Flustered by her sudden action and the warmth of her body, John obeyed. He leaned down and timidly placed his lips against her's.

Again, the unexpected! She opened her mouth, reaching into his with her darting tongue. Now he knew what Mered meant about getting excited. He felt the erection in his groins, ready to explode. Her closeness was more than the casual touch of an instructor.

Just as quickly, she released him and darted away. Reaching the side of the ravine, she called back.

"Practice your shooting with the bow so that you can go

with the hunters. And you need to practice your kissing. You are a poor lover. Maybe, someday, I'll give you another lesson!"

With that, climbing quickly out of the ravine, she was gone, running in the direction of the village.

John couldn't move. Overcome by this brief but unexpected pleasure, he stood helpless. This girl had stirred a passion unknown, until this moment. Was it simply that, a physical reaction between two bodies, one male and one female? He had been taught the facts to some degree, and had heard the language of his peers, plus the stories of the priests about intercourse. He had not been cautioned or told about the bursting emotions, other than Mered's reference to "excitement."

Not knowing what to do next, he sat down on the shady side of the ravine. Nibbling on the sweet cake he had brought with him, and drinking water from the skin bottle, his mind raced back and forth over the details of this brief encounter. Was this simply a matter of "growing up," or was this a part of a plan for his life, something to be taken seriously, something in which Yahweh had a hand?

Suddenly he realized he had brought up the name, Yahweh, something he had vowed to put out of his mind. Yahweh would have to come to him, he had said! Well, so be it! Yahweh would have to let him know. In the meantime he had work to do, something not involving girls. However, he had to admit it. She was a good teacher!

The afternoon was ending when John gathered up his arrows and released the string from the bow. He could shoot! He could shoot with a good degree of accuracy. Now, he was a hunter! Surely, the hunters would accept him. Tomorrow he would demonstrate his skills.

Returning to the villa, he arrived just in time for the evening meal. This time he washed and bathed according to the prescribed ritual. Although the others were not aware of his thoughts, he wanted to calm his emotions, wash away the sweat of emotions and practicing. The cool water was precisely what was needed!

Tobiah, having suggested the place for his practicing, wanted to know the results. The hunters would not be back until dawn, so he could ask John about his afternoon.

"How did it go? Was the ravine what you expected, a private place with no distractions or audiences?"

John wasn't about to tell anyone about Debra's presence and help. He simply spoke of his progress.

"I think I have improved! You were right. It was an excellent place for privacy, just what I needed. Tomorrow, when the hunters are back and up, I will let them see what I can do. I think they will be pleased."

He couldn't help but look down the long table, spotting Debra at the far end. He couldn't be sure, but along with her smile, and the smiles of the others, there was a brief wink. Their encounter was their secret, at least for the present.

# CHAPTER 8

*. . . he who walks in wisdom will be delivered . .*

Proverbs 28:26b

The hunters were dubious. A few days ago John could hardly find the target. Now he insists he can. He says he can hit it dead center!

"That can't be true!"

"He is wasting our time!"

However, they did appreciate his acquired skills at making the best arrows. They were willing to give him another try. If he had improved that much, he would go on the next hunt! Also, there was a degree of curiosity about one so young and so inexperienced, yet so confident. They were doubtful, but hopeful. They would see.

Following the morning meal and the daily rituals at the pool and in the atrium, Tobiah had them gather in the field above the village. Jakan, the elder and head hunter, had set up a target. Now it was time to see what this young man could do.

"John, if you are as good as you claim," declared Jakan, "you will enjoy the best cut of meat from our next deer!"

With that, they handed John his bow, letting him pick his first arrow. For a moment he closed his eyes for what he didn't mean to do, call silently for Yahweh's help. Then, fitting the arrow to the string, pulling it back as far as possible, aimed along his arm and let go with his two fingers.

The shouts of his audience were evidence of his success. His arrow hit the target, dead center! Two more arrows followed, with equal success. The first was no fluke, no accident. John had come through! Led by Jakan and Tobiah, they gathered round, slapping John on the back. He would go on the next hunt. If he could do that with a deer he would truly be one of them!

Once the congratulations were over, John looked back toward the others, including wives and children. Standing in the background, but taller than most, was Tobiah's daughter, Debra. Even at that distance he took note of her knowing smile and, he was sure, the wink of her eye. How would he be able to give her credit for what all assumed to be a "man" thing? If it had not been for her, he would have never succeeded. "Thanks be to . . . . Yahweh?"

Three evenings later John was invited to go! They were heading out for a night of hunting. Actually, they departed late in the afternoon, wanting to be in place at the rising of the moon. It would be past full, but would provide sufficient light for their purpose. Carrying bows and arrows, knives and ropes, water and dried fruit, they were prepared for a long night of walking, climbing and waiting. Anticipating success, they were bringing their woven bags for carrying the meat and skins.

It was a clear night, as most nights were close to the Salt Sea. Myriads of stars filled the sky. From time to time a shooting star streaked across the heavens. Some called that a good omen. Others said "No!" They saw it as something bad. Those seeing the good were in the majority. They were taking a new member on his first hunt. He would kill a deer!

The first part of their excursion was familiar to John. He and Mered had traveled the same route, ending up at the waterfalls. However, the hunters gave that wadi little attention. Moving on to the east, they entered another one just behind the Qumran village, heading toward the distant hills.

At this point in their travels, they could talk to one another. Later, silence would be essential. Walking with Mered, John asked about the cliffs ahead, those closest to Qumran.

"What are those openings in the walls of the cliffs we are passing? I've never seen anything like that anywhere else."

"Those are caves, mostly small and mostly empty. Sometimes wild animals, like the rock badger or the fox, even the wolf, raise their young in such caves. But, you never see such animals any more in this area. They are too close to Qumran. Wild animals don't like people!

"A few of the caves closer to the level of the wadi have fire wood in them. Sometimes the shepherds sleep there when the weather is bad. They build a fire and gather their sheep inside for the night. A few are connected to other caves by narrow passageways. Sometime, when we have a free day we could climb up to some of the larger ones."

John was thinking of his encounter with the robbers.

"I don't like caves! Those mauraders who attacked us the night I came to Tobba, were hiding in caves. I'm not afraid to climb up and explore a cave, but it would bring back some bad memories. I would just as soon forget them!"

Before long they entered another wadi, branching off the first one. There they climbed over a high ridge and dropped down to a larger valley. Up ahead, on the wall of a steeper cliff was another waterfall, larger than the one visited by John and Mered. Up and down the length of the valley were many more trees, some in groves. Here was more undergrowth, as well as tall grasses growing across an open pasture. The water from the falls provided a small stream. It ran most of the length of the valley before it disappeared into the ground at the end nearest the Salt Sea. The thing that impressed John was the movement of the grass. With a light breeze blowing, the tall grasses shone like silver in the evening sky.

This would be their stopping point, hopeful the coming moonlight would bring out the deer. It was now time to be silent, with the group finding hiding places near the falls. On earlier trips the hunters had erected blinds of sticks and branches, enough material to keep the deer from spotting them. More important, most times the breezes blew away from the falls toward the end they had entered. Also, the noise of the falling water would cover any sounds of movement by the men. It was time to relax and wait.

As they were leaving the village, Jakan had cautioned John concerning his first attempt at killing a deer.

"You may be unable to shoot the first time. That's not uncommon. Most of us, on our first try, freeze. Why we do that is not clear, but it happens. If possible, you will be given the first shot. Don't feel badly if you fail tonight. There will be other opportunities. However, whatever happens, you must be quiet!"

With these instructions fixed in his mind, John settled down with the others. Actually, he could not see anyone else. They were well hidden. He made sure his bow was strung and his best arrow was at his fingertips. He was ready, so he thought.

The waiting was difficult. After the excitement of the past days, the preparations for this hunt and the long walk, John was sleepy, hardly able to keep his eyes open. It would be a long night! Only the shriek of an owl, the buzzing of the insects and far-off call of an unknown animal kept him alert. Would he hear or see an approaching deer?

With time to think, trying to keep alert, John could not help but question his life at Tobba. The harder he tried to shut Yahweh out, the more he thought of his future. Yahweh was to let him know what Yahweh wanted of him, but when? As far as he could tell, Yahweh was silent, as silent as the stars passing overhead.

He simply could not see anything in his present situation

that was Yahweh-related. Here he was, among strangers, and with both parents dead; far away from Yahweh's house, the Temple! Where did Yahweh want him to live and work? When did Yahweh want him? Where was Yahweh? Was he cooped up in the Temple's Holy of holies, or was he far above the dome of the night sky, as some had suggested?

At the same time, he had to be honest with himself. He was still young, at the very beginning of his adult life. He had a lot to learn! He had a lot to learn about people . . . and girls! Where are girls supposed to fit into his life, girls like Debra? Why did he get so excited when she was near, wanting to touch her? Every time he thought about her he wondered. Was she merely playing games with him, having fun at his expense? She wasn't much older than his age of 14, now nearing 15. At her age she should have grown up, just as he should have grown up back there in Jerusalem. It could be that Yahweh wanted him to learn patience, as well as learning a lot more about people.

Jerusalem! That brought back other memories, happy memories as well as sad ones. He wondered about Eljah, what he was doing tonight. And, Jonathan! He missed him. They were the ones trying so hard to help him grow up, and they did help. Then, there was that stranger from Egypt. Where was he tonight?

With those thoughts running around in his head, and almost asleep, John was alerted to movement down the valley. The waning moon was up, throwing long shadows across grass and trees. Tree shadows made it difficult to see any deer and the only indication of their presence was sound, a buck snorting where the small stream disappeared into the ground. John, along with the others could only wait, alert, waiting for the animal to mover closer toward the falls.

Could that be the same buck, now approaching the grassy pasture? Were his eyes playing tricks? Where were the other deer, or were there any other deer? John could not be sure. All this was new to him. Not only that, he wasn't sure he wanted to do any killing. Sacrificing animals in the Temple bothered him. It always would.

Yet, he had to realize the purpose of this hunt. Those scribes, writing hour after hour, were copying Yahweh's Word on deerskin scrolls. Who was he to say those words would not touch the lives of people, sometime, somewhere? Perhaps his night of hunting would be a way of spreading Yahweh's message. His muted prayer was right to the point. "Yahweh, show me what to do!" These men took this hunting seriously. They certainly weren't playing games. There was a purpose in their lives. That's what he needed, a purpose for his life!

There it was, standing still and tall, not thirty paces away, a deer, a large deer, a deer with tall, beautiful horns. John reached for the arrow at his knee, moved into position without any noise. The arrow was slowly pulled back as far as he could pull. Sighting along the length of his arm, he released the horn-tipped arrow, pointing directly at the deer's shoulder.

The deer tried to run, but fell where he stood. John's arrow had done its work well. The deer was dead!

Trembling with emotion, John's face was wet with tears. Unable to move, he sat down, laid his bow aside and waited. He didn't know whether to shout or to keep quiet. What would come next?

He didn't have to wait long. All the hunters gathered about him with their congratulations. There had been, according to Jakan, only three other deer, all does. After John had felled the buck, the rest had fled up the valley. There was no need to stay.

Making a sled of green branches, the deer was tied on, with the hunters taking turns dragging the carcass until they were out of the valley. Once on the other side of the ridge, they stopped to dress out the deer. They did not want the scent of the slain deer left in their hunting valley. With ropes and bags of woven cloth they divided up the loads and started home.

John was grateful for his restored health. His full strength had returned and, although younger than all the others, he carried his share of the load. The way was clearer now, under the shining moon, but the walk was long and tiresome. It would be good to rest, after a dip in the community pool. No ritual bathing this time! John wanted to clean the dirt and dust and sweat from his tired body . . . and sleep!

The hunters assured him they would take care of the cleaning and storing of the gear and meat. The meat, for the most part would be hung up to dry. Preservation was a problem. However, there would be a celebration meal the next evening, taking note of John's success with the bow. Enough meat would be cooked for that feast, with the whole community taking part.

Yes, John had the right to bathe and sleep. He was the successful hunter, the killer of deer! It took no urging to comply. With the village now asleep, he undressed at the pool. The water was fine, still warm from the day's sun. Lazily he bathed, dried himself, slipped on his loincloth and headed for his bed in the old barracks. Tomorrow he would wash his tunic he had worn for the hunt.

Entering the darkness of the barracks, he realized he was not alone. The smell was disturbingly familiar. It was Debra, waiting for him.

John tried to sound angry.

"Why are you here? Don't you know you are supposed to be in your bed at this time of the night? And another thing, this building is off limits for you. I heard your mother tell you that when I first moved in here. What if your father misses you and comes looking? Anyway, I'm tired and need sleep!"

"That's a fine thank you! After all, I was the one who made all this possible. I heard you killed the deer, with one arrow. I wanted to congratulate you! Don't you think you owe me something, something more than your fussing?"

"I'm sorry! I really didn't mean to fuss, but you really shouldn't be here. I don't know what to make of you. You don't know what you're doing to me! You bother me when you you get close, and that's not right! I want to do things I know I should not do. I think you better leave."

Debra looked down, tears in her eyes. Then she looked up at John and smiled.

"I'm glad I bother you! I want you to hold me, kiss me, do whatever you want with me."

With that Debra pushed herself tightly against him, pushed him down on his bed and reached her warm hands under his loincloth.

The emotion of the day, the night of hunting, the killing of his first deer, and now, this, was too much. John pressed his lips hard against her's and reached for her breasts. Rolling her over underneath his body, he lifted her tunic.

It was too much! Before he could do what he intended to do, his erection ended in a sudden spurt of semen.

Embarrassed by the unexpected, disturbed by his immaturity, John rolled over on his side, sat up and turned away from Debra. He was speechless, wondering what this beautiful, passionate girl would think of him now, wondering what she would say.

After a long silence, she laughed! It wasn't a scornful, derisive laugh. It was a soft, understanding laugh.

"I love it! For a time I thought you were not human, that you had no feelings for me or for anyone else. You frightened me with your seriousness. You were the mysterious stranger from Jerusalem, far too good for the likes of us. You were the man of the world. You knew everything we didn't know. I was determined to see if I could reach you, break through to the real you. Thank you!"

He couldn't believe what he was hearing. This girl was full of surprises. One minute she was ready and anxious for intercourse with him, but now she's laughing, not at me, but accepting me as I am. She likes me!

"John, would you let me stay, just a little longer. No one in my family wakes up in the middle of the night. If they did they wouldn't miss me. I have my own little corner where I sleep, alone. Please, hold me in your arms and tell me about yourself. I promise! I won't try to get you excited again tonight. Please!

For more than an hour John told his story. He talked about his birth, being the child of elderly parents. He told her about the encounter his father Zechariah had with Yahweh's messenger, Gabriel. He told her about the predictions given by his father at the time of his naming and circumcision. He described his home, his village and his life as the problem child of the community. That was interrupted several times by Debra's giggling.

"That sounds like me, so I have been told. I was into everything! We do have something in common. But, go on. I want to hear more!"

"Everyone seemed to think if I would go with my father to the Temple when he was on duty, it would relieve my mother and keep me out of trouble. It did help my mother, but it didn't do much for the priests trying to do their work at the Temple. I was a real problem! Sometimes I would free the birds in the cages, those to be sacrificed. I think I must have been more trouble there than at home.

"Finally, a young priest by the name of Eljah offered his services. He would try to help me grow up. Eljah tried, but had little success. I don't think things would have changed or improved if I hadn't run away one afternoon. Down below the lower city I met a stranger, an Egyptian who seemed to think I was special. He said great things would happen in my life. I didn't understand him, but it made me think about those predictions.

"That was just before my mother died. When that happened, I had to grow up. I believed Yahweh did have something for me, something that would touch the lives of many others, the lives of all our people."

By now, John's arm holding Debra was asleep, numb. He sat up, propted himself against the adjacent wall and had her lay her head against his chest. It was not an act of passion, but his need for support in vocalizing his thoughts.

"You pretty well know the rest, the decision to bring my

father here and the tragedy which prevented that. Now that I am here, what comes next? You people worship Yahweh in your own way, trying to do what you think he wants you to do. That's my concern, too, doing what he wants, but Debra, what does he want? What does he want of me, and when? I suppose that's why I seem so serious. I need some answers!"

"John, I can't give you any answers, because I don't know. My family and my village worship Yahweh, seriously, intently. For myself, all that really doesn't interest me. It never has. I want to deal with the things I can see and touch."

Again, Debra, laughed. "I like to touch you! But, seriously, how can we help you? Does Yahweh want you to live here, marry, have children? Or, does he want you back in Jerusalem, or somewhere else? For me, I want you to stay! I want you to love me, marry me, give me many children."

Debra surprised herself. She had never wrestled with problems like that. She had never met anyone like John, never felt so passionate about anyone else. Developing into womanhood she had her fantasies about men, flirting with the young men, but nothing like this. At the same time, she sensed something was different. What was the word . . . something spiritual . . . something, as the elders would say . . . something holy?

By now, both John and Debra were worn out. They stood up and embraced. With a final, light kiss, Debra slipped out. Almost before she disappeared, John was asleep.

Just before the light of a new dawn, John sat up. Out of a deep sleep had come a question and an answer. Should he stay in Tobba, or must he leave? He must leave! He would have to go! He didn't know where, but he would have to go!

Debra, going back to her own space and bed, could not get to sleep. John had said she bothered him, but what about me, she wondered. "John, you bother me, far more than you will ever know!" Startled by her thinking and trying to put to rest the things of the past hours, the intimacy, the thoughts and the spoken words, she was frightened by her conclusion. At the same time John had awakened to his question and answer, Debra said it, too, in a trembling whisper, "John will leave us!"

# CHAPTER 9

*. . . and became strong in spirit . . . .*
                              Luke 1:80b

How would he tell Tobiah he must leave? He and the people of the community had been so gracious in welcoming John. They had saved his life, restored him to health. They had taken him in, given him a home. He had earned an honored position with the hunters. The celebration on the night following the hunt was for him. He was the hero! In his speech honoring John, Jakan had insisted that Tobiah make John an official member of the village family, and everyone agreed. Tobiah, as well as the entire group, voiced their approval.

The burning question, of course, was "why?" Why should he leave? There was no logical, rational reason for leaving. If his father had lived he would not be considering such a move. Even now, now that his father was dead, he felt sure the Division leader Jonathan would question his departure, and so would Eljah. In their eyes, as well as in the eyes of these newfound friends, leaving would make no sense.

Also, if he left, where would he go? Jerusalem held no real attraction for him, unless he was headed for the priesthood. As for his own village, there was nothing there, no relatives, only the tomb where his mother was buried. Tobba was his home!

Then there was Debra. He knew how she felt and, to some degree, even with his mixed emotions, he knew how he felt.

Sure, he did not know what the future might hold in their relationship, but the impact of her presence said, "stay!" There was a desire, almost a compulsion, to stay in Tobba.

Yet, and John couldn't explain it, he felt he was being pushed out by a strong, but unidentified hand. He must leave! What created this disturbing idea was the picture that flashed into his mind in that early morning awakening. It was a picture described by Rabbi Hilkiah, preparing John and others for adulthood, the story of their father Abraham.

The ancestral family had moved from the Babylonian valley up to a place named Haran and it was there Yahweh had spoken to Abraham. And what did Yahweh say? "Leave your father and your mother, leave everything you have, what you possess, and go to a land I will give you, an unknown land, a foreign land. There I will bless you!"

Was that it? Was Yahweh now creeping back into the picture? Is Yahweh saying now is the time for me to prepare for what he wants of me? Sure, the Rabbi was reminding them of Israel's calling, called to be the people of Yahweh. Yet, it started with that one person, their forefather Abraham. Yahweh called him to go into the unknown!

The unknown! The wilderness! That was it! Somewhere out there was the answer. Out there would come the preparation for what would be his Yahweh-given destiny. There would be no other influences on his life, only Yahweh's. There would be no Jonathan, no Eljah, no Tobiah and, yes, no Debra, none to sway him or change him. Alone, he would prepare for what Yahweh had in mind. Yes, this was Yahweh's call to him, John, the Yahweh-promised child of Zechariah and Elizabeth. Yahweh had not forgotten him!

At the same time, and this was making it so difficult, he was being torn apart by the agony of what that might involve. It was scary! His life at Tobba had grown more comfortable with each passing day. After all the trauma of home and village and Temple, here was security, a safe haven. These were caring people. And Debra? She wanted him to stay. She wanted him!

And Yahweh? Had he really given him a clear signal for the immediate future? Could it be all this speculation over Abraham might be just that, speculation? Were his thoughts about leaving spurred on more by trying to escape his distubing relationship with a girl, rather than by what Yahweh had in store for him? He wanted to shout, cry out:

"Yahweh, tell me what to do!"

Some days later, and after much thought; wrestling with his dilemma, John went to Tobiah. Following the morning's bathing ritual, he asked if he had time to talk. He needed Tobiah's help and advice as the leader of Yahweh's people living in Tobba. He needed his help, not in the cleansing of the body, but in mind and spirit!

Walking out to the edge of the village, they sat down in the narrow shade of a palm tree; one planted some years before by the Roman farmer.

"Tobiah," John began, "I'm not sure what Jonathan told you about me and my father, other than the need for a home for us."

"He told me very little," Tobiah responded, "other than that."

"He did assure me you were good people, good servants of Yahweh. He said that your father was one of Yahweh's outstanding priests. He had served his whole life in the Temple, but was now old and feeble, needing a new home. Concerning you, he felt confident that, someday, Yahweh would use you for his purpose. However, he did not elaborate."

"He was right," John continued, "concerning both my father and me.

"The story is well-known in Jerusalem and in my home village. My birth was part of Yahweh's plan. My mother, Elizabeth, and my father, Zechariah, were old, far too old to be having a child. Everyone knew that! By themselves, without Yahweh's help, my birth would never have happened.

"But, it happened. Yahweh's messenger, Gabriel, came to

my father at an Evening Sacrifice when my father was serving at the altar. He told him my mother would have a baby boy. At the proper time he should give the boy the name of John. Because my father didn't believe him, and said so, Gabriel told my father he would remain speechless until I was born.

"It happened, exactly as Gabriel predicted. After my birth and at my naming and circumcision, my father spoke again, for the first time in nine months, giving me the name John. At the same time, he talked about the birth and about me.

"Some of his first words were these: 'and you, child, shall be called the prophet of the Most High.' He said much more, but the point was made, I would be a called servant of Yahweh, called to speak for Yahweh.

"I know you and your people living here see Yahweh in a somewhat different way from us, we whose lives were tied so closely to the Temple. However, Yahweh is our Lord, yours and mine, and we must serve him as we think best. Isn't that so?"

"Yes, John, you are right. At the same time I am puzzled. I did not know about the miracle of your birth, or the Yahweh-centered purpose surrounding it. We do believe in signs and yours is a powerful one. If that is so, and I believe what you are saying, how can we help you? What do you think Yahweh has in store for you? What does he want you to do for him?"

"That's the problem, Tobiah. I don't know. Yet, one thing I do know, I must leave! I think I must leave soon.

"No, please, I see your response coming, your objection to what I'm saying, but I must leave. I must wrestle with this by myself, without your influence, or Mered's, or Jakan's, or my close friends back in Jerusalem. I must find a place out there for myself, somewhere out there, alone!"

"John," Tobiah objected, "you don't know what you're saying. Out there is a desert, a wasteland, a dangerous place. You wouldn't survive. Between the Salt Sea and the Judean hills there is nothing but barren hills and valleys, where very little grows. There aren't many trees, little shelter except for caves. Water is scarce, hard to find. Food is scarce, very hard to find. You can't grow crops out there! No one lives out there, except some hermits and wild men, robbers. There are wild animals, dangerous animals. What you're suggesting is impossible!"

"Tobiah, you live here near the shore of the Salt Sea where very little grows. As you say, on the other side is that wilderness which is desolate and dangerous. Yet, you and others like you have managed to survive. You have learned to live under very harsh circumstances. You have developed this desert land, clearing more area than you had when you first came. You, if you had to, would be able to move away from this place, farther into the wilderness and still survive, would you not?"

"Yes, I suppose so. I've never really thought about it, but with our skills and knowledge, what we have learned over the years, we could do it. But you don't have that knowledge! You are new to this rugged life."

"That's what I'm asking. Help me by teaching me, showing me how to develop my skills in desert living. You will admit I learned to make bows and arrows, good bows and arrows, and to use them!"

"John, there's no question about that, about your ability to learn. Your deer hunting skills proved that. I still don't understand how you did it, but your shooting improvement was unbelievable. How did it happen so quickly?"

"Tobiah, do you remember my asking for a secluded spot for practicing? It was there I improved. I never told anyone, but your daughter Debra followed me and showed me how to aim accurately. I didn't say anything because hunting was a 'man' thing and I wasn't sure just how the hunters would take it, knowing that a girl was my successful teacher. Your daughter knew what she was doing, but she wanted me to keep it secret."

John was not about to tell more about Tobiah's daughter, Debra. That would have been disaster! Some things were best left unsaid, and he was sure Debra would not say more, even with her father's questions.

"Well, I never! I knew Debra had a lot of ability in things

women were supposed to do, but how she learned to use the bow and arrow is a mystery. You are right; the hunters would not have apprecated what you are telling me. Hunting, to them, and rightly so, is a 'man' thing.

"However, I'm not sure just how we can help you. If you are so determined to leave, to live out there alone, we must try to help, but do so without telling your plans now. We will say you want to develop a greater knowledge of our way of life, including our ability to live in the wilderness which is all around us. Since you are one of us, it would be reasonable.

"In fact, there is the requirement of a testing period for any person wanting to be one of us. That was not mentioned the night we celebrated the killing of your first deer. We simply overlooked it in our enthusiasm of welcoming you. Sooner or later some of the elders will remember and raise the question. Yes! That will explain what you will be doing! Let me give it some thought. At the proper time we will have to make a formal announcement. If Yahweh is directing your life we dare not interfere!

"But, that brings up another question. Are you positive Yahweh wants you to leave now? Has he given you a sign? I have to accept what you have told me concerning the predictions at your conception and birth, but you are still young. Also, in order to serve him you need both training and experience as a prophet of Yahweh. When and where will that come?

"No, Tobiah, I can't say for sure that Yahweh has given me a sign, other than this feeling I have. It is as though I am being pushed along in a new direction, and I must be ready to move. I also must find help in my training, but I have no idea as to where I will find that. I know, there are more questions than answers at this point, but I have to be ready when Yahweh calls!"

John was pleased with their conversation. He would be a good student! Keeping eyes and ears open to this desert world surrounding them, he would make his plans for departure. In the meantime, his daily prayers to Yahweh would include his questions.

"How, O Lord? When, O Lord? What, O Lord, am I to do?"

With that, he entered into the daily life of work and worship at Tobba. The daily ritual of bathing, along with the fixed prayers, strengthened his determination to improve his skills for the future. He learned to pray according to the Essene's ritual. At the same time he offered his own prayers of supplication: "O Lord, show me your way for me!"

The women of the village laughed at his request to help in the bake house, but were willing to teach him. He finally met their approval, baking good unleavened bread according to their recipes.

He stayed away from the small vineyard and wine storage yard, unwilling to get involved with the winemaking. He believed that was not for him, unnecessary. There would be no place for strong drink in the desert.

The fields of grain and the garden drew his attention. Both were small, but provided needful food. The grain was harvested and ground into flour. From the garden came a few vegatables, some lentils, onions and other greens. He learned how to plant, care for and harvest both grain and vegatables. Along with that, there were a few wild plants, either holding water or having a soft, pithy center that could be chewed. If needed, these could help sustain life. The leaves of some wild, scrubby plants could be cooked, like greens. In an emergency they could be eaten without cooking.

If he wanted seasoning for any food there was the Salt Sea. He learned to extract the salt by evaporation. Small amounts could be set in shallow vessels, set out in the hot sun until the water was gone. There were a few shallow pools of water near the sea, brackish water holding a few small fish. These could be scooped up and cooked whole.

The tanning of hides was a distasteful task, but one needed for preparing garments for wilderness life. He could set traps for small animals, cook the meat and cure the skins. Sewn together, such skins could provide clothing and sandals. He learned to tan the skins.

Cooking would be a problem, but using hard flint, a fire could be started with dry grass. There was always plenty around that could be protected by storing it in a pouch. All this kept John busy, quite busy. His days were full.

He passed his 16th and 17th birthdays. Now, larger and taller than ever, stronger than ever, he was accepted in all phases of community life. The hunters welcomed him into their group, expecting him to be with them on every hunt. He killed more deer than anyone else. He had an uncanny ability to spot the animals first and his arrows were always straight and true! He knew how to move quietly and could creep closer to the deer without being spotted. His eyesight was exceptional, at night as well as in the day.

John's appearance was changing. His beard was beginning grow. It wasn't much, but with a sharpened knife he kept it trimmed, giving him, according to the women, a handsome appearance. They were happy to have him around each day, enjoying his company. He always had something nice to say to each one he met. He had changed, was more congenial than before, and, seemingly, less serious. Little did they know the intensity of his feelings. His warmth and friendliness came from an inner assurance of being headed in the right direction, Yahweh's direction. However, the seriousness was still there, deeply imbedded inside.

There was one disquieting element of his new life. Debra was avoiding him. She was polite and would speak, but beyond that there was little or no contact. Many times, whenever he was involved in village affairs, especially those with the women present, she would leave. That disturbed John and he tried more than once to get an answer.

Walking out after an evening meal, he met her just outside the room that was the library in the original villa. Now it was used as a storage room for miscellaneous supplies. Taking her by the arm he pulled her inside and closed the door.

"You've been avoiding me, Debra. I need to know why. Have I done something to offend you? As you are well aware, I really don't know how to act where girls are concerned. I do know I have treated you badly. Is that it? Tell me!"

Debra's eyes avoided his, looking down at the floor. Then the tears came, spilling down her tunic. She started to speak, but couldn't. There were too many tears.

John reached out, put his arms around her and waited.

Finally she stopped, cleared her throat, and in a weak voice, almost a whisper, answered.

"You are leaving us. After we were together, the night of your first hunt, after I left you, I couldn't sleep. I knew then, you would leave us. Oh, John, I love you and I don't want to lose you! What am I supposed to do?"

"Debra, my life is in Yahweh's hands. You should know that! At this point I'm not sure what he wants, or where he wants me to live. I'm not sure when he will want me to leave, or if he will want me to leave. Right now there are too many unknowns, and I simply don't have the answers. I do know I must be prepared for whatever might come.

"For the present I need to learn all I can in order to live here or elsewhere. Your father is aware of my concerns and has promised to help me develop those skills needed for survival. I've told him the time may come when I will have to live alone, somewhere out there, in order to hear what Yahweh wants. If Yahweh calls, and he will, I cannot be influenced by anyone else, including you. You are special to me, and I don't want to hurt you, but I have to do what I believe to be in keeping with Yahweh's plan for my life! Debra, please! Don't avoid me, but help me!"

"John, I told you before, I believe in things I can see and touch. I am happy when you hold me, like this. But, I will not interfere and will try to help you."

With tears wiped away, replaced by a little smile on her

face, Debra pulled John's face down to hers and kissed him. This one was like the first time back in the ravine, the warmth of her darting tongue against his. With that she slipped out of his arms, calling back as she went out the door.

"Maybe, just maybe, I can have some influence on Yahweh, persuading him to leave you alone!"

As the days passed, John waited for Tobiah's response and recommendation on his request. He needed to give it a try, this living alone, but he needed the opinions of those able to evaluate his progress. At this point, could he survive, alone?

Tobiah did come up with one surprise. He took him aside one morning, inviting him into the room where John had talked with Debra, the old library. Although it had been in a mess, with various and sundry supplies stacked and scattered around, Tobiah had cleared one corner. There was a chair and a desk, actually a tall lectern. Next to the furniture were open shelves, filled with scrolls stuck into a number of cubbyholes.

"John, you spoke of the necessity of knowing what Yahweh had to say. Why don't you begin here! Our scribes at Qumran have prepared these priceless records of Moses and the prophets. These Scrolls written on skin, mostly deerskin, represent years and years of dedicated labor. Needless to say, it is essential they be preserved.

"Deeply concerned for their preservation, the leaders at Qumran have entrusted these to our care. As they have said many times over, if the 'sons of darkness' attack them, destroying what they have at Qumran, these will survive. Now, at my request, they have agreed to your reading and study. Here, as you find time, is Yahweh's word for you. I'm sure I don't have to remind you to handle these as holy things!"

John was overwhelmed with emotion! He had seen the Temple Scolls many times, but had paid little attention to their importance for himself. They were simply a part of daily worship. This was different! Here was more, much more than the books of Moses. Here were the words of the prophets, including the greatest of prophets, Isaiah. Also, there were some other writings that seemed to speak directly to today's concerns, concerns about darkness and light. He, for a moment, was speechless!

"I don't know what to say, Tobiah. This is a treasure, a wonderful treasure, and I am most grateful to you, and grateful to the men at Qumran. How can I ever thank you!"

"Thank us by being a good student while you are here. If Yahweh is calling you to be his prophet, study these as you have never studied before! Who knows when you will take the next step? If you must leave us it will be good for you to have knowledge of the scriptures in your mind. It is good you know how to read Hebrew and Aramaic. Also, you should be able to help us, as we try to interpret what Yahweh has to say to us. This place will be your private classroom, where you will not be disturbed."

With that, Tobiah closed the door, leaving John to stare at his good fortune. He was confident the Temple did not have all of what was before him in these cubbyholes. He was richly blessed!

Starting at the top of the cabinet, John pulled out the first Scroll. It was the words of the prophet Joel. Carefully unrolling the skin he began to read: "the word of the Lord that came to Joel" . . . fearful words, frightening words . . . words about destruction . . . words about devouring locusts . . . then, shortly, these words, "Alas for that day! For the day of the Lord is near; it will come like destruction from Yahweh."

It was a call to repentence, Yahweh's words of warning to a stubborn, sinful people. Only the faithful will survive. John had never read such before, the words of this ancient prophet, words of warning.

Pausing to give thought to what the prophet was saying, John had a sinking feeling in the pit of his stomach. If what these people in Qumran and the adjacent villages were saying about Israel was true, the words of the prophet Joel must be repeated, now! They needed to be spoken by some one called of Yahweh. Could it be this was meant for him?

Eagerly he read on, until he had finished the Scrolls in the one cubbyhole, the entire book of Joel. Absorbed in his reading and his thoughts, he payed no attention to the time, until there was a knock on the door. Debra pushed open the door, beckoning with her finger.

"I was told not to disturb you, but the noon meal is ready, now. You have to stop and eat."

"Debra, look! Here are the books of Moses! Here are the laws of Yahweh! Here are the words of the prophets! How can you talk about food with all this at our finger tips?"

"I know," Debra replied, "father told my mother what he had given you, telling all of us not to disturb you. But, you have to eat. All those Scrolls will be here tonight, tomorrow. You will have plenty of time to read and study.

"Anyway, I want you to take your time, lots of time. That way you will be here a long time, with me!"

This time she gave John her brightest smile, took him by the hand and led him to the community dining area. Just before they reached the opening, she stepped back and let him enter, alone. It was only after he was seated, she came dashing in for the meal. Making her apologies for being late, she sat down, bowed her head, waiting for her father's prayer.

John had a lot of choices to make, dividing his time between learning wilderness skills and reading from the Scrolls. He was amazed at the delicate, careful work of the scribes. He couldn't begin to imagine the hours, the days such men had spent at their tasks of writing, of copying. Some, he was sure, had given their entire lives to this monumental task, truly a labor of love!

At the same time, he was engrossed in the messages unfolding. Yahweh was the creator of the heavens and the earth, giving to the world what was good and perfect! Even as men and women disobeyed Yahweh, he still cared for them. He would not tolerate evil, but he was always willing to give his people another chance. His compassion was stronger than anything else!

He would save his people, from themselves and from their enemies. He would bring about a Day of the Lord, a day of salvation. He would send a Messiah, an Anointed One, to deliver his people! In what the scriptures spoke of as "the fulness of time," this Saviour would come. Then, there was the other side, the warning of destruction for those unwilling to repent! The Day of the Lord, for some, would be a day of darkness! Yahweh had spoken!

Such was the message of the prophets, condemning the wicked; calling Yahweh's people to repentence! It was a message the people must hear in every generation. As John wrestled with what he was reading, he became convinced this was a message for his own generation!

In the midst of all that, John was brought up short, thinking about his own life. Would that be his calling? Was this what Yahweh had in mind for him? Was Yahweh preparing him to be the messenger? He, certainly, was not the Messiah! Yet, how could he be the messenger? He was an unknown. Sure, his was a miraculous birth, with Yahweh's hand in it, but Yahweh used great men, Abraham, Moses, Samuel, King Solomon, King David, Isaiah, Jeremiah and others. Those were the ones called to speak and write, to act for Yahweh. The record spoke for itself. Yahweh called great men to do great things!

With the questions outweighing the answers, John would roll up the Scrolls, place them in their proper pockets and close the door behind him. It was time to think of other things, matters concerning survival. Along with the reading and the study there was the wilderness out there! He had to reach the point of knowing he could survive.

On such days he would disappear, slipping away without being missed. While most of the community assumed he was in the villa library, he would be out among the rocks, the boulders and the scrubby growth of the desert, exploring a world that seemed so forbidding.

Most times he stayed within sight of the village, but as he became more familiar with the surrounding area, he moved farther out. Tobiah was right. It was a desolate place. Yet, all this was exciting to John. Alone, with no sound of a human voice, he thrilled at the cries of the birds, especially the soft sounds of the turtledove. Here they were free, not cooped up, waiting to be sacrificed.

Then, there was the sound of the wind blowing along the high cliffs. Even the buzzing of the many insects had a music all its own. Overhead were puffs of white clouds being pushed along by the wind. This was Yahweh's created world, a world free from the imprint of human frailities. Here he could breathe! Here he could listen to the voice of Yahweh, the creator. Here, he was certain, he would be ready to hear the Yahweh's call, the molder of his own life. The big question, of course, was the time. When would he hear, when would he know Yahweh was calling him?

Somewhere out in the midst of this beautiful creation, Yahweh was waiting, preparing to beckon him on. Of that he was certain!

# CHAPTER 10

*. . . and he was in the wilderness, until . . .*
                                Luke 1:80b

Tobiah called the community together for the formal announcement. He and John had discussed the matter, and after months of preparation and study agreed there was no point in waiting. Continuing to put off his departure would make it that much more difficult to leave. Tobiah realized John's anxiety. He would not be at ease until he knew what Yahweh desired of him. He had to wrestle with that, alone. That would be impossible at Tobba.

Also, Tobiah was confident of John's ability to survive. He had learned his lessons well, lessons essential to living alone in the wilderness. Having seen him develop into one of the best of hunters, he was confident John could secure food, both plant and animal. Others had shared their positive evaluations of skills in the bakery, in the garden and in the grain fields.

From time to time Tobiah spent the day away from the village, teaching John about the terrain, the plants and the grasses. There were edible plants, but there were others to be avoided. There were good insects and there were bad insects. There was one, a large insect, a locust, which was edible, if needed. There were lessons in weather conditions. There were the stars overhead, helping one find direction for movement at night. Their night sessions were made easy in that most nights were perfectly clear.

In addition, Tobiah was happy with John's retention of the scriptures as found in the Scrolls. He could quote from Moses and the prophets without hesitation. He had caught the sense of urgency as spelled out by the Essenes. As with Jeremiah, it seemed to be as a fire burning within him. Whenever he talked to Tobiah about a particular passage of scripture, Tobiah couldn't help but notice John's eyes. They seemed to brighten intensely, taking on a far away look, as though he was seeing beyond the walls of the building. For Tobiah it was an out-of-this-world, experience. The word was "awesome", something he had never encountered before.

Following an evening meal in late Spring, Tobiah reminded the villagers of their vote of confidence in their newest member, John. He talked about his first hunt and the killing of his first deer. With that, they had welcomed John as a full-fledged citizen. He was now a member of the village of Tobba. However, they had overlooked one requirement. Those desiring to live in Tobba must be deemed worthy. There was a test, one established long ago. It was an initiation required of all candidates for residency. For a period of three years the life and activity of the initiate would be under scrutiny, a probation period. Following that, each candidate must spend a full year alone, living apart from the settlement. It would be a test of survival.

Knowing what was coming, Tobiah paused and waited. The response came, immediately! Both men and women interrupted him.

"If you mean John must leave us, we object. He is one of us! Anyway, he has been living here over 3 years. That's enough!"

"He is one of our best hunters. We think he has passed all the necessary tests!"

After everyone had his or her say, Tobiah began again.

"No one is exempt from the rules. I know that and you know that. We, as a community, made those rules and we will follow them. We must abide by them!

"Yes, John has been with us more than three years, and nothing in all that time would make us want to deny him membership. He is an excellent hunter. He has entered into all our activities. He is a devout worshipper of Yahweh. He has worked hard, learning our ways, learning to use all the resources necessary for survival.

"Now it is time for the next step as he approaches his 18th year. Now is the time for him to fulfill this requirement, a year of isolation. I trust no one will question my decision. We do this out of love and respect, not as a punishment. Until he leaves, we will enjoy being with a young man I would be happy to call my son!"

The applause was unanamous! All held John in high regard. He was, indeed, a part of the community. All were confident that once he met the final requirement, he would be one of their future leaders. After all, one year is not such a long time. The years since his arrival had passed so quickly. How time flies!

None of that, of course, took away the uneasiness in thinking about the future. Although it had been years since they had been faced with this final requirement, no one could predict the results. According to their memory, one individual had succeeded, but one had failed. He had disappeared, somewhere out there! From all indications he had died, alone.

The hunters wanted at least one more hunt, but there was a problem. It was the wrong time of the year. The newborn fawns would be with the doe, still dependent on their mother's milk. Hunting was out of the question. Maybe they could set up a tournament, a contest of skill with bow and arrow. They all knew John would take first prize, but the others could compete for second place. Such thinking simply reflected their restlessness.

Several members of the community, along with the hunters, deluged John with both ideas and gifts. The gifts were those items each believed to be essential for that desolate world out there, the wilderness. Along with gifts came the instructions, telling John over and over what he should or should not do.

There was no way for John to make use of all they offered.

He had more than enough. He thanked them, one by one, and went on with his own selection, carefully packing what he felt to be needful for his upcoming journey. As to their suggestions, he listened to each one with patience. He knew and appreciated their good intentions and their concern for his safety.

After a few days, those directly concerned with John's daily activity began to wonder. Tobiah had said nothing about a date for John's departure. What was the proposed schedule? One by one they approached Tobiah, unwilling to ask John.
"When will he leave us?"
"Will it be soon?"
"Will we have a big sendoff, enjoy a final meal together?"
"What about special prayers and rituals? He will need that!"
For every question Tobiah's response was not very satisfactory, making no commitment as to date and time.
"All is in Yahweh's hands. John will leave when Yahweh wants him to depart. You must be patient and, please, let him have some time to himself. He is still busy with his study of Yahweh's word, the writings the Qumran community have entrusted to our care."
John sensed their continuing uneasiness and wished he could be on his way. In spite of Tobiah's reminder, a number kept dropping by, bringing either some little item or simply wanting to make small talk. They said little or nothing about his plans for leaving, the date of departure. There seemed to be an invisible wall in that regard. All wanted to know, but were afraid to ask.
John had to be content to leave it at that. He and Tobiah had discussed all the possibilities. When the time came, when John was ready, he would simply slip away. There would be no big event, no sharing of farewells. At this point John needed no tearful goodbyes. It would be a solemn moment in beginning this important move in his life. If only Yahweh would make things clear and specific!

Once he had made his selections for his life out in the rugged countryside, he turned his attention to the Scrolls. Far into the night a lamp was burning in the old library. Having gone through the books of Moses and having dates and places and people in mind, he turned his attention to the prophets. These held him spellbound. It was as if Yahweh was in the room at times, making sure John was aware of the prophetic role Yahweh demanded. These writings were, indeed, holy! He must read until all these were burned into his heart and mind. Nothing should be permitted to come before that!

Debra noticed it first, and fussed at John. He was not eating. He had lost weight. All this attention to his preparations, especially his late hours of reading and study, was taking a toll on his health. That was not good! He had to build up his physical strength before leaving. Physical weakness was dangerous and could lead to disaster. Her orders were given over and over. He must listen!

John smiled, agreed, and changed nothing. His preparations went on as before. He must be ready when the time came. Actually, John had no date in mind. He believed he would know when it was right, the time to leave. He and Tobiah had made the decision about his leaving. He would slip away in the small hours of the night, before anyone was awake. There would be no final farewells!

Summer was approaching, and the days were growing longer. After a long day of walking into the west, going far beyond the ravine he remembered so well, John made the decision. Perhaps it was the smell of the warming countryside. Perhaps it was the sounds of nature, the soft wind blowing off the Salt Sea, the tall, lanky birds walking among the reeds, the cries of the eagles soaring overhead. All seemed to beckon him to make the final move. Tonight, or early tomorrow morning, he would be on his way. It would be done quietly with no fanfare. It was time to go!

At supper he tried his best to maintain a normal outward appearance. His conversation gave no indication of his decision. After the evening meal he excused himself, went by the library to read, as many assumed he would do, and then went back to his quarters in the old barracks. No one seemed to notice anything different. All was quiet and no one came by.

Sleep did not come easy. He knew he must rest because he would rise early. Tossing and turning he finally gave up, falling into a deep sleep. After a time he was dreaming, reliving his years at Toppa. Faces of many of the residents passed before him. Then he saw Debra. She was showing him just the right way to hold and point the arrows.

It was all too real. He could even breathe her smell, her scent, as though she was in the room. Restless, turning over, he realized that was no dream. Debra was there! How did she know he was leaving? There was no way she could have known, but she had come!

As his eyes focused on her tall, slim figure reflecting the light coming through the small window above, she unfastened her dress, letting it slide slowly to the floor. There was nothing underneath. Her arms, legs and breasts seemed so very white. Her beauty overwhelmed John as she leaned over him, her long, dark hair spilling across his face. Then she was there, lying on top of him. Sensing his movement of protest, she put her fingers to his lips, reached down, and pulled him on top of her, opening herself up to him.

Almost before he realized what was happening, he responded. He held her as tightly as he could until it was done. His muffled cry was the only sound as Debra met him fully, completely. Finally, totally exhausted, unwilling to release each other, they both slept, arms entwined.

It was still dark when John sat up. For a moment he wasn't

sure. Had he dreamed about Debra, or had she really come to him? It was no dream! They had done what they should not have done. He had violated the very basic law of Yahweh. He had sinned! He had done what was evil in the sight of Yahweh! Now, how could he do what Yahweh wanted of him? Would Yahweh want him now? Would Yahweh be willing to use him as his father Zechariah had predicted?

In his misery, John wept, weeping tears of remorse and guilt! Without Yahweh's assurance, life would be meaningless, worthless. He would have to pay a price!

There was only one answer . . . the wilderness! There he would either die or survive. Survival would mean that Yahweh had not deserted him, that Yahweh would, in his own time and way, use him. As Gabriel had reminded his father long ago, "With Yahweh all things are possible!" Also, he knew he could not face the people of Tobba, not after what had happened. He had to go, regardless. He had to go, now!

Debra had disappeared. He had no idea as to when she had slipped away. He had no time to seek her out and ask her forgiveness. He regretted he might never have that chance. He might never see her again, but that could not be helped now. All that would rest in Yahweh's hands. It was time to leave!

John had prepared carefully for this moment. His backpack was full! It was heavy, but he was confident he could handle the weight, even over the rough terrain. Slinging that across his back he put his knife in his belt, his arrows in their sheath and his bow over his shoulder. Over his other shoulder was his skin of water.

Stepping outside, he paused to look around. The villa and village were quiet. There were no lights to be seen. The moon had already set. Pausing for one brief prayer to Yahweh, a plea for both care and forgiveness, he moved out slowly toward the west. His greatest burden was his sense of guilt. Would he be able to live with that? Would Yahweh let him live? Would Yahweh watch over him and, someday, use him? He felt like the psalmist, asking the same question: "Where can I flee from your

Spirit?" Yet, he knew such was impossible. Yahweh would either save him, use him, or Yahweh would destroy him!

With those thoughts running through his head, he moved westward, working his way through the underbrush. Turning away from the Salt Sea he headed in the direction of the towering cliffs. As he had discovered earlier, there were breaks in the rising terrain, making it possible to move north into the uninhabited wilderness. The climb would be steep, but not insurmountable. He knew he would not have to scale the first row of cliffs in order to reach a stopping place beyond. Having scouted this area of the land some time before, he was confident of his route. He could move rapidly, and he wanted to be as far as possible from Tobba before the light of the approaching dawn.

Sure enough, there was the wadi he had spotted earlier, an entrance to a small valley. The cut in the towering cliffs, invisible from the road running along the Salt Sea, opened the way northward and westward. However, by this time John was slowing down. He was tired! The intensity of his preparations, plus the events of the night, had drained his energy. He must find a stopping place soon, a place to hide and rest.

Moving slowly up the small valley he spotted some foliage, a few small trees, at the upper end.

It seemed to take forever, but it was the nearest place suitable for his purpose. Finally reaching the cover, he had to stop, remove his heavy load and regain some strength! Just as the light of the new day brought everything into focus, John crawled into some tall grass under the trees, laid his equipent and supplies aside and collapsed into sleep. He was now alone!

# CHAPTER 11

*. . . the voice of one crying in the wilderness . . .*
                                            Matthew 3:3a

How long had he slept? He had no idea. It was afternoon, according to the position of the sun. Sitting up, stretching his arms, yawning, he started to rise, but stopped. Over to his left, sitting under the nearest tree, was a man. He looked like a man, a short man. John's first impression was that he was seeing an animal with a human face. His hair was long and unkempt. His face was covered with a long, straggly beard. Obviously, he had never used a comb or brush, at least not in recent days. A few twigs and brown leaves were knotted in the tangle of hair.

The man was dressed in animal skins, roughly sewn together. There was no design in the clothing, and he was barefooted. From what John could see, he carried no weapon. In his right hand was a staff. Leaning against it, he made no move to rise or speak. His eyes never wavered. He was staring, watching John.

Not quite sure how to handle this intruder, John remained on one knee, his mind filled with questions. Who is this? Does he mean me any harm? Is he alone, or are there others nearby? Perhaps I am the intruder and this is his territory. Perhaps the first thing to find out is our ability to communicate!

Minutes passed, until John's legs were cramped and stiff. Realizing this could not go on much longer, he moved to stand erect, doing so slowly and carefully. He wanted no confrontation with this person.

"My name is John. I come from the east, from the village of Tobba. I am looking for a place to live, where I can be alone. I assure you, I mean you no harm."

Silence. The man held his position, eyes focused as before, watching John as though he had not heard or understood him.

John tried again.

"Do you live nearby," he asked. "Do you live alone, or are there others in your community? Do you come here often?"

Silence!

Finally, the man moved. Using his staff as leverage, he stood up. John was right. He was short, barely coming up to John's shoulder. Slowly, cautiously, he approached John, moved his staff to his left hand and extended his right one in greeting.

"I am Rekem, from the village in the cliff. We call it Yahweh's holy mountain, Eden. No, I do not come here often. I have never ventured this far before. Our lives are given to prayer and meditation where we live, in the cliff. We leave only when we have failed to live without sin."

Puzzled by the reference to "living in the cliff," and "without sin," John asked. "Where is this place? I have never heard any reference to a cliff village in this desert, this wilderness. What do you mean 'without sin'?"

Rekem laughed. "This is no desert, no wilderness. This is Yahweh's dwelling place, his kingdom, where he watches over his faithful people, where he cares for his trees and bushes and plants and animals and birds and insects. He created all this, far from the evil ones."

"Who are the evil ones," John asked. "What have they done that is so wrong? I do not understand you."

"You, of all people, should know! You are Yahweh's chosen, are you not? You have sinned, have you not, driven out by your own guilt? Otherwise, why would you be here, running away?"

John was dumbfounded! How could this man, this creature, know him, or anything concerning his past life? It made no sense. It was frightening, and it made no sense! What would Yahweh have to do with this creature?

Looking up at the sky, noting the position of the early afternoon sun, Rekem's response was a suggestion.

"It is getting late and we have some distance to travel. Do you need help with your things? I will be glad to carry some of your load."

"Where are we going, and why should I go with you?"

"We are going to the village in the cliff. Now that I have been purified, I can return. There we will try to answer your questions, you who should know the answers."

John thought for a moment. Perhaps it would be best to give up and follow the man. He could find no reason to linger. It was getting late and he had no place suitable for another night. Picking up his pack, his water skin, his weapons, he nodded to this stranger Rekem.

"I must trust you. Go ahead, lead the way."

Rekem crossed over to the eastern side of the short valley, seemingly headed for the cliff beyond. To John's surprise, there was another break in the vertical face, a passageway. Traveling between narrow walls, they finally emerged into a wider valley with more cliffs ahead. And there was another surprise, water. There was a narrow, shallow stream of clear water coming down the valley and finally disappearing in the brush below.

Just before darkness began to creep into the valley, John saw it, the village. It was high up the wall of the cliff, smoke rising from the openings, the windows in the wall. There was a large open area, with people leaning over a low parapet, looking down at them. These people, or someone, had built a town in the side of the mountain, even to the point of adding stonewalls and parapets!

"Are we going up there?" asked John. "Perhaps that's a foolish question, but I see no path, no ladder."

"Oh, there's a path, steps cut in the face of the cliff," replied Rekem. "But they go only so far. At the top of the steps will be a ladder. They let it down from the village."

With that, Rekem started up the steps, after calling for a rope and basket that was quickly lowered. He put John's belongings inside. Those above raised the load easily to the village level. Without the back load it was easy to follow up the steps and then up the lowered ladder. Just as the sun was setting and darkness enveloped the valley, they arrived. Rekem was home, bringing with him a stranger who was quickly surounded by the curious villagers.

Breaking through the human ring, a man came to the center of the circle. Taller than most of the others it was obvious he was an elder, perhaps the leader, the head of the village. He greeted and welcomed John to the village that he called Eden.

"On behalf of the people of Yahweh, I welcome you to our home. We are honored to have one of Yahweh's chosen visit us. We will eat and then we will talk. However, before we eat, I must return to my prayers."

With that he disappeared through one of the doorways cut into the cliff. Others came forward and showed John where to wash for the evening meal. Before long Rekem joined him. To his surprise, the garment of skin was gone, replaced by a white garment, matching those worn by the others. His beard had been trimmed, combed and cleaned.

"You don't wear the garment of skins all the time?" questioned John. "You look different."

"I am different," answered Rekem. "My sins have been forgiven and my old garments of sin have been discarded. I am clean! I know you don't know our ways, or understand them, but we believe we are Yahweh's chosen people. We are the righteous ones. Here, in this hidden village, we strive for perfection.

"To be sure, we don't reach perfection. We know that, but we come closer than other believers. None of this is bragging, for that would be a sin. It's simply a fact of life. We may live isolated lives in this village, but we know what takes place in

Jerusalem, in Qumran, in Tobba. In all those places, sin works havoc, the sin of owning and having things, things not needed. He knows what we need and he supplies our needs. When we strive for more we sin!"

"And what was your sin?" asked John. "What did that have to do with your being in the place you met me?"

"Almost two months ago I went to our leader, Jeriel, and made my confession. In the midst of my daily prayers and meditation, I had questioned Yahweh's provision. Our water supply was low and I began to worry. How could we improve the situation? What would we have to do to make sure we had plenty? The answer I worked out in my mind, confident in our ability. We would build a dam; divert the water from the other side of the valley. We could take care of it ourselves. Sure, it would take a lot of work, but we could do it!

"I should not have done that. I should have trusted Yahweh, that he would meet our needs. With prayers of supplication I should have sought his answer. I did not do that. I sinned."

"But, Rekem, we all do that, at one time or another. If that is sinning I am guilty, more than anyone else. Yes, I'm supposed to be one of Yahweh's chosen, but I keep raising questions. When and where will he call me? What does he want of me?"

"Exactly! I know that and Jeriel knows that. Yahweh knows that! That's why I was waiting for you, to bring you here. It is time for your cleansing, the cleansing of your sins.

"Jeriel decided on my punishment. In keeping with our requirements I gave up my life here for 40 days. I was sent out in garments only Yahweh could provide, animal skins. I was sent out without possessions, no weapons. I would live off the land. The only thing I carried was my staff and a small hand knife. The staff was something to aid me in my walking. The knife was for cutting and preparing edible plants and leaves, even small animals and insects.

"As you can see, I survived. I went out, putting my trust and faith in Yahweh. I was not harmed and I did not go hungry. With Yahweh's provisions of food and drink, I was able to spend my time in prayer and meditation, reminding myself of Yahweh's gracious love. I was able to be an instrument in Yahweh's hands, waiting for you and bringing you here."

John couldn't believe what he was hearing. How could these people know anything concerning his life and his relationship to Yahweh?

"Are you telling me all this is a part of Yahweh's plan for my life, and that he has chosen you people to make it work?"

"Yes! This is true. However, I will stop there. It will be our leader, Jeriel, who will talk with you this evening. He will tell you Yahweh's plan for your life."

With that, Rekem led John through another doorway, into a larger space filled with rough-hewn tables. This was the dining area! When all had gathered and were seated, Jerial raised his arms for attention. When all was quiet he offered the prayer for the evening meal, pieces of unleavened bread and a broth of lentils and greens. It was not much, as John saw it, but it seemed to satisfy those around him, and it was filling. When finished, John had to admit it was enough.

There was little or no conversation during the meal, but after the tables were cleared, and as the people were leaving, they began to talk with one another. Jeriel indicated he wanted John to stay seated. Waiting for all the others to exit, he sat quietly, eyes closed. John had the distinct impression that Jeriel was praying.

Finally, when all was quiet, Jeriel opened his eyes and smiled.

"We have been waiting for you to come. I know this is hard for you to believe, but Yahweh is now ready for you to take another step toward your final preparation. You were right about leaving Tobba. You had to leave and you had to prepare for living alone. For a long period, the time was not right, and Yahweh wanted you to discover that, and get past your immaturity.

"Your problem had to do with your impatience, trying to get Yahweh to give you a sign before he was ready. Part of that was your age. Part was your working through your grief over the deaths of your parents, especially the death of your father. Part was your own wrestling with your human emotions as a man, emotions relating to a girl, Tobiah's daughter. A larger part had to do with your lack of knowledge in regards to Yahweh's holy word.

"Now, as I said, you are ready to begin your serious preparation, the next step toward becoming what Yahweh wants of you. Tobiah made it possible for you to have access to Yahweh's revelations given through Moses and the prophets. I understand you have done well in that regard. You have grasped the sense of urgency for the future. Marvelous things will take place in the lives of Yahweh's people, both the faithful and the unfaithful. That will come, but not immediately. It will come when Yahweh is ready!"

As Jeriel stopped talking for a moment, John was shaking his head in wonderment.

"How can this be? How do you know so much about me? How has Yahweh revealed so much to you, and how will you be of help in the days ahead? What you have said leaves me almost speechless!"

"John, do you remember what was said to your father Zechariah, at the time of his offering the Evening Sacrifice in the Temple, before you were born?"

"Yes, as I remember the story, one of Yahweh's messengers came to him, telling him that my mother would bear a son. They were to name him John. That would be me. I would be called to serve Yahweh. I was told the name of Yahweh's messenger was Gabriel."

"Precisely! Now, with your leaving Jerusalem and coming to Tobba, this same messenger of Yahweh has revealed the rest to us, through me. He did so with the understanding we would help in preparing you as Yahweh's spokesman. We were to be a part of your story.

"We do not know the details of your life, but that's not important. We don't know how you worked through your relationship with Tobiah's daughter. I can suspect, but that is your concern, not mine. In many ways you have sinned, just as we have sinned. What is important is the manner in which we deal with our sins, the cleansing process. Just as Rekem worked though his, we trust you will work through yours. The important thing, John, is to place all these things in Yahweh's hands. Let him hold you and guide you.

"But, now, it is late and we must rest. You have had a long, busy day and I know you are tired. Tomorrow we will go on with what Yahweh wants of us, especially what he wants of you."

Calling Rekem, Jeriel left John with him and went to his own quarters. Rekem took John to his, providing a pallet. It was late and John was tired. However, sleep did not come easy. The hard floor didn't help. Also, there were too many questions to be answered, questions which kept bumping into each other. Finally, trying to put those aside, he remembered to pray. It was a brief, simple prayer, but to the point.

"Yahweh, help me!"

With that, he slept well, better than in recent weeks.

The next morning John was awakened by the sound of singing. Half asleep, he thought he was back in Jerusalem. The singing was from the psalms, something the priests would use for their morning worship. He could hear the leader giving the response loud and clear:

*Hear, O Israel, the Lord is one!*

Then the others would repeat the psalm of praise.

But this was not Jerusalem. This was a village cut into the side of a mountain, a village of Yahweh's people singing Yahweh's praises far away from Jerusalem.

After the singing there was silence. Rekem entered, prepared to waken John.

"You are awake! That's good. We invite you to join us in our prayers. After that we will go about our daily tasks. For you there will be more sharing with Jeriel. Please come."

In the large room with the tables, the entire village had gathered, all except the small children. The tables had been pushed back, with everyone sitting on the floor. All heads were bowed and everyone was silent. With eyes either closed or lifted toward the heavens all were praying.

John followed Rekem as he pointed to an empty space. Sitting cross-legged on the floor, John bowed his head, ready to join with the others in prayer. However, nothing came to the front in his consciousness. His mind was blank! Almost coming to the point of panic, John realized he was faced with something new. There were no more questions of Yahweh, the how, the when. He simply could not articulate any of those. He suddenly realized that's what Yahweh wanted! How did the scroll read?

*Be still and know that I am Yahweh!*

Everything was blank. His mind was empty. He was open to whatever would come, and it came. It was as though he was hearing a voice calling him from far away, but a voice of assurance. It was the voice of Yahweh! For the first time, it was the voice of Yahweh! Incredible! After all the years of asking, seeking, begging for some word, Yahweh was now speaking to him!

"John! John! Hear me, John! I have created you and I will use you. Now, I must prepare you for that. Your life will not be an easy one. Opposition and tragedy will follow you. Yet, know that among men you will be the greatest, for you will point men to me through the Promised One who will come after you. I will not let you go! Put your trust in Jeriel's instructions for what comes next.

"After your brief time in the village in the cliff, I will lead you farther into the wilderness. There you will live, pray, meditate on the Scrolls, and wait for my voice. There will be a time of cleansing, but also a time of service, helping others in need.

You will learn that I am Lord of all! You are in my hands and I will not depart from you.

"You will touch the lives of many people. Many will enrich your life. Some would do you harm. Others will love you, thank you. Now, listen to Jeriel. He will counsel you and send you forth in my name."

John was amazed at the passage of time. He was stiff from sitting on the floor. Rekem reminded him it was almost the middle of the day. Surprisingly, he felt refreshed, ready to take on new experiences, whatever might come.

Again, Jeriel called him aside. It would be his final instructions for John. Seated near the low wall that looked out over the valley, he began with a question.

"Did you hear the voice of Yahweh this morning? Did he remind you to be ready for my directions for the future?"

"Jeriel, I can't explain it and it is hard to describe, but I heard a voice. It had to be Yahweh's voice. He reminded me my life will not be an easy one, but to it he has called me. I can only follow and obey. I must try to clear my life of all that is wrong, of all that would keep me from my mission. I will have to live somewhere out there, letting Yahweh take care of my daily needs.

"I do not understand my mission, but it has to do with the Promised One. That would have to be the Messiah, would it not? I will go before him, pointing to him as the One spoken of by the prophets. Help me understand that!"

"John, you are, indeed, a chosen vessel. As a human being, I would question that. Your past leaves much to be desired. Yet, I know now, after years of prayer and medition, Yahweh's ways are different from our ways. He knows what's best. He will use you as his messenger to the world, proclaiming the Redeemer!

"Now it is time for you to leave, to be on your own. We may never see you again, but we will know you are in Yahweh's hands. None of this will be easy. At times evil ones will surround you, but Yahweh will not let you go, not until your task is done. May you go in peace, always ready to be open to Yahweh's call and instruction! It is good to know you have reached this point of understanding.

"There is much more to come, but all that will be revealed in Yahweh's own time and way. You may not know this, but the One to come is Yahweh's own Son, but born of a human mother. Her name is Mary, your own mother's cousin."

John's mouth dropped open. He could not speak. His mind raced back over the years. There was Elijah's story of the young boy in the Temple. There were all the conversations about a possible boy cousin living, so he thought, somewhere in Galilee. It was all beginning to fit together!

"Do you mean to tell me the Messiah, the Promised One, is related to me through my mother? How can this be? How do you know that?"

"John, do I have to remind you again? Yahweh has revealed this to me through his servant Gabriel! Trust me. I am telling you the truth! You will be the one to go before the Son of Yahweh, the one called Jesus. I hope you grasp the importance of your task, the need to prepare! Out there, in the wilderness, Yahweh will guide you, instruct you. You must listen and obey!"

John sat in silence, his heart pounding, his eyes filled with tears. In silence he turned Jeriel's words over and over. Beyond all doubt, the time had come. He must take the next step in his call and appointed mission. He hardly heard Jeriel's final words.

"I see no reason to hold you longer. You must go, fulfilling Yahweh's call. May Yahweh bless you and keep you!"

Jeriel stood up, turned away and left. The meeting was over.

John spent the rest of the day alone. Seated in an alcove overlooking the valley below, he brought up in his mind's eye, Scroll after Scroll. He relived the lives of many of Yahweh's chosen, great leaders of old. He looked intently at their calls and their missions. He searched, again, for Yahweh's word of promise, the promise of a Messiah. As he turned over and over in his mind what he had read and studied so avidly, he searched his own soul, wondering if he was fit to join the long line of faithful messengers. Surely, Yahweh could have picked someone far more worthy than he. The exciting thing was what Jeriel had revealed about family, his own cousin. He would some day speak to the world about him. Surely, he would need to see him, talk to him, and let him know what Yahweh wanted of John!

They did not disturb him. They did not call him to the evening meal. He sat, alone, all through the night, meditating, agonizing, and praying. He was alone and Yahweh was silent! The one word that blazed again and again into his mind's eye was "patience." He must learn to be patient, waiting for Yahweh's call, no matter how long that would take.

As the rays of the morning sun burst through the openings in the walls of the village, John stood up. Alone, with no other person present, he bowed his head for a final prayer. He, in spite of no sleep and no food, knew he had been cleansed, refreshed. His prayer was one of both praise and thanksgiving.

Above all else, he was aware of the power of Yahweh, as well as his purpose. In contrast, he was keenly aware of his own limitations. If he were to fufill his calling it would be only by Yahweh's strength. He would take a young man named John, in spite of all his weaknesses, and do what he purposed. Yahweh was Lord!

Following the morning meal and prayers, Jeriel rose, embraced John and called for Rekem. Little else was said. It was time to go. Rekim would see John on his way. Helping gather his belongings, he reminded John he might not need all he was carrying. Yahweh would provide. He would provide far more than one might think. At the same time, he put an additional item in John's pack. It was a gift of unleavened bread.

They descended the ladder as the villagers waved their farewells. Going down the steps cut in the wall, they found John's pack already lowered to the valley floor. Rekem helped carry some of the load, and leading the way, moved away from the direction they entered the valley two days before. Heading north and west, the path led them up the long valley. Climbing over some low ridges they came to the opening of another valley leading more directly west. After an hour's walk Rekem stopped and said his farewells.

"John, there is an enormous world out there. You will find no villages and very few people. You might meet a hermit, or you might meet some of the wild ones. Most likely you will see neither. You will be alone, but always remember! Yahweh will be with you, no matter where you go. Be open to his will. Be prepared for his voice. It will come!"

Rekem embraced John, shook his hand, and headed toward his home, Eden. He did not look back.

Peering in the opposite direction, John moved down into the new valley. His first concern was to find shelter for the night. As he moved onto the valley floor he came to a small stream of water flowing toward him. Going upstream toward the far upper end of this long valley, he came to a smaller branch, apparently coming down from the cliff on the north side of the valley. Turning in the direction of the mountain he found the perfect spot. Adjacent to the small waterfall, the source of the small branch, there was an opening to a small cave. Apparently it had never been occupied, at least not in recent months. It was there he would spend the first night, perhaps more. It could be this was his new home! Stowing his possessions in the back of the cave, he drank from his water skin and ate some of the unleavened bread.

Sitting at the entrance to the cave, he took time to look back over his life, all the way back to his first years in his home village. Memories flooded in upon him as scene upon scene came into his thoughts. There were sad moments, but there were happy moments. There were people he could never forget, people who had touched and changed his life. He had been richly blessed!

As the sun settled in the west, the darkness began to spread over the valley. With his cave in the first shadows, he was ready to relax. Pulling his cloak from his pack, he tucked it around him like a blanket, closed his eyes and went to sleep. It was time to rest!

# CHAPTER 12

> *. . . streams in the desert.*
> Isaiah 35:6b

Just as the setting sun had cast first shadows over John's side of the valley, so the rising sun cast its first rays into his cave. He was awakened by a brilliant burst of light shining in his face. Tonight he would move farther back.

Fully awake now, John stood up, opening his eyes to the beauty of the landscape within the valley. With his keen eyesight he spotted a small herd of deer in the far distance. They were grazing peacefully, undisturbed. Overhead and on nearby tree branches were the birds, both large and small. High above all the rest were the soaring eagles, seemingly aloof to all going on below. It was Yahweh's world, a beautiful world. For John it was comforting assurance. Yahweh was in control!

Yet, the comfort was mixed with anxiety. John's present world, although including all that lay before him, was also a world of hurt and guilt! He had never felt this way before. To be sure, there were other heartaches and uncertainties over the years. He had shed many tears, tears of fear, tears in the deaths of his parents. He had felt the hurt in the progression of his father's declining health, dealing with the unrelenting changes. His life, at times, had not been an easy one. He had been forced to grow up, as he saw it, far too soon. Back in his home village he never had close friends his age. His world, for the most part, was an adult world.

The strong image for the moment was Debra, what had happened between them. He had given in to his human emotions of passion and desire. He should have been strong. It was the more disturbing as he remembered the pleasure of her closeness, the ecstacy of intercourse. How could such pleasure be so terribly wrong? Trying to balance his mixed emotions went nowhere.

What was he supposed to do now? Here he was, alone, waiting for Yahweh to show him what lay ahead. Sure, Yahweh had finally spoken, reminding him that he was in control; that he would care for him, direct him. He spoke of John's place in Yahweh's plans. Great things were in his future. Also, Jeriel had assured him that he was in the right place. He had assured him Yahweh was with him and would lead him. The startling news was Jeriel's talk of relationships. His cousin was Yahweh's own son, but born of his mother's relative. How could that be? No one had ever known such a miracle. He needed to know more.

Yes, he knew he would have to wait, but how was his patience supposed to play out in this place? At the moment there was nothing, other than a beautiful valley and Yahweh's created doing what creatures do. Should he stay here or move on? Would this be the best place for finding answers, or must he seek them elsewhere. When, where, would Yahweh speak again?

Finally, trying desperately to shut out the confusion racing through his mind, he was surprised to reach a level he had reached the day before. Seated on the ground, he closed his eyes, and without any effort on his part, everything went blank. It was as though his very being, his personhood, his consciousness, had left his body. His mind was, again, like an empty vessel. Into that emptiness came the voice!

"John! John! You are in my world, precisely where I want you. You will relate to it day by day. You will explore this world and will appreciate my provision for your daily needs, as well as the needs of others. I will provide. Just remember these words, eternal words: 'Wait on the Lord!'

"Here you will meet others. Some will laugh at you. Some will want to do you harm. Most will not understand you. Some, many, will need your help! It will be in these contacts, you will come to understand my mission for you, to proclaim the coming of my Son, the one of whom Jeriel has spoken, your cousin Jesus. Your lives are woven together in the fabric of the prophetic word given long ago. As the world sees it, you and he will share the same fate. At the proper time you will meet him, speak with him, and learn from him."

In the silence that followed there came another surprise. John saw the Qumran Scrolls, the history of Yahweh's people and the words of the prophets. It was as though he was holding each one in his hands. One by one they were unrolled before him. He could make out the texts he had read over and over again. Again, the words were burning into his heart and mind, words of both assurance and warning. Yahweh would fulfill his promise! One in particular filled him with anticipation. It was Isaiah's vision in the Temple, the vision of Yahweh and Isaiah's response: "Here I am! Send me!" Yes! Yahweh would use him. Also, he was confident, Yahweh would speak to him, again!

The vision faded. John opened his eyes. Surprisingly, as it happend in the village in the wall, the time had slipped by rapidly. It was noon; the sun was overhead. Conscious of a physical hunger, John went back into the cave and found the bread Rekem had placed in his pack. Breaking off a small amount he went down to the stream and refilled his water skin. Sitting in the shade of an overhanging limb he ate the bread, washing it down with the water.

Feeling satisfied, John went back to the cave, picked up his bow and arrows, and headed west. He felt the need to exercise. For the moment his mind was at rest. He felt he was at peace, at peace with himself and with his world. All things were, indeed, in the hands of Yahweh. Later he would have time to reflect on the startling events of the morning, a new element, a pleasant surprise. He did have a cousin, but a divine cousin! They would, in good time, meet.

Walking felt good! He needed the physical action and this was the answer. Taking long strides he covered a lot of ground. Along the lower level of the valley there were no boulders or rocks. There were few bushes, only some tall grass that did not impede his movement. Almost before he knew it, he had reached the spot where he had seen the deer.

They had disappeared, but he could see their hoof prints near a small spring of water. Apparently this was a favorite place for them. Here was food and water, plenty of grass and foliage.

Continuing on, he almost stumbled into a brood of dark grey hens. They startled him as they flew up and away. Knowing his need for food he quickly fitted an arrow in the bow. Moving forward, he stirred them again. Almost without any effort his first arrow hit the mark, a large fat hen. Tonight he would build a fire. The bird would be roasted over hot coals!

His other need, he knew, was for lentils or edible leaves. He had been given a small clay pot in which he could cook such things. His problem was to find greens suitable for cooking. Looking around he saw nothing he could use. It was time to move on.

Again, with long strides, he continued westward until he came to the far end of the valley. There seemed to be no way out until he climbed up and over a fairly high ridge. Beyond, stretching out of sight was a plateau. Here there were fewer trees, but larger ones than those behind him. In the distance, almost out of sight, was a tiny plume of smoke rising above what appeared to be a tent. He was not alone! There were others in his wilderness.

Assuring himself of Yahweh's watchful care, he made the decision to investigate. The afternoon was passing, but he felt confident he could return to his cave before dark. Approaching the tent with caution, he called out before getting close.

"My name is John. I am alone and mean you no harm."

For several minutes there was no response. Then the flap of the tent was thrown back and a woman came out, facing John. She was old, wrinkled and bent over. Looking directly at John she responded with a plea for help.

"My husband is old and weak and we have little to eat, only a bag of lentils. These we have in large supply, but we need water. We need meat! My husband needs to regain his strength, but we have no meat. In order to cook anything, we need water. There is a stream to the south, but I dare not leave my husband. Anyway, I do not have the strength to travel that distance, to carry the water skin. Could you help us? Please do not harm us! We are old and have nothing of value. Would you help us?"

John smiled in reassurance. Seeing the tears in her eyes, tears beginning to roll down her dark cheeks, he stepped forward.

"Here!" he said, "Here is water and meat."

With that he handed her the hen. Taking his skin of water from his shoulder, he asked:

"Do you have a pot or some container into which I can pour this water? You are welcome to what I have and I will see that you have more. Let me empty this and I will go for water."

Following her into the tent, he poured some of the water into a large clay pot sitting next to a small fire. At least they had fire and a little wood. Lifting the pot onto the rocks surounding the fire, he added wood, stirred the coals until the fire blazed up. The water would soon be hot.

Then he turned his attention to the husband. He was lying on an old frayed rug. Although he was covered with a rather heavy woven blanket, he was shivering. John felt his forehead. It was hot! Remembering that Debra's mother had laid out some roots and powders in his pack, he tried to remember which was good for fever. She had gone over the list carefully, trying to hold John's attention.

"Someday," she insisted, "you will have need of these medicines. Mark my word, you will want to know what each will do!"

She was right. He needed something for this man's fever. He would have to return the next day, perhaps sooner. Now he had to make sure the man's wife could fix some food. Seeing a larger water skin near the tent's entrance, he headed for the distant stream.

"I will be back as soon as I can. In the meantime I want you to clean that hen. Get it ready for cooking. Don't cook it over the fire or in the coals. Cook it in the hot water. Once that is done, you can add the greens, or the lentils. Do you have any salt? That will give you a good broth which you can feed your husband."

"Don't tell me how to cook," the woman smiled. "I was cooking broth long before you were born, young man."

John laughed and headed south. At least the wife had a sense of humor, in spite of their bad situation. Surely Yahweh had sent him to this place! What had Yahweh said? "Some people you meet will need your help." These two did!

It was a long distance, but John moved rapidly. Avoiding the rocky shoulder to his right, he dropped quickly to the lower level, heading for the stream. The route took him along side some scrubby trees, some dead and dried. Here would be a source of wood for their fire.

Making very little noise as he raced south, he surprised a deer, a large buck. The deer bounded to his right, climbing quickly the rocky shoulder, disappearing down the other side. Here was sufficient meat, John thought. He might be able to do much better than a small hen.

Reaching the shallow stream, John filled the larger skin until it was tight. The skin was old, very old, but it did not leak. There would be sufficient water for several days. Slinging it over his shoulder he hurried back to the tent. By the time he arrived he could smell the meat. The woman knew what she was doing! Obviously, she had the helpful seasoning on hand. John was hungry, and the odor intensified that feeling.

Entering the tent, the man's wife responded without looking up, reminded John the wood supply was low.

"Go! There's wood, dry wood, down toward the stream. If you expect me to feed us, including you, I must have some more wood! I can't cook without wood."

Amused at the woman's demands, John left again. Taking a long rope from the side of the tent he headed south again. Gathering up as many branches as he could carry, he returned. Stacking most of the wood outside, he took the rest inside. There would be plenty for cooking the meal and more! Sitting down, watching her bending over the pot, he asked:

"Tell me your name, and your husband's name. As I told you my name is John. What is yours?

"Our names are not that important, but, if you must know, my husbands name is Maacah and my name is Sarah, a good Hebrew name! You must be the son of Zechariah, the priest, if your name is John."

John could only gasp at what he was hearing. How did she know his family, his father Zechariah? Here were two elderly strangers living far away from other people, isolated out here in the desert, yet they seemed to know far more than anyone would ever expect!

"How would you know my father's name? You are right. I am the son of Zechariah."

"Young man," responded Sarah, "we have lived a long time, and we have seen many things. We have traveled south to the great desert of sand, and north to where we have seen the mountain of Baal, shining white with the frozen water. For a time we lived near David's city. That's where we heard the story of the miracle, a child born to elderly parents. Not only that, the story was told of the naming of that child. He was not named for his father, but was named John. He would be someone about your age, and few men carry the name John. Zechariah had to be your father.

"Don't get too excited over the obvious! It's time to share this meal while it is hot. We will eat first, feed my husband, and then we will talk."

Digging into a large woven basket, Sarah pulled out small

clay dishes, 3 small dishes and spoons. One of the dishes was bronze. Using a large ladle she shared the broth, filled with pieces of meat and lentils. It was good! It was only right that John had Sarah pause as he thanked Yahweh for his gifts. The hand of Yahweh was with them!

Then it was time to feed Maacah. John propped him up, his arm under his shoulder. Sarah, with much care and patience, fed her husband in very small amounts, giving mostly the liquid. Then, before she was through, she fed him a few, small pieces of well-cooked meat. From time to time Maacah would open his eyes, eyes filled with questions and wonder. John was a stranger!

Being unable to eat very much, it was not long before Sarah had John lay him back down. Maacah closed his eyes, asleep to the world. John wasn't sure, but Maacah's forehead was not quite as warm as before. It was a good sign.

"My husband Maacah," Sarah began, "is a Aramaean. His family goes all the way back to Abraham, to Abraham's brother. Strangely enough, his name was given to both men and women. Why, I don't know. Although he understands Hebrew, he speaks Aramaic, a language which is more ancient than Hebrew. Even today, Aramaic is used by a lot of our people, especially in the area called Galilee."

"Yes, I know," responded John. "I know that to be a fact. I, too, can use and understand the language. My father, along with other priests taught me. In fact, I think I have a cousin living in Galilee and, I would assume, speaks Aramaic. Someday I hope to find him and find out if that is so."

"Would your cousin be the son of a woman named Mary," Sarah questioned. "There's a marvelous story about her, and about her son. Have you heard it?"

For the second time John was startled by what he was hearing. How did these people know anything about the woman called Mary, the one who visited his mother so long ago? It had to be the same person!

"Tell me, Sarah, what do know about a Mary from Galilee, and what is this marvelous story?"

"Up in Galilee, the story is well-known, that her son, the one called Jesus, was born in a city more closely to us, the town of Bethlehem. As the story goes, his was an unusual birth, predicted by Yahweh himself! The father's name was Joseph. He was a carpenter, but died a couple of years ago. He must have been much older than his wife Mary. As far as we know she is still living there, in the town of Nazareth, and her son must be carrying on his father's work as a carpenter. We were in that area last year, but haven't had any recent news."

John, staggered by all this new information, stirred by all he had gleaned from Eljah, Jeriel and Yahweh, sat silent. While Sarah was cleaning her dishes, he had little to say. She was busy with her chores, busy with Maacah, and hardly noticed John deep in thought.

That was interrupted by Sarah's question:

"Where will you stay tonight? The sun is setting and it will soon be dark. Before you leave I would like you to go for more wood, enought for the night."

It was late! Going outside John made a decision. He would get the wood, but would rather not walk back to his cave. The distance was far. With no moon tonight it would not be safe. Concerned, also, for Maacah, he thought it best to stay.

Going back inside he asked about staying.

"Sarah, how did you get here? I see you have no animal to carry your belongings, your tent. Surely, you were not able to travel alone, just the two of you. How long have you been here?"

"We have a grown son. He has never married, but lives with us. At our age we are totally dependent upon him. Two days ago, he and a friend of his left, hoping to buy some food supplies, cheese, nuts and dried fruit. We have an old camel that our son is riding. His friend has a donkey. Hopefully, they will return soon, probably in the next few days. I believe the cheese and the fruit will help my husband. Actually, we are shepherds. We earn a little by caring for other people's animals. Also, we know how to weave the wool into cloth, a skill very few people have these days. We get by."

John, shaking his head over all that information, headed south again, looking for wood. It would soon be dark and he wanted to finish that task while he could see the way. By now he was tired and would have no trouble falling asleep!

Bringing more wood into the tent, checking on his hosts, making sure Maacah was no worse, he found a corner in the tent for himself. Given a robe from one of the baskets he bade Sarah goodnight, closed his eyes, and slept. Tomorrow he would try to sort out all he had learned, from both Sarah and Yahweh. Somewhere in all that, he had some decisions to make, one involving a possible journey north! He had to know more about his mother's cousin and her son. his own cousin. The pieces of the puzzle were beginning to fall in place!

# CHAPTER 13

*. . . the wilderness and the dry land shall be glad .*
*. .*

Isaiah 35:1a

John was awakened more than once during the night. Sarah, concerned for her husband's condition, kept stoking the fire. It wasn't so much the need for heat, but the light of the fire made it possible to check on Maacah. She did her best to make sure she didn't disturb their guest. John tried to cooperate. If she really needed him she would have called.

At the first suggestion of daylight, John moved about the tent. Sarah was sound asleep and Maacah's breathing seemed better. It was time to leave. He would return to his cave and, before the day was out, be back with the medicine, the powder Tobiah's wife had given him. Before settling down for the night, he made sure Sarah knew he might leave while they were still asleep.

Outside, the stars were fading with the rising of the sun. It was not yet visible over the eastern hills, but the glow marked the beginning of a new day. It was the hour John liked best, the beauty of Yahweh's world in the stillness of the dawn.

Slinging his bow over his shoulder, John moved rapidly. Leaving the higher plateau he crossed the ridge and dropped down into his valley. Passing the spring where he had spotted the deer, new tracks indicated they had been there during the night. It would be easy to provide additional meat for his Sarah.

At the cave he found his possessions intact. Nothing had been disturbed. It was nice to know the security of Yahweh's world out here; a far cry from Jerusalem. Perhaps the citizens of Qumran and the surrounding villages were right. They didn't have to worry about "things." The better argument was the village "in-the-wall," Eden, where possesions were far less important! He felt sure he would learn that for himself in the days ahead.

Knowing that time was not critical, John wanted to pause and consider future plans. He needed to sort out what he knew about the person Sarah referred to as Mary. This Mary had to be his mother's cousin, and her son was the child Eljah had seen in the Temple! He had to be the one Yahweh spoke of yesterday. How did he put it?

"One person in particular you must meet! Your lives are woven together."

If this was Mary's son and his cousin, John wanted to find him, meet him, and talk with him!

He needed solutions to the many unknowns; things he believed would have direct bearing on his own life. Yet, the problem was time, Yahweh's time. He would have to be patient.

Sitting at the entrance of the cave, leaning against an outcropping of smooth rock, John tried to get a mental picture of the information he had acquired over the years. There were facts of which he was certain, facts concerning his family and his mother's family.

Yaheweh had planned his birth. As Yahweh's messenger told his father, Elizabeth would bear a son. Then, during the time she was waiting to deliver John, his mother's cousin Mary came down from Galile. She, too, was pregnant! Her husband Joseph, a carpenter, came with her, but did not stay. Of all this he was sure.

The rest was only hearsay that Joseph and Mary had to come south to Joseph's hometown, Bethlehem. It was Sarah who had suggested it was there the son was born, the one named Jesus. If so, why did they go back north to Galilee, to the town of Nazareth?

So, here was a mystery. How long were they in Bethlehem? Why didn't they stay, if that was the father's home? Obviously, according to Sarah, they did go back north. Again, from what she had said, it was there the father, Joseph, died. Above all else, how was Yahweh working this out in his scheme of things? This divine plan, this miracle of Yahweh's son, staggered John's imagination! If Jesus was really Yahweh's own Son, how did Joseph fit into the picture? Could a human mother give birth to a divine son?

What was it Yahweh had said, back there in the village in the wall? He spoke of a "Promised One who would come after you." That would confirm the idea that John would, in fact, be a forerunner, preparing the way for his cousin. Is that the mission Yahweh has in mind for him? More important, what would be his cousin's mission?

John closed his eyes and began to think through the Scrolls, trying to get a mental picture of Yahweh's promises for the future. Somewhere there was a clue. There had to be! The prophet Isaiah had said a young woman, an unmarried woman, a virgin, would give birth to a son. He would be given the name of Immanuel. That name, he knew, meant "Yahweh with us."

How could that be? Weren't Joseph and Mary married? Did they have a child before they were married? Is she the one, the unmarried woman with child? How would Isaiah have known that? Again, what about the name, "Yahweh with us?" Was Yahweh really in his cousin? It was a puzzle, a huge puzzle. He must go to Galilee!

This time, in spite of the questions, and with difficulty in clearing his mind, he sat quietly and waited. He was not disappointed. Yahweh spoke:

"John, hear me! You are and will be a chosen vessel. Yes, when the time is ready you will go before him, my son Jesus. He is my son, born of woman, born of Mary, but he has no earthly father. He is different. You were born of earthly parents, but with my presence and power. He was born of and through the power of my Spirit. He is holy, separate, my son! He is in me and I am in him. That is a mystery and neither you nor anyone else will be able to understand that. You accept this on faith, faith in me, and faith in my promises. Someday, he will be described as both Yahweh and man, and that will be correct.

"He is the Promised One who will be the salvation of the world. You have read the story of my creation and the story of human rebellion. I created everything good, but from the beginning my people disobeyed me. They did wrong! They missed the mark I set for them. We call that sin. Yet, I had a plan. The first ones failed, but I would send my own son and he will not fail! I made a promise and you have read about my promise. It is the story of faith, of faith in the promise that I would send a Savior someday, when I was ready. It is now close to that time. In just a few more years it will be your mission to tell the world about him. You will be given a message of warning, but also a message of hope. He, my son, will give himself for your sake, for the sake of the world. He will explain this to you.

"Now, it will be good for you to meet him, see him, visit with him. Then, you will return here and wait. Here you will prepare, and be ready when I call."

Opening his eyes, John shook his head in wonder. Yahweh's unfolding story was almost too much! If all this was true, and it had to be so, his life would be changing, drastically. However, for the present, he had more immediate concerns. It was getting late. The sun was now in the western sky. It was time to return to the tent before dark. In addition to his weapons and his water skin, he was carrying the rest of the unleavened bread and the medicine for Maacah. The way was somewhat easier in that it was now a familiar path. He had no need to stop, seeking directions. Going past the spring and up over the ridge he soon spotted the plume of smoke rising from the tent. Sarah had kept the fire burning. However, the wood supply must be low. He would have to find more before dark.

Maacah appeared to be better, but John insisted he take the healing powders, the medicine for fever. Debra's mother had assured John this would help. It would, in a very short time, reduce the fever. This time Maacah was alert enough for Sarah to introduce John. He could tell Maacah appreciated his speaking in Aramaic. In response to John's words of greeting, he smiled.

"Sarah tells me you have been of much help. We thank you! We thank you in the name of Yahweh. Yahweh is good!"

"Yes," answered John. "Yahweh is good. He will take care of you; make you stronger. We will try to help. I must see about the wood now, but I will be back shortly. In the meantime, you should rest and let the medicine do its work."

John headed south, in the direction of the broken branches. He would tie together as much as he could carry, making sure there was a sufficient supply for the night. Tonight he would, again, sleep in the tent, sharing their food. After that would come his plans for travel. Tomorrow would be time for that, the planning and the preparation.

For this trip he was forced to cover more territory in his search for dry wood. In this part of the wilderness there was a real scarcity of trees. The farther south he went in this bleak, forbidding region, the more he was concerned for Sarah and Maacah. How would they survive in this desolate land? They did have a son, but John had to wonder about him, leaving his parents alone.

Some of his questions were answered as he came back to the tent. Tethered outside were the two animals, the donkey and the camel. Their son had returned. Stacking some of the wood outside the tent, John carried a load inside for the fire.

The son's name was Mibsam, an ancient name in Hebrew history. His friend's name was a more familiar one, Daniel. Daniel was quiet and soft-spoken. He had little to offer to the conversation. John saw him as a shy person, somewhat unsure of himself.

Mibsam was just the opposite. He was loud and boisterous, and quite jolly. He carried a very positive outlook on life;

including the assurance his parents would be fine. He would take care of them! As he talked he slapped John on the back, voicing his appreciation for a stranger's assistance. If he could do anything for John, he had only to ask. It would be done!

John couldn't help but like this man. He might have some faults or failings, but he meant well. Whenever he had an opportunity to get in a word, John explained about the wood, the medicine and his intent to find additional food, deer meat. After that, he would leave the parents in the son's hands. He would be gone a number of days, uncertain as to when he might return.

"Mibsam," he asked. "What else can I do to be of help? Your parents are dependent, unable to do the things of former days. They will need you here! Were you able to find any cheese, nuts and fruit? All those will help give your father strength."

"Oh, yes! We had to go as far as Hebron, but we found what we needed, enough for a number of days. That, plus the lentils, will provide enough for all of us. Now, if you are able to kill a deer we will be fine."

Mibsam had his doubts concerning a deer, wondering about the skills of this young stranger.

Howver, John reassured them the deer would be no problem. The important thing was the care of Mibsam's parents.

"Will you stay close by, watching over them? I'm concerned about others who might come by, wild ones who might do them harm."

Mibsam laughed.

"Don't worry so much my friend. We have survived this far. Yahweh watches over his own, especially old people and children. Didn't you know that?"

He seemed to show little concern for John's worrying, but John wanted to make sure the son would really care for his parents. He believed Mibsam loved his parents, but he tried to stress their needs. Hopefully, there would be no problem while he was away.

Again, Sarah prepared the evening meal, a broth with the lentils and the hen, plus some cheese and bread, and John's bread. It was enough for all. Maacah ate very little, only some of the broth.

As Sarah cleaned the dishes following the meal, setting the large pot off the fire, she began to tidy up for the night. Maacah dozed off. John and Mibsam began to talk. John was curious, wanting to learn something about the land to the west, in the direction of Hebron.

"How many days travel to the village of Hebron?" he asked. "Is that the best way north, toward Jerusalem and Samaria?"

"It's the only way north, unless you want to take the long route by the Salt Sea to Jericho. That would be far out of your way. It isn't an easy trip to Hebron, but not too bad if you follow the valleys going west. I think you will have little difficulty if you watch for the tracks of other travelers, their camels and donkeys. Just stay off the ridges. That would be quite tiring. Just this side of Hebron there is another well-traveled road, going north and south. Once you leave Hebron, traveling north, that will take you by way of Bethlehem.

"As to the size of Hebron, it is not just a little village, It is a large town, a center of trade. It is famous for its grape vineyards and olive groves. The oaks of Mamre are reminders of the days of Abraham. Did you know he and his wife Sarah are buried there, along with Isaac and Jacob? King David was crowned there. For many, many years it was a walled city, one of the cities of refuge. You will like Hebron. Walking? Allow two days, at least two days."

"Yes," responded John, "I must make a journey north to find some relatives of my mother. This is my first opportunity to do so, and I want to find the best route, all the way to Galilee."

John did not want to go into the details, sharing with Mibsom his reasons for the trip. That was John's concern and Yahweh's direction. He felt Mibsom would not understand.

Thanking Mibsom for his information, he had one request of Daniel.

"Tomorrow morning I want to collect more wood. I will be

up early and would like to use your donkey to carry the wood. May I do so?"

Daniel agreed, but insisted it would be a problem. He had a stubborn donkey, one unwilling to do anything for strangers.

"You are welcome to take him with you, but I have my doubts. I don't think he will want to go with you. He doesn't take well to strangers. Be careful! He might try to bite you."

John laughed. "Anyway, I'll be up early and I'll try to get the donkey to obey me. If not, I'll bring back a smaller load. Then you and Mibsom can gather more later on."

Now it was time for rest. John was tired! It was not so much the physical exercise, but his encounter with Yahweh, sitting still so long at the entrance to his cave. Each such experience was exhausting! This last one was especially so, filled with Yahweh's amazing revelations concerning his son, Jesus. Yahweh was right. One accepted such mysteries only in faith.

Finding his robe of the previous night he excused himself, found an empty corner away from the family and fell asleep. The last thing he heard was the murmur of voices, Sarah, Maacah and Mibsom talking with one another. Daniel's voice was silent as he sat and listened to the others.

The next morning John was awake and stirring while the others slept. Even inside the darkened tent John was aware of the dawn of a new day. It was time to be up! Life was precious! One must live it to the fullest. Thankful for Yahweh's watchful care over him, aware of the possibilities ahead, John saw each moment as a wonderful treasure. He wanted to be alert, active, doing what was set before him while there was time. Some would have thought him to be some sort of fatalist. John thought in terms of opportunity, Yahweh-given opportunity. There was work to be done. First of all, plans had to be made for a journey northward.

His first move was another trip, looking for wood. This time he had a carrier, the donkey. John had a way with animals and the donkey went willingly, without his usual braying. Hanging a basket from each side and with plenty of rope he was ready to travel. Today's route was farther to the west, rather than directly south. With his keen eyesight John had spotted some larger trees in that direction. The distance was much greater, but John felt confident he would find wood. This time the sun would be at his back, at least on the way out.

It was a long walk. By the time John reached his destination, the sun was high in the morning sky. Approaching the grove of trees John was surprised to find a caravan in the area. There were several tents pitched under the trees near a spring. Men were moving about, feeding the camels. From what he could see, they were beginning to pack up their gear, getting ready to depart.

As John came near, the men stopped, waiting for him to approach. They seemed undisturbed by this stranger coming out of the east. Being alone, he could not be a threat. They raised their hands in greeting. Then, one of them spoke; speaking in a language John could not understand.

"My name is John and I come in peace. My home is far from here, far to the east."

Surprise! One of the men in the background turned away from entering the largest tent and came forward to speak.

"John, do you remember me? I am Makir, the one who led you back toward your Jerusalem. I can't believe it! You were such a small boy then, but look at you now. You are a grown man, a tall, handsome young man."

With that he came forward and embraced John.

"Our esteemed leader will be surprised, but will be so happy to see you again. At the moment he is resting inside. You must understand! He is older and not well. We are on our way south, returning to the land of the flooding river and the monuments of stone. From all indications this might be his last journey to your land."

John was dumbfounded, yet pleased. He would see, again, the man of mystery, the one who had turned his life around. He could almost feel the man taking his hands and placing them on his head. John remembered how he trembled at his touch and the explanation of Makir:

"He sees in you a holy person, one through whom great events will take place."

Leading John into the darkness of the huge tent, he spoke to the man resting on the cushions. With little light from the one lamp, it took several minutes for John to adjust to the semi-darkness. As Makir talked to his leader in his own language, John could see the man's eyes brighten, the man who had knelt before him years before. Now old and bent he struggled to rise and beckened Makir to help him, but John rushed forward, took his hands, kissed them, and placed them on his own head.

Makir tried to stop John, but his leader waved him away. With John kneeling and the other one seated, they looked steadily into each other's eyes. For several minutes there was silence, then the man spoke, slowly, deliberately, with long pauses. Makir interpreted:

"My heart is at rest! My eyes have seen the fulfillment of my vision. No, your mission is not complete, but only beginning. But you have accepted what your Yahweh has set before you. You have come of age. You will do what your Lord has called you to do.

"Also, I am confident you will see her, the young woman I met long before I met you. Tell her you have seen me. She will know of what I speak, and will be glad."

As he paused and leaned back against the cushions, John could see he was exhausted, not only from the speaking, but also from the sudden encounter with the one he had called "holy." It was an emotional moment for both.

"My lord," said John, still holding his hands, "my Yahweh has touched my life in many ways. Whether you know it or not, he touched me through you. That night I met you in your tent below the walled city my life was changed, drastically. I grew up! Returning home, I found that my mother had died during the night and I would have to become a man, responsible, first of all for my father; then for my response to my Yahweh. He had a purpose in my birth and I am striving to fufill my calling, what you saw in describing me as a 'holy' person.

"Since that night in your tent I have been on a long journey, a pilgrimage, seeking to learn what my Lord has in store for me. Slowly that is unfolding before me. I will try to be faithful to what he wants of me. I thank you for what you did, touching my life as you did."

Makir responded, after completing the translation.

"See, he is nodding, but he is exhausted. In a few moments he will be asleep. He tires easily. It is best we leave him now."

Quietly John opened the flap of the tent and stepped outside, waiting for Makir. He could not linger long.

When Makir joined him, John thanked him for his help, for letting him share a few moments with the one who had touched his life in such a special way.

"Would it be good for me to wait, or would it be best for me to move on? If I can be of help I will stay."

"No," replied Makir. "He will understand. He is content with what has taken place. We have changed our plans and will stay one more night before resuming our travel south. The additional rest will be good for him. As you are well aware, our paths may never cross again, but that will not matter. You have met once more. Your hands have touched. Your lives are bound together, forever!"

As John turned to see about Daniel's donkey, before saying goodbye to Makir, he was pleasantly surprised. The men had gathered the wood John was seeking. The donkey's baskets had been filled and tied down. It was time to depart.

Thanking Makir again with a hearty embrace, shaking hands with the men gathered around them, John turned eastward. Before he crossed the first little rise, he turned and waved. Yahweh, again, had reinforced his calling. A part of that confirmation lay in the hands of an Egyptian, an old Egyptian nearing death.

# CHAPTER 14

*The Lord watch between you and me,*
*when we are absent, one from the other.*
                             Genesis 31:49

Seeing Maacah's and Sarah's tent in front of him, John felt he was coming home. The time spent there had been pleasant. He had been able to help those needing his assistance. It was as though he had become a part of the family. As he approached he noticed the camel had wandered some distance away, looking for any clumps of grass. Even being hobbled, he was always looking for food, always hungry. Everything else was the same.

Calling to those inside he had Mibsam and Daniel help him unload the wood. Daniel was amazed at his donkey's willingness to travel with a stranger. That had never happened before.

Inside, Maacah was up. He had color in his cheeks and the strength to move about. Standing beside the fire in the center of the tent, he welcomed John.

"Thanks be to Yahweh for your safe return. You are welcome in our midst. We hope you will stay for the evening meal."

"Yes, I will be happy to stay, but I must make preparations for my journey north. That means I will have to return to my cave, deciding what to leave and what to take with me. I can leave some things there. I'm confident they will be safe. Or, if you plan to stay here any length of time, I could bring such items here, leaving them with you. That's really not important and I certainly don't want to burden you."

Maacah was insistent!

"By all means, leave your things with us. Even if we move, it will not be a problem. We will be most happy to be of help, just as you have helped us."

"I thank you, and I may do that, but I do have one more task. Tonight, after the evening meal, I will try to find a deer. You can dry the meat over the fire and I will be able to take some with me. Dried meat can be eaten as it is, or added to the pot when cooking. Either way it will help all of us."

Both Mibsam and Daniel were excited over the idea. They wanted to go with John! He was dubious about their being able to keep up with him, and he was rather doubtful about Mibsam's ability to keep quiet. However, if the hunt would prove successful, they could help carry the deer back. Finally, after impressing upon them the rules of the hunt, he agreed. They would eat early and, as soon as it was dark, travel to the east, where John had spotted the first deer. Sarah and Maacah, of course, would stay behind.

John reminded the others to limit their eating. Deer hunting on a full stomach was not good. It was too easy to fall asleep while waiting. One had to be alert every minute, once the hiding places had been chosen.

The way Sarah prepared food it was hard to do, eat as little as possible. Sarah was a good cook and the food was tasty. However, they did try and at John's signal, gathered rope, baskets and water. It was time to go! Daniel wanted to bring his donkey, but John quickly ruled that out. Another animal's noise and smell would keep any deer away. The men would have to carry the load.

Moving eastward, John led the way. Neither Mibsam nor Daniel had ever been over the ridge into the next valley. This time, once they had crossed the ridge, John led them south. He wanted to be downwind from the deer. If they did come to the area of the spring, they would not catch the scent of the men. Also, there were several low bushes on that side of the spring. Here they could hide and wait.

Mibsam questioned their hiding place. It seemed so far from the spring. How would they be able to see the deer? And, even if they saw them, how could John kill one from such a long distance?

John smiled and assured both men. He would be able to see and his arrow would find its mark. The main thing for them to remember: "Be still and keep quiet!"

Hours went by. More than once John had to remind Mibsam to be quiet. It seemed he had to talk whenever he was in the company of others. Finally, John heard the deer, long before the others. In fact, both Mibsam and Daniel were dozing, unable to remain alert. Deer hunting at night was not for them.

It was not long before John saw them approaching the spring. There were several, one large buck, two smaller ones and three doe. Carefully, slowly, John knelt on one knee, fitting the arrow to the bow. Selecting the smaller of the two bucks he waited until there was little movement in the herd. Then, sighting at the proper angle, high for that distance, he released the arrow. He could barely hear the thud of the arrow striking the deer, but he knew it was an accurate shot. The deer fell immediately, and the others bounded away.

The noise of their hooves on the rocky ground awakened the two sleepy men.

Mibsam whispered: "What was that noise? Have you spotted any deer?"

John laughed out loud.

"Yes, I spotted some deer. In fact, one is lying on the ground, the one I was able to kill, even from this distance."

Mibsam looked at John with greater respect. This young man was something special. He could find and kill deer as though he did that sort of thing every day. It was amazing!

Going forward to the spring, John removed his arrow from the carcass. Taking his knife he cut it out. It was a shot that had penetrated to the deer's heart. With the other's help they made a sled from several tree branches. As always, John wanted to move away from the place of the killing. They would dress out the deer near the family tent. The odor of the dead animal and the skinning would be far from the gathering place for the other deer. They would return.

Mibsam and Daniel were excited over the night's hunting and were anxious to be of help. John was happy to let them pull the makeshift sled back. Outside the tent, John had them rig up a tripod of limbs and hang the deer off the ground. It was time to go to work, skinning the deer and cutting up the meat. Once they had finished, saving the parts wanted, as well as the skin, they could take the rest some distance to the north, leaving the head, the legs and the unwanted parts for the wild animals and birds. Yahweh's other creatures would have their share!

It was almost dawn when they finished. Sarah had woven a green branch rack for the meat drying, once it had been cut into strips. The rest would be cooked the next day, or dried in the sun. Mibsam suggested taking some to a village much closer than Hebron. Perhaps they could sell or exchange meat for grain. John was agreeable, but Mibsam would have to make the trip. Both he and Daniel could ride the camel, making better time, but they should leave right away. Spoiled meat would not sell!

They agreed! Wrapping the meat in large palm leaves and putting their load in bags, they mounted the camel and headed west, just as the sun was rising. Sarah and Maacah were still asleep and John joined them. He would get in a short nap before the sun was high.

Sarah awakened to the smell of meat strips drying over the coals. This would be faster than the drying out in the sun, and time was important. However, there would be plenty for outside drying, after John had departed. She wondered about the absence of their son and Daniel, but did not try to awaken John. She let him sleep.

He finally stirred, rolled over and got up. The meat did have a delicious smell, reminding him of his hunger. Having eaten little the night before, he was ready for some food. Perhaps there was some leftover broth!

"Well, my hunter of deer," asked Sarah, "did you lose two men last night?"

"No, we all came back, with one deer, a young buck. We kept the good meat and put the other parts out in the desert, far north of us. That will feed some of Yahweh's creatures. Mibsam and Daniel wanted to sell some of the meat, or trade for grain. If they keep moving they should be back by late evening. We did save the hide, if you would like to work with that.

"You made a good rack for indoor drying. As you can see, it is working already. You will have plenty of time for the slower drying outside, in the sun."

Sarah was delighted.

"You are quite a hunter, John. We thank you for helping us. This meat supply will last for a number of days. The dried meat will keep and I can continue to use it to make a good broth for Maacah. It will give him strength. Sure, I can take care of the hide. I will be able to clean and tan it. We will be able to use the leather.

"Now my concern is for you. What are your plans, John?"

"As soon as the men are back, I will make a final trip back to the cave and get what I need. In the meantime I will gather more green wood for the outdoor drying. This other meat needs to be cut into strips for that. If you will do that, I will go for the wood. Maacah should be able to turn the meat drying in the tent, don't you think?

"Be on your way, John. We will take care of things here. We do need more water, if you will take the skin with you. There should be some slender green twigs near the water supply."

John picked up the skin, put his knife in his belt and headed south. He would bring water and wood. Green wood, slender growing branches, made excellent racks, something he had learned back at Tobba. Strange that he suddenly thought of Tobba. What were they doing today? How was Debra? Did she miss him or think of him? Would he ever see her again?

With those thoughts running through his mind, it was time to reach a decision. As much as he would like to see his friends, the people of Tobba, he knew he must not travel by way of the Salt Sea and Jericho. That would delay his journey north. Also, seeing Debra and the others would not be helpful, not now. Once he left Maacah and Sarah's tent he would travel west to Hebron. From there he would turn north, going through Bethlehem. Galilee was his destination and he must be on his way, now! It was time to find Mary and her son, Jesus.

Arriving at the stream, John filled the skin with water. Moving along the bank he selected and cut a number of supple, green branches. These would do fine in providing a rack for the drying meat. After a brief rest, watching the eagles soaring high overhead, he was ready to leave. He was ready to leave his friends and deal with his own destiny. Just as the eagles soared free overhead, so Yahweh's people would be freed in days to come. How did Isaiah say it in the scrolls?

> *They shall mount up on wings like eagles.*
> *They shall run and not be weary.*

The evening meal was over before Mibsam and Daniel returned. They were exhausted from a trip longer than anticipated. However, they did sell the meat for a good price, one shekel, the equivelent of four denarii. With two denarii they bought a bag of grain and a small amount of cinnamon for Sarah, something she would use as seasoning. A friendly vineyard owner had shared a large bag of grapes.

There was little talk after Mibsam and Daniel shared the news of their journey. They were tired, ready for a night's rest. John indicated he would be up early, returning to his cave. He should be back before noon. Tomorrow afternoon he would be on his way to Hebron.

As before, John was awake first. Moving quietly about the tent, he picked up his water skin and knife. Stepping out into the dawn, he paused to give Yahweh thanks for the beauty of his creation. It would be a good day. It would be a momentous day, marked by Yahweh's direction to find the one he would "go before." He still wasn't sure just what that meant, other than this is what Yahweh had called him to do. It was time to leave.

The trip back to the cave was uneventful. His things were as he had left them. Gathering up what he thought he would need, he was ready to return to the tent. The rest he moved to the back of the cave. He would not have his friends worry about his things. His meager possessions would be safe!

He would miss the beauty and quietness of his valley, but, perhaps, he would return here. There would be, according to Yahweh, a waiting period, a time for preparation, and he could see no reason for waiting elsewhere. He believed he would come back to this place, his wilderness home.

John was back, just as the others were rising. They had slept well and long. Attentive to John's desire for an early departure, Sarah had prepared some lentil stew and bread the night before. Warming that up was done quickly. John would be well fed for his journey.

Sarah also filled John's pouch, filling it with food. There was dried meat, bread, dried figs, nuts and grapes. He would not go hungry. As she embraced him, saying her goodbye, she pressed two coins into his hand, two denarii. Sarah saw John as another son, one she had come to love. She, more than the others, would miss him!

The family gathered around John, each saying their farewells in their own way. Maacah held him close, asking Yahweh's blessings on John and his journey. Mibsam and Daniel shook his hand.

"Don't forget," declared Mibsom, "you will have to teach us how to hunt deer when you return!"

John spoke to each one, with one more embrace for Sarah.

"Mibsam, you are responsible for your parents. You and Daniel take good care of them while I am away. Will you do that?"

Mibsam nodded. He would do just as John had asked.

"Trust me!

With nothing more to say, John shouldered his pack, fastened the pouch to his leather belt, put his knife in the sheath, next to the pouch, slung his water skin over his shoulder. With a final wave to everyone, he laughed, leaned over Daniel's donkey as though whispering in his ear. He then scratched the donkey's long ear and headed west. That, and their responsive laughter, broke the tension. John was on his way. At the first rise, he turned, and with one final wave, disappeared.

# THE SCROLLS

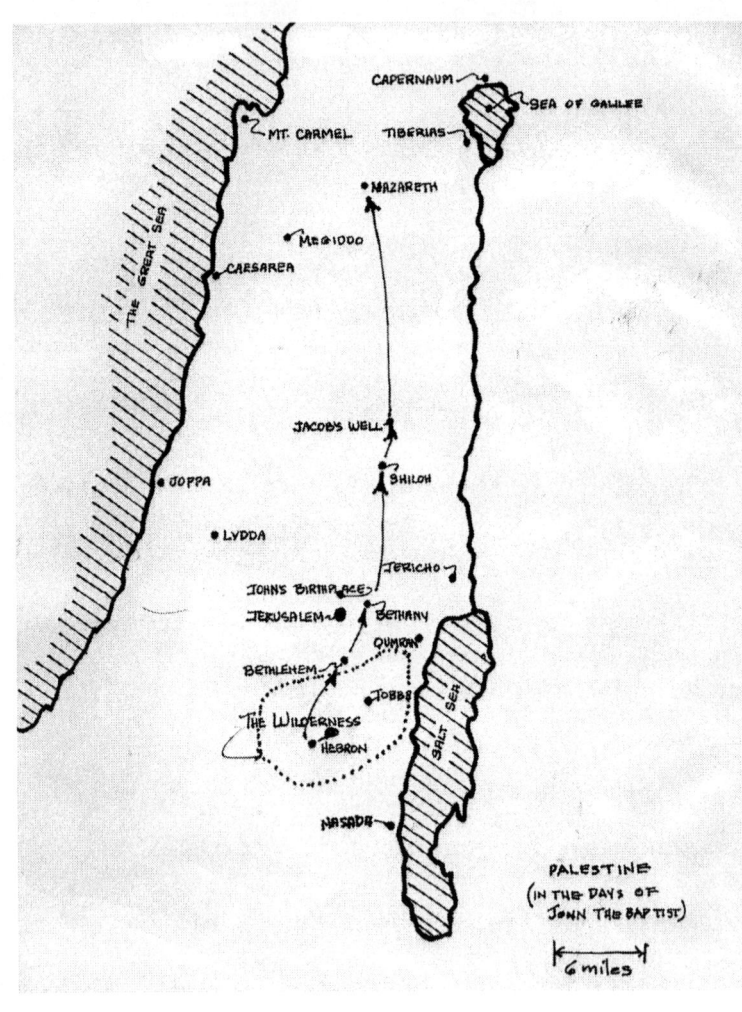

# CHAPTER 15

*. . . I have made, and I will bear;
I will carry and I will save . . .*
                                        Isaiah 46:4b

John was confident he could be in Hebron by the next evening. He would have to keep moving, but with his long strides he should have no trouble. From Mibsam's description it should not be a difficult walk. As long as he stayed in the valleys he could move rapidly. As he well knew, ridges were seldom good for walking. The view was nice, but it made for slow travel.

It was painful to leave his friends. They were now family, and he was concerned. Hopefully, Mibsam would watch over his parents. He did promise he would be a supportive son and John had to trust him. All were in Yahweh's hands.

Also, he had to admit, there was a sense of apprehension in beginning this journey north. There were so many unknowns ahead. Was he doing the right thing in trying to find his mother's relatives, his cousin? Would he really be the one he was seeking, the one Yahweh had described? Sure, Yahweh had suggested it, outlining the relationships with both Yahweh and John, but all this was unknown territoy. What would they say to each other? For himself, he was still wrestling with his mission in life. What about the specifics, the pertinent details for him?

For the first hour John followed the same path he had traveled before, when looking for wood. In the distance he spotted the grove of trees where he had encountered the caravan and his Egyptian friends. He was sure they had departed. Coming closer he saw there was another tent near the spring. This one was much smaller, of poor material. Obviously, this was the property of a shepherd family, herding sheep. Even at a distance, one could hear the sounds of sheep.

With the sheep milling around the spring, muddying the water, John did not stop. He waved to the family and continued on his way. Mibsam's directions were to turn north for a short distance and then west again, entering the adjoining valley. Here, the land opened up without any high hills or peaks. There were grassy areas on the sloping hillsides and he could see several flocks of sheep in the distance.

It was easier walking now and John was quick to notice the difference. This was a well-traveled path, branching off the north and south route that the Egyptians must have traveled. Makir had talked briefly about that, indicating they would not go through Hebron on their journey south. Their leader had wanted to avoid the towns. He was going home!

As the hours went by, with the sun sinking in the west, John encountered more people going in the same direction. They were hurrying to reach a resting place for the night. One man on a camel had paused long enough to share information about such a place. John was assured he could find water and a sleeping place within the hour.

The man was correct. A few houses, three to be exact, had been built near a spring. Only one was occupied. A family from Moab lived there, selling what they had on hand, cloth, salt and bread. For those wanting a sleeping place inside, there were the other two buildings. One could sleep inside for a small fee.

Arriving at the spring, John noticed a number of people stopping a short distance away from the buildings, preparing to camp for the night. With the sky clear and the weather warm, most were settling down outside. Some were lighting fires, heating water. There were a few donkeys, some carrying the loads of their owners. There was one ox and cart belonging to a trader heading for Hebron. It was interesting to John; he was carrying a load of leather hides, soft brown skins. It looked as though some might be deerskins.

It was a friendly gathering of people and John had the opportunity to meet and talk with several. One was a youg priest, returning to his home in Hebron. He had just begun his service at the Temple and was on a brief leave. He had learned his father was not well and had been given permission to take care of family needs. He would have to return to Jerusalem as soon as possible.

John invited him to eat some of his bread and dried meat for the evening meal. He had enough for both. The young priest, Ishvi, was grateful, not only for the food, but for the company. Traveling alone, concerned for his father, a friendly voice was most welcome. When John offered a prayer of thanksgiving for the food, asking Yahweh's blessing upon his father, he was touched.

"Are you a rabbi? You seem so young, but so mature! You pray as though you really know Yahweh. Sometimes the prayers in the Temple seem so ordinary, so impersonal. Surely, you are not a priest."

John smiled.

"Do you know a young priest by the name of Eljah?"

"Yes, I know him. But how do you know him? Do you come from Jerusalem? Are you, were you, a priest . . . or a rabbi?"

"My father was a priest, some years ago. From time to time I would visit him in Jerusalem. I met several of the other priests, including Eljah."

John did not want to go beyond that point. The story was too long. The story, to this young priest would be incredulous. He was determined to leave it at that.

"Tell me about Eljah. How is he doing? I would like to see him again."

"He is fine and has been of much help to me. Under our Division leader, Jonathan, he has helped so many of us coming into the priesthood. When I see him, I will speak of you and your kindness. Tell me your name."

"My name is John. I think he will remember me. But, tell me about yourself. How did you come this way, if you are going back to Hebron? This is out of your way. Shouldn't you have come down by way of Bethlehem? I have never traveled that way, but friends have instructed me on the best routes."

"You are right, but I left the main road to make a brief visit to a friend in Tekoa. When I left there I came down the wrong valley, a little east of the main route to Hebron. So, here I am; but almost home. We will be in Hebron tomorrow afternoon.

"Do you have family in Hebron, John? Are you staying long, or are you just passing through? I would be most happy to have you stay with us if you need shelter. It would be good if my parents, my brother and sister, could meet you."

John, thinking about his travel plans, accepted the invitation.

"Thank you, my friend. I have no family there, and will be on my way north the next day. My plans are to go through Bethlehem, all the way to Galilee. My mother, now deceased, had a cousin living in Nazareth. This is my opportunity to try to find her. I will be grateful for a place to spend the night, meeting your family. Also, I would like to see your father."

Both John and Ishvi had blankets for sleeping. John had started a small fire that would provide some warmth as they settled down for the night. It would be comfortable under the stars. Tomorrow Ishvi would be home, bringing a young stranger with him.

Mibsam was right. Hebron was more than a small village. It spanned both valley and ridge. Some parts of the town reminded John of the lower city below the walled city of Jerusalem. It was a busy place, with shops and markets all around. The odors of fresh meat, wool, spices, grapes, olives and dried fish were quite strong. The smell of grapes and newly fermented wine hung in the air. On the outskirts, south of the main town area, were the tents of those passing through. Camels and donkeys and oxen gave out the strong pungent smell of the farm.

There were a number of permanent homes, some of stone and others of mud and wood. All had flat roofs. Grape vines provided shade for outside work. Here there was a sense of prosperity, a town with a degree of wealth.

Nearby was a military square, the quarters of a Roman garrison. A small part of a Legion was stationed there, in charge of both people and property. People with trade goods, either residents or those passing through, were required to pay taxes. In spite of their grumbling, the appointed tax collectors took their share. In Hebron, as well as in all other towns, the tax burdens were heavy.

John and Ishvi arrived earlier than expected. They had walked steadily since early morning. As usual, John was an early riser. He awakened Ishvi and had them on their way before many of the campers were awake. They were in Hebron in the middle of the late morning activity in the markets.

Ishvi wasted little time in the center of the town, where the main road went north and south. With John following close behind, they went farther up and west. On the edge of the town, high on the ridge running north and south, were several larger homes, set apart from the others. One of the largest was Ishvi's family home.

As they approached the walled entrance, a servant came out to greet them and provide water and towels for washing their feet. With a brief smile and greeting, he ushered them inside.

"Your family will be most happy to see you, Ishvi, especially your father. He is not well."

Ishvi hurried in, pulling John behind him. With a word of warning he called out:

"It's me, Ishvi, I'm home. I"ve brought a visitor with me. Come and meet him, a good looking young man."

With that announcement echoing through the house, his younger sister dashed in. Seeing John, she stopped, blushed, and then hugged her brother.

"Welcome home, my priestly brother. Introduce me to your handsome visitor."

"Miriam, this is my friend John. I met him on the way here and invited him to stay with us. He will be here one night, before he travels north. He provided an evening meal for me last night, for which I am most grateful.

"Now, remember your manners, young lady, and don't pester him. Do not make eyes at him. He doesn't want to be bothered by little girls."

"Ishvi, you ought to be ashamed of yourself, talking like that. Anyway, I am not a little girl! I'm almost sixteen. John, please ignore him. I will make eyes at you. You are so much better looking than Ishvi!"

She smiled her best smile at John and, without catching her breath, dashed from the room.

"Mother, Ishvi is home, bringing a handsome man with him. Come and meet him, now!"

The mother, Naomi, entered hurriedly, anxious to greet her son and visitor.

"Miriam, don't make so much noise. Thank goodness, your father is sleeping. Sir, please excuse my daugher's outburst. Welcome to our home."

Embracing Ishvi, she began to cry.

"Ishvi, what are we going to do? Your father doesn't improve and the local rabbi, the one who is supposed to know so much about healing, hasn't been of any help."

John, anxious to be of assistance, asked if he might see the father, Simon. He knew a little about illnesses, and might have something for him. Remembering the things Debra's mother had given him, along with her explicit instructions, he hoped he just might have the right thing. That, with Yahweh's help, might be what the father needed.

Entering the darkened room, he heard the rasping breathing

of the man on the bed. Feeling his warm forehead he knew he had a fever, perhaps the same he had found in Sarah's husband, Maacah. Would it be right to give him the same medication? Not quite sure, he bowed his head and prayed silently, asking Yahweh's presence, blessing and guidence. He was confident the powder would not harm but, with Yahweh's blessing, would help.

Asking for his backpack left at the entrance, he found the medicine. Assuring the family, he had the servant bring a cup of water. Mixing the medicine in the water, he lifted Simon's shoulders so he might drink from the cup. They would know by evening if this would help. Again, John prayed it would be so.

Leaving Naomi with her husband, John followed Ishvi into the back couryard. It was a beautiful, well-cared-for space, lined with shade trees. In the center was a fountain, filled with flowing water. Down below there was a small pond containing fish. Benches placed around the pond provided a resting place, a good place for talking.

"Mother tells me she doesn't know where my brother Nehum might be. He seldom stays at home any more. He travels a lot, going as far south as Beersheba and, as far north as Samaria. I suspect he has been all the way to the Sea of Galilee. Nehum is a trader, mostly in gold, silver and bronze. We think that is a very dangerous business, but he is the older son and should be able to care for himself. We suspect he bribes the Romans for their protection. To us that is sinful, but we cannot tell him what to do. Apparently he is quite wealthy."

John, disturbed by what he heard, responded.

"Our people suffer greatly at the hands of the Romans. We pray constantly that the Promised One will come to save us from the hands of our enemies. Yahweh has spoken many times concerning a Messiah for his people. Many of us believe that will happen soon, in our lifetime."

"Oh, yes," responded Ishvi. "We hear that all the time in Jerusalem, but we are not so sure. So many years have passed, and we are still in bondage. Yahweh remains silent. I'm doubtful."

"Please, Ishvi, don't give up hope. Yahweh will have the last word. He will do what he says he will do. The Torah, all the books of Moses, confirm that. I can testify to that in my own life. He will do what is best for your father. Just wait and see!"

With that word of encouragement, John asked to see more of Hebron, in particular the burial place of Abraham and members of his family. It would be a moving experience to stand at their gravesites. He also remembered David was crowned king here in Hebron by the prophet Samuel.

Ishvi, anxious to please, gave John a tour of the town, pointing out his route for the next day, the road north to Bethlehem.

Abraham's grave, as well as the graves of Sarah, Isaac and Jacob was on the north side of town, toward the oaks of Mamre. Here John stood quietly for several minutes. Ishvi waited patiently, until John turned away. For John there was a flood of memories, Yahweh saying to Abraham, "Leave your homeland. Go to a place, a land I will show you and give you." He was confident this was Yahweh's message for him. Now, he was on his way, on a path unknown, just like Abraham.

From there they walked through the busy market, where the many merchants were calling out their wares and bargains. They had no desire to buy anything, wanting only to watch the many people buying and selling. It was a busy, exciting afternoon. A few of Ishvi's friends greeted him, embraced him, and asked about his father. They also wanted to know about Jerusalem and the Temple. Ishvi was now a celebrity, a traveler to distant places!

Taking their time, returning to the home late in the afternoon, they were greeted by Ishvi's excited sister.

"You won't believe it, but father is so much better. He is sitting up and mother is feeding him some soup. We think he will be just fine!"

Turning to John she smiled and thanked him.

"You are not only good looking. You are a wonder worker. You have performed a miracle!"

Making a face at her brother, she laughed and spoke again to John.

"You can't leave us tomorrow. I think I'll keep you. Ishvi can leave for Jerusalem, but I want you to stay!"

Their mother, following behind her daughter, invited John to speak to Simon. Her husband wanted to thank this stranger who worked miracles.

It was a good evening. Naomi had the cook prepare a delicious meal, including fruits and nuts. There was plenty to eat, more than enough. John finally begged for deliverence. Everyone wanted him to taste what he or she thought to be the best. He was, as he laughingly described it, "stuffed!"

Many were the words of appreciation. The husband, and father, was so much better. His fever was gone. He was sitting up a little, regaining his strength. All were certain he would recover, fully. They could not thank John enough.

After the evening meal, Isvhi invited John to walk, moving across the western side of the ridge. From there they could look toward the Great Sea, where the Judean hills dropped down to the valleys below. Although they could not see it, they were looking in the direction of the territory of the ancient Philistines.

Sitting on an outcropping of limestone, Ishvi wanted to talk. As the shadows of night began to move down the slopes below, and as the stars began to sparkle in the night sky, Ishvi asked for John's thoughts.

"You intrigue me, John. All along the way I have observed your confidence in what you are saying and doing. You were able to provide what my father needed, and he is on the mend. Also, you spoke concerning the Messiah. You seem so sure as you spoke of him coming soon. What makes you speak in such a positive way?

"Sure, I hear the elders in Jerusalem say the expected things, but they seem to have no clue concerning future events. I want to know what you think, what gives you reason to hope."

John was hesitant to tell all, but he wanted to give his friend both hope and assurance.

"Ishvi, the Scriptures contain Yahweh's promises for the future. If you haven't read all that, you will. You should! Study the writings carefully. Yahweh has promised the Anointed One will come. He will come when Yahweh is ready.

"I am certain that time is drawing near. I will be involved in sharing that message of hope. You see, Yahweh predicted my birth, through his messenger Gabriel. My father Zachariah received that word while offering the Evening Sacrifice in the Temple. That is a matter of record and your leader, Jonathan, will confirm that. Ask him.

"My father and mother were quite elderly when I was born. My mother was old, much too old to bear a child, but she did. It was Yahweh's doing. Then, at my naming, my father was given words of prophecy, words that spoke of my place in proclaiming what Yahweh would do. He would send a Saviour!

"This, too, has happened. A young woman of Nazareth, my mother's cousin, gave birth to a son, Yahweh's own son. She was betrothed at the time, to a man named Joseph. She had known no man! This was Yahweh's doing, also predicted by Yahweh's Gabriel. He spoke to the young woman, Mary, and to her betrothed, Joseph. Believe me, that is true fact!

"He and I are about the same age. I am on my way north, hoping to find him, meet him, and talk with him concerning these things. Hopefully, he will know what I am to do, and when he will come forth as our Messiah. His name is Jesus, which means 'Saviour.'

"I know all this is difficult to take in and believe, but it is so. When he comes we will be delivered from our enemies. Our people will be restored to freedom, brought back to faithfulness under Yahweh's rule and direction. Israel will be great once more."

Ishvi said nothing. His eyes were fastened on John's. His mind was in turmoil. He could not fathom what he had heard! Yet, he believed John was not making up this unbelievable story. He shivered, shook his head and stood up.

"Do you mean to tell me Yahweh is now ready to act, to give all this land below us, back to us? Are you saying we will be great again, free to worship Yahweh, with no fear of those who rule over us? Are you serious, pointing forward to what some have called the Day of the Lord? I can't really doubt you, but I need to see it happening."

"You will, I promise," John answered. "He will come!"

Ishvi led the way back to his home, in silence. At the door to the guest room, he embraced John. With tears in his eyes, he thanked him. His final words were brief.

"We will see. Only time will tell. Let us live in hope!"

John went to bed; happy he had been able to share his story. Ishvi might not be fully receptive to what he had heard, but the rest was in Yahweh's hands. John was confidant Yahweh could handle that, and would!

# CHAPTER 16

> *. . . but you, O Bethlehem, Ephrathah,*
> *who are little to be among the clans of Judah,*
> *from you shall come forth for me,*
> *one who is to be ruler in Israel . . .*
>
> Micah 5:2

John chuckled! This seemed to be the story of his life. It really wasn't that funny, but here he was, leaving again! He was saying goodbye to newfound friends. As he had discovered several times before, it was never easy. After a night of relaxed conversation with a very grateful family, an intense discussion with the young priest, and a good night's sleep, he wanted to linger, but could not. It was time to depart Hebron and head north.

Everyone came out to see him off, Simon, Naomi, Ishvi and Miriam. Simon shook hands, thanking John for his quick recovery. It was amazing! Two days ago he could hardly move, racked with fever. Now, here he was, outside, feeling so much better.

"You are truly a man of Yahweh! You saved my life!"

Naomi and Miriam embraced him. In spite of her mother's embarrassment, Miriam kissed him. She was certain it was love at first sight. He would have to come back!

Ishvi wrapped an arm around his shoulder.

"We are grateful for all you have done for us. We will never forget you. Please! When you come south again, come by way of Jerusalem. From what you tell me, Eljah will be happy to see you, and so will I. I'll share with him what you did for my family, especially my father. We will miss you. May Yahweh watch over you while we are apart, one from the other.

"As to what you have shared with me concerning Yahweh's plans, I must wait and see. I will have to think much more about that. I trust Jonathan will be of help. I pray so!"

Over John's protests, all repeated their gratitude, waving to him until he was out of sight. It was not easy to say farewell!

Moving quickly through the town, ignoring the many offers of the merchants, he left Hebron. His next stop would be Bethlehem. It would be an all day walk. If he lingered along the way, it would be more. He had hopes of spending the night there. He had hopes of finding anyone who might remember Mary, Joseph and a baby. He wasn't sure about the exact year, but it had to be at least eighteen years ago. Surely, the birth of Jesus might be remembered by some of the older residents of the town. They would have to remember the census ordered by the Roman emperor, Caesar Augustus. To be sure, the decree came from Rome earlier, but when the order finally reached Judea, Samaria and Galilee, a large exodus of people took place; all citizens forced to return to their hometowns. Bethlehem would have been a very busy place!

With those thoughs spurring him on, John moved on up the valley. Passing the oaks of Mamre, he thought through again the epic of Abraham, and his wife Sarah. It was a marvelous story, especially the coming of the three visitors, Yahweh telling Abraham and Sarah they would have a son. He had never thought of it before, but that was the story of his own life, Yahweh's messenger coming to his parents in their old age. They were informed they would have a son! Could it be Yahweh's way of reminding him of Yahweh's presence and purpose for him? Yes! It helped confirm what he believed to be true! In Nazareth he would learn the rest!

Although John left Hebron early in the day, he was not alone. This was the main route north, well traveled. A number of homes were scattered along the way, as well as a few small villages. There were grain fields of millet. Such crops were important for making bread and as a source of income. People with grain to sell went either south to Hebron or north to Tekoa, Etam or Bethlehem. A lot of people were on the road.

Another small town along the way was Zior. According to local tradition, Easu was buried there, in one of the many tombs. No one could really identify the particular tomb, but they were sure it was here. Stopping in Zior for a brief rest, John was assured it was the truth. That, too, was of special interest, as he recalled the Scrolls and the history of Moses. The story of Jacob and Easu was a part of that history. For John it was a reminder of the conflicts of life, the darkness that always seemed to threaten Yahweh's people.

It was late afternoon as John approached the hills of Bethlehem. The main part of the village straddled a rather high limestone ridge. On the south side there was a steep drop and an old donkey path leading down toward the Judean wilderness and the Salt Sea. Perhaps, just perhaps, that might be a shortcut when he returned south. That, he believed, would be a part of Yahweh's plan for him, a return to his wilderness.

As John climbed the ridge and entered Bethlehem the merchants were already putting away their goods. It was getting dark and the streets were deserted. Only one man, a young man, remained. On a low table there were several items for sale. There were two small loaves of bread, several strips of dried meat and a few dried fish.

"Sir," he called to John. "Wouldn't you like to buy what I have left? My mother baked the bread this morning. It is good bread! The dried meat and fish you can carry with you. It will keep. I can tell you are a stranger. You have never been here before."

John wasn't quite sure how he might answer. How would he know he had never been in Bethlehem? As to the dried meat and fish, he still had with him his own dried deer meat, enough for a few more days.

"Why are you still here," John asked, "after all the others have departed? You can come back tomorrow and sell what you have left."

"That's my problem. I didn't sell very much today, and I won't tomorrow. The merchants try to discourage people from buying from me. Only people like yourself, strangers, will stop to talk. You see, I'm not from Bethlehem. I'm from Samaria, north of Jerusalem. My mother and I moved here last year, after my father died. My uncle took possession of our home, claiming my father owed him money. He made it very hard for us and we had to leave.

"I don't know why I'm telling you all this, all my problems. But, you seem to be someone I can talk with. It has been a very frustrating day and I need to share this with anyone willing to listen."

John assured him he had time to listen and would be willing to hear his story.

"My name is John. What's yours?"

"My father insisted I be named Shemuel. Why, I don't know. It was not a family name. Perhaps I should have been named David, because of what I do now, watching, taking care of sheep. When I'm not here I help a friend with his sheep.

"Anyway, we decided it would be best to get a new start somewhere else. We are not Samaritans, but we did live there, in the town of Shiloh, a day's journey south of Jacob's well. My father was a stonemason, and a good one. He could find work anywhere.

"Here, we are strangers, and these people don't seem to welcome strangers. We are told this goes back a number of years, when so many had to come here to be registered by the Roman government. It must have been a stressful time, but I really don't know what happened. There are stories, but we don't know if any of them are true. I guess they just don't like strangers!

"It's difficult to make a living here, but we don't know where else to go. My main work is helping with the sheep. Those who are shepherds and have sheep of their own, try to help us out, giving me some work when I might be needed. They understand our situation, because they, too, aren't welcome in Bethlehem either. The wealthy people, especially, look down on shepherds.

"I do have some skill with stone work, learning that from my father. However, since coming here, few want me to work for them. The shepherds live mainly in tents and have little need for stone houses. They do try to get me work with the residents, but have had little success."

John had difficuly taking all that in. Shemuel's story was hard to follow. Surely, some of the residents of Bethlehem were nice to strangers.

"Tell, me, Shemuel. Where do you live? If they don't welcome you here, why do you come?"

"We live in one of those caves north of the town, close to those who have sheep. We have to do our best to earn a living. When we have something to sell I bring it into town. But, I talk too much and it is time to go home. Are you sure you won't buy what I have left?"

John thought for a moment and then made a suggestion. This young man just might be of help. He and his mother had not lived here very long, but, perhaps, their friends, the shepherds, might help with his questions about his relatives.

"I'll buy what you have here, if you will do something for me. Could you and your mother give me a place to sleep? I'm on my way north, but I need shelter for the night. I'll give you a danarii for what you have here, and for a place to rest. Agreed?"

The young man grinned.

"It's a bargain, but really too much for what we have to offer. But, I won't argue with you. I'll take it. We can use the money."

Sweeping the table clean, giving all the items to John, he picked up his belongings. With a brief "Follow me," he headed north.

It was a long walk, a slow walk because of the darkness. Overhead the stars shone brightly, but there was no moon. The path was packed hard, but there were lots of rocks. Shemuel, warned John to be watchful. The ground sloped steeply on both sides. The path was right on the top of the ridge.

In the distance John could see a fire, partly hidden by some sort of barrier. It was a low wall built out from the side of the hill. That was Shemuel's stonework. Overhead there was a shelter of vines and branches. On the other side was the wide opening to a cave. This was home. His mother, Tamar, was waiting.

"Shemuel," she called. "Why are you so late? You need to eat something and rest. Joel will be expecting you later tonight. His sheep are on the east slope, just above the upper line of olive trees. Tell me, son, what kept you in town. Did you sell my bread?"

"Yes, mother, I sold your bread. In fact, I sold all I had! I want you to meet the man who bought everything that was left. He gave me a whole denarii for the bread, dried meat and fish.

"Mother, this is John. He is asking for a place to spend the night. He is on his way north and needs our help. We can do that, can't we? John, this is my mother, Tamar."

"Of course we can! Welcome to our home, John. It is not much, but it is our home. We are grateful to have a place to live. Someday, when Shemuel earns enough, we will build something better. He knows how to do that."

"I thank you for your hospitality, taking a stranger in on a moment's notice. As to your home here on the hillside, you don't need to make excuses. I was born in a home that was part cave. Don't make excuses for what you have. It is not the building, or the cave, or even the tent, but who you are and what you do with what you have.

"Shemuel tells me the residents of Bethlehem aren't so gracious, that they don't welcome strangers. That really comes as a great surprise. There is a story about the town, about a special child being born here, the child of strangers. That would have been years ago, but you would think they would remember that!"

Tamar wrinkled her brow, trying to think of what she might have heard about a special child.

"There is a story, but we are not sure of the details. It has to do with a child, or, rather, children. Some tragedy took place, something no one wants to talk about. That was a long time ago, and we have not lived here long. You would have to ask someone else.

"But, it's late. We will share what we have with you. There is bread, some cooked greens and a little dried meat, mutton."

They moved into the edge of the shelter, with John suggesting they thank Yahweh for his gifts and blessings. Sitting on rough benches they shared the simple, but filling meal.

After a few minutes of silence, Tamar spoke.

"John, you wanted to thank Yahweh for this food. When we lived in Shiloh, and my husband was living, he did that at every meal. Neither Shemuel nor I pray anymore. My husband died and we were forced to give up our home and leave. Since that time we have had to struggle to survive. Why did Yahweh let that happen to us? If he is so great, why do things like that go on?"

Tamar's eyes filled with tears, remembering the past. Here they were, far from their home of many years, living under very difficult circumstances. She had no husband, with no hope of marrying again.

John waited, closing his eyes in thought and prayer, a silent prayer.

"Yahweh, help me say the right thing."

He stood up, looking up at the bright stars overhead. Then he turned back toward Tamar and Shemuel.

"I'm not sure that I can answer all your questions, but let me try. What we have, the sky, the stars, the moon, the land, the water, the plants, the animals, all these things were created by Yahweh. Yahweh created us. In the very beginning he made it known that all this was good, very good. Yahweh is good and gives all these good things.

"At the same time, there are those who don't want to live under the goodness of Yahweh. Some become very selfish and mean. They hurt other people.

"Shemuel tells me your husband's brother took your home after your husband died. Even if your husband did owe him money, it was wrong to drive you out. However, he was the one who did that, not Yahweh. I don't know how that will work out, or what might happen to your husband's brother. I do know Yahweh still loves you, cares for you. Also, out of the bad there can come good. I believe that. I know that. It has happened in my own life. Out of bad things have come good things."

With a smile, he added: "See, Yahweh is good!. I met you and you welcomed me into you home."

Tamar couldn't help but smile in return. She wiped her eyes on her robe. Little did she realize John was special, that he had a way of making things look better. Little did she know John was called of Yahweh, called to do good. He had a way of helping those whom he met, no matter the situation.

"You are right, young man. But it is hard, so very hard to believe what you say. Shemuel, we will do better, but right now it's time for you to find your sheep. Joel will be waiting!"

"Yes, mother I'm on my way."

Turning to John, as he picked up his cloak and staff, he said: "Sleep well. I'll see you in the morning. Don't leave before I get back!"

With that, Shemuel disappeared in the darkness. They could hear him as he headed toward the upper line of olive trees. It was not so far and they could see the outline of the taller trees against the sky.

"I'm certain Joel will stop by soon. Shemuel will be filled with his latest news about you, and Joel is always curious, especially about strangers. He likes to talk and he doesn't get much chance, not with the people of Bethlehem. Perhaps he can help you with your questions."

John responded. "That's good. I would like to meet one of your friends. I would like to find out what he knows about the past history of this town. Surely, if he has lived here long, he would know something."

Tamar was right. It was not long until Joel showed up, whistling as he climbed the ridge toward the home. By the time he arrived, Tamar had cleaned all the dishes and put away the food. Inside the cave she showed John where he might sleep. Of course, with Joel there, none of them might get much sleep. Tamar was convinced that shepherds slept very little!

"Joel, we have a visitor, a very nice young man, a stranger to our area. In Bethlehem he bought the rest of what Shemuel had to sell, looking for a place to sleep tonight. Shemuel offered our home, so here he is. He will sleep here before he moves on north.

"By the way, he is looking for information about something that happened here long before we came. Perhaps you can help him."

Joel was big, tall and broadshouldered. He could have picked up both John and Tamar at the same time. You could sense the strength in his arms and legs, even though his hair was turning grey.

John reached out his hand in greeting. For a moment there was no response. Joel looked at John, looking into his eyes, almost staring. Then, with a big grin, he grasped John's hand, squeezing it until it hurt.

"Welcome, my friend, to Bethlehem. Well, this is not really Bethlehem, but we are close!"

With that, he laughed, the loudest laugh John had heard since leaving Mibsam.

"Come, let's sit down. Tamar, get us something to drink, perhaps a little goat's milk. I am thristy after getting all those sheep to settle down for the night. Shemuel should have little trouble tonight. All was quiet when I left him."

John didn't really care for the goat's milk, not this time of night. He did ask for some water. Water always reminded him of Yahweh's provision of the basic needs of life.

"Joel," he began, "I was born near Jerusalem, of very elderly parents. They are both dead now. My mother had a cousin named Mary. This Mary lived far to the north, in a town called Nazareth. She married a carpenter named Joseph. It turns out that Joseph was of the family of David, King David, one of his many, many descendents. When the Roman emperor ordered all our people to be counted some years ago, every male had to go, take his family with him, go back to his hometown.

"That meant that Joseph had to come all the way south to Bethlehem. I was told his wife Mary was expecting a child and that child was born in Bethlehem. I have no idea how long they stayed here, or when they went back to Nazareth. I have never met my mother's cousin or any of her family. Others have told me that her husband, Joseph, is dead.

"Now that I have time, I am on my way to Nazareth, hoping to find my relatives, but here in Bethlehem I had hopes of learning more about them, something about the birth, something about what happened to them."

"John, you ought to know a lot of babies have been born here, babies born to visitors as well as to the residents of the town. It would be hard to get much information now. You say this had to do with the emperor's orders? That was a long time ago, and it took more than a year for all of our people to comply with the new law."

"Yes," responded John, "This would have happened about eighteen years ago. You see, this baby was born just about the time I was born. I'm led to believe the baby was a boy, a very special boy, and that Yahweh had something to do with what I am telling you."

Joel's eyes widened, and then narrowed down to a thin slit.

It was evident he was remembering, startled by John's story. For a long time he was silent.

"John, I am going to share something with you I had vowed I would never mention again. Tamar, I want you to listen carefully, too. This will be of miracles and mysteries. It will also explain to you why Bethlehem doesn't take kindly to strangers. I don't pretend to understand what I saw and heard, but it had to be of Yahweh's doing. It had to be! Also, and I can't explain it, you are special, John. Somehow you fit into this story, more than just being a relative. Having met you, I can believe there is something here concerning you. I can see it in your eyes!"

He really didn't need an answer and John kept silent, sitting closer to catch every word.

"About eigtheen years ago, I think it was about eighteen years ago, we were doing what we have always done, herding sheep. I was rather young then, just learning how to care for sheep. Frankly, I didn't see much future in being a shepherd. I wanted to be a hunter!

"Anyway, I remember the year because it did involve a lot of people coming into Bethlehem in order to obey law about the census. There were people everywhere, with most of them sleeping outdoors or in tents. There simply were not enough houses to care for all who came. As you can imagine, the citizens were not too happy about the crowds. It was disturbing!

"For us, we had to move our sheep farther away. Frankly, we were afraid some would be stolen. We didn't know any of those strangers, and we didn't trust them. We moved our sheep and our tents, which was a lot of trouble. Just when I wanted to go hunting, we had to work that much harder.

"Finally, we had everthing in order. The weather was good, not too cool. It was just right for watching the sheep, making sure no animal would try to attack them. At night we took turns. Some would sleep while others had to stay awake. There were times when all would nod, unless there was a problem, a sudden noise or a sheep bleating.

"That's when it happened. A bright light, almost like sunlight, surrounded us. There were voices, voices singing about Yahweh's glory. Startled as we were by all that, we didn't catch all the words, but we remembered some, and we shared that later with those we met.

"However, there was one voice we heard quite clear. I can still remember the words. It went something like this:

> Don't be afraid. We are bringing you good news.
> This news will bring great joy to all of you,
> to everyone! A Savior has been born tonight
> in Bethlehem.
> You will find him, wrapped with his birth bands,
> lying, not in a bed but in a manger of straw.

"Then there was more singing about the glory of Yahweh. Finally, they disappeared. After that we hardly knew what to do. We were afraid! None of us had ever seen anything like that. None of us had ever heard anything like that.

"After a bit, after we had calmed down, our curosity got the best of us. My father suggested we go down to the village, try to find this baby. So, we did. We found him in the big stable for animals on the south side of the town. Actually, it was an open cave. Sure enough, there was a baby, sleeping. He was asleep on some fresh straw. There was a man and a woman present, obviously the baby's parents. From the way they were dressed, my uncle thought they were from the north, possibly from Samaria.

"Again, we would not have thought much about a baby born there, except for those who spoke and sang to us. My father said they had to be Yahweh's messengers, Yahweh's angels. So, as we went back to our sheep we told everyone we saw what had happened. We were filled with joy; just thinking Yahweh had sent us the one promised long before. Yahweh's messengers called him the Messiah! The next day, and the next, we kept telling our story.

"But, do you know what happened? Everyone we met, everyone we talked to, said we were crazy, that we had probably been drinking too much wine. They laughed at us. They ignored us. They wouldn't bother to check out what we had been telling.

"Finally, my father and my uncle got all of us together and told us what not to do. We would not tell anyone else about what we had seen. If this was Yahweh's doings, and they believed it was, Yahweh would be the one to spread the good news. We would keep our mouths closed.

John interrupted.

"You mean to tell me no one else saw anything special about this baby born in that stable? No one else helped them, gave them a room where the baby could be born in a house, and not in a stable?"

"That's right," replied Joel. "As far as we could find out, they were pretty much ignored. There was one family who let them use a small house on the edge of town. Their son had moved away and the house was vacant. I believe the father of the baby was a carpenter and he did some work for that family, in exchange for using the house. They stayed for some time, waiting for the mother to regain strength for the journey north.

Again, John broke in.

"How long did they stay in Bethlehem? Did you get their names? Did anyone ever do anything for the family?"

"As I remember they stayed several months, perhaps a year. Then, suddenly, they disappeared. I really don't know who helped them during that time. As to their names, I did hear the father was called Joseph.

"That brings up the rest of the story about the unfriendly people in Bethlehem. After the baby was born and most of the strangers had gone back to their own homes, we traveled farther north and west, taking our sheep to better pastures. When we returned to the area of Bethlehem, we heard about some other visitors. These were real strangers, men from another land far to the east. They came on camels, the biggest camels the people had ever seen. They were looking for this same baby, we were told. Not long after that the family just disappeared. One day they were there and the next day they were gone.

"Shortly after that some soldiers, Herod's guards they were, came, looking for the baby. Not finding him, they took all the very young baby boys from their mothers, and from what we understand they killed them! How many there were, I never learned, but there must have been several. They were trying to destroy that baby born in the stable!"

"You see, there was one other thing which made all this a mystery and a miracle. The night this baby was born, a new star appeared in the sky. We didn't see it at first because of the brightness when Yahweh's angels came to us, but when they left, and by the time we started down to Bethlehem, we saw it. It was a star we had never seen before. It was a star brighter than every other bright star, stars we had watched all our lives. It seemed to hover right over the town, right over the stable, shining brightly night after night. It was only after we had returned from the other pastures that it disappeared.

"Now, John, you tell me what this is all about. We wanted to learn more about this affair, but we couldn't get anything from the people of Bethlehem. After those young boys were taken away and killed, no one would talk, and they will not welcome strangers, even to this very day!"

John thought for a long time, until Joel asked again for help in understanding. Finally, slowly, putting his thoughts in order he responded.

"Joel, Tamar, Yahweh's hand is in all of this. He is directing my life, leading me to something I'm not able to fully understand. However, I will try to explain what I do know and how it relates to the town of Bethlehem. Joel, you have been truly blessed. You witnessed a miracle, Yahweh's miracle, the night those heavenly messengers came, and the night that baby was born.

"The story begins with my parents. My father was a priest, serving in the Temple in Jerusalem. He served many, many years, until he was quite elderly. He and my mother, Elizabeth, had been married many years, but had no children.

"One evening, when my father was offering the Evening Sacrifice, one of Yahweh's messengers came to him, telling him my mother would have a son. This son would grow up and be a prophet of Yahweh. Because my father would not believe him, this messenger, Gabriel, told him he would not be able to speak again, not until the baby was born. Then, at the birth, the baby would be named John."

Joel interrupted the story, shouting

"You are that John! That is hard to believe, but, along with all the rest, it begins to make sense. I think it begins to make sense. That's why you are here?"

"Yes, it all fits together. You see, about that same time, this messenger of Yahweh, Gabriel, went and spoke to a young, unmarried woman living in Nazareth of Galilee. Her name was Mary. She was betrothed to a carpenter of that town, Joseph by name. However, before they were actually married, Gabriel told her she would have a baby, not by Joseph, but by Yahweh's power, by his Spirit. Because of that they should be married right away. Also, after the wedding, she should travel all the way down to where my parents lived. They would meet my father, Zechariah, who could not speak, and would visit with her cousin Elizabeth who was pregnant. She and Joseph would be convinced this was Yahweh's doing.

"They did come, traveling all the way down to Judea, to my paren't home just outside of Jerusalem. They found it to be true! Elizabeth was carrying a baby, a baby boy, me. Joseph must have returned to Nazareth right away, but Mary stayed longer. By that time eveyone knew she was pregnant, carrying Yahweh's child. Of course, they didn't know it was Yahweh's child.

"Obviously, Mary returned to Nazareth, but by that time Caesar's orders had arrived. That's why they had to come all the way back down, not to Jerusalem, but to Bethlehem. Joseph was of the house of David, King David. The rest of that story you know. You were there the night this child was born, the one, as I understand it, was named Jesus.

"The rest of the story is rather complicated. Both my parents are dead now. I have been living down near the Salt Sea and, more recently, living alone, trying to understand what Yahweh has in mind for me. Growing up, we had no contact with my mother's cousin, Mary. It is only now that I have been able to make this journey. I am on my way north, traveling to Nazareth, hoping to find Mary and her son.

"There is one more part to this story, you need to know, difficult as it may be to understand. Yahweh has spoken to me several times, directly, as well as through other people. He has convinced me he has a mission for my life. I'm not fully sure what, but it relates to my cousin Jesus. Two things I must do. I need to meet my cousin, and I must be patient, waiting for the next step. I believe I will have to return to the area of the Salt Sea and, alone, wait for Yahweh's guidance and instruction."

John stopped, looking intently into Joel's and Tamar's eyes. Did they understand? Did they think he was a fanatic, telling a story no one could believe? Or, were they convinced, as he was convinced, Yawheh's hand was at work here?

Tamar spoke first.

"Well, I never! John, I knew there was something special about you, the minute I first met you."

Joel agreed.

"It does make sense and I believe you, John. Yahweh does some mighty strange things. I don't understand all you have said, but we will just have to wait and see. We all know, or should know, the old prophets spoke of a promised Messiah long ago. Maybe, just maybe, he would drive those Romans out. Just think, we have met someone who has heard the voice of Yahweh!"

"Joel, you heard his voice, long before I heard it. You heard his messengers here, on these very hills. You have seen him, the Messiah! Your names will be remembered, long after we are gone. I'm convinced of that."

"I don't know about that," responded Joel, "but I do know that for once I'm talked out. It's time for me to shut up. All of us have a lot to think about tonight. I know you are tired, too, walking all the way from Hebron. Let's get some sleep."

Joel said goodnight and headed back to his sheep. Saying little more to each other, Tamar and John found their places and were soon asleep. Overhead the brilliant stars gave promise of a clear day ahead.

# CHAPTER 17

*. . . and when they came to Bethlehem,
the whole town was stirred because of them . . .*
                                        Ruth 1:19

John was up early, but not ahead of Tamar. She was busy, heating water over the fire. Set outside, the smoke filtered up through the vines. Inside the cave, in the sleeping area, it was still dark.

As John stepped outside, Tamar greeted him with a smile.

"I trust you slept well, after all that talk last night. Joel sure doesn't know when to stop. But, seriously, you have given us so much. You have brought us hope! I'm not sure I can take it all in, but I'm trying. You will have to share this with Shemuel when he comes home. He will be amazed, too. My big question is this. Where do we go from here? Where do you go from here?"

"Tamar, you and Shemuel should stay right here. I know this is not an easy life, but I think I know what you want. You want security for yourselves and I'm sure that will come. You want friends, people with whom you can relate. You have good friends in Joel and the other shepherds. They are nearby and will help anyway they can. Perhaps, as time goes on, the people of Bethlehem will accept you, too. That would be good, for them as well as for you.

"As for me, I must move on. I will continue north. I do not

plan to stop in Jerusalem, but will go on through Samaria to Galilee. I must find him, the one born here years ago. That is my immediate mission, to find my cousin Jesus, to talk with him. After that I must do what Yahweh calls me to do. I'm confident he will direct my next move. Be assured of one thing, when Yahweh takes his next step, the world will know it! You will know it! You, too, will be blessed!

"However, before I leave, and I'm thinking about staying with you one more night, I want to see Bethlehem in the daylight. I would like to find the stable where he was born. Do you think that's possible? Do you think Shemuel would go with me? Would it be alright with you, if I stayed another night?"

"John, you know we will be happy to have you stay, even longer than one more night. We wish it would be possible for you to live here. You have already meant so much to us! But, now it is time for you to eat. I've been heating a delicious broth for us. Shemuel will be coming any minute. Do you like warm goat's milk?"

"It's not my favorite, the goat's milk, but, yes, I will drink some, along with whatever you might have. I really don't eat a lot early in the day."

As they began to set the table, Shemuel came striding down the hill and up the ridge. He was ready for the morning meal.

"Well, my friend," Shemuel began, "did Joel talk your ears off last night? Isn't he something, the way he carries on sometimes; and what is this you were discussing? He wouldn't tell me much. He said you would fill me in. He called it good news."

As John responded, he expressed concern for Shemuel's night duty with the sheep.

"Do you want to catch up on your sleep first, or do you want to talk? I can wait if you need a nap."

"Not at all. It was a very quiet night with no problems. Both Joel and I slept, that is, until the sheep began to stir early this morning. By that time, Joel's cousins had arrived, ready to move the sheep a little farther west. So, Joel sent me on my way, knowing you might leave today."

With the food and drink ready they sat down to enjoy Tamar's cooking. John thanked Yahweh for his wonderful gifts, including the food. At the end of the prayer, both Tamar and Shemuel added their "Amen."

As Tamar cleared away the dishes and utensils, Shemuel suggested they move outside, finding a seat under an olive tree some distance from the cave. There they would enjoy the warmth of the morning sun.

"Mother, we don't mean to exclude you. Join us as soon as you can. I'm sure John will be sharing what he told you and Joel last night; or, we can wait until you are through here."

"Yes, Shemuel, I want to hear it all, again. Talk about other things until I come. Is that agreeable to you, John? I want to make sure I remember everything!"

With John nodding his agreement, he began to question Shemuel about the town. Did he know any of the residents well enough to talk with them? Were there any who would talk, if you were to ask questions?

"We've been here long enough so that some do speak to us. Whenever I go in to town, either to sell or buy, a few will ask about my mother. However, these are the poorer residents. Those who are wealthy, especially those big merchants, ignore me. However, I think that has more to do with my trying to sell things. They don't like any competition. Overall, I think they are just suspicious of strangers. I do know they don't like questions about their town."

John tried to reassure Shemuel, suggesting patience.

"People are like that, sometimes not very considerate of those they don't know well. I think that after a time you will see a difference. There is more to that here in Bethlehem. When your mother comes I'll try to explain."

Waiting for Tamar's arrival, John asked Shemuel about the work of stonemasons, wondering how the stones could be cut so square. It took a long time for Shemuel's explanations, but he was happy someone was willing to listen. He did have some skills in that regard and seldom did he have the chance to share his knowledge.

"One must use iron chisels to cut a series of holes in the rock. Then wedges of hard wood are driven into the holes. Once those are in place, water is poured over the wood, making it swell. All that takes time, but if the work is done superbly, the rock will crack and split as the wood expands. It's a lot easier to use stones from broken down structures, but such is not always available."

By the time he was through his mother had come. Sitting next to Shemuel she suggested John share his story.

Carefully, slowly, taking note of Joel's part in the story, John tried to make sure Shemuel understood all they had discussed the night before. As he unfolded the details, Shemuel's eyes seemed to open wider with each word. Amazed at what he was hearing, he could hardly contain his excitement.

"Are you telling me Yahweh's own son, named Jesus, was born here, in Bethlehem, and that those people didn't believe it, didn't accept the truth? They didn't do anything for the child or for his parents? I can't believe that!

"And you, John, you are a part of Yahweh's plan? I knew you were special, but I had no idea how special."

Shemuel let out a long shrill whistle. Standing up, he walked back and forth, too excited to sit still. Just think! Yahweh sent his own messengers to his friend Joel, to those shepherds! Now, his friend sitting here will be one of Yahweh's messengers! He could hardly contain himself.

"Tell me what will happen next. I don't think it will involve Bethlehem, will it?"

"Shemuel, I really don't have all the answers. Only time will tell all Yahweh will do. It will involve Bethlehem, just as it will involve our people everywhere. Yes, it will involve me! I will learn more about that when I meet him, Jesus. We will have to be patient. We will have to wait for Yahweh to speak again, and act.

"In the meantime, you need to stay here, caring for your mother, selling what you can in the market, helping Joel with the sheep. You will have plenty to keep you busy! I hope you will get the chance to do some stonework in the area.

"Also, I want to see if we can find that stable. Surely, it is still there, a place where people keep hay and straw, and their animals."

Shemuel was ready to go. He, too, wanted to see the place. He had heard a few stories, but before today had paid little attention. No one had ever suggested that Yahweh was involved.

Leaving Tamar behind, they moved down the ridge and entered the town. In the center of the town square the merchants were set up, their wares on display. A number of people were already milling about, looking for bargains. As always, they were intent upon finding the best at the smallest cost. For the most part they paid little attention to those they did not know. Neighbors took time to chat with neighbors, ignoring the others.

It was a typical market square, filled with the smells of meat and fish, of spices and wines. The stronger odors came from the onions, olives, olive oil and dates. It was a busy and noisy morning.

However, as John and Shemuel entered the square and were noticed by some, the noise of conversation became muted. Most knew Shemuel, but no one knew John and they wondered about him. Here was someone they had never seen before. Why was he here? What was he doing with the young man from Samaria? You could sense their curosity.

After a few minutes an older man, one of the merchants, approached them.

"Young man, you are a stranger here. Are you a relative to Shemuel? Do you want to find a place to sell? If so, I should tell you something your friend already knows. You will find little business here. We are a small town and new businesses don't do too well."

John, understanding the reason for the man's words and his

obvious hostility, smiled, put out his hand in greeting and introduced himself.

"No, I'm not here to sell anything, other than the love of Yahweh, and that's not really for sale, is it? Yahweh loves all of us, regardless. My name is John, son of a former priest in the Temple, Zechariah. He is dead now. I'm just passing through."

His response and warmth of greeting startled the merchant.

"I really meant no offense, but we are very cautious where strangers are concerned. That's a long story, one that goes back a long time. You wouldn't understand that. You are too young, and you have never been here before."

"I think I do understand. It started with Caesar's orders which brought a lot of people to Bethlehem, didn't it?"

"How would you know that?"

John's answer came as a surprise, a shocking surprise!

"Yes," continued John, "a lot of people came, including an expectant mother, traveling with her husband. They had to settle for the big stable. That's where the child was born. That's the night the shepherds came down, later telling their story which no one wanted to believe. Do you want me to go on?"

By that time several others were pushing in close. John's words, although not spoken loudly, had caught their attention. Those nearby had lost all interest in the affairs of the morning market. Disturbed by what this young man was saying, they came even closer, waiting to hear more.

"That night a new star appeared in the sky, remember? And it stayed until that family left. You had other visitors, some time later. These were men from a far distant country, riding on big camels. They found that baby boy, living in a little house on the edge of your town, a house one family had let them use. You may not know it, but they came to worship him. They brought him gifts.

"Then came your tragedy, the one no one wants to talk about, the killing of several little baby boys by Herod's guards. Although they didn't know it, the other child, the one born in the stable, had vanished, he and his parents.

"You have lived with that heartache all these years, suspicious of any and every stranger. The real tragedy now, is that attitude. Be assured! Yahweh grieved with you. I would remind you that child born in that stable was a special child, now reaching manhood. I don't know all the answers about him, but you will know when Yahweh is ready. Your town, Bethlehem, will be remembered long after you and I are gone, remembered because of that one child, the one born in a stable. That was about eighteen years ago, wasn't it?"

John's words left them speechless. Amazed at his knowledge, startled by his revealing talk about past events, tragic events included, they didn't know what to say. Looking at each other, shaking their heads, they began to realize how much they had lost. Their Bethlehem had developed a reputation. So concerned for themselves, they had closed their hearts and minds to others. So wrapped up in their own losses, they had refused to be an open town. Their suspicion of others had become a way of life. This stranger had disturbed them but, at the same time, had opened their eyes.

One resident, another one of the merchants, finally spoke.

"Young man, I don't know who you are, but if what you say is true, tell me something. How do you know all this and how do you fit into this story? Are you saying you are speaking for Yahweh? If you are, are you saying we have shut him out of our lives?"

"Sir, I have no right be pass judgment on any of you. I have enough faults of my own, but I do know Yahweh wants us to respect others, to love others, even as he has loved us. Sure, there are those we don't like because of what they do, but we don't need to follow their examples. Doing good is far better than doing bad. I hope you believe that.

"As for my part in all this I am doing what I believe Yahweh wants me to do. I do believe he is preparing me to speak for him some day in the future. I assure you, I'm not trying to brag, or put myself above you. Pretending to be something you are not never works, does it? Yahweh uses whom he wants to use.

Only time will tell how that works out. At the moment I have to be patient, studying his word. Both you and I have to be ready to serve him. Right now, the best way to do so is by serving others. What do you think?"

With a broad smile on his face, John did his best to look everyone in the face. Hopefully, what he was saying was getting through. There was much he knew he could not tell, but he wanted to make sure Yahweh would touch their hearts this morning.

As the crowd milled about, talking with each other, John noticed a couple of men talking with Shemuel. He was delighted! Perhaps this was the beginning of some change in attitudes. Wanting to pursue that, he spoke again.

"My friend here, Shemuel, was kind enough to give me a place to sleep last night. He and his mother made me welcome in their home. They don't have much, having been forced to leave their home up in Samaria. After Shemuel's father died they came south, settling here. I learned that his father was a stonemason, and Shemuel has some skill in that. There aren't many of those around, except for those in Jerusalem, working on the Temple. If any one here needs a stonemason, Shemuel is available. Also, in spite of what some may think, he and his mother are not Samaritans. They, too, are good Jews. I hope you will give him a chance."

Hearing that, others began to talk with Shemuel. One merchant wondered if he might work some for him. From time to time he had to travel to Jerusalem. Once in a while he went down to Hebron, buying those items he could sell in Bethlehem. While away, could Shemuel manage his shop?

Delighted with the results of the conversations going on, John stepped aside. He wanted Shemuel to have the attention. Perhaps he and his mother would be accepted into community life! His silent prayer to Yahweh was one of gratitude and thanksgiving. He could leave Bethlehem with a light heart!

Yet, there was one more thing John wanted. He felt the

need to find the stable where his cousin Jesus had been born. Would it still be there, used as a stable?

A younger resident, came up and began to talk with John.

"I remember my parents talking about those events, the things you mentioned. Apparently it was about eighteen years ago. I was just a small child and really didn't know the details. They, my parents, were talking late one night, talking about Herod's guards. They were saying how thankful they were, that I was older, that they did not take me. They also talked about a baby, a baby born in that stable, wondering who those people might be.

"The next day I tried to ask them about what I had heard, but they wouldn't say any more. They said I must have been dreaming. I did find the stable. Some older boys told me about a baby being born there. They were laughing. They thought it was funny, that people would go to such a place to have a baby. If you want to, I'll be glad to take you."

"Yes," responded Johm. "I would like that. As soon as Shemuel is ready we can go."

Finally, Shemuel rushed over.

"John," he cried, "I have two job offers. The merchant, Kemuel, wants me to be available to manage his shop whenever he is away. Another merchant wants me to enlarge his house, adding a courtyard. That will keep me busy for a long time! John, I can't thank you enough for what you have done for us!"

"Shemuel, I haven't done that much. It was just a matter of sharing what I know and what I believe. Most people will respond to that, just as these people have. You will do just fine. I'm sure of that.

"Now, if you are through, this young man is going to take us to the stable, the one where Jesus was born. Let's go!"

With a wave of his hand, John excused himself, following Nathanael, the one offering to take them to the stable.

It didn't take long. On the east side of the village the ground began to slope down toward the valley below. On the side of the hill, adjacent to a few smaller houses, there was an opening, a large opening. It was the cave!

Entering, they found it empty. There were no animals inside, but there was a lot of straw. There were several stone troughs, or mangers, in the back. It had to be in one of those a new baby had been placed after birth. The thing that struck John was the quietness. Here, inside, you could hear nothing of people or even animals passing by. And the smell! It was pungent, strong, the odor of earthly things. Yahweh had come to earth, here, in this place! This was holy ground!

Pausing to reflect on what he had learned, he was touched by what he had been told, that here Yahweh's son had been born, away from the noise and confusion of a world dominated by Rome. Would that world ever know that Yahweh had a hand in the order of a Roman emperor which sent Joseph and Mary south, all the way to a little town called Bethlehem?

Suddenly he remembered! There was a passage about Bethlehem in the writing of the prophet Micah. Closing his eyes he began to bring up mental pictures of the Scrolls in Tobba. Yes! Micah had talked about Bethlehem, Yahweh's prophetic word:

> *But you, O Bethlehem Ephrathah,*
> *who are little to be among the clans of Judah,*
> *from you shall come forth for me,*
> *one who is to be ruler in Israel,*
> *whose origin is of old, from ancient days.*

That was it and here was the place! To this place Yahweh had come, placing his own son in human hands. John trembled at the thought, remembering also Yahweh's call to him. He would be a part of Yahweh's plan for his people!

Again, John closed his eyes, offering up his silent prayer:

"Yahweh, Lord of heaven and earth, you have come

to this place with your ancient promise of salvation. Help us to see that. Help me to obey your will for my life. Amen!"

John was reassured! Yahweh was fufilling his promise given centuries ago. It began here, on this spot. In Yahweh's own time and way, the whole world would know and, hopefully, believe.

# CHAPTER 18

*. . . a voice was heard in Ramah . . .*
Matthew 2:18a

John's second night with Tamar and Shemuel was one of celebration. Shemuel couldn't stop going over the events of the day. John had done wonders in getting the people of Bethlehem to welcome him, offer him work. One day the merchants let him know he was not wanted. The next, today, they were offering him work, plenty of work.

"Mother, you should have been there. You should have seen their faces as John began to talk. Not only were they startled by what he was saying, but they finally realized how badly they had been acting all those years. He made them see that, not by condemning them, but by smiling, offering them a chance to respond. It was a miracle!"

For Tamar, even with what she was hearing, it was difficult to accept. How could it be, this change of attitude? She had been snubbed so many times, enough to avoid going into Bethlehem. Would it be different now? They kept assuring her it would!

At the same time, John reminded them change comes slow. There would be those reluctant to accept them, even with what had taken place in the marketplace. They must be patient! Just be gracious in dealing with all they met. With Shemuel working in town, attitudes would change!

Joel joined them before the evening was over. He would have stayed longer, but promised to take Shemuel's turn with the sheep tonight. It was only right for Shemuel to celebrate. Joel, too, was overcome by what he had heard. Even he and the other shepherds would see a change in attitude. John was positive of that!

As with Shemuel, Joel saw it as a miracle! He kept looking at John in wonderment. How could this young man accomplish so much in only one day?

John's answer was quite simple:

"Yahweh can do marvelous things. He can change our hearts, even the hearts of stubborn and stiff-necked people."

He laughed! "They sure were stiff-necked. I thought the merchant Kemuel's eyes would pop out as I described past events and present attitudes. He couldn't believe what he was hearing. Yet, you have to give him and the others credit. They did change! I'm happy for all of you. Most of all, I am grateful to Yahweh. He is gracious!

After Joel left, saying his grateful goodbyes to John, they took little time in going to sleep. The day they would long remember had been full. Shemuel had slept none since coming in from the pasture early that morning.

Both Tamar and John were up early. John was anxious to be on his way. Although difficult to do, he had to leave. It would be a long and difficult journey, nights of sleeping in strange places. It was time to move on.

Again, Tamar insisted he eat something. This morning it was some of her fresh bread and honey, along with a strip of dried mutton. This he washed down with goat's milk. It was good! Before he was through, Shemuel joined them. He would have slept longer, but wanted to see John before he left. He, like Tamar and Joel, knew his indebtedness to this young visitor. He had brought hope into their lives, something they had lost when forced to leave Shiloh.

As John was gathering his things together, putting his blanket into his backpack, he questioned Shemuel about the best route. He would not stop in Jerusalem on his way north. At this point he wanted no delay!

"You really don't have to go back through Bethlehem." Shemuel responded. "Follow this ridge beyond the first grove of olive trees and then drop down into the valley on your left. That will take you in the direction of Jerusalem, into the Kidron Valley. Once you see the Temple, go up the eastern slope to the Mount of Olives. There is a small village on the ridge. It is called Bethphage. Don't go to your right. That path will take you to a differnt town, Bethany. If you move along at a steady pace you should reach Bethphage in less than two hours. By that time you will want to stop and rest. Don't take the road leading left of the city. That's the long way. Everyone going north knows going across the Mount of Olives is the best way around Jerusalem

"There is a man there, in Bethphage, who raises and trains work animals. My father knew him, back when he had to move building supplies north to Shiloh. The man's name is Joshua. If you need any help, or further directions north, he will be glad to help you. He was always willing to assist my father at little or no cost. I remember him because my father's name was Joshua. Also, he helped us move our possessions here. You will like him!

"It will be impossible for you to go as far north as Shiloh today, but you should stop there. It is an easy, well-traveled road toward Galilee. The best place to stop for tonight is Ramah. You could get to Bethel, but it would be dark by the time you arrived. Plan to stop in Ramah."

Thanking Shemuel for his help, and thanking Tamar for her hospitality, he was ready to leave. Tamar hugged him, giving him a package of her bread. He had plenty of dried meat, having purchased some from Shemuel. He and Shemuel embraced, but said nothing more. He could see that Shemuel's eyes were filling with tears, tears of gratitude. With one last look and wave he disappeared above the line of the olive trees. The ripening olives were getting larger, soon to be harvested.

Dropping down into the valley to the west, John moved easily along the road, another well-traveled one. It was the same road he had traveled from Hebron. Southward, the road went all the way down to Beersheba and the Wilderness of Zin. Somewhere in that desolate territory Moses had brought Yahweh's people out of Egypt.

To the north the road went by way of Jerusalem, through Samaria and on to Galilee. He was finally on his way!

Shemuel was right. In the distance the Temple and Temple Mount stood high above everything else. In the morning sun it was a beautiful sight!

> *Come into his presence with singing . . .*
> *Enter his gates with thanksgiving . . .*

How many times had he heard those melodious words, songs of praise! Even as a small boy, a very rebellious boy, he always stopped to listen. As the years went by he added his voice to the others.

Entering the lower end of the Kidron Valley and pausing to take in the sight of Yahweh's Temple, those memories flooded in upon him. The temptation was strong, almost overpowering, the temptation to enter the city, find Jonathan, and find Eljah.

Yet, he would not! Reluctantly, he turned east toward the olive groves lining the slopes and the top of the Mount of Olives. There, just a long stone's throw from the valley, was the little village nestled among the trees, the village of Bethphage.

He had no problem finding Joshua. He was working with his donkeys and oxen in a large enclosure. Off to the north was another enclosure with a higher wall. Here there were a few horses and camels. All were for hire!

John called to him as Joshua stopped to mop his brow. It was getting hot.

"Sir, my name is John. This morning I left friends of yours

near Bethlehem, Tamar and her son, Shemuel. They send you their greetings."

"John, you are most welcome. Come let us sit in the shade and drink a bit of very light wine. It will do us good!"

John thanked him, declined the wine and asked for water.

"Water? Water is no good. Most of it is polluted. You should drink wine!"

"Really? I don't drink wine, and I have some good water here in my water skin. I'll be glad to share it."

To John the wine looked pretty strong. It smelled strong!

With that, Joshua began to talk and ask questions.

"Young man, you say your name is John, a rather unusual name around here. I remember a story about a boy named John. I think his father was a priest in the Temple. If I am correct, his father was quite old when the boy was born. The boy would be about your age. I wonder whatever happened to them. Would you be that John?"

"Yes, I am that John, grown up now. My mother died when I was about twelve years old. My father and I moved away after that, moving down toward the Salt Sea. His health was very poor and we all hoped the change in climate would help, but he died shortly after we moved. Now, I'm on my way north, looking for some of my mother's relatives. From what I know they should be living in Nazareth."

Joshua whistled.

"That's a long journey and you're traveling alone. That could be dangerous. You better not trust those Samaritans! Where have you been living since your father died?"

"We had friends living in a little village, Tobba. I've lived there a number of years. Now, I'm on my way north, following Shemuel's directions. He wants me to go through his home town, Shiloh."

"Tobba! Isn't that one of those villages where the pious ones live? I've often wondered about them, bathing all the time, filling skins with their writing day and night. They do make good wine, some of the best. Actually, they have others do their selling. They don't want to be made unclean with contact with the likes of you and me, I guess."

"No, it was not quite like that in Tobba. They have a lot more freedom. In fact, we were the deer hunters, preparing deer skins for the scrolls. Whole familiies lived there, raising animals, planting crops. Those were very nice people!"

"Well, how can I help you? I have to get back to my work and earn some money. I'll be glad to let you borrow a donkey. That way you could ride, all the way to Nazareth. Then you could drop off old Neco on the way back. He's not much. That's why I call him Neco, after that Egyptian king. He was not much, either, from what I've been told, something to do with one of our kings, a long time ago."

This conversation was going nowhere and John had enough rest. It was time to be on his way if he expected to reach Ramah before dark. Thanking Joshua for his hospitality and declining his offer of a donkey, John headed on up the Mount of Olives until he could see the main road which some called the Damascus Road. He had no intentions of traveling that far, but this was the main road to the northern territories. As soon as he spotted it he dropped down into the valley. Again, he was on his way, traveling this time with a lot more people. In fact, he had not encountered so many in all his travels. Listening to a number of conversations he learned that many of those traveling were returning from a festival, the Feast of the First Fruits. How could he have forgottern that one! Sure, it was a minor festival, but important to a lot of people. He remembered how busy they were in the Temple.

By now, even after the rest stop in Bethphage, John was slowing down. He had to force himself to maintain his morning pace. There was one smaller village along the road, a good excuse for another rest. This was Gibeah. John tried his best to remember what he had read about Gibeah, but nothing came to mind.

Sitting on the side of the road, resting under an old olive tree, John drank water from his skin. It was warm, but it was all he had. He hoped to replenish his supply in Ramah. There should be a well in the town. Here there wasn't much shade, but enough to keep off the afternoon sun. It was good to stop for a moment, drink the water and nibble on some of Tamar's delicious bread.

John was picking up his pack, when an older couple, a well-dressed couple, approached him. Surprisingly, they were alone. It was obvious they needed rest. They looked tired.

"Sir, I see you have some water. May I ask a favor for my wife? We have been walking from Jerusalem, on our way home, and we neglected to bring water. Would you sell me some for my wife? She is not feeling well today."

"Of course not! This water is not for sale. It is for sharing. I will be glad to give you what you need. Let your wife rest here in the shade. It's not much, but I think it will do. Take what water you want. I do have to warn you, it is not very cool.

"I have a better idea. Let me pour some water into this large cup I'm carrying. Then I will go into the village over there, Gibeah. Surely, they have a well. I'll be back as soon as I can."

Over the man's protests, John headed into the village, a short walk. Sure enough, there was a well in the center of the town. The town had been built around the well. To protect the well there was a low wall, as well as a cover overhead. Good wells had to be protected.

John had to wait his turn. There was a bucket because the well was rather deep . It made John think of Jacob's well, but that was farther north, above Shiloh. From what he had been told, Jacob's well was quite deep.

There were several women drawing water, but no men. John had learned long ago that men didn't draw water from wells. That was woman's work. However, seeing one youg girl struggling with the full bucket, John stepped forward. He took the rope from her hands, pulled up the bucket and poured the water into her clay jar. With that done, John smiled at the others, lowered the bucket and brought up the water for the next girl. By that time, he had attracted quite a crowd. The men passing by stood on the outskirts of the gathering, laughing.

"Look at him, a woman in man's clothes. He can't be a man. He's drawing water from the well."

John laughed in return.

"I guess none of you men are strong enough to pull up the bucket."

He knew he shouldn't have said that, but he was provoked. And, he got results. The men tried to show off their strength, trying to see who could draw the most water, quicker than anyone else.

Now, it was John's turn to laugh. All the women had their water, and John had his, the water skin filled with fresh, cool water. He thanked the men, bowed to the women and headed back to his couple waiting in the shade of the olive tree.

Again, pouring water into the cup, the man's wife now had good water, cool water. Smiling her thanks, she suggested it was time to go. It would be dark before they reached home, unless they kept going. She assured them she felt much better.

"How far do you have to go?" John asked. "If it is too far you should find a place to sleep here, in Gibeah."

"We know no one in this village," the husband responded. "Anyway, it is not far. We live in Ramah and we can be there before dark."

"Not if you have to support your wife and carry your load. Let me help you with that bag. I'll make sure you arrive safely in Ramah.

Carrying his load and the man's bag, John struggled to keep moving. Most times the weight would have been no problem, but John was tired. Yet, he tried to be of assistance, supporting the wife's arm on the opposite side.

There it was, the town of Ramah, lying on the western slope of the ridge going north. It was larger than Gibeah, and the houses looked more prosperous. In fact, there were several villas to the north of the town proper.

John was surprised to see the couple headed for one of the

larger ones, inviting him in. By the time they reached the courtyard several servants welcoming their master and mistress home surrounded them. These were wealthy people!

As they waited for the servants to bring water for washing their dusty feet, the man turned to John, inviting him into their home.

"You told us you are traveling north, but planned to stop overnight in Ramah. We insist you sleep here, in our home. You have been so very kind to us, and we want to repay you. This is the very least we can do."

With his wife adding her words of appreciation and invitation, John accepted. He would stay the night. Immediately, a servant picked up John's backpack and led him to a room that opened on the other side of an enclosed courtyard. It reminded John of the villa in Tobba, but this one was far more elaborate. There was a marble table, a comfortable chair and a large bed. On the table there was a bronze mirror. Next to the mirror were several sweet smelling creams and ointments. The entire floor was covered with a beautiful rug. It brought back memories of the Egyptian and the rug covering the floor of his tent.

Adjacent to this large, airy room there was a larger space with a tile floor. In the center was a bathing pool filled with water. It was a far cry from his desert home, the cave!

Pointing the pool out to John, the servant offered to take his clothing. He would have his garments washed and returned. It didn't take John long to remove tunic and loincloth. The water was warm and delightful. It was a pleasure John had not enjoyed since leaving Tobba. With the pool large enough for movement, John swam back and forth, happy to relax his sore muscles.

He would have stayed in longer, but another servant entered, bringing a large towel. He reminded John that the master and his wife were expecting him in the dining area overlooking the valley. They would eat there. Drying himself John found clean clothing in his backpack. The tunic was wrinkled, but it would have to do. Then he noticed a light colored, well-pressed tunic lying across the bed. His hosts had thought of everything! Also, someone had cleaned his sandels. He was ready to join his hosts.

"Let us introduce ourselves," his host began. "I am Joseph and this is my wife Ruth. We welcome you into our home and we trust you will be comfortable here. Yahweh has blessed us in so many ways and we place all we have at your disposal.

"We don't want to pry, but we are curious. You tell us your name is John and that you are traveling north to Galilee. Are you traveling in your business? I ask questions like that because I have my own businesses and am always interested in what other men do. My wife says I shouldn't do that, that I am too nosey, but that's one of my bad habits."

"Yes, I keep telling him so, that he should not ask such personal questions, but he just ignores me," responded Ruth.

She was smiling as she talked. She, too, was curious about this helpful stranger.

"No, I am not a business man. I'm on my way to find and visit relatives, a cousin of my mother. Her name is Mary. She married a carpenter of Nazareth. His name was Joseph. That was years ago and I have never met them. They had a son and, probably by now, other children. I was told that the father died a few years back. It is their first-born I want to meet. He would be about my age."

John was hesitent to go beyond that point. How could he explain to these people Yahweh's involvement in his life and what might lie ahead?

"We wish you well on your travels and your search. It should be a joyful time when you find them."

John thanked him and asked his questions in return.

"You said you have your own businesses. That means you are involved in more than one enterprise and I am curious. What do you do?"

Joseph chuckled, warning John this would take some time.

"While we are waiting for our dinner to be served, let me begin my story. I grew up in the hill country of Ephraim, in a very small village, Arimathea. My forefathers had large land holdings on which they planted olive trees, many olive trees. By the time I came along and had to take over the business, we had added our own caravans. We take our olives and olive oil to the large markets, even down to Egypt and as far north as Damascus. Our caravans go as far as Haran, far beyond the source of the river Jordan. From these markets we bring back other trade goods, spices, perfumes, cloth, rugs, even gold and silver. We buy cedar, the best, near Haron. These are our businesses.

"Finally, after Ruth and I were married and had children, we wanted to move closer to our own largest city, Jerusalem. There our children would get the best education and we could worship in the Temple, Yahweh's Temple.

"However, even though we have a house in Jerusalem, we missed the country. Jerusalem was just too noisy, too dirty.

So, we built here, in Ramah. You see, Arimathea is very close to another town called Ramah. This Ramah reminds us of that one. The other one really has a longer name, Ramahim-zophim, but to us it's simply Ramah.

"Here we are close to Jerusalem and that is good. We can be in the Temple for all the feasts. Also, I have been elected to the Sanhedrin. When the High Priest calls a meeting I can be there in short order. If necessary we can stay over in our Jerusalem house, but here is our real home. We plan to stay here as long as Yahweh gives us life!

"I suppose our main concern is peace, peace for our people, even under Roman rule. Our hope is that Yahweh will bring that peace. Some day he will send us the Messiah, the One promised long ago, the one talked about by the prophet Isaiah."

Finally, with a sigh, Joseph added: "I hope he will come soon!"

Hearing Joseph's story and his wishful words of hope, John knew he had to share his own story. It, too, would be long, but he believed that Yahweh would approve.

"Joseph and Ruth, I told you my name is John, and that is correct. Now, I should tell you my father's name was Zachariah.

He was one of the Temple priests, serving there for many years. His wife, my mother was Elizabeth, daughter of Elkanah."

Joseph, eyes opening wide, interrupted.

"I know that story. Your parents were quite old when you were born. You were an only child, and your birth was predicted by one of Yahweh's messengers. He spoke to your father at an Evening Sacrafice! For nine months he was speechless, but, finally, when you were born, he spoke again. You would be named John, and not Zechariah as Yahweh had directed. Above that, you would be called a prophet of Yahweh! I can't believe it, that we have met you, John, son of Zechariah! We are truly blessed!

"But, tell me, what happened to you father? We did hear about your mother's death, when you were still quite young."

"After my mother's death, my father's health began to fail. Physically he was doing very well, but his mind was going. He really became a problem for his Division leader, Jonathan. Finally, on the advice of some of the elders, it was suggested we move away, down close to the Salt Sea. We would live in a small village, Tobba. It would be a much quieter place than Jerusalem and the climate would be warmer. This was the land of the pious ones, the Essenes. However, Tobba was differnt from Qumran. In Tobba there were wives and children and some of the men were deer hunters. They provided the skins for the Scrolls the pious ones were writing and copying.

"Our plans were tragically interrupted on the way to Tobba. Traveling down the road to Jericho, just before the road forked toward Tobba, we were attacked by robbers. My father died! Apparently his heart just gave out. I was wounded, rather severely, trying to resist. It was only through the skill of the elders at Tobba I was nursed back to health. After that I remained in Tobba for several years, learning how to hunt and kill deer, learning how to survive in the wilderness."

Joseph interrupted again. This time it was for the serving of the dinner. It was time to eat.

"Let us eat now," he suggested. "We can continue our

conversation later. Ruth and I want to hear the rest of your story. I think you might have some surprises for us! First, however, let us now ask Yahweh's blessings, thanking him for these provisions for life."

His brief prayer was sincere. Yahweh had blessed them, richly so!

The meal was excellent. The main course was pheasant. Fresh greens were at every plate, along with sweet breads, as well as unleavened bread. There were nuts, grapes and olives. Wine was served and offered, but John asked for water.

Servants were at each place, waiting to meet any need. Bowls of water were placed beside each person, along with a linen towel. John was amazed at the abundance of food, as well as the care that was evident on every hand. Joseph and Ruth were proper hosts!

Once the meal was over, they retired to a smaller room off the Reception Hall. Here there were comfortable chairs. Finally, after a bit of small talk, Joseph asked John to continue his story.

"At Tobba I began to question Yahweh, why he let my parents die. If what my father had said at my birth was true, if what Yahweh's messenger had told my father at the Evening Sacrifice was true, when would I know what he wanted? When would he call me to be his prophet? I must admit, this was a most difficult period in my young life.

"However, after those early days at Tobba I became convinced I had to move away, out into the desert. I wanted nothing to distract me as I waited to hear Yahweh's voice. Finally, I did. I know it is hard to explain, but Yahweh has spoken to me, several times. He wants me to prepare the way for our Messiah. Before moving away, the leader of Tobba put into my hands copies of the Torah, Moses books, also the Psalms as well as the words of the prophets. These I have read and studied. I know most of them by heart. For me, the central thrust is that promise, the promise of a Messiah. He will come!

"That brings me to the more incredible part. The Messiah is here, not ready to begin his work, but waiting for what Yahweh's says is 'the fulness of time.' This Messiah is Yahweh's own son. As Isaiah predicted long ago, the son would come, born of a woman, born, not by a man, but by the power of the Spirit of Yahweh. That son is the one I want to meet and must find, the son of my mother's cousin, Mary!"

"John!" Joseph interrupted again. "How can that be? That's impossible!"

"No, it is not impossible. I learned long ago that Yahweh can do anything he wants. When Yahweh's messenger Gabriel spoke to my father in the Temple he went to Nazareth and spoke to a young, unmarried woman, my mother's cousin, Mary. He told her what would happen and he told her husband-to-be Joseph what would happen. They both accepted it.

"To prove this was no dream, Yahweh had them come all the way down to our home, meet my speechless father and visit my mother Elizabeth who was carrying me.

"That was followed by Joseph and Mary having to go down to Joseph's home town, Bethlehem, obeying the orders of Rome for the registration. That's where my cousin, Jesus, was born. I've just come from Bethlehem. I met a shepherd who was there at the time. He told me just two days ago about the event, how Yahweh's angels came to them that night, sang to them, told them to go down into Bethlehem. There they would find, the newborn baby boy. They did so and they found him! There's more to that story, but that is enough for now. I have been told Joseph is dead, but that Mary and son, and perhaps other children now live in Nazareth. I am on my way to find them!"

Joseph closed his eyes, was silent for a long time. His wife Ruth said nothing, staring into the darkness outside, waiting for her husband to speak.

At last Joseph responded, careful in voicing his reaction.

"John, I said before, a few moments ago, all that is impossible. At my age I have trouble taking in something new, especially something so startling. I do have my hopes, and I hope what you say is true. I do not doubt your story, but I must wait and see. I do know Yahweh's ways are not our ways, but I will wait for Yahweh's sign for me.

"You have blessed us by your kindness and by what you have told us. We are most grateful. May Yahweh keep you and use you! Now, let us rest. The day has been long and we are tired. We will see you in the morning, before you depart."

Ruth, again, thanked John for his kindness.

"We are so very grateful to you. You have been a blessing to us, and if what you tell us is true, you will be a blessing to many.

With that, Joseph and Ruth excused themselves. John returned to his room, ready for sleep. It had been a long day. Also, the strain and stress of telling his story was difficult. Had he said the right thing? Did Joseph believe him? He wasn't sure.

# CHAPTER 19

*. . . and the Lord appeared again, at Shiloh . . .*
*I Samuel 3:21*

When John awoke the next morning he found his washed and pressed clothes lying across the chair. Most times he would have wakened if someone entered the room, but not last night. He had slept soundly! Anyway, the thick rug on the floor muted all such sounds. He was thankful for a good night's sleep.

However, before he drifted off, he did remember one passage from the Scrolls, from the words of the prophet Jeremiah. Here he was in Ramah and Jeremiah had spoken of Ramah:

> *A voice is heard in Ramah, lamentations*
> *and bitter weeping. Rachel is weeping for*
> *for her children; she refuses to be comforted*
> *for her children, because they are not . . .*

How could that be? That would apply to Bethlehem, not Ramah. It was there they wept over the deaths of the very young! Would there have been a mother there named Rachel? Regardless of that, the tragedy would be remembered for all time.

Yet, there had to be something else Yahweh had in mind, something Isaiah had predicted long ago. It had to do, not only with Ramah, but also with other towns nearby. That included Gibeah. Now he remembered! It was Isaiah who had mentioned the town with the well in the center of the village. Yahweh was promising the restoration of the remnant of Judah. Assyria would be the invading force, used of Yahweh to punish his people for their sins. But, finally, they would be forced out. Although there would be much destruction in places like Ramah and Gibeah, Yahweh would bring his people back to Zion. Yahweh would be triumphant! No wonder there was weeping in Ramah, and everywhere!

With that picture running through his mind, John slept. When all was said and done, and when all enemies would be driven out, Yahweh's people would be secure, safe in Yahweh's hands. The time was drawing near.

Gathering up his things, John asked one of the servants where he might find his hosts. He was ready to bid them farewell. He was led through an open colonade to the back courtyard. The sun was up, but several beautiful willow trees shaded the area. Seated on benches, adjacent to a marble table, were Joseph and Ruth. Joseph stood up as John entered the garden area.

"Greetings on this lovely morning! We trust you slept well. Were you comfortable? Were you disturbed by any unnecessary noise? Sometimes our neighbors stay up late, talking into the early morning hours."

"No, nothing disturbed me and I slept well. I want to thank you for your hospitality. You and your wife have been most kind, taking me into your home. I am grateful."

Joseph insisted it was nothing.

"It is time for our early morning refreshments. We have some nuts and dried figs. The figs are sweet and most delicious. Also, we have fresh grapes. These come from our vineyards near the river Jordan. Come, enjoy these, and sit with us for a moment before you leave.

"We are the ones who should be thanking you, helping us

along the road near Gibeah. You were most considerate! Also, I want to thank you for your story, your words concerning the Messiah. I can assure you, that intrigues me. After you went to bed I sat in our room for a long time, trying to recall some prophetic words concerning a Messiah. I do remember a passage, something about a ruler arising out of Bethlehem, but cannot remember the source."

"Sir, that was the prophet Micah."

"How do you know the Scriptures so well? You are hardly twenty years of age. I'm sure few of our rabbis are so knowledgeable. I am impressed. More than that, I am disturbed, not quite ready to believe all you are telling me."

"My lord, last evening, in telling my story, I talked about Tobba and Qumran. Most people think these pious ones are, at the very least, strange, unable to deal with reality. I'm convinced they are dealing with reality better than most. We, as a people stand under the threat of destruction. Rome rules our land, our way of life and, if possible, would control our religion, our worship of Yahweh.

"The ones living in those remote communities are deeply concerned. Sure, they might see Yahweh in a different light, but they live in hope, hope that the Promised One will come. For years and years they have been making copies of all the records. Their Scrolls contain the books of Moses and the Law, the Psalms, the Prophets. From these they speak of the One who is to come. Yahweh and his true followers have the light. The enemies of our people, even some of our own people, are sons of darkness.

"These I have read, over and over. I am convinced the promise of Yahweh is being fulfilled. Soon, the Messiah will begin his ministry. He will come to you and to all our people. Then you will know and, I trust, will believe."

"You amaze me, young man! I hope you are right. As a member of the Sanhedrin we have to deal with false messiahs, men who give us nothing but trouble. I'm sure you can understand my doubt. We are constantly in fear of some individual, or group, stirring up a rebellion against the Roman authority, claiming Yahweh's approval. That would be diasterious for all of us."

"Yes, I know and understand. I appreciate your reluctance to believe, but Yahweh is now ready to act, fufilling ancient prophecies. Why not now, or soon? Our nation, our people are in darkness and bondage."

John's hopes were high. Someday Joseph would believe!

Now it was time to go. The morning visit and refreshments were nice, but it was time to go! Again, expressing his appreciation for their hospitality, he gathered up his backpack, moving on toward the main entrance.

Accompanied by Joseph and Ruth and a few of the servants, he started out the open archway. Then he turned, paused to ask one more question.

"Why were you two traveling alone, all the way from Jerusalem? That was not wise. You had no servants with you. Your wife, Ruth, was walking, not riding. You could have employed carriers for her. I don't understand."

This time it was the wife, Ruth, who answered.

"We were going to Yahweh's Temple and we were no better than anyone else going to Yahweh's Temple. Most pilgrims were traveling alone, without servants. Most were walking. We would do the same. Joseph wanted me to ride, but I refused. It was the least we could do."

John had to come back. He embraced Ruth, shook hands with Joseph and waved to the servants. With a final lifting of the hand he turned away and walked rapidly toward the road to Bethel and Galilee.

This was hill country. Ramah was situated on the high slope of the ridge running north. John had to drop down to the west, following the connection to the main road leading toward

Bethel. Today there were fewer people on the road. By now, those attending the Festival had moved on.

There were a number of carts on the road, pulled by oxen. Most were headed toward toward Jerusalem, carrying supplies to be sold in the markets. One cart was filled with clay jars of oil. Another was packed with baskets of dried fish. You knew this because the smell of dried fish was rather strong. Asking about the source of the fish, one traveler said they were from the Sea of Tiberias, caught near Capernaum on the north shore.

Several were leading sheep south. Isaiah had said something about leading sheep to the slaughter. At the moment he could not recall the reference, but he felt sure it would come to him. Yahweh had a way of opening his mind when needed.

John passed some priests, accompanied by two pharisees. They were on their way to Capernaum, but would not go through Samaria. At Bethel they would turn east toward the Jordan. There they would cross the river, going up the east bank. Priests, pharisees and rabbis wanted no contact with Samaritans! To them, these people were unclean!

John laughed at that, walking that additional distance, just to avoid a particular people. Sure, Samaritans were descendents of those marrying other peoples, those whom their enemies had brought in to live in the area. However, that was long ago. Yahweh created them, and most Samaritans worshipped Yahweh. Shemuel had shared that information back in Bethlehem.

In Bethel travelers would be reminded of other ancient practices involving Yahweh's own people. The northern kingdom of Israel had a worship center at Bethel. Under evil kings there was pagan worship. Being unable to worship in Solomon's Temple they were led astray. That was the beginning of the downfall of Israel, ending with the Babylonian captivity. The words of Jeremiah spoke of that awful sin.

*Because your fathers have forsaken me,*
*says the Lord,*
*and have gone after other gods,*

> *I will hurl you out of this land,*
> *into a land which neither you nor your fathers*
> *have known . . .*

To John it was a reminder of human fraility, his own as well as that of others. Only Yahweh could change that.

Having had a good night's sleep, John moved on at a good pace. Passing other travelers, he would wave, smile and continue without stopping, moving rapidly toward Bethel. As he walked he thought of those who had come this way. One, in particular, was Jacob, running away from home, trying to escape the wrath of his brother Esau. They finally came to terms and made peace years later, but it was to Bethel Jacob had come. There he had his dream of angels ascending and descending to and from heaven. It was there Jacob renamed the place Bethel because in his vision he had seen and heard the voice of Yahweh. It was there Yahweh had promised to be with him and, as with Abraham, promised to bless him, he and his descendents.

John had no idea about any possible descendents for himself, but he was certain of Yahweh's blessings. Yahweh's promises had been given to him, also. Yahweh would go with him. In Nazareth he would meet him, Yahweh's own son!

Along the way there were two small villages, but John did not stop. He was determined to reach Bethel by mid-morning. This road along the valley made for easy walking. Although the ridges to the right were still rather high, the land toward the left began to open up into fertile plains. In that direction one could see fields of grain in the far distance. Closer at hand were sheep grazing along the road. Higher up on the steeper hills were olive trees. Farmers and shepherds were busy at their work.

Arriving at Bethel about the ninth hour, John stopped for a brief rest. Sitting on the steps of the ruins of the ancient temple, he drank from his water skin and nibbled on some of the last of Tamar's bread. He wished he had more. While sitting and resting, several children stopped to stare. Some of the older ones began to ask questions:

"Who are you? Where are you going? What is your name? Why are you stopping here? Do you have any family? Where are your parents? Where do you live?"

John tried his best to respond, knowing they were only curious children. After answering most of their questions, he thought he would tell them a story.

"How many of you have been in your synogogue?"

With several raising their hands, he continued.

Have you been there when the rabbi read Yahweh's word from the Scroll?"

Again, several hands were raised.

One older child responded: "The rabbi teaches us about those things. He has told us about the Torah and the words of the prophets. Why do you ask?"

"What are the writings on, papyrus or skins?"

"We don't know. We never asked."

"A lot of the Scrolls are written on skins, animal skins. Some are on deerskins. You asked where I lived and I will tell you. For several years I lived near the Salt Sea, east of Jerusalem. That's a long distance from Bethel. There we hunted deer, large deer. It provided meat for the people and the skins were scraped thin, softened and dried. We did that so the writings of Yahweh could be placed on soft skins which could be rolled up, just like those in your synogogue."

With that, the children came closer, asking more questions.

"How did you hunt the deer? How did you kill the deer? Did you kill any deer? Did you use spears or swords?"

Again, John answered their questions, telling about his experiences. They were fascinated!

When he rose to leave, they begged him to stay, hoping for more tales of life down by the Salt Sea.

The best he could do was to encourage them to ask their rabbi, their parents and their elders about the world around them. The important thing was their education, learning! This is Yahweh's world and you need to learn about his world and, more important, about him.

"Promise me! Will you try to learn all you can about Yahweh and his world?"

Even with their responsive "Yes!" they still didn't want him to leave. As he moved on, they followed close behind, all the way to the edge of the town. Several times, in response to their calls, he turned around to wave.

Between Bethel and Shiloh there were only a few small settlements, no large towns. There were more shepherds in this rather desolate territory. Someone pointed out the ruins of an ancient town, high on the ridge to his right. There had been a temple erected on the high slope, a temple of Baal. The town was Baal-Hazor, now deserted. Thanks be to Yahweh! Baal had been defeated long ago!

He was now moving into the heart of Samaria, although he was quite some distance from Shechem and Mount Gerizim. He would not arrive there until tomorrow. As he walked steadily on he met a lot of people of the area, mostly Samaritans. In response to his greeting and smile some gave a feeble wave. Others would not respond, keeping their heads lowered. They hardly knew what to do with this outgoing stranger from the south. Most Jews would have ignored them!

It was the middle of the afternoon before he reached the larger town of Shiloh. John had a decision to make. Should he stop here for the night, or move on? He asked and soon learned there was little between Shiloh and Shechem. He would, most likely, have to sleep outdoors if he moved on. Darkness would catch him on the road.

The other decision involved his Bethlehem friends. Should he try to find Shemuel's uncle? Would that do any good? What could he say?

There was an inn nearby. It would cost very little, if he didn't mind sleeping in a room filled with a lot of travelers.

Sitting on some old stones on the side of the road, he had

time to think. He had water and he had food, some dried meat. Eating was no problem.

Shiloh! This was holy ground! Here Joshua, according to the history of his people, had divided the land for the twelve tribes. Moses had died, far to the south, and Joshua had brought his people to this place. Not only that, there was a worship center here, where Hannah had prayed for a child. And Yahweh had granted her wish, answered her prayers. Samuel was born, the child given to Yahweh. Samuel, like John, had lived and served in Yahweh's Temple. However, there was no real Temple at Shiloh, only a tent of worship. But it was Yahweh's tent, or tabernacle! And Samuel lived here! He had anointed kings!

The more he thought about it, he reached another decision. He would try to find Shemuel's uncle. It would do no harm to let him hear of Tamar and Shemuel. After all, they were family.

So, in the center of the town, near the well, he asked several about the home of Joshua, the husband of Tamar. One or two shook their heads. They knew of no one by that name. Another stopped, stared for a moment, and then turned away without speaking. Finally, an older man answered his question.

"They don't live here anymore. Joshua died and his brother, Ira, took the house. Tamar and her son Shemuel moved away. Where, we don't know."

John thanked him for the information and asked directions to the house.

"I can assure you Tamar and Shemuel are doing well. I met them and stayed in their home a few nights ago. They live near Bethlehem, below Jerusalem. Shemuel has work, both as a shepherd and as a stonemason. I wanted to share that with Joshua's brother."

The man thought for a moment, expressed his joy over the news of former neighbors.

"I'll show you the house, but you may not get to talk to Ira. He had an accident last week. Trying to hitch up his oxen to a cart, one of them trampled on his foot. He is in great pain, with a badly crushed foot. There is no skilled doctor in Shiloh and the rabbi doesn't know what to do."

The house was like most of the houses in Shiloh. There was an open area behind a low wall. Overhead was the traditional grape arbor for shade. There was one long room across the full width of the building, with three other rooms around an open court. Outside steps led to the flat roof of wood beams and hardened clay. Overall, it was larger than most of the houses along the street.

John approached the one door visible on the street side. He knocked on the wood door and waited. Seeing and hearing no response, he called out: "Is there anyone here?"

In a few minutes a woman opened the door.

"Who are you? What do you want? My husband is not well and does not wish to see anyone."

John tried to assure her he wanted nothing more than to see her husband, to bring him news of Tamar and Shemuel.

With that, she opened the door wider and invited John inside.

"You are an answer to a prayer. My husband believes he is being punished for what he did to his brother's widow. This was his brother's house until he died. My husband took it from Tamar, with some story about Joshua owing him money. Now he has been injured and blames it on himself. Yahweh is punishing him for his sin.

"But, who are you, and how do you know Tamar and Shemuel? Tell me about them."

"My name is John and I live far to the south near the Salt Sea. I'm on my way to visit relatives in Galilee. Two days ago I came through Bethlehem, below Jerusalem, and met Tamar and Shemuel. In fact, they invited me to stay with them, which I did, for two nights.

"They have had difficulties in settling in a new community. Strangers are not always welcome, not at first. But all that has changed. They have made friends and Shemuel has found work, plenty of work. He also helps some shepherds care for their sheep. Also, he will be working with a merchant in the town. Shortly he will be doing some stone work for another merchant They are doing well.

"Shemuel was kind enough to give me directions north, hoping I would travel through Shiloh. So, here I am. Would it be possible for me to see your husband? I know a little about broken bones and might be able to help. If he has regrets about what he did, the news from Tamar and Shemuel might help."

"I'm not sure how much you can help him. You look so young. You're not a priest or rabbi, are you?"

"No, I'm neither, but where I live, we have to take care of all our needs. On the edge of the wilderness there are very few skilled in medicines, but I learned some things from the one who set my broken arm. Let's see what I can do."

She took John across the enclosed courtyard and into a room on that side. With only one small shuttered window, there was little light. Lying on the bed was a tall, gaunt man, obviously in great pain. Groaning, he was turning from side to side.

"Sir, that is not good for you, turning like that! I want you to drink this when your wife brings me a cup of water. Then you are going to sit up and we will put your foot in a pot of water. Once we have washed it with soap, we will wrap it, tightly. Very soon you should feel better."

Ira's wife was speechless, amazed at her husband's reaction. With John speaking with firm authority, her husband was doing precisely what John asked, without any argument. Then, responding to John's directions to her, she hurried to bring both the cup of water and a large pot of warm water.

John took off his backpack, found the medicine Debra's mother had given him, medicine for pain. He also found some cleansing soap. Mixing the pain medicine in the cup he had Ira drink it. It was bitter, but he drank it without hesitation. Sitting up, Ira extended his injured foot over the pot, where John could wash it.

John was in no hurry to touch the foot, not until the medicine had eased the pain. He asked his wife for cloth with which he could make bandages.

"It will have to be torn into narrow strips. I know cloth is valuable, but we will have to wrap his foot very soon. Can you find what I need?"

"Yes. I will bring the cloth. We have plenty. My husband buys and sells cloth. There is no reason why we can't use some like you say."

John noticed Ira's eyes. It would not be long until he would be drowsy and the pain would be less. It was time to talk.

"Sir, my name is John. I am a friend of Tamar, Joshua's widow, and her son Shemuel. They are now living near Bethlehem, below Jerusalem. They are doing quite well, making friends. Shemuel is working, earning money. I wanted you to know that, before I move on north to Galilee.

"Your wife tells me you think you have been injured as a punishment for sin, for what you did about your brother's house. If you took this house wrongly, that is bad. But, Yahweh did not punish you by having your foot crushed. That was an accident. If you want to blame anyone, blame yourself, or your ox. Yahweh loves you, your wife, your sister-in-law, your nephew, and he loves me. He wants us to love him in return. We do that by loving others.

"If you are ashamed for what you did after your brother died, you could pay a fair value for this house, sending the money to Tamar. What do you think?"

Ira could only shake his head in wonder. How was it that this young stranger, appearing out of nowhere, could provide the one answer he so desperately needed? Ever since Tamar and Shemuel had moved away, sleeping had been a problem. He knew what he had done was wrong. Could it be that Yahweh would forgive him?

By now, he was almost asleep. John was able to use the soap, washing the foot clean. He was sure that one bone was broken, but the only thing he could do was to wrap it tightly. After a week some of the swelling had gone down. He let the foot dry, wrapped it and helped Ira lie down. By this time he was asleep. John knew he would sleep most of the night.

Talking to the wife, asking her name, he also asked if he could stay the night. He wanted to be near when Ira waked up. He would rewrap the bandage before leaving.

"Praise be to Yahweh for sending you to us! My name is Martha and I would be grateful if you would stay. I had cooked broth for Ira, but I also have bread and lentils. We will eat in the courtyard. There is a large jar of water near that other door, water for washing. If you think it necessary, you may sleep here, in this room or, if you want privacy, there is another room next to this one."

"If you are sleeping here, Martha, I will sleep in the next room. I will do so if you promise to call me when he wakes. I will want to check the wrappings. Also, I want to make sure he has no fever."

The meal was a good one. Martha knew how to cook!

As they sat at the table in the courtyard, John asked Martha about her husband, what he did for a living.

"He is a trader. He really doesn't have a shop as such. He travels a lot, buying and selling goods, things like cloth, olives, olive oil, always the best grade. He buys and sells grapes and wine. He deals in animals, sheep, goats, and oxen, even camels. He has done well.

"After we moved into this house, he sold ours for a good price. Now, he will have to pay Tamar for this one, if he does what he promised you. He is a good man, really. Sometimes he lets his desire for wealth control the way he acts, but he is a good man. Only since the accident has it been difficult living with him. I'm sure it's the pain, plus his feeling of guilt. Maybe the accident was a blessing."

John assured her things would work out. He would ask Yahweh's blessing on them, just as he asked his blessings upon them at the beginning of the evening meal.

As John prepared to sleep, after checking on Ira, he prayed again, thankful he had been led to find Tamar's Shiloh family.

# CHAPTER 20

> *. . . and he went and dwelled in a city called Nazareth, that what was spoken by the prophets might be fulfilled . . .*
> Matthew 2:23

John had to be up once. Martha had called him. Ira was trying to sit up. Checking for fever, John gave him a drink of water. His forehead was cool!

"Sir, I want you to lie back down. You are doing fine. Your foot will be sore for several days. If you will stay off the foot for the next two weeks, you will be able to move about. However, you will need a crutch so that you do not put your full weight on this leg. Will you do what I ask?"

Ira nodded, lay down and went back to sleep. Again, Martha was impressed.

"John, I don't know how you do it, but he does everything you ask. I don't know what I would have done without you!"

"I think he responded so well because he was desperate for some relief. Sometimes, it is best to be firm. All that helps, but let's give Yahweh the credit. He does wonders when we are in need. Don't you think so?"

Martha could do nothing but smile and nod in agreement. She knew Yahweh was lord of all, but this young man had a way, which brought results, good results.

With the sun rising over the eastern ridge, John shared a light meal with Martha, a few fresh grapes and bread. While he was getting his backpack in order, she heated some of yesterday's broth for her husband. By now he was sitting up, wanting to get up.

Once he had eaten a little, John helped him sit up. Going outside into the street, John stopped a young man, asking for his assistance. Together they lifted Ira, carried him out to a chair in the courtyard. John thanked him for his help, wondering if he might be able to locate a crutch. He was sure Martha would pay for his services.

"No," he said. "My father was the one you met yesterday, when you were asking directions. At my father's suggestion I was coming to check on him, seeing if I could be of help. I want no pay in responding to a neighbor's need. From what I see, he is much better. My father will be pleased to know that. Before the day is out, he will be stopping by. Also, we will find a crutch."

Thanking him again, John walked with him to the street.

"You may tell your father that Ira regrets what he did about the house, and he plans to do what is right for Tamar and Shemuel. He has assured me he will. I think your father will be happy to hear that. Yesterday, when I met him, I could sense his disappointment in his neighbor's actions. Just make sure he comes. The two of you will be of much help in moving Ira, until he can get back on his feet. We thank you!"

Back in the courtyard, John removed the bandages, washed and dried the foot again. It looked better. As he rewrapped the foot, he told them what to do.

"Remember to stay off the foot. Martha, you will need to wrap the foot each day with clean cloths. Each time use the soap I am leaving with you.

"Ira, I'm going to have you drink one more cup of water with this medicine in it. That will ease the pain for the day. I know it will be uncomfortable, but each day you will see much improvement. Will you do as I suggest?"

Ira had difficulty in responding. Tears filled his eyes. Trying to control his emotions, he finally answered John.

"You, sir, work miracles! Yes, I will do what you ask. You say my neighbor and his son will help me move about, and I am grateful for that. Martha will appreciate their help. It would be impossible for her to move me."

Martha had difficulty speaking, but nodded her head.

Ira continued to speak, making sure John understood the change in his life.

"I remember what I promised to do. I will send money, the fair amount for this property. You can be sure that will happen. How else can we thank you?"

"You have already thanked me in what you will do for your sister-in-law. That is enough. There is, however, one more thing. Be faithful to Yahweh in all your dealings. You have been blessed in what you have. Be a blessing to others!"

Shaking Ira's hand, embracing Martha, John moved on out into the street. The road in front of him would take him to Galilee and to Nazareth! Hopefully, he would reach a halfway point before evening. He knew he could not reach Nazareth before tomorrow, not unless he walked all night. That would be foolish.

He dropped down the slope east of Shiloh, moving up the valley that led to the northeast. He really needed to go northwest, but this was the road, unless he wanted to climb up and down a lot of hills.

He was able to move rapidly. There were no towns along this main route north. There was one family living at the joining of two small streams coming down from the hills on the left. Their home was small, but did offer a place to rest and sleep, if needed.

John did stop long enough to drink some of his own water supply, speaking to those living there. The man's wife was at home, with two small children. Her husband was with his sheep on the other side of the ridge. He would be bringing them back before evening.

Continuing up the valley, the road finally made an abrupt left turn. Shortly after that, the route took John up the slope of another ridge and onto a higher plateau. By midday he was there, at Jacob's well!

It was obvious this was a popular stopping place for travelers, not because of Jacob, but because of the well. It was deep, deeper than anything John had ever encountered. It had a good taste, and it was cool! Here he could refill his water skin.

At the middle of the day, the place was crowded. There were several priests resting under the olive trees. There were merchants, moving their wares by donkey or ox carts. There were a few Roman soldiers, pushing their way into the area of the well. They had little respect for anyone else. There were shepherds. You could see their flocks down the slope. There were women from the nearby town of Sychar, waiting their turn at the well. These were Samaritans.

John waited patiently, waiting until all had drawn water. With the sun moving past the midday hour, most of the travelers had departed. Refilling his water skin, John, also, was ready to move on. Talking with one man who had just arrived from the town of Samaria, John knew that could be his stopping place for the night. This was the main Samaritan town, and he believed he could find lodging. He should be able to enter the town before dark. Just west of Sychar was the larger town of Shechem, but there was no need to stop there. The road skirted the nearby mountain, Mount Gerizim, and then led west into another valley. With a small stream flowing west toward the coastal plain, the road was easy to follow. Crossing the stream, John paused long enough to put his feet in the flowing water. It felt good. The sandals were fine, good for walking the dusty, rocky paths, but it was good to remove them at stops along the way. It was a pleasant interlude.


Samaria! It was big, a large town. It was a busy town. Even in the late afternoon, the market was busy. Larger than most towns in this northern territory, Samaria was a center of trade. There were many shops around the town square, far more than in Bethlehem or Hebron. On the outskirts there were several large homes. Some were two stories high. In the distance were the ruins of what appeared to have been a sort of fortress. John learned that had been the home of some of the kings of Israel. The most notable one was King Ahab. He and his wife Jezebel had lived there. John remembered that story. King Omni had established the town and given it the name Samaria. Ahab followed him. Both kings were evil kings, worshippers of Baal. He recalled the battle, or the contest, between Yahweh's prophet Elijah and the prophets of Baal. He remembered how Yahweh defeated them. Elijah had to flee south after that, but, eventually, Jezebel was killed after Ahab had died in battle. The Scrolls contained that story, Yahweh's victories over evil!

There was one shop attracting John's attention. He could smell bread, freshly cooked bread. It was displayed in large loaves. The Samaritans preferred the leven. John admitted it tasted better! A copper coin was enough for two loaves. In the shop he asked about lodging, but was told there was little to offer travelers. That seemed odd for such a large town, but John took him at his word.

The shopkeeper did espond with a suggestion.

"'There is a widow living near the road toward Ginaea and Dothan. She offers a place to sleep on top of her house. Steps go up from the outside. There is a trellis, which gives some protection from the sun, but not from the rain. At this time of the year that should be no problem."

Then, as John thanked him and started to leave, the man laughed.

"She will probably offer you a place inside, a good looking fellow like you."

That unexpected remark was puzzling to John. However, if he wanted to stay in Samaria he would have to find the house. Otherwise he would find a spot along the road, out in the open. He wondered why there were no more inns in such a large town!

It was still light, giving John a little time to explore the town. John wanted to see the ruins of the old fortress, the home of some of the kings of Israel. He walked in that direction, curious to see why there were no houses built close by. Was there a reason for that?

"You should not come any closer!"

John was startled by that sudden, unexpected command. Turning to his right was a man, an old man standing in the shadow of a large tree. He seemed to have appeared out of nowhere.

"Why do you say that? And why doesn't anyone build here? Back there the houses stop. I don't understand."

Coming closer, the man asked: "Have you never heard the story about King Ahab?"

John nodded his head.

"Yes, that is a part of the record of the kings of Israel, after the kingdom was divided. I know the story well. Why do you ask?"

"What was the evil of King Ahab and his wife Jezebel? Let me refresh your memory. She was a worshipper of Baal, bringing the prophets of Baal with her when she married Ahab. After the prophet Elijah defeated her prophets, and had them killed at Mt. Carmel, the vineyard of Yahweh, she vowed to kill Elijah.

"It never happened. Later she had Naboth killed, the one who owned a vineyard here, near these ruins. Ahab wanted it and Jezebel killed for it. She was an evil woman, but she would pay for her evil. The dogs would lick up the blood of both Ahab and Jezebel. Yahweh made that prediction through the prophet.

"It happened! Ahab was killed in battle, brought back here to be buried. The dogs licked up his blood, as his servants washed it from the king's chariot. Jezebel lived a number of years after that, but she, too, was killed, thrown down from the upper story of the palace. The dogs licked up her blood. Then the entire household of Ahab was killed."

John assured the old man he knew the story. He had read it in the Scrolls.

"Why do you tell me this? That was centuries ago."

"I tell you because this is an evil place. The spirits move over these ruins. The blood of evil people has soaked this ground. No one will build here, or even live close by. You should come no closer! Your life is in danger, too. I can see it!"

"My friend, my life is in Yahweh's hands. He will determine my fate, not evil spirits from the past. I am curious. How and why do you say such things? Are you a prophet?"

"My ancestors were prophets, sons of prophets they were called. Many of them did wrong, telling falsehoods, trying to please evil people. Now, I tell the truth. You will see.

"You are carrying fresh bread, baked today. I know the shop. What did the man say about a place to sleep?"

"He told me there was only one place, a house on the road to Ginaea and Dothan, a house owned by a widow. She rented space on the roof. He did say something about sleeping inside, but I didn't understand that."

"That's because she sells her body! She is an evil woman. Do not stop there! There are other places, where you can stay. The shopkeeper lied. He works for her."

John, disturbed by what he was hearing, was silent. He knew there were women who did that, and he knew there were evil men who would lie. What was he to do?

"Sir, I thank you for your information and your warning. I had forgotten there were such people around us. I will move on while there is still some light. I will be fine and will find a place to sleep outdoors. Yahweh will watch over me!

"But, you should remember also, at such places as this one, evil does not rule simply because of what happened in the past. Evil lives in evil people, not in things. There are good people and there are bad people. Yahweh calls us to be good. Be assured! With Yahweh's presence and power, good will overcome evil."

Trying to make sure he had the attention of the old man, he came closer. The darkness seemed to hide him in the shadows.

Suddenly, he realized he was talking to an empty space. The man had vanished. There was no one there.

Shaking his head in wonderment, puzzled by what he had heard, he moved on down the road. He would find a place to sleep somewhere along the way. First, he would put some distance between himself and Samaria. He had an uneasy feeling about the town.

By now there were only a few houses ahead of him. He could hardly see them in the darkness. Suddenly, hearing voices behind him he wondered. Who would be traveling this way after dark? Would he have company? There was no torch, no light, and that was most unusual. Honest travelers would be carrying a light. Stepping into the shadows he waited.

As they came closer, he could hear them talking and laughing, two men.

"If that stupid young man is sleeping on the roof, we can handle that. We can take what he has and kill him. Either way we will have something to sell tomorrow."

"Yes!" said the other man. "If he is sleeping inside, she will take care of him. Once he is asleep, she will call us."

Hearing that, John wanted to rush out. He had the strength to handle both, and he had the element of surprise. He could injure both, even kill them! Evil was in this place! How could he let them go?

He did nothing. As they went on down the road to the widow's house, he waited. Then, he moved off the road and up on the ridge to his right. Sitting under a tall cedar tree he kept watch. Finally, he could hear the two men returning, heading for Samaria. John couldn't hear all they were saying, but they were grumbling. There was no man at the widow's house. As they moved out of earshot, John came back down to the road, moving cautiously in the darkness. Once he was back on the road, it was easy to follow. There were no others traveling that late. Thankful for his keen eyesight, he moved rapidly toward his destination. He was alone, but Yahweh was with him.

It was late! The old moon was beginning to rise in the east. If there were others on the road, or lying in wait for unwary travelers, they could be spotted, easily. Watching for a good and safe place, John slowed his pace, looking carefully to each side of the road. At last, he spotted a clump of trees and some large rocks to his left. It would take some climbing, but it seemed to be a good place.

Sure enough, the rocks above the trees were quite large and at the higher level there was an opening, a small cave. There he could not be seen. Another advantage was noise. Anyone climbing up toward the rocks would tumble the smaller ones down the slope. He would be safe.

Sleep did not come soon. His experience in Samaria was distressing. The world was in conflict, darkness against light. Was there an evil force, separate from people doing evil? There was the record of Satan, but where did you find him? Could you see him? Did his spirit move over places of evil, as the old man had suggested?

Sure, Yahweh was the Creator, the only one able to watch over and care for us. He had his angels, like those who sang over Bethlehem, and he had his special messengers, like the one who came to his father and to others, the one called Gabriel. Did Satan have his own angels, his own messengers? If so, how do you fight against them? Should I have attacked those two men bent on evil? Would Yahweh have approved?

That raised the larger question. What should Yahweh's people do about the Romans? Should they fight with weapons, or should they be submissive to those who ruled over them? What would Yahweh want them to do? John was convinced trouble would come. Yahweh's people would be in great danger. What should they do?

Then, there was the matter of the Messiah. What will he do, when he is ready to act? Will he be a warrior like King David, or will he be submissive to others? It was a puzzle!

John didn't know when he went to sleep. He vaguely remembered the late moon rising high in the night sky. However, he finally slept, longer than intended. When he opened his eyes and peered out of the shallow cave, he could see a number of travelers on the road. It was already busy.

Using a little of his water to wash his face, he poured some in his cup. Drinking that, he chewed on a strip of dried meat. In addition, he had the bread he had purchased. It was good, even though an evil man had made it. Thinking on that, John came to one conclusion. Life, to a large degree is what you make of it, what you do with it. Things like bread or meat or grain or cloth are not evil in themselves. People are evil, or good.

It was time to go. Today he would reach Nazareth! Making his way down to the main road, he was joined by others traveling north. As he learned, some would stop in Dothan. Others would stop in Nazareth. Others would go as far as the northern sea, the Sea of Galilee. A few would end up in Damascus.

John greeted all he passed, walking at a faster pace than most. The nearness of his final desination spurred him on. He had traveled a fair distance from the outskirts of Samaria during the night and had camped near the end of the high ridge running parallel to the road. As best he could tell he had walked about five miles in the dark.

He wanted to be in Nazareth by the end of the day. He wanted to find the home of Mary, the home of his cousin Jesus before dark.

Leaving the higher ridges behind, the land spread out into lower, rolling hills to the west, toward the Great Sea. Here there were larger fields of grain. There should be a good harvest. On his right, the slopes were steeper. He could see sheep and goats grazing under the watchful eyes of the shepherds. There were trees, but most of those were in the valleys, along the several small streams they passed.

Although there were many farms along the way, and houses

on those farms, there were no towns. The first one, and the first one large enough to be called a town, was Dothan. It really wasn't much, but it provided an excuse to stop and rest. There were a couple of shops and an open market. A few people were there, looking for bargains. There was a well, located adjacent to what was left of an ancient wall. At one time there must have been a wall around the town, and a gate, a place for the elders to sit and judge cases.

Dothan! This was the place! Joseph had come here, looking for his brothers caring for Jacob's sheep. Here, his brothers had intended to kill him. They would have, except for the plea of one brother. He had said "No!"

That's when they sold him into slavery! He was taken far south, all the way to Egypt. What a story, how Yahweh watched over Joseph! Through him, Yahweh's people were fed in the days of the great famine. To be sure, they all ended up in slavery, but that started with brothers thinking evil in their hearts, and doing evil. It was the same old story. Evil begets evil! Good begets good!

Moving on, after talking with a man and his servants coming down from Nazareth, John came to a disturbing conclusion. He could not reach Nazareth tonight. If he could fly like that eagle soaring overhead, it would be easy, but he was no eagle. He would have one more night on the road.

The question was, where? Where could he stop? From what he learned, there were no other towns, other than one very close to Dothan. That would not help.

One traveler suggested Nain. It was just to the right of the main road to Nazareth, but it was a nice town. The people were friendly, mostly Jews. There, he was assured, he could find a place to sleep.

With that in mind, John picked up the pace again. He would stop and sleep in Nain. Hopefully, someone would take him in for the night. Of course, he could sleep anywhere. If he could survive in the wilderness he could survive on the Damascus road. The only difference, as he had learned, the wilderness was much safer.

Sure enough, the sun was setting when he arrived in Nain. It would soon be dark! If he was to find an inn, he had to do so soon. Small towns had few. Most times the so-called inn was space in someone's home, sometimes a space with the animals in the inner courtyard.

There was an inn, a fairly large home near the center of town. The husband was dead, but his wife and son took in travelers. Anxious to earn a living, they didn't charge too much. John was assured it was a good place to stay. The door to the street was still open and John entered, asking about a room. The woman greeting him, smiled. There were no private rooms, but once all were inside for the night, there would be space for him. If he had a blanket or cloak he would be fine. If he wanted food, it would be an additional cost.

Food was no problem. John still had his own. Most of the bread he had purchased in Samaria was still in his bag. There was the meat, the dried strips, plus some dates. Sitting in the open courtyard of the house he enjoyed the evening meal, offering to share with those who might go hungry. Tonight there was only one other traveler and he turned up his nose at John's simple fare. He would pay for a full meal.

With so few present, John had the opportunity to talk with his hostess, the widow.

"Do you have many customers at this time of the year? You are not on the main road to Nazareth. Does that make a difference?"

"No, it doesn't. Most travelers coming from the south come this way. You see, this is the road to Tiberias on the Sea. It is most unusual that we have so few. A lot of traders come this way, also a lot of Roman soldiers. Of course, they don't stay here, but they do travel this route."

"How long has your husband been dead?" John continued. "It must be very difficult for you."

"Yes, it is, but my son is growing up and will be able to take charge of things in a few years. Men do better at this. In the meantime I do what I can."

With the hour growing late, the woman assigned John and the other man their space, room to spread out their blankets. John rolled up his cloak and placed it under his head. Before long all were asleep.

The next morning, John hastened to be on his way. Paying for his lodging, thanking his hostess for her kindness, he moved back down the road to the connection with the road to Nazareth. He could have cut over a ridge, but was content to stay on the level road. He would be in Nazareth by noon. Getting on his way early, he met few people. They would come later, once the sun was higher up. It was a beautiful morning, not too warm for a summer day. This was lower Galilee, but the elevation helped keep the temperatures down. It was easy walking, at least for the first hours.

Then the road began to climb. The steeper road meant a slower road. He was climbing up to Nazareth! Rounding a bend in the road he was there. Nazareth sat on the edge of a valley to the west. Above, on the right, the town spread out toward the ridge. Farther up, the ridge ran directly north, high above the village.

Arriving in the center of the town, just above the town's well, John stopped to rest. For the last hour he had walked faster than his usual pace, but, at last, he was here! Walking down to the well, he drew up fresh water.

Now it was time to find Mary and his cousin Jesus. Most of the women of the village had already come to the well. He would have to find someone else and ask for directions. Sitting by the well, waiting patiently, trying to collect his thoughts, he was approached by a resident.

"Sir, you must be a stranger here. May I be of help? The shops are below you, on the way to Sepphoris."

"Yes, I am a stranger. I have never been here before. I really don't need the market. I am looking for a relative of my mother. Her name is Mary, the widow of the carpenter Joseph."

The man raised his eyes in surprise.

"Then you must be John, her son's cousin! Would that be correct? He kept saying you would visit someday. How he knew that, none of us could decide. They will be happy to see you. Let me show you the house. I was a good friend of Mary's husband.

The house was large, well built. You could tell the builder knew how to construct a house.

The man approached the street door.

"Mary, I have a surprise for you! You have a visitor, a visitor from Jerusalem!"

In a moment the door opened. It was Mary! For a moment she was silent. The bright sunlight of the street was blinding. Then, she rushed forward, embraced John and began to weep.

"John! John! You have come! Jesus knew you would come. He kept saying you would come. Now, you are here! If only you could have met my beloved Joseph, but he is gone. He died two years ago."

Clinging to John, the tears continued to flow, her shoulders shaking as she sobbed. John did his best to comfort her, not speaking, but holding her gently in his arms. Finally, after a long time, she wiped her eyes on her dress, took John by the hand, thanked her neighbor, and led John inside. Closing the door, she embraced John again.

"I can't believe it! You have come, all the way from Jerusalem. That is a long, long, journey. I know. I have traveled it before, years ago.

"But, come. Let us go out to the courtyard, and to the shop. Jesus is there, busy with his work. You will have to admit, he learned well from his father. He is a good carpenter!"

Moving through the room, out into the courtyard, he saw

him coming out of the shop. Jesus stopped, brushed off wood shavings, smiled, came forward and held out his hands.

"Welcome! I knew you would come!"

# CHAPTER 21

*. . . is not this the carpenter's son?*
*Is not his mother called Mary?*
*And are not his brothers James and Joseph*
*and Simon and Judas?*
Matthew 13:55

John was speechless! His mouth wide open, eyes fixed on Jesus; John was speechless! For months, yes, years, John had wrestled with his decision to make this long journey. Was he doing the right thing? Would this cousin really be the one, the one Yahweh suggested he meet. If he were Mary's son, the one born of Yahweh's Spirit, how would he be received? Many times he had tried to envision this moment, coming face to face with the one he believed to be the Messiah!

Now, he is greeted without any great fanfare, without any amazement over his arrival. It was a simple "I knew you would come."

In his travels John had met a lot people, touched the lives of many. He had heard them say, in response to his assistance, "It's a miracle!" Now it was his turn, thinking to himself, "It's a miracle!"

Finally, after what seemed an eternity, John responded with a smile and an embrace.

"Thank you! Thank you for your warm welcome and for the assurance Yahweh was right. Certainly, you of all people, would have known I would come!"

Jesus laughed.

"Tell me about yourself. Sure, I knew you would come. My father assured me you would come. That I understood, and I told my mother and brothers, you would come. I know, it sounds incredible, but my father does incredible things!"

It was John's turn to laugh.

"From the very beginning! Yahweh does do incredible things. I can attest to that; what he has done for me, from the beginning of my life.

"My story is a miracle. I know and understand that now. It started out that way, Yahweh's messenger coming to my father Zechariah in the Temple, telling him his wife Elizabeth, my mother, your mother's cousin, would have a baby, even in her old age. Your mother came to see her before I was born."

"Yes, how well I remember!" Mary interrupted. "That same messenger, Gabriel, told me to go, make that visit. I would find it to be true, including the prediction that your father would be unable to talk. As I recall, all your neighbors were amazed. They couldn't believe your mother was expecting a baby. It was a miracle!

"I stayed as long as I could. Then I had to return to Nazareth. It would not be long before Jesus would be born and I needed to be in my own home for that. Of course, at the time, I did not know we would have to travel south again, all the way to Bethlehem. However, that is another story."

"Perhaps you heard," John continued, "my father's speech returned when they brought me to the Temple on the eighth day. That's when he gave me the name John. That also created quite a stir. The neighbors insisted I should be named for my father, but Gabriel had said in the beginning I would be given the name John!

"What followed was hard on my mother and father, but especially on my mother. At her age she had difficulty in dealing with me, an overactive, getting-into-everything little boy. First of all they had to find a wet nurse to feed me. Then, as I grew older, my mother had trouble keeping up with me. I was into everything, at home and all through the village.

"Finally, after a lot of complaints from the neighbors, my father's Division leader suggested I come to the Temple whenever my father was on duty. For a long time that was a disaster, until a young priest took me under his wing. Actually, things didn't improve much, even then, not until I ran away and met an Egyptian down below the lower city. Would you believe it? He turned my life around! He said he saw in me a holy person, that he had seen only one other person who had touched his life like that. I know now he was talking about you.

"Mary, I saw him one more time, on the edge of the wilderness, not too far from Hebron. His health was failing! He and his followers were on their way home to Egypt. He sent you a message, his greetings, as though he knew I would find you. You were that young girl!"

"John, that was long ago, before you were born. A camel caravan had stopped in Nazareth for two nights, something that had never happened before. My friend Miriam and I were so excited. As young girls we dreamed of adventure, of traveling like that, of living in big cities, far away. We would marry handsome men like those Egyptians.

"The morning they departed, they came to thank the elders of the town for their hospitality and the use of our well. The leader, with two others, stopped when they saw us and smiled. Then, as they were turning away, he came back, looked me in the eyes, bowed and knelt down before me.

"It was exciting, but it was also disturbing. It was not until later, when Yahweh's Gabriel came to me on the hill above the town, that I put the two things together. Yet, I really didn't understand. I was too young. I'm sure it was the same with you. It must have been, for both of us, a way of impressing upon us what was ahead. Yahweh wanted to get our undivided attention, using that mysterious Egyptian to do so."

"He certainly did that for me." John remembered. "When I found my way back home, life was different. I was finally growing up. However, the first thing I had to face was a tragedy. The night I was away, my mother died. The years caught up with her! I was devastated!"

"Yes, John, we received that news. It was some time later, but other friends from Jerusalem shared that with us. For me it was a very sad time. Later, on our annual trip to the Temple, we wanted to check on your father, but that year Jesus went with us and we had no opportunity. You see, we had quite a scare. He was missing for three days. We thought he was with our large group heading home, but he wasn't. He stayed in Jerusalem, in and near the Temple. He was so anxious to get on with his father's work! Weren't you, son?"

Mary smiled as Jesus responded.

"You kept reminding me to be patient, and you were right. I'm still impatient, but I've learned to wait, even as you, John, must learn to wait. It is not easy, is it?"

"No! It is not easy, but wait we must. Your father Yahweh keeps reminding me of that. Did you know I was at our home when you came that year? I was closing up our house, getting ready to move away from Jerusalem. I missed the Passover, and just missed seeing you. My young priest friend, Eljah, told me the story when I returned. He had seen you in the Temple and was so excited. He was delighted with the way you disturbed those who thought they knew so much.

"The question I could never answer was this: 'If I had been there, what difference would it have made?' What do you think? If I had met you then, would I have realized who you were?"

Again, Jesus laughed.

"I don't think so. We were both too young, and none of that would have been revealed to us. But let's stop talking. I see my brothers coming in. I want you to meet them, all four."

Approaching his brothers, he started the introductions.

"Here is the oldest, next to me. His name is Joseph, named for the best carpenter in all of Israel! Here is Simon and James and Judas. My brothers, this is your cousin John. He has traveled for days, just to meet you!"

They all gathered round, shaking hands with John after giving their mother hugs and kisses. They had been over to Cana, taking furniture their brother Jesus had built for a newly married couple. Mary told John later that evening that Jesus did that sort of thing for a lot of people and, if they were poor and could not pay, it was a gift. He loved to work with his hands, a work he had learned from Mary's husband, his Nazareth father. Also, she gave the younger sons credit for their support. They helped in the shop by bringing in lumber for drying. They always kept a good supply on hand. Joseph, in particular, was going to be another gifted carpenter, just like his father.

Also, they helped by working in the grain fields at harvest time. Some paid them with grain, while others paid the usual daily wage. With all working, they did well, even with so many mouths to feed. They were good sons, attending to their mother's needs. Mary was proud of all five!

"John, you probably don't know I have a daughter. Sarah was born after our son Joseph was born. She is married and now lives with her husband and his family over in a small village, Bethlehem. Isn't that interesting, another Bethlehem! He is a farmer. We don't see her very often. There was another girl, Mara, whom we raised in our home. Both her parents died when she was just a baby, so she lived with us for several years. Now she is living with her aunt and uncle in Sepphoris. We do see her frequently."

With night approaching, Mary began to prepare the evening meal. John dug into his stock of food, adding to the supper. There was one loaf of bread left, plus several pieces of dried meat and a bag of nuts, both almonds and pistachio nuts. Those were real delicacies, adding to the meal of stew and lentils Mary had cooked that afternoon.

Since there were seven for supper they sat at the larger table under the tamarisk tree, one their father had planted. After Jesus' blessing there was little conversation. Six hungry men wasted no time in talk. That would come later. It was a good meal at the end of a busy day.

All helped in clearing the table. The dishes were washed in short order. As soon as possible they moved inside. One neighbor had stopped by while they were eating, but did not stay. He would come back tomorrow and get acquainted with John. Nazareth people were very friendly.

John thanked Mary for the meal, assuring her it was the best he had enjoyed in recent days. Then, at her request, asking about his father, he resumed his story.

"My father is dead. He died not too long after my mother's death. That was the turning point in his life. Physically he was fine. However, his mind began to go. He would do things at the Temple he wasn't supposed to do. He became quite forgetful. At times he would interfere with the work of others. The High Priest wanted him to retire, right away!

"It took a lot of persuasion on his Division leader's part to keep him in Jerusalem. We knew retirement to our home would be fatal for him. Without his dear Elizabeth, he would not live long. So, with the advise of the elders, Jonathan made the decision for us to move to a community near the Salt Sea. I objected, knowing something about the Essenes at Qumran. As a young boy I wanted no part of their rituals, their pietistic life. However, Jonathan assured me it would not be like that in his friend's village, Tobba. In Tobba there were families, men, women and children. In Qumran there were only men.

Also, some of the men in Tobba were hunters. They provided the deerskins for the scribes copying the scriptures at Qumran. Altogether, they had a lot more freedom, free to travel if they so desired."

"And did that work out?" Joseph asked.

"Yes, it finally worked out for me," John answered, "but not for my father. Just before our group of travelers reached the fork in the road near Jericho, robbers attacked us. One of the men died in the skirmish. My father died of shock. I think his heart just gave out. I tried to resist, but was wounded severely for my troubles.

"How terrible," Mary spoke, voice trembling. "What a tragedy! You were so young, too young to lose both of your parents. How were you able to deal with that?"

"It was not easy. Later on I questioned Yahweh, wondering whay all this happened. Can you imagine, a fourteen year old arguing with Yahweh?

"However, it could have been worse. We all could have been killed. Those who were to meet us arrived just in time and drove off the thieves. They carried us, me and my father, to Tobba on a threshing sled. For two or three days I didn't know anything, whether I was dead or alive, but those were wonderful, caring people. They nursed me back to health and accepted me into their community. It was very pleasant, living in an old Roman villa."

Judas interrupted him.

"What did you do in Tobba? It must have been boring for someone your age. Were there any boys your age?"

"There were lots of small children and a few young people a little older than myself. One boy was about sixteen. He taught me how to find the best wood for making arrows, also bows."

This time it was James breaking in.

"Did you get to go hunting? Did you kill any deer? What was it like, to go with those men, the hunters?"

John spent the next several minutes sharing his arrow making and deer hunting experiences. Jesus' brothers were fascinated, hanging on every word. John had done something every boy dreamed of doing. He was a hunter! Between a lot of questions and his answers, John was able to give a vivid description of life with the people of Tobba, holding everyone's attention. All the brothers, caught up in the hunting stories, wanted to hear more.

After a while, Mary called a halt.

"We have worn John out. It is late and time to call it a day. We will have plenty of time to hear more tomorrow. Now it is time to rest. Jesus will share his room with John."

Reluctantly, the brothers agreed.

"Don't forget," Simon reminded John, "we want to know

more about Tobba. You spoke of a Roman villa and we want you to describe it. You will do that, won't you?"

"Yes," John assured him, "I'll do my best."

It was dark now, quite dark. The old moon had not yet risen. Even when it did, it would be only a sliver of light. The brothers extinguished the lamps on the table and on the post at the street door. Jesus carried one lamp to his room, showing John where to put his things and where to sleep. There was one narrow bed and one pallet on the floor. Over John's objections, Jesus insisted he would sleep on the floor.

"That should be my place to sleep," protested John. "In the wilderness I sleep on the ground. I'm quite accustomed to harder beds than this pallet!"

"You will again," Jesus replied, "but here you are our guest. Please, enjoy the bed.

"As to what else lies ahead, let me share something other than a soft bed. Now comes the difficult, the hard times for you. Both you and I will have to endure much, but that is why we have been placed here. That's why you have come to see me, to prepare for what comes next.

"When you think back over the months and years, you really didn't have any doubts about me or my mother, that we were your relatives, did you? You knew, deep down inside, who we were. The real question was your mission, what my father's messenger, Gabriel, had in mind when he talked about the Holy Spirit. Also, your father said you would be called a prophet of the Most High. You wrestled with that one, wondering what that meant, didn't you?

"I do know my father has spoken to you, more than once, either directly or through others. He has already given you some insight into your calling. That is why he encouraged you to come here, to meet my Nazareth family and me. Our lives, linked together, will be a part of my father's plan for the world.

"Jesus, you are so right. And that is my great concern, what your father has in store for me. What are his plans and, in particular, how are these plans to be accomplished? What am I supposed to do for him, and for you?"

"John, I really don't know all those details, not yet. My father has not revealed everything to me, not even the time this mission will begin, neither yours nor mine. I do know this! I am to obey everything he asks of me. I am to be perfectly obedient. There will be temptations, but my one mission is to do what my father wants me to do, not what other people want me to do."

"How can you do that, Jesus, do no wrong, do only what your father asks of you? I can't! That is a part of my problem. I have done wrong things, bad things. Does he still want me to be a part of his plan, have a part in your mission? He has said 'yes,' but I stilll have to wonder."

"John, you are a human being. Human beings do wrong things. People, all people, disobey my father. That is why I have come from him. I know this is hard to explain and hard to understand, but we are different. Yes, I was born here. I was born in Bethlehem, according to prophecy. My mother is Mary, your mother's cousin. In that relationship I, too, am human. I laugh. I weep. I have to eat, sleep. I get hungry. Sometimes I eat too much of my mother's wonderful cooking.

"Yet, I come from him, Yahweh. He sent me to be born here. Sure, I can do wrong. I could disobey my father. I will be tempted to do just that, but that is why I have come, to obey him, to do what you and all others cannot and will not do. I will do that for you and for all people. I must not fail! It will involve sacrifice, but I must not fail!

"In your reading of the scriptures do you remember what the prophet Isaiah had to say? He was talking about me when he said:

> *Surely he has borne our griefs and carried our sorrows*
> *He was wounded for our transgressions*
> *All we like sheep have gone astray;*

*We have turned every one to his own way;*
*And the Lord has laid on him the iniquity of us all.*

"It was the prophet's way of saying I would obey, not sin. I would take your place. I would be faithful. Through me and because of me, you will be declared good and righteous."

John thought for a long time, all the while looking at Jesus. It was difficult to grasp! How could Yahweh be satisfied with people like himself? He was not good. Neither was he righteous. He had sinned! He had committed adultery! Could Jesus erase all that? How was that possible?

Yahweh could use him. Yahweh could call him to be the one to come before his son, to be the messenger for his son, but that would not change facts. He was unworthy!

"How will you be able to erase my sins, make me righteous? How can you do that for the whole world, even our enemies?

"Jesus, this is an evil world, filled with a lot of evil people, and I can understand Yahweh's concern. According to the writings, He would send a Messiah, a deliverer. It seems to me that would require a purging, a cleansing. You should come in strength, not in sacrifice! You are Yahweh's son! You are the one to fight against evil, destroy evil! Yahweh's Law must be obeyed! That's your mission!"

Jesus shook his head. With a wry smile he suggested they get some rest.

"We will talk more tomorrow. You are right. There is far too much evil. That's why I have come. However, we will have to do it my father's way, not the world's way. Right now, it is time to rest. Let's get some sleep."

From what John could tell, Jesus was asleep, immediately, but not so for John. There was too much jumbled up inside. Surely, Yahweh would reveal his plans while he was in Nazareth, plans for both himself and Jesus. He, John, would come first with a Yahweh-given message, a message that would point to the Messiah, that is, Jesus.

There was a suggestion of that somewhere in those Scrolls. Where was it? Staring into the darkness, he did his best to envision which prophet and the message. Isaiah! It had to be Isaiah. Yes! Now he remembered

> *In the wilderness prepare the way of the Lord,*
> *Make straight in the desert a highway . . .*

Then there was something else about this voice, what this voice had to say, something about "grass," that people were grass. People, evil people, would wither, fade away, but the word of Yahweh would stand forever. Yes! Yahweh would speak, first through him. Yahweh would give him a message, the message about the one to come, the Messiah. When Yahweh was ready, John would call the people to repentance, to return to Yahweh. The rest would be up to Jesus. What he did and what he would say would be Yahweh's choice. For John, that was the great mystery. He had to accept what Jesus was saying, in faith.

Also, now convinced more than ever, he would have to return to the wilderness and wait! He would have to wait somewhere out there, until Yahweh called, calling him to speak that word which Yahweh would give him. However it worked out, he would be led to say it! It would be about him, Jesus. He would 'prepare the way of the Lord, the Messiah!'

But, what would Jesus' message be? How else could he come, other than an avenger, a destroyer of evil? The evil in the world must be stopped, but how would that make people good and righteous? That was the burning, the disturbing question.

It was a long night. John tossed and turned. On his back, looking up into the darkness, he could see a lot of different possibilities. He was convinced that between the two of them, John and Jesus, they would turn their world upside down. Finally, with visions of marching armies filling his thoughts, he fell asleep.

# CHAPTER 22

*. . . can anything good come out of Nazareth?*
*John 1:46*

For a moment John wasn't sure. Stirring, he wondered. Where was he? He had been traveling for days. Days and places were now running together in his mind. How many nights had he spent on this journey north? Where had he stopped? Which stop was this one?

Opening his eyes, seeing the empty pallet, he remembered. Jesus! He was already up and out. Yes, he was in Nazareth, in the home of Mary and her sons. Jesus had slipped out without waking him! That was most unusual, others up while he was still in bed. It took a minute for John to realize and accept the fact he was satisfied to stay put, in no hurry to get up.

Searching for the reason, his willingness to be lazy, he saw it somewhat as the calm after the storm. To some degree, it was a normal feeling of "mission accomplished!" He had arrived, safely, at his destination. He had found his aunt and cousin. Yet, he was a bit confused and disturbed. Jesus should have had all the answers. Wasn't that the purpose of this long journey, Yahweh suggesting he come? He had been so confident Jesus would explain everything.

The answers were not as John had envisioned, the firm assurance they, together, would set things straight in their world.

They would be the strong, firm, powerful messengers of Yahweh, bringing people back to Yahweh.

Last night's conversation didn't point that way. Jesus kept speaking of sacrifice and service, of restoring us to righteousness. Yahweh would do what we could not, and would not do. He would give and not take. Jesus had hinted of suffering, something John had not anticipated, not to the extent he feared. Surely, it would not come to that! Would Jesus' life be endangered for the cause? Jesus couldn't die! He was Yahweh's own. As with the Word of Yahweh and Yahweh himself, Yahweh's son would live forever!

Still lying on his back, elbows out, and hands under his head, John stared at the ceiling. Almost without breathing, he whispered a silent prayer to Yahweh and waited. Surely, he would come and speak.

"John, listen! You have not wasted your time in coming. You have been called, chosen to prepare the way for my son. You will do so where you started your journey, in the wilderness. This time of preparation will be long, longer than you would want or expect. When the time is right, I will call you forth. You will, like so many others in the past, speak for me. It will be a word of warning, but it will be also a word of assurance. The assurance will come through you as well as through my son. He will come to you. There you will hold him up as the One promised of old, the Messiah. Once that is done, your task will be over.

"He will increase and you will decrease. At the same time, you will be known, you will be remembered as the firm, strong, prophetic voice of Yahweh. You will be called great! You will be known as the greatest man ever born of woman. At the same time, everyone hearing and accepting that voice will be just as great in my kingdom, but it begins with you. As to what happens to him, you will not see. He will suffer, but he will accomplish his mission. He will be victorious, not on your terms but on mine.

"Very soon, you must leave. The time draws near for you to

depart. As you journey south remember that whatever comes, I will not let you go!"

The voice faded. Silence! John opened his eyes, again. Stunned by what he had heard, he wrestled again with his understanding of things to come. What did Yahweh mean when he said I would not see what would happen to my cousin? What about my calling? How would it end? What would I do after that? Also, both Jesus and his heavenly father keep talking about suffering.

Suddenly John shivered. He felt cold, as though a winter wind had swirled into the room. It was time to rise, find his Nazareth family. He felt the need for company, for conversation, something to turn his mind into another direction.

Mary greeted him first.

"We knew you were tired, so we tried to be quiet and let you sleep. Jesus is in the shop and Joseph is helping him. The other boys have gone to cut wood for future use. They will be back this afternoon. Let me fix something for you to eat."

"Mary, I'm really not hungry! I was tired and I thank you for letting me rest. Jesus and I talked at length, before we went to sleep. Afterwards, I had difficulty getting to sleep. There are just too many things on my mind. Then, this morning, I heard his father's voice.

"I know that's hard for people to believe, that Yahweh talks to me, but he does. He has done so before. Some would say I was dreaming, that it's my imagination. Do you believe me?"

"Of course I believe you, John. I have not heard him directly, but he has spoken to me through his messengers, beginning with Gabriel. Actually, it began with that stranger, the one from Egypt, but that made no sense at the time. Another one was a devout man, Simeon. He spoke to us in the Temple, at the time of my purification. Also, a prophetess named Anna was there, speaking of my son as the redemption of Israel. Oh, yes, his father speaks, quite clearly. I believe you!

"But what did he say to you this morning? I think, perhaps, you are disturbed by what you have heard, both from my son and from his heavenly father. Would you share that with me?"

"Mary, I am disturbed! Knowing that the world is evil, I believed our mission was to combat that evil, wage war against it. To me that meant confronting the Romans, as well as those of our own nation, those who have not been faithful to Yahweh and his commandments. Fight we must!

"Yet, what I am hearing is something quite different. Both Yahweh and his son know about the evil. That is why Jesus has come. However, I am being reminded Yahweh's ways will be different. He will be giving, not fighting back! There is talk of sacrifice and suffering. How can that be? Yahweh's son cannot, must not suffer! He is good and righteous. We must stir our own people to rise up and fight. Sure, we will have suffering, but that happens in war."

Mary was silent. She was thinking back, far back to that first Temple encounter. What was it old Simeon had said directly to her?

*and a sword will pierce through your own heart . . .*

She must share that with John. He should know! He will have to realize Yahweh sent his son to fight, not by arms of might, but with arms of love. He would suffer and she, his mother, would suffer, and, if she understood anything about human affairs, she was sure John would suffer!

"John, this is not easy to say, but you need to know. My son, Yahweh's son, will suffer. It is not clear, by any means, what that will involve. Fighting evil, as Yahweh wants to fight evil, is quite different from the ways of men. Men want to use swords and spears. They, the evil ones, will use swords and spears; whatever they think it takes to fight against the good.

"When we were in the Temple for the first time after my son's birth I was warned of that. An old devout man told me in no uncertain terms, my heart would be broken over what would happen to my son. He, my son, has come for the fall and rising of many in Israel. In other words, he will be the center, the focal point of the conflict. He will suffer!

"There is one more story few people know. After Jesus' birth in Bethlehem, in that stable, in that cave, we lived in a house for several months. His birth had not been easy on me. I was so young and so small. We needed time to recover before making that long journey back here. While we were still there, some strangers came to Bethlehem, looking for us. They had seen the bright new star and had come with some special gifts. They, in their own way, saw in our son, a king. They believed they were worshipping a king. The gifts were special, some gold and spices, frankincense and myrrh. Remember? Frankincense is for anointing one for the priesthood, Myrrh is for anointing the body at burial. Gold is the gift for kings.

"We learned these men from the East had come by way of Jerusalem and had talked with King Herod. He, as most everyone knew, would permit no threat to his own throne. He would destroy any newborn king, if there were such a person. He had done that before, killing his own sons. So, he planned to send his guards to Bethlehem and have all the young male children killed, and he did!

"However, before they arrived, Yahweh sent his messenger to us, warning us to leave. We did so, quickly, not going north, but going south across the desert, all the way to Egypt. We stayed there until we heard that Herod had died. It was not an easy journey, but it was the only way to save Jesus from evil men."

John let out a long shrill whistle, something he had picked up from Shemuel, back in Bethlehem. It helped express his astonishment.

"No, I did not know that you went into Egypt. In Bethlehem I learned about the strangers coming, riding on huge camels. Beyond that, there was nothing. The people there said you simply disappeared.

"When I came through Bethlehem they had a strong distrust of strangers. You could appreciate that after what they had been through, the terrible tragedy of Herod's action. However, I think they finally resolved that. Yahweh helped. Before I left they seemed to understand they were special in Yahweh's sight.

"Yet, I still don't understand what is to come, and the way Yahweh will do things. I don't understand how he has permitted you to suffer so much already. Your Joseph is dead. The two girls are no longer here. You have had a hard life, with more to come. How do you deal with that? Surely you have your questions that continue to disturb you! For myself, I know I will need to trust more. Hopefully, my learning will come to me, not only here, but back there, in the wilderness. That return trip, I'm afraid, will have to be soon, very soon."

"John, you must understand all of us are in Yahweh's hands. Sure, I have my bad days. I weep whenever I think of my husband and my girls. Mothers need daughters, but I love my sons. They have been good to me!

"We will certainly miss you. You have been a blessing to us. All you have told us helps us understand a little more of what lies ahead. My cousin Elizabeth would be happy to know her carrying and delivering a son was, and is, a part of Yahweh's redemptive planning. You and Jesus will provide Yahweh's salvation for a hurting world. Be assured of that, even if you don't understand it all.

"Now, let me get Jesus from the shop. He gets so engrossed in what he is doing that he forgets to rest."

Mary walked quickly across the inner court, calling her son's name. Both Jesus and Joseph came out, brushing off the wood shavings. They had been busy, cutting and shaping an oxen's yoke.

"Well, our visitor has come to greet us on this beautiful morning!" Jesus called out. "We knew you were tired from your travels and from our talking so much. So, we let you sleep. Mother, have you given our cousin something to eat?"

"He said he was not hungry," Mary replied. "We will have a big meal this evening. There are some grapes on the big table. Why don't you two rest a minute and tell John what you have been doing."

"Joseph, how many of these yokes did our father make?" Jesus asked. "It must have been hundreds!"

"Yes, I think that was my first memory of the carpenter shop, yokes, that and the carrier saddles for the donkeys. Later, as we grew up, I learned why he made so many. They were the best.

"Farmers and traders would travel long distances just to get our father to meet their needs. His reputation as a skilled carpenter was well known, especially the yokes which were light on the oxen's neck. Now, we are trying to follow in his steps."

Joseph was eager to show John the shop and the work they were doing today, and John was impressed, not only by the magnitude of the work, but by the order and cleanliness of the shop. These were caring young men. Sure, there were a lot of shavings on the floor, but there was a proper place for tools and lumber. He was certain all would be clean at the end of the day.

"Joseph, your mother tells me you want to be a carpenter, just like your father. From what I can see you are doing that quite well. What about your younger brothers? What do they want to do? Will they continue to work with you, helping you and Jesus?"

"John, I really don't know. Simon is getting restless. He seems to be more interested in traveling. He thinks Nazareth is too small for him, that his opportunities here are limited. We've suggested farming, but he shows no interest in that. Someday he will leave, looking for work elsewhere. He does get along well with people, and that would be good in whatever he does. Frankly, I think he would do well as a trader, buying and selling.

"Both James and Judas want to be of help to Jesus. None of us are sure of his future, but we do know he is special in Yahweh's sight. We've known that, all of us, from birth. Jesus will be called of Yahweh someday. He will be the one to speak for Yahweh, not just here in Nazareth, but out there, in all the towns and villages across our land. We don't understand that, and we, too, have to be patient and wait. Someday, I think, I will be alone in my father's carpenter shop."

"Joseph, you have a big responsibility here. I'm certain you will be equal to the task, and you are right. Jesus is special and Yahweh will call him when the time is ripe. All our lives will be touched, and that includes your mother. I surely don't have all the answers, but I am assured those will come. We, all of us, must be firm in our faith. Above all, we must be patient!

"You also need to know I must leave soon. Since that is so, I need to find and talk with Jesus. There are a few more things we should discuss before I go. I'll let you get back to your work while I take him away from helping you."

John and Joseph walked backed to the large table where Mary and Jesus were waiting. Sharing the grapes, they asked John for more details of his early life in and near Jerusalem.

"Tell us what you remember about your father Zechariah," Mary asked. "and what did you do while he was on duty?"

Trying to remember, John began to talk about those early days. It wasn't easy, recalling childhood activities, childish ways.

"The first thing I remember was the size of the Temple. It was enormous! It was rather frightning, especially the areas where there was little light. The one thing that really impressed me was the singing, the voices of the priests. That was the one thing that kept me quiet. You knew the Temple was a holy place!

"At the same time you can imagine what a little boy did, especially one full of energy. I was into everything. I was trouble! I thought birds and animals ought to be free, not cooped up in cages. Whenever I had the chance I would let them out. That created quite a stir, and a lot of stern talk. My father was not happy with me. It got so bad they assigned a young priest, Eljah, to watch over me; hopeful I would learn and grow up.

"I do remember my father's influence in the Temple. He was a respected teacher and leader. He had served in the Temple all his adult life and knew the right way to do everything. Everyone knew the Division leader, Jonathan, looked to him for advice. I was proud of my father.

"As I told you last evening, I did grow up, finally. However, that was closer to the end of my father's service in Jerusalem. Yet, even with that, I don't think I would have made a good priest. I did not appreciate all the rules and regulations that made the worship of Yahweh so rigid and formal. Some of those serving in the Temple seemed to think more of what positions they held and how much they gave, both in offerings and in fasting. It seemed to me there was much more interest in themselves, rather than in the worship of Yahweh.

"Remembering those early years, I am reminded of what we have to do, Jesus. We must turn all hearts back to Yahweh, your father. Somehow, we have to get the priests to be better leaders for our people. That will be your task, and mine! Don't you think so?"

Jesus laughed.

"John, you are right, but I don't think we can make anyone, especially the priests, do what we want them to do. My father will use us, but only in his way. It will be the way of love, not the way of force. Both of us will have to remember that. It will not be easy, but we will do what my father wants of us. Be reassured, my friend, he will teach us and show us.

"But, enough of that for the moment. John, I want to show you more of Nazareth before you have to leave. Mother, will you and Joseph stay here while we walk through the town?"

"Yes, son. Take your time."

The first stop was the village well. Jesus recalled his mother's stories about the one well in the town, where she and her friend Miriam met each day, filling their jars with water. It was that well that provided the water for the Egyptians and their camels. It was the well where his mother's betrothed, Joseph, met her and carried the water for her, the day he was finally convinced Mary was pregnant with Yahweh's son. That was the day they began to make final plans for an early wedding.

Moving on through the village, they were greeted by many of the r esidents. Jesus introduced John to each one; careful to make sure they all knew the relationship. "This is my cousin, John, from Judea."

As they continued on, it seemed only natural to stay on the path toward the high ridge north of the town. With Jesus suggesting they climb to the top, John was impressed with the view, the unfolding panarama below. Again, he whistled, enthralled with the 360-degree view. There was the lake! That had to be the Sea of Galilee. The mountain to the southeast! That had to be Mount Tabor. With Jesus' help John was able to spot the ancient site of Megiddo, far down the Esdraelon valley. To the west was Mount Carmel, where the prophet Elijah defeated the prophets of Baal.

"This is wonderful," John shouted. "I had no idea one could see so far from this ridge. Yahweh's world is a beautiful world!"

Jesus smiled. "Yes, it is beautiful. My mother and her friend Miriam would come up here as often as they could. This was their special and private spot. More special than all that, this is the place my father's messenger, Gabriel, met my mother. It was here he told her she would bear a son, me, Yahweh's son. It was here she accepted that miracle-to-come.

"Sometimes, even now, mother will disappear, but we know! She comes here, alone with her own thoughts. Each time she comes, she returns more radient, more confident, renewed in strength. Her life has not been easy, much more difficult after her Joseph died. She misses the girls, terribly so! Yet, she is able to carry on, taking care of our needs day by day. She is truly a blessing for all of us."

"Thank you, Jesus, for bringing me here. You are right. You have a wonderful mother! You and your brothers and sisters are richly blessed! It would be a greater blessing if all of you could live out your lives in this quiet village, but, unfortunately, that will not happen. It is time to prepare for the work before us.

"This morning I shared with your mother the words of your heavenly father. He spoke to me, again, before I was out of bed, reminding me of what lies ahead. He also reminded me it was time to leave, to go back to my wilderness, and wait. That, both the leaving and the waiting, will be hard. I would like to stay longer, but I must not.

"Jesus, I still have many concerns. I came looking for answers to the things I've wrestled with, but they haven't come, not the ones I expected. Also, I know I'm too impatient. I seem to know less now, less than before. Where do we go from here? What am I supposed to do when the waiting is over? What are you supposed to do? When and where will we meet again? Can you help me with all that is bothering me?"

"No, John, I really can't. I do not have a timetable for the future, not yet. We can only wait until my father calls us. Wait we must. He will show us the way. You can depend upon him.

"Now it is time to leave this place. My brothers should be back by now and we will eat soon. You will need to get a good night's rest because I am suggesting you leave in the morning. Do you agree?"

John was taken back by Jesus' suggestion, wondering again why he should leave so soon. Yet, as he thought about it, there was no reason to linger. Staying longer would make leaving harder. They had met and talked. They had shared their thoughts. He had met Mary and all her sons. He had heard from Yahweh again. He must leave. The time had come for the next step in his life. In response to Jesus' suggestion, he nodded his head in agreement.

"Yes! You are right. I do have to leave, but now let's go back to your family. I'm hungry!"

# BOOK TWO
## The Fulfillment

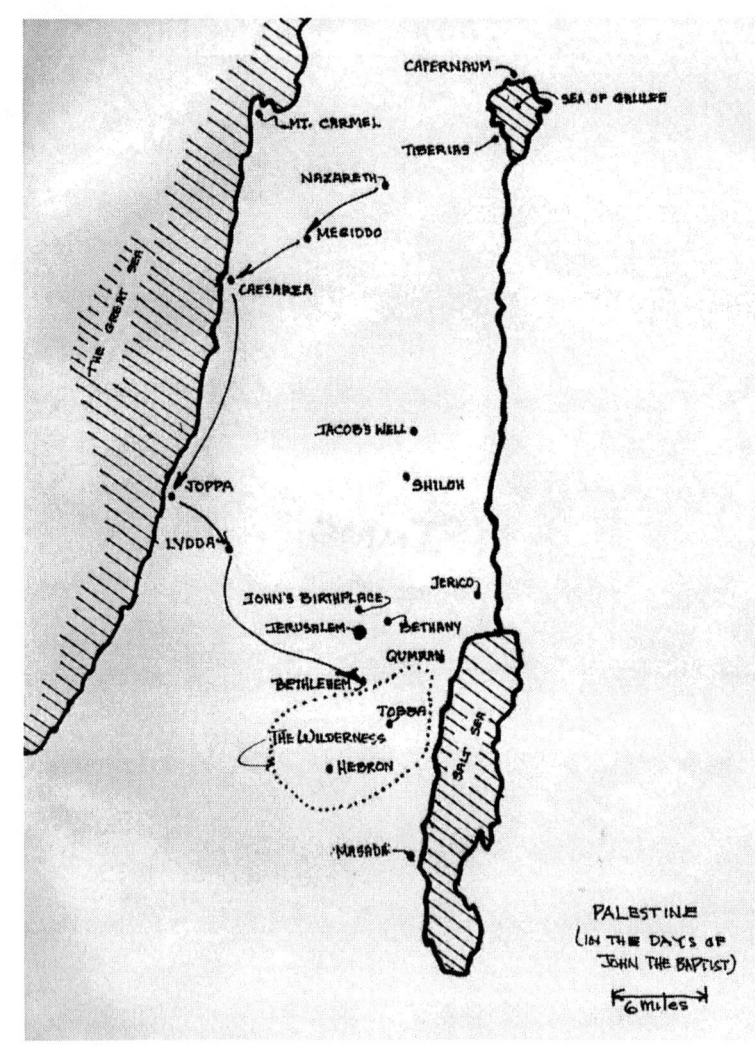

# CHAPTER 23

> *. . . along the borders of Manasseh were*
> *Taanach, Megiddo and Dor . . .*
> *the descendants of Joseph,*
> *son of Israel lived there . . .*
> I Chronicles 7:29

The evening meal was a delight. Mary, with the help of her sons, had prepared dinner. Clean plates and empty serving dishes were evidence. Neither her sons nor their guest could eat more. The bountiful table was one to remember! John, was impressed.

No one wanted to talk about John's departure. He stayed longer than intended, but everyone understood. He was family! They had insisted he stay and celebrate his nineteenth birthday. That was only right. Birthdays should be observed with family.

Also, Jesus' brothers kept reminding John of his promise to describe the Roman villa, now a part of the village of Tobba. They wanted to know about his life there and, in particular, his hunting experiences.

"That's a pretty tall order," John responded, "but I'll try. First of all, the village, like Qumran, is near the Salt Sea. The color of the water is unbelievable, a deep blue. From what I'm told, the water is very deep. Yet, nothing grows in that water. The salt content must be high, along with other bitter minerals.

Salt is mined by letting the sun dry up the water placed in clay trays."

"You mean there are no fish in that sea?" Simon asked.

"Why not? There are plenty here, in the Sea of Galilee."

"The water is full of minerals. There are a few small fish in the brackish water along the edge, but none in the main lake. Fish can't live in that water. I suppose the main difference is the water flow. I'm told that up here there are springs feeding your lake. Then the water flows out, down the Jordan River. The Salt Sea has no outlet. Why, I don't know.

"As to the village of Tobba, it was built around an old Roman villa. The owner wanted to farm the land, but had little success. Neither he nor his workers knew much about planting crops. He did have some success with a vineyard, but the income was not enough to meet his costs. Also, his family was unhappy with the climate and isolation. They finally moved away, abandoning the place.

"The villa is nice. There are large areas under roof, well lighted, a central hall, a reception hall and a library. There are several rooms for sleeping, one for meals. Outside there is another eating space, under a trellis. Trellises are everywhere, providing shade.

"Let's see, there is a large bathing pool. That is used mostly for the ritual baths. There is the kitchen, a bake house, a wine storage yard and an enclosure for farm animals. I slept in a separate building. It was an old barracks built for the servants and slaves. Some worked in the villa and some were farm workers. Others took care of the animals. You would have to see the place to appreciate it."

James broke in with another question.

"How many days would it take for us to travel to Tobba? I sure would like to see the village, and the Salt Sea! Oh, I know that is out of the question now, but someday . . . just maybe, someday . . ."

His voice trailed off, with his brothers nodding in agreement. Mary smiled, knowing the possibilities were limited. Only John would be heading south. She wanted to say more, but tonight she would let the others talk about their interests.

"What about the deer?" Judas wanted to know. "You promised to talk about hunting."

For the next several minutes John shared his deer hunting activities, beginning with his search for wood. They laughed over the description of his frustration in trying to reach accuracy in using bow and arrow; how a young girl became his best teacher. They were intrigued by the account of his first hunt.

This part of John's story was difficult to share. It brought up memories of the personal struggle with his emotions, his wrestling with relationships, his questioning of Yahweh's purpose in his life. In the recounting, a number of faces kept creeping into view, Tobiah, Mered, Jakan and Debra. What were they doing tonight? Were the hunters looking for deer? Had Debra forgotten him? He didn't think so. He could not forget her!

Simon changed the subject, asking about the deerskins and their use as scrolls.

"Did they really need that many deer hides at Qumran? What were they writing that took so many skins?"

The conversation went on far into the night, Jesus' brothers wanting to learn more concerning far away places. Their cousin was special in more ways than one! No one wanted to bring it to an end. However, after a few yawns, Mary suggested they all get some sleep. John needed to be ready for tomorrow. He would be leaving!

John's departure was difficult. These were his family, his mother's family! He did know he would see Jesus again, but wasn't sure about the others. He would miss them! Sure, he could have stayed longer, but he knew he must be on his way.

With a warm, lingering embrace for Mary and a brief hug for each of Jesus' brothers, John left them standing in their courtyard. Jesus walked with him to the outskirts of the town, talking as they moved along.

"My prayer is for your safe return to your wilderness, John. As you have been told we will meet again, when my father is ready. Neither you nor I know when or where. We will have to wait and see. In the meantime you will follow his instructions. He will guide you each step of the way.

"You will have some difficult times ahead. At times you will be in danger, but my father will be with you. He will not let you go! His power is greater than all others. Never forget that!"

With that, Jesus smiled, gave John one last embrace. With no backward glance, he walked back into the town. He had a carpenter's work to do, the work his earthly father had taught him.

Before going to sleep the night before, John had tried to think through possible routes home. Should he retrace his steps or explore new roads? Jesus and his brothers had shared their knowldge of all the possibilities and John was intrigued by what he had been told. Now he must decide.

Although there was a sense of urgency in his thinking, John resisted retracing his steps. Looking to the southwest, as the hills of southern Galilee flattened out into the fertile Jezreel valley, he could see the fields of grain reflecting the morning sun. Sheep were grazing on the slopes. In the far distance he could see the mound of the ancient fortress of Megiddo. That sight beckened him in a new direction! He would travel southwest to visit Solomon's bastion city. It was there David's son, Solomon, had secured the northern borders of Israel, stationing chariots and horses.

He would visit Megiddo and then take the main coastal route southward. Joseph, Jesus' brother, had reminded him ancient armies from both Egypt and Syria had traveled that road, many times. Also, in the period of the Judges, there had been a successful battle against Sisera, the Caananite king. Following that victory, when the chariots of Sisera had floundered in the waters of the Kishon River, Israel had occupied

Megiddo. The Lord had given them the victory! John was drawn in that direction.

Moving down the slopes into the fertile plain, heading toward Megiddo, John remembered the hunters of Tobba talking about arrowheads of flint. Traders coming through had found them in abundance near Megiddo, excellent flint already shaped for their arrows. He would look for some for himself and for the hunters of Tobba!

Yet, as John settled into his long strides of walking, he wondered if he would have much use for flint arrowheads in the months, or years, ahead. Where would he be living? What would he be doing back in the wilderness? Would he have to be hunting, or would Yahweh supply all his needs, as he did for Elijah? It was easy to think about Elijah. Over to the west he could see the ridge of Carmel, where Elijah had defeated the prophets of Baal. That was one of the accounts he remembered so well, reading the Scrolls back in Tobba.

John thought about climbing the ridge to Carmel, but decided against it. That would take him in a more northly direction, away from his destination. Megiddo would be his stopping place for the night. From there he would head directly south, through Caesarea and Joppa. He didn't know what he would find in those places, but they were on the coastal route south. Also, he had been to Caesarea once before, when he was a little boy. Eljah's family had brought him along on that trip. He wondered how much he might remember.

His first encounter with a town was Sarid, a reminder he was leaving the ancient territory of Zebulun. The tribal area had been given to the tenth son of Jacob, a son born to his first wife Leah. If he remembered correctly, one of the Scrolls spoke of the territory having twelve towns and their villages, but now, apparently, most had disappeared.

It was a small, quiet town with few people around. Most were working in the fields and vineyards. Some were moving their sheep westward, toward Carmel. The name "Carmel" seemed significant. It was the "vineyard of the Lord."

There was one shop in the center of the town. Unsure of his stops ahead, John purchased a loaf of bread. Outside the town there was a small clear stream. John replinished his water supply and continued on his way. It was a comfortable day, not too hot, good for walking. By afternoon he would be in Megiddo.

As the valley flattened out and as the path dropped lower toward the plain, John was surprised to see rising hills ahead, extending far south of Elijah's "Carmel." His mental picture of this part of Galilee had envisioned a gradual slope all the way to the Great Sea. He did remember being told Megiddo was built on an elevated site, but this was unexpected. How could he reach the coastal city of Caesarea? The mountain range ahead was blocking his way.

He did remember the stories, the records, concerning this ancient fortress. Here Barak had defeated a Caananite king with the help of Deborah, Yahweh's chosen. Then, long after the death of Solomon, two kings of Judah, King Ahaziah and King Josiah, had died at Megiddo. King Ahaziah had been wounded by Jehu's men, and taken to Megiddo. King Josiah had tried to stop the advance of an Egyptian army under the Pharoah Neco. This was a place of war and conflict. Megiddo straddled two main routes, one east and west, the other north and south. Generations of people and many armies had passed this way, fighting to take control of both land and people.

Yet, there was the question. How did they get to the coast through that mountain range? Where was the road going west? Wrestling with that, John came to the river Kishon. Here Barak had fought and defeated the Caananites. Their chariots had floundered in the swollen stream. However, on this day the stream was narrow, easy to cross.

Where was the access to the coast? The hills rising in front of him seemed to block the way. Crossing the little stream, John sat down in the shade of a grove of willow trees. They were not very tall, but did provide some shade from the early afternoon sun. It was an ideal spot for rest and refreshment. With his supply of fresh bread and some leftover dried meat, he had plenty for a middle-of-the-day stop. While resting he could decide on his next move.

John did not have to wait long. Looking toward the west, in the direction of the mountain range, he saw a rising cloud of dust. As it came closer, he realized he was seeing something new, horses and riders. Moving rapidly they were at the river before John could be on his way. These were Roman soldiers.

To his surprise, they came to a sudden stop, just beyond his resting place. They had stopped to water their horses. Somewhat fearful of this unexpected encounter, John kept silent, sitting still. He had no reason to converse with Israel's enemies. Assuming they would move on, once their horses were watered, John was startled by one of the men coming toward him, obviously their leader.

"Young man, the road north? How is the road north? I cannot help but believe we need to be going more to the northeast. We need to be in Tiberias tonight! None of us have been this far north before and those stupid men at the Caesarea garrison weren't much help. Their directions were confusing. Can you help us?"

John, knowing very little of this northern territory, was hesitant to give directions, but decided to try.

"Sir, I left Nazareth early this morning. I do not live in Galilee and have never been to Tiberias, but the town is just over the ridge from Nazareth, on the inland lake, the Sea of Galilee. On my way north I stopped overnight in a closer town called Nain. It is on the main road to Tiberias.

"Do you see that rounded mountain standing out by itself, the one over to the northeast? Yes, that one. That is named Tabor. There is only one village this side of that hill, the town of Nain. You can be there shortly. In the town there is a widow and her son. They run an inn for travelers, and they can put you on the road to Tiberias. They will give you the right directions. You can depend on it! I'm confident you can reach Tiberias tonight."

"I believe you and I thank you, but I am surprised, your

willingness to help us, we who control your land. Most times I would be distrustful of someone like yourself, but I believe you. I can see it in your face. You are an honest man."

John blushed. "Sir, I think you will find most of us are honest people. We believe in our Lord Yahweh, the one who created us and taught us to do what was right and honest. The idea might be foreign to you, but this is what we believe. If I would be dishonest with you, I would be dishonest with myself. Does that not make sense?"

The officer paused, thought for a moment, and then laughed.

"Young man, you have taught me a good lesson, one I must remember. I am a Centurion, a Roman soldier. I think I am a good one, and I appreciate what is right and honest. Yes, that does make sense. I must learn more about your Yahweh before I leave this land.

"Now, we must be on our way to Tiberias. Once my mission is finished, I will have to return to Jerusalem by way of Caesarea. There is little time for rest these days. Our Procurator will want to hear from me as soon as I return. Is there anything I can do for you?"

"Yes! You said you have come up from Caesarea. I have never traveled this way before and those hills seem to stand in the way. How do I get through them to the coast?"

Again, the Centurion laughed.

"At Megiddo there is a mountain pass. You can't see it until you are almost at the foot of the old fortress. That's why Megiddo was so special, so I have been told. It guards the pass that was so important. Today, of course, there is nothing there. Megiddo is deserted. No, you won't have any trouble getting through. May you have a safe journey! May your Yahweh protect you!"

With that, the officer waved his appreciation and quickly mounted his horse. The soldiers were again on their way, moving rapidly in the direction of Nain. Following John's directions, and with the help of the widow at Nain, they would be in Tiberias by dark.

John was puzzled by the Roman's comment concerning Megiddo. He said it was deserted. How could that be? He had assumed there was a town of Megiddo. If there were no town or village, where would he stay for the night? He really wasn't worried about sleeping outdoors, but this was unknown territory.

He would soon find out. Leaving the banks of the little river, he strode rapidly in the direction of the fortress mound. Moving along the road traveled by the Roman horsemen, he suddenly realized something was missing. It gave him a sense of uneasiness, difficult to define. Finally, he broke stride, paused and stopped. What was it? What was different? What was missing?

There was no one on the road! That was it. There was no one on the road! Sure, there had been the Roman soldiers, but no one else. On every other road John had traveled in his long journey to Galilee he had met people, a number of people, but not here. Since leaving Sarid he had met no one. Was it the time of the year, the time of the day? Or, was it the place, this place called Megiddo? Did his people avoid it? Were they fearful about it, somewhat like the king's place at Samaria? If so, why?

There was only one thing to do. He had to be on his way! He wanted to be there before the sun set; find a place to stay. It was new territory to him and he wanted some security for the night. Surely, there would be someone, some family, perhaps a village not too far away.

There was no one, not a soul at the foot of the mound! The place was, as the Centurion said, deserted. There was an erie silence everywhere he turned. There was only the wind, rattling the palm fronds overhead.

After a brief rest, not quite sure what to do next, John began to climb the hill, curious to see the top of this huge and broad mound. Here and there, protruding from the dirt and weeds, were huge stones, cut stones, stones that had been prepared by some ancient stonemason. These had to be what was left of Solomon's old fortress. If the Scroll records were accurate, hundreds, even thousands of people, had occupied this place.

Solomon had built this enormous frontier city, protecting Israel from foreign invaders. Here he had kept his warriors, his chariots, and his horses. Now, there was nothing left, nothing but a deserted mound of rubble, the ruins of long ago.

Yet, it was not completely deserted! Sitting down on one of the larger stones near the top, John heard the sound of animals. At first, he thought of sheep, but it was not the bleeting of sheep. It was the distinctive sound of goats, lots of goats. Standing up, climbing on to the very top of the hill, John was startled by an amazing sight. Down below, in a center depression, there was a herd of goats. Sitting in the middle of the goats, holding a baby goat in his lap, was a man. Looking up at John, he waved, inviting John to climb down.

"Welcome to Megiddo," he shouted over the noise of the goats. "You are the first visitor we have had in a long time. We welcome you! My friends welcome you!"

As John approached, the man stood up, gently placing the young goat on the grass. Reaching out his hand he introduced himself.

"I am called Josiah, son of Abner. They named me, not for my father who died just before I was born, but for an ancient king who died here at Megiddo, King Josiah. Why, I don't know. I was not born here. Isn't that odd?

"Now that I am old, the only one living here, perhaps that is fitting, odd but fitting. You see, with no one else around I am Josiah, king of Megiddo! I suppose you could say these are my subjects. Actually, they are my friends."

Having given his welcome and explanation, he sat back down, picked up the goat, and invited John to sit nearby.

"Who are you, young man? What brings you to this place? Why in the world did you climb this deserted hill? No one else bothers. No one ever comes near. Tell me about yourself."

"My name is John. I've been visiting in Galilee, and now I am on my way home. I live down near the Salt Sea, east of Jerusalem. Like you, I live in my own little world, alone. But you have what I do not have, your friends. Yet, I am not really alone. Yahweh watches over me and takes care of me, just as he takes care of you."

Josiah was silent for a moment, not knowing what to say in response. How did Yahweh get into this conversation? There was something unusual about this young man, but what?

"Tell me something," he responded. "We are Yahweh's people, his chosen people. I was taught that long ago. The people who lived here and fought here were Yahweh's people. They prayed to Yahweh. They offered sacrifices to Yahweh. They brought their offerings to Yahweh. Now all that is past. We are in bondage. I sit on the ruins of our nation. We are not a special people anymore. We are lost! We have been abandoned!

"I'm sure you saw those Roman horsemen earlier today. It was the sound of conquering powers. They rule our world. Where is Yahweh? At night, when the wind blows across this desolation, I don't hear Yahweh. I hear ghosts, ghosts of a world that no longer exists!"

As Josiah continued to talk, his voice became louder. Pacing back and forth in his small open space, tears began to spill down his face. Finally, he sat back down, buried his face in his hands, shoulders shaking.

It was John's turn to stand up, wondering how to deal with this man's despair.

"Josiah, I know how you feel, because I have wrestled with the same. Even in my young life I have cried out for Yahweh's deliverance. At times I, too, have wondered, 'Where are you, Yahweh?' Why did Yahweh let bad things happen to his chosen ones? When will Yahweh deliver us? When will he help us?

"The prophet Isaiah talked about our people sitting in darkness, and there has been a lot of that. Yet, at the same time, Yahweh gave a promise, repeated over and over again. It is the promise of salvation; that he will deliver us, free us from our enemies. He will send a Deliverer, a Messiah! Josiah, that will happen sooner than you might think.

"As to what happened in the past, many of our people and kings did what was bad. They went astray and our nation suffered.

That was not Yahweh's fault. That was our fault, the fault of the people of Yahweh.

"I know that because Yahweh has called me to help share this message of hope. Believe me! Sure, I don't know how all of this will work out, or when. However, we must be patient, and we must not give up hope. The Messiah will come! I know that is hard to believe, but that is the truth. You can depend on it!"

Josiah looked up, wiped his eyes, staring at John.

"Are you trying to tell me you are a prophet, a prophet of Yahweh, a prophet like Amos or Jeremiah? No! We don't have prophets any more. We don't have a nation any more. There is nothing left, nothing but darkness and despair. We are lost! We are like Megiddo, deserted and desolate and destroyed. Don't talk to me about prophets!"

Taken back by Josiah's outburst, John closed his eyes and prayed. He needed Yahweh's help and he needed it now! How could he deal with this old man's troubles?

There was a long period of silence, no one speaking, but when John opened his eyes, he was touched by what he saw. Josiah's eyes, opened wide, were staring intently at John, eyes not filled with despair, but with longing. John believed this stranger before him was looking desperately for help. He wanted some meaning for his life!

"Josiah," he began. "Tell me about yourself. Where were you born? Where did you grow up? Tell about your family. You said that your father died and you were named, not for him, but Josiah. What about your mother? Did you have brothers and sisters? How did you get here, living alone?"

John knew he had to find some point of contact, something that would reveal the one thing bothering Josiah. If he could get him to talk about his past, he might discover what that might be. With Yahweh's help, he would soon know.

Again, there was a long period of silence, with Josiah staring into the distance, and beyond. John was sure he had touched a long-fogotten memory, but he would have to wait.

"Young man," Josiah blurted. "You ask too many questions!

I'm not sure what you are up to, and I'm not sure I want to talk about my past. It's painful, even thinking about it. Yet, there is something different about you. I don't know what it is, but you are different. Even if you are not a prophet, I believe you want to help.

"You have to travel north, some distance north, in order to reach my home town, where I was born. There was no lovelier village in all of Galilee, the village of Cana. As to its size back then, I was too young to be interested in that. If I recall, there were a lot of houses and several shops. Built on a hill overlooking the Plain of Asochis, the town had to have cisterns for catching the rainwater. The nearest stream was some distance away. I do remember the trees, the olive trees. There were lots of olive trees. Then there were the vineyards. Down in the plains a lot of wheat was grown. To the west, toward the Great Sea, there were forests, both cypress and cedar trees. These were cut for lumber. There were some sheep, but more goats. Goat hair was woven into cloth.

"My father died before I was born. He was a stonemason, one of the best. As such, he was conscripted by Herod and taken down to Caesarea. While there, working on Herod's ampitheatre, some falling stones crushed him. They brought him back home to die. We received nothing for his work!

"After I was born, we were forced to move away, over to Sepporis. My mother's brother lived there and offered to take us in. That went well for a time, but then my two older brothers were ordered into Herod's guard. Both were killed in a skirmish with some rebels fighting against Roman rule. Again, we received nothing. I had no sisters and my mother died in poverty. To Herod, life was cheap!

"I, too, once I was old enough, was ordered to fight for Herod, but I escaped. For several years I lived in Sidon, far up the coast of the Great Sea. I became a sailor and had a number of successful voyages. We all shared in the profits, according to our years and duties. It wasn't much, but it helped keep me alive.

"After more years had passed I became homesick and returned to Cana. Yet, it was not the same. The Romans still ruled the territory, and I learned I was a wanted fugitive, even after all those years. For a time I was hidden by a cousin. I remember he had a son named Nathaniel, about your age I would guess. He really wasn't much fun, always complaining about the future, wondering what would happen to all of us.

"Getting tired of that, despairing of any help for any of us, I left again. This time I was captured and put in Herod's prison on the coast. I would have died there if it hadn't been for a storm. We were forced to work on the breakwater for a harbor, regardless of the weather. It was killing work, but a giant wave washed me out to sea. Luckily, they had released us from our chain, and I was pulled down the coast. Finally, I waded ashore far south of Caesarea.

"Later, I learned I was listed as dead, which was fine with me. At night I worked my way north, until I came to this place, an excellent hiding place. No one knows I am here! Anyway, with my age and long hair and beard, no one would recognize me.

"But, what good is that? I have no family. I live alone, except for my faithful goats. The Romans are still in control. I dare not return to Cana. Our nation is no more. There is no one to stand and fight for our people. Yahweh has deserted us! Now you come, in the face of all that, and talk about hope. What do you know?"

"Josiah, you are not alone. Everywhere I travel I hear your story, people with a lot of heartaches. I know that is no consolation for you, but we are a people hurting. We have to live with that, but we have to live as the people of Yahweh. We have to do our best to help one another, even those we don't like. Yahweh is the Lord of righteousness, and he wants us to do what is right and good. Others might do bad things, but not us!

"Yahweh has promised he will send One to set us free. He will come and help us! I am convinced of that. I ask you to believe this. I am always helped when I pray to Yahweh.

Sometimes it seems he doesn't hear, but he does. You can always speak to him. He will hear and he will help!"

"Young man, I don't know how you can talk with such confidence. You are either mad, or dreaming. How is it you can talk about hope? I've lived a lot longer than you and I can find no reason to hope! Can you prove what you are saying?"

What could he prove? Josiah's query was like cold water in his face. He couldn't prove anything. He had tried to convince Joseph of Arimathea, but he had little to back up his story. Josiah's question was forcing John to look ahead, to the time Yahweh would call him to speak. How could he, an unknown coming out of the desert, get anyone to believe his story? If he couldn't get Josiah to believe him, how could he persuade others? What could he say?

With a plea, a silent prayer to Yahweh, he began:

"Josiah, it is a long story, hard to believe, but a true story. Do you remember what the rabbi told you about a Messiah? You did go to the synogogue when you were young, didn't you? What did he teach you?

"Sure, we heard all those stories, but none of that made any sense, not with Herod's men around. How could Yahweh, or some Messiah, deal with that? Yes, we heard, but we weren't too impressed. Anyway, for us, my family, it went from bad to worse. As far as we were concerned those stories were not real, only make-believe."

"Very well, Josiah, let's start with something that is real, me! Am I real, a real person? When you talk to me, are you talking to the wind, or are you talking to a man? Sure, you know the answer. So, begin with me, the facts of my life, the fact I was born to parents far too old to be having children. That's a matter of record. Others can attest to that. So, why was I born to parents far too old to have children? The answer came from Yahweh himself."

With Josiah now listening intently, narrowed eyes focused on him, John began to tell his story, beginning with his father's encounter with Gabriel. As best he could, he recounted the story of his birth and the birth of his cousin Jesus. He went on to recount Eljah's story of the young Jesus coming to Jerusalem. Omitting much of his life at Tobba, he talked about the Scrolls, his life in the wilderness, his determination to find his cousin, his conversations with Yahweh. Finally. he talked about his trip to Nazareth, his encounters with people all along the way. He told him the story of Bethlehem.

"Josiah, I am on my way back to my wilderness. There I will wait for Yahweh to call me forth, just as he promised to do. How long will I have to wait? I don't know, and Jesus doesn't know, but when that happens, everyone will know. The promised Messiah will come!"

Josiah sat still for a very long time. He was not looking at John. His head was bowed. For a time John thought he might have dozed off.

The sun was setting as he finally looked up, and smiled. Rising on one knee, and then standing erect, he laughed.

"Young man, I said you were either mad or dreaming, but there seems to be one other option, that you are a real prophet. So, if you are a prophet, I must believe what you are telling me! If I believe what you are telling me, it is because of faith; no proof, just faith. Can you believe that? I will have to live by faith!

"Somehow, from the beginning, I knew you were different. I still can't put my finger on it, but you are different. I believe you! I have to believe Yahweh has not deserted us and, someday, will set things straight. That brings back a lot more memories, memories of all those psalms we had to learn in the synogogue, psalms filled with the promises of Yahweh. In his name, I thank you!"

With that, Josiah bowed his head, eyes brimming with tears of joy. Then, at his suggestion, they sat down to eat, sharing bread, meat and fruit. There was little talk. As the darkness moved in, the only sound was the wind rattling the dry palm fronds. There were no ghosts!

# CHAPTER 24

*. . . he went down to Caesarea . . .*

Acts 25:6

As the light of a new day burst across the hill called Megiddo, John was awakened by the sounds of goats, Josiah's goats. It was a muted sound and no goats were to be seen. They had disappeared. John threw aside his blanket, stood up, searching for Josiah and his animals.

Walking slowly across the top of the hill, in the direction of the sound, John came to the edge of a deep ravine. Down below, Josiah was filling his water skin. There was a spring, or, rather, a pool of water. Some of the goats were drinking, while others were climbing up and down.

Seeing John peering down from the crest of the mound, Josiah called out.

"Come down, but be careful. I don't want you to fall. I want you to see this, a marvel of construction, a tunnel."

Making his way down, John was surprised to see ancient steps. Sometime in the past these had been set for a purpose, but he wondered for what reason? If it had been a well, a rope could have been lowered to the water below. However, at the bottom he found the answer. There was not a spring, but as Josiah said, a tunnel. Peering into the darkness, he saw a sliver of light in the far distance. Along the floor of the tunnel there was a stream of water.

"Have you ever seen anything like this?" Josiah asked. "This was dug when Megiddo was a walled city. The spring, the only source of water, was located outside the walls. When enemy forces surrounded the city, their water supply was cut off. So, they dug an underground tunnel to the spring and then covered it with a roof. They could reach the water, but invading forces could not. I heard the story as a child, but no one really believed it.

"At the far end, at the spring, some of the old roofing has fallen in. If you are small and agile, you can climb out that way. That would be my escape route, if any one came looking for me."

"Josiah, you are full of surprises! I am impressed. However, now that this is a new day, I must leave you and your friends. There is a long journey ahead and it is time to go. I trust you will be fine here. Perhaps, someday, you will be able to return to Cana. Surely, Herod's people have forgotten you. Anyway, another Herod is in charge and he seldom travels far from his town north of the Sea of Galilee.

"Remember, Yahweh has not forgotten you. The Messiah will come! I will pray that Yahweh will keep you safe!"

"Young man, how can I thank you for your assurances? You are a prophet! More than that, you are a miracle! You have touched my life. You have changed my life. Now, what can I do for you?"

John smiled, thinking what he might say as he departed.

"You can do good things for other people, as you have for me. I thank you for your hospitality. You welcomed me into your home, and I am grateful.

"I almost forgot! There is one other thing. The people I lived with near the Salt Sea hunt deer. They provide meat for the community and the deerskins are preserved for writing. They become the Scrolls on which the words of Moses and the prophets are written.

"For the most part their arrowheads are made of bone and they become brittle and break. Seldom do they find flint. I have been told there are stone arrowheads in this area, left from an earlier day. Have you seen any? I would like to take some back to those hunters, if it is at all possible. Have you seen any?"

It was Josiah's turn to laugh.

"Why didn't you say so? I have collected hundreds. They are all around us, some you can see easily. Others are hidden in the dirt. I will give you as many as you want."

Josiah was as good as his word. At the top of the mound he filled a leather bag with stones, perfect flint arrowheads. Giving them to John, he thanked him again. Knowing John was determined to be on his way, he made no effort to detain him. Waving his goodbye he headed back down to his goats.

Shaking his head in wonderment, John gathered up his belongings, slung his pack over his shoulder and started down. The next stop would be the coast and the city of Caesarea. Leaving the high mound behind him, he turned west, following the well-traveled gap through the mountain range toward the coast. As he saw it, this was the beginning of the end, the return to his wilderness. There he would wait for Yahweh's call. He hoped it would be soon.

For the first hour of his journey, John was surrounded by hills, the mountain range reaching south from Carmel. However, it was easy walking. He was now traveling over a road that had been worn by many generations. According to the Scrolls, many marching armies had come this way.

Now, the scenery was changing. This road was well traveled, and today was no exception. More than once John had to step aside as horses raced by. He encountered a lot of travelers. There were carts pulled by oxen. A few were guiding their sheep and goats, going to the markets of Caesarea.

John had no idea what he might find in this large seaport. He knew it was, for the most part, occupied by foreigners, a Roman center of government. Would he find any of his people there? Would there be a place of worship, a synagogue? Where could he stay for at least one night before he continued south? There was no need to linger; his wilderness awaited him!

Some distance away from the seaport city, he could see some of the structures standing out against the skyline. There was a stone wall on the inland side of the city. One structure, as he learned later, was a temple, a temple dedicated to Caesar. To his people he was divine. This was a pagan city! However, he was impressed by Roman skills.

Some distance from the city he crossed an aqueduct. It was bringing water down from the mountain range. Built of stone, it carried water into the city. Where the land dropped below the level of the water flow, the aqueduct was supported on stone arches. As John walked alongside, he couldn't help but admire what had been done. Yet, at the same time, he remembered the tunnel at Megiddo, also the water brought to Jerusalem from the pools of Solomon. Stone pipes carved out by his own ancestors carried that water. Yahweh was no respecter of persons. He had given good minds and abilities to all people and all creation should give Yahweh the praise. To bow down before man, or man-made gods, was not only wrong, it was sinful!

Entering the city through the northern gate, John had difficulty moving along the crowded street. There were people everywhere! He had never seen such a variety of clothing, not even in Jerusalem. Continuing along this main thoroughfare he had to step aside when others, especially the Roman soldiers, confronted him. They had little regard for anyone else! Pushing and shoving people out of their way, they did not hesitate to use their long staffs and spears.

Before he knew it, John became the center of their attention, something he had been trying to avoid. Walking slowly, entranced by the goods in the open market, he failed to step aside. A sharp blow on the head sent him sprawling. He could do little but crawl to the side of the road. Reaching his hand to his head, he realized he had been cut. Blood was dripping down his face and into his hand. Digging into his pack, he tried to find a cloth. Dizzy from the brief but traumatic encounter, he had little success. Trying to clear his head, he could do nothing but sit still, hand pressed against the wound.

Suddenly, a warm wet towel was placed against his head. Someone behind him had pulled his hand away, covering his wound.

"Do not move, my friend," was spoken quietly in his right ear.

"We don't want to attract any more attention. In a few minutes we will stand up and move into the shop across the street. I'll give you the support you need."

With the cloth pressed against his head, almost covering his face, John could do little but follow instructions. The unknown rescuer helped him to his feet. Holding John carefully by the arm, he guided him, moving quickly to the other side. Later, after his wound was dressed, he was told they had waited until the street was empty, that is, empty of Roman soldiers. Few saw them as they entered the shop.

"We regret you had such a rude welcome to our city. It could have been worse. We are thankful it was not. Someday Yahweh will deliver us from our enemies. Someday we will be the rulers and they, those pagans, will have to serve us! When the time is right, Yahweh will send a Messiah, even greater than King David."

By now, John could open his eyes and see the one who had come to his rescue. Even though his head was throbbing from the blow, he believed he was in good hands. He did wonder about the man's dress. His tunic was of fine linen, but not belted at the waist. It hung loosely over his shoulder. The Romans called it a toga.

"I thank you, my friend, for helping me, bringing me out of harm's way. I can imagine what those Roman soldiers might have done if they had stayed around, waiting for my reaction. You saved my life! I am grateful for one of our own nation, one willing to risk his own life for a stranger."

His rescuer smiled.

"Would it make any difference if you knew I am not, as you say, 'one of your own nation'? Actually, I am by birth, Greek. My people settled generations ago in the territory of Celicia, far north of here. My parents live in the city of Tarsus, where all the citizens were granted Roman citizenship. The Greek background goes back to Alexander the Great, when he was the conquerer of this part of the world. That's the name they gave me, Alexander.

"My father works in the cloth industry in Tarsus. Although he is getting old, he still helps, sharing his skills with the young workers. It was in Tarsus he and my mother met some of your people. There was a large community of Jewish people living there, also workers in cloth. My parents were intrigued by the worship of Yahweh. Roman and Greek gods did nothing to give them peace or hope. Belief in your Yahweh did! They became proselytes to the Jewish faith, attending worship in the local synagogue.

"When I brought my family south to live and work in Caesarea, we quickly found the Jewish community. All were so helpful and supportive. And isn't that typical of the followers of Yahweh? We try to help friend and stranger alike."

"I can certainly agree with that, in the wonderful way you have helped me! But, tell me, what do you do here? I haven't had a chance to look around. Is this your shop?"

"Yes," Alexander replied. "Selling cloth from Tarsus has given me a good business. In spite of the Roman taxes, we do well. The Roman leaders and the local authorities know me as an honest man, an asset to the city. They also know I am a Roman citizen. Herod the Great would have seen things differently, I'm sure, but he is dead. Thanks be to Yahweh!"

"Alexander, you amaze me. Yahweh amazes me. He provides miracles, and you, my friend, are one of those. That's the story of my life. I, too, am one of Yahweh's miracles. My name itself, is indicative of that, rather unusual for a son of Abraham. My name is John!"

With that, John put out his hand in greeting. Then, still feeling the effects of his accident, dug into his pack, looking for the medicine for pain. Asking for a cup of water, he downed it quickly; confident he would feel better soon. However, for the moment, the buzzing in his head would not go away. It hurt! He asked if he could rest.

"Forgive me, John, for ignoring your needs. Let me help you upstairs. There is an open room overlooking the harbor. There you can rest. We will let you have time to recover. When you feel better we will share an evening meal. Once you are up, I want my family to meet you. Also, your name interests me. Hopefully, we can talk about that.

"This dressing and the salve I've put on it, has stopped the bleeding. I believe you will be fine."

Alexander helped John up the stairs. It was cooler, just what John needed; sea breezes blowing in from the west. Almost before Alexander reached the bottom of the stairs, John was asleep.

The sun was setting as John opened his eyes. Sitting up, he witnessed something he had never seen before. It was the sun sinking slowly into the Great Sea. The sun was huge, but he could look directly into its orange glow! Yet, almost before he could savor its beauty, it was gone. The blue of the broad expanse of water was replaced with streaks of gray, rapidly turning darker.

Another sight was just as intriguing, a ship heading away from the coast into the setting sun. As with the large orange orb of light, it was there and then, before he could blink, it was gone! It had disappeared, as though it had dropped off the edge of the sea. How could that be? Where did it go? He would have to ask his host.

Watching, conscious of both the beauty before him and the quietness surrounding him, he felt a sense of calm and wellbeing. Yahweh had created a marvelous world. In spite of the evil he had encountered, Yahweh watched over his own.

Somewhat reluctant to stand, wondering if his dizziness would return, he lay back down and closed his eyes. In a moment he heard the voice of Yahweh.

"John, you need to share your story with these people. Do not hesitate to speak. They will be helped. Yes, you were in trouble with those soldiers, but I sent Alexander to help you. Now, before you leave Caesarea, tell them what is to come. Those who hear you will wonder. Some will have their doubts. Some will not believe you. However, the day will come when they will remember and rejoice."

Silence! The next thing he heard was Alexander's footsteps on the stairs.

"I've come to check on you. I trust you have rested well, and I sure hope you are feeling better. If you are, we will share our evening meal downstairs. My family is looking forward to meeting you! Also, we have invited some of our friends to drop by. They've heard of your accident and are distressed."

Alexander helped John to his feet, making sure he could manage the stairs. Thankful for the rest and Yahweh's assurance, John was ready to try. He did feel better, much better!

The throbbing in his head had gone, and he was hungry.

Alexander's wife, Clarice, met them at the foot of the stairs.

"Welcome to our home! Alexander has shared your story with me, your terrible encounter with those men. We are so sorry, but thankful it was no worse. They could have taken you away, put you in prison. Thay sort of thing does happen, and we can do nothing about it. But, enough of that! You are safe now, and we want you to eat with us. It is not much, but we trust it will be sufficient."

The meal was more than sufficient. There was an abundance of fruits and nuts. The bread was fresh. The unfamiliar was the meat, fish. According to Alexander, these were cuts from very large fish caught offshore. Clarice explained the process, soaking the meat in oil, and then broiling over an open fire. Sometimes, as she explained, they prepared the fish as a stew.

John was offered several possibilities of drink. Standard was the wine, but John declined. Believing the local water might be suspect, he was inclined to drink from his own supply. Yet, at the insistence of his hosts he did accept the goat's milk. It had been cooled and was tasty.

Alexander and Clarice had two children, a boy and a girl. The daughter, Dorcus, was a beautiful young lady. Approaching maturity, she did her best to act "grown-up," wanting to impress John with her social graces. Beyond that, she wasted little time with the meal, asking to be excused as soon as it was proper. She and her friends would gather at a neighbor's home. After a brief visit all would be accompanied home. It was not safe to be out, unescorted, after dark.

The son, Rufus, was younger. He was much more interested in asking John about his travels. He kept asking about "adventures" in far-off places John might have visited. He wanted to be a sailor, the captain of a ship. He would sail on the Great Sea, carrying grain, oil and wine to distant ports.

In response, John asked about the ships sailing out of the harbor at Caesarea. From the upper level he had seen a ship drop out of sight. How was that possible?

Alexander did his best to explain.

"There was a time when people were afraid to sail out beyond sight of land. Some are still afraid to do so. They think ships drop off the edge of a flat surface. They do not trust the truth, that our world is not flat. Greeks, knowledgeable in such things know the world is not flat, but curved. Ships do not fall off an edge. They simply disappear from sight as they travel west, going beyond our line of vision. I know it looks as though they fall, but they don't."

Laughing, he reminded John that his people, the Jews, would never make good sailors. They still thought the world was flat. Also, out there, over the edge, there were great fish to devour those who dared go out. There was water above, in the firmament, and water below. One should stay where Yahweh had put them, on dry land! Water, especially the sea, was foreign territory.

"But, John, tell us something about yourself. You said your

name John was unusual. Also, you said you are one of Yahweh's miracles. What did you mean? We would like to learn more, where you have been and where you're going. We don't mean to pry, but would you satisfy our curiosity?"

"Yes, I am one of Yahweh's miracles and I'm confident there is more to come. Let me begin with my birth on the outskirts of Jerusalem. My father, Zechariah, was a priest, taking his turn in the Temple worship. He married the daughter of a priest. Her name was Elizabeth. However, their marriage was missing one thing, children. They wanted children and they prayed about it, but no children. Finally, after they were quite old, and had given up any hope of having children, one of Yahweh's messengers came to my father in the Temple. As he was offering the Evening Sacrifice, he surprised him with the prediction Elizabeth would have a child. He should be named John!

"Because my father wouldn't believe him, insisting this messenger was talking to the wrong person, Gabriel told him he would lose his voice until the baby was born.

"I was that child. He went on to say I would, someday, be a prophet of Yahweh. It happened, just as the messenger said. After my birth, and after they took me to the Temple on the eighth day, my mother said I would be named, not after my father, but John. It was then my father spoke again, for the first time, saying, 'He will be named John.'

"Also, this same Gabriel visited a young woman of Galilee, my mother's cousin. He made an unbelievable promise, that Yahweh had chosen her to carry a child, Yahweh's child. He would be born to her. He told her, also, that she should travel all the way to my parent's home; find my father speechless, proving he was telling the truth! She did! It was true! Her story is a miracle. I have been visiting her in Nazareth, and am now on my way back south."

Alexander and Clarice were spellbound; both with eyes and mouths open wide. Even Rufus was quiet, waiting to hear more.

Alexander was the first to speak.

"John, this is unbelievable! We do not doubt your word,

but we have never heard anything like this before. There must be more, if what you are telling us is so. What about the young woman from Galilee? What comes next for you? If Yahweh's hand is in all this, where will you go now? What is it he wants you to do?"

"Alexander, Yahweh has suggested I share this story with his people living here in Caesarea. The Sabbath begins tonight and that means you will go to the synagogue tomorrow. Isn't that right?"

With Alexander's nod, John went on.

"It will be good to gather with Yahweh's people. If you don't object, and if the head of the synagogue agrees, I will tell the whole story then. Some might not believe what I will be saying, but Yahweh wants me to speak. Again, that might be difficult for you to believe, but he does talk to me. He has done so a number of times. In fact, it was his suggestion I travel all the way to Nazareth. And, would you believe it! Yahweh also told me he sent you to rescue me!"

Alexander stared even harder. It had to be true! Something had told him to go look out into the street. He had been busy with one of his workers, rearranging supplies in the very back of his shop. He had no time for or intention of looking outside; until something, or someone, had told him do so. It was only then he spotted John sprawled on the other side of the road.

"John, I have to admit it. I'm trembling! I have never felt this way before. I hardly know what to say. I am not an old man, but I have encountered a lot in my life. I have been told many things, but nothing like this! Yahweh's hand is being held over us, all of us. This is holy ground!"

The silence was intense! No one had anything to say, not until Dorcus dashed into the room, returning from her visit to her friend's home.

"Why is everyone so quiet? What's going on? Let me tell you the latest news, what I heard tonight. You won't believe what people are saying . . . ."

Before she could finish, little brother Rufus grabbed her by the arm, pulling her toward the upper terrace.

"Come on sis. These old people are talking about other things; so let me hear the latest gossip. Anyway, do I have something to tell you!"

Rufus could hardly wait until they were at the top of the stairs. On the open terrace, he tried to share what he had heard. John was a prophet, Yahweh's prophet! Yahweh had spoken to him! Also, John's father had been a priest in the Temple in Jerusalem. One of Yahweh's own messengers had spoken to him!

Dorcas didn't know whether to believe her little brother, or not. Surely, Rufus couldn't make up such a tale. What was going on downstairs?

"Rufus, if you are trying to fool me with a story like that, I'll throw you in the ocean tomorrow; no, not tomorrow. That's the Sabbath. I'll do it the next day."

"Sis, I'm telling you the truth. Let's go back down. You'll see I'm not lying or making up a story."

By the time they came down, some of the neighbors had arrived. They had heard about the accident and they wanted to check, even though it was getting late. Alexander welcomed them, introduced them to John, but said little about his story. That would have to wait until the Sabbath.

Clarice served sweet cakes and nuts, offering small cups of wine to their guests. One by one they expressed thanks for John's narrow escape and then said their "good-nights." It was getting late! They would see the family and their guest tomorrow in the synagogue. It was time to extinguish the lamps and go to bed.

Dorcas wanted to stay up and hear John's story, what her little brother had shared with her, but her mother would have none of that.

"Dorcas, you should have stayed in this evening. You will just have to wait until we go to the synagogue tomorrow. John will be invited to speak. Now, let's get to bed!"

Dorcas wanted to object, but knew better. She headed for her room without saying "good night."

John was offered the couch on the upper terrace and he was soon asleep. It had been quite a day!

The synagogue was an imposing structure. Built in the traditional style of post and lintel, it represented the finest in Jewish architecture. Double doors were set between stone columns. The walls of cut stone, brown in color, had aged well. It was an old structure, one of the first synagogues of Israel. Wealthy Jews had insisted on the best for worship and instruction. There was no way of missing the synagogue. Carved into each of the two doors was a seven-branched lamp stand, a reminder of an ancient and important festival, the Dedication of Lights.

Inside, there was very little in the way of furniture. The one essential piece was the Torah shrine. Some called it an Ark. The Torah Scrolls, the Scrolls of the Law, as well as a number of prophetic Scrolls, were kept in the shrine, hidden from the people by a screen. The leaders of the synagogue sat in front of the screen. Next to the shrine was a raised podium, the Bema. This was for the reading of the lessons. Rows of stone benches lined three sides. Worshippers sat around the walls, the women separated from the men. Here, in Caesarea, the right side wall was reserved for the women. The children were gathered together in a side room, the synagogue's library. Here, as schedules permitted, the children were taught the rudiments of the faith and the history of their nation.

As they entered, the head of the synagogue greeted each family. He presided at the Assembly and had the task of assigning readers of the Scrolls. Alexander made sure John would have an opportunity to speak, as well as read a passage of his own choosing. He introduced him as the son of the elderly priest Zechariah, now deceased.

"Jarah, this young man, according to what he has told us, is one of Yahweh's special people, called to be a prophet. It is hard for me to believe, but it must be so! We have to hear what he has to say."

Jarah remembered what Alexander would not have known, the story circulated years earlier, the story of an old priest and an elderly wife becoming the parents of a child, a child promised by one of Yahweh's messenger.

"Alexander, I can't believe this is the same person, the son born to the priest Zechariah! That was the talk of our people, both in Jerusalem and beyond. The last news we heard was the death of his mother. After that there was nothing. Later I did hear from one man, someone who traveled a lot in his trading business. He was told the father and son had moved away. If this young man is that John, we must hear what he has to tell us! I agree. I will call upon him to speak."

For several minutes there was both noise and movement. Those gathered for worship wanted to greet one another, sharing their news. There was always concern for those unable to attend. Jarah, the current head, had the wisdom to give time for those moments of socializing. It made for better response once the worship began. Sometimes, when the reader or the speaker failed to excite those present, or talked too long, there was grumbling, as well as nodding heads. Today Jarah wanted all to be in an attentive mood. Alexander had stirred his interest in their visitor and he was curious. This young man, as he remembered the story, would deserve everyone's full attention. Also, Jarah being a good judge of character knew there was something unique about their guest.

At his nod, the Hazzin, the minister, raised his arms for silence, beginning with the traditional Shema: "Hear, O Israel, the Lord thy Yahweh is one!" All responded with their murmuring of agreement, their "Amen." Several brief prayers by another leader, known as the messenger, followed.

Then Jarah stood again, introducing Alexander's guest.

"We are honored to have in our midst the son of Zechariah, one of Yahweh's renowned priests. Some of you may recall the story coming out of Jerusalem years ago, almost twenty years ago. Zechariah, up in years, approaching retirement, was offering the Evening Sacrifice in the Temple. Suddenly one of Yahweh's messengers appeared to him, predicting his wife Elizabeth, also quite elderly, far too old to have children, would give birth to a son. They would give him the name John.

"This son would grow up to be one of Yahweh's prophets. As a prophet he would turn Yahweh's people back to him, preparing the way for Yahweh's Anointed. He is here, in our midst, John, the son of Zechariah! We are honored to have him worshipping with us. He will read and speak Yahweh's word. I trust all of you will give him your undivided attention!"

As Jarah sat down and as John stood up there were gasps, muted sounds coming from those present. All were wondering what this might mean. Surely, this young man could not be one of Yahweh's prophets! He was too young! He comes to us out of nowhere. Can he prove he is that John born years before? Some looked at him in anticipation. Others were doubtful, skeptical.

John was well aware of the range of attitudes. He had seen that before. Silently he lifted up his prayer to Yahweh: "You have told me to speak, share my story. Help me!"

After giving his audience time to relax, John began with words of appreciation. He was grateful to Alexander and his family for their kindness and hospitality. It was an honor to be given the opportunity to speak in this renowned synagogue.

Then, bowing before Jarah and the elders, he asked for the Scroll of the prophet Isaiah. With Jarah's nod of approval, the Hazzan went behind the screen and retrieved the requested Scroll. With a formal bow he handed it to John. One could see his questioning expression, but he had to honor Jarah's orders. With the precious Scroll in John's hands he sat down. Did this one know what he was holding in his hands? Would he handle it with the utmost care?

Carefully, John opened the Scroll, resting it on the Bema, and began to read:

> *Again the Lord spoke to Ahaz, 'Ask a sign of the Lord your Yahweh; let it be deep as Sheol or high as heaven.' But Ahaz said, 'I will not ask, and I will not*

> *put the Lord to the test.' And he said, 'Hear then O House of David! Is it too little for you to weary men, that you weary my Yahweh also? Therefore the Lord himself will give you a sign. Behold, A young woman shall conceive and bear a son, and shall call his name Immanuel.*

Pausing for a moment, John unrolled until he came to the next place he wanted to share. He resumed his reading:

> *There shall come forth a shoot*
> *from the stump of Jesse,*
> *and a branch shall grow out of his roots,*
> *and the Spirit of the Lord shall rest upon him,*
> *the spirit of wisdom and understanding,*
> *the spirit of counsel and might, the spirit of knowledge and the fear of the Lord.*
> *And his delight shall be in the fear of the Lord.*

Again, John paused, closed the Scroll and handed it back to the Hazzan with a warm word of thanks. John's care of what was a holy treasure impressed the Hazzan! In spite of his doubts, he was ready to listen to what this stranger might say.

Sitting down, as was the custom, John began to speak.

"Friends, sons and daughters of Abraham, proselytes, I am confident of your knowledge of Yahweh's word given through Moses and the prophets. The great prophet Jeremiah echoed Isaiah's words I have just read, as he spoke in terms of a new covenant, a new agreement with Yahweh's people. Jeremiah said: 'Behold the days are coming' when all this will take place. He, too, spoke of a branch, a righteous Branch, one who will execute justice and righteous in our land. When he comes Judah will be saved and all Israel will live in safety.

"In his first book Moses explains why a new day is coming. He records the history of Yahweh's beginning creation, Yahweh creating men and women, men and women who disobeyed

Yahweh. Yet, in that recorded history, you find Yahweh's words of promise. He would send a Deliverer, a Saviour, one who would bring Yahweh's people back to him. He would do so when he was ready, not before.

"This one would be Yahweh's Anointed, one who would set things straight, one who would do what our first parents would not do, obey Yahweh. He would bring light into our darkness. He would set us free from our enemies and from our bondage to sin. He would restore us as his people. He would bring us peace, this righteous Branch of Yahweh."

Stopping for a moment, trying to sense the group's reaction to what he had said, he was startled by a demanding response. One of the men stood up, pointing his finger at John.

"What do you know about freedom and peace? We don't have any peace. Those hated Romans rule our land and us. They tell me they treated you rather harshly yesterday, knocking you to the ground. They would do the same for any one of us, if we stepped out of line. Yahweh may have made a promise, and I don't doubt that, but it has never been fulfilled. Most likely it will never be fulfilled in our lifetime."

With others voicing their individual beliefs and questions, Jarah called for quiet, reminding those present they were out-of-order. The rules of the synagogue were clear. The speaker must not be interrupted. He was sure John would answer any questions, once he was through speaking.

Even with Jarah's admonition it took several minutes to calm everyone, and for him to nod to John, asking him to proceed.

"My friends, I have raised those same doubts, many times. Most likely I will ask them again. We suffer greatly under these pagan Romans. I, like you, yearn for the day, the Day of the Lord. I ask Yahweh that it might be soon. But, we also know Yahweh's times and ways are not ours. He will act when he is ready to act. In fact, he already has, many times over.

"For me it began with Yahweh's messenger, Gabriel, speaking to my father in the Temple. His wife, my mother, Elizabeth, would bear a son, even in her old age. Because my father didn't believe Yahweh could do that he was struck dumb for nine months. He did not speak again until I was circumcised on the eighth day and given the name John. Temple records confirm that truth.

"Just about the same time, this messenger Gabriel spoke to a young woman of Nazareth, a woman who had known no man, just as Isaiah described it. This young woman, named Mary, descended from David, was betrothed to a man named Joseph, also of the lineage of David. He told her she would bear a son, not Joseph's son, but Yahweh's son!"

Before he could continue there was another outcry of voices, voices raised in both wonder and doubt. How could this be? "The Lord our Yahweh is one!"

"Please!" John asked. "Let me finish. Then I will try to answer you. In order to convince both Joseph and Mary Yahweh's hand was in this, Gabriel suggested they go ahead with the wedding and then travel to see my mother Elizabeth and meet my father who was unable to speak. This Mary and my mother were cousins, both expecting baby boys at that time. All that worked out as Gabriel had told them.

"I was born in my parents home. Mary's son, named Jesus as instructed by Gabriel, was born in Bethlehem, Joseph's hometown. By order of the Roman government they had returned to Bethlehem for Caesar's census. Yahweh's messengers, or angels announced his birth to plain, ordinary shepherds. I have been through Bethlehem and have talked with one of those shepherds. He confirms that story!

"Also, I have traveled to Nazareth and have met Mary, my kinswoman, and her first born, Jesus. He knows what lies ahead, but like myself, has not been given the time or place when we will tell the world about him. Yahweh has called me to be the one who goes before him, to prepare his way. Remember! Isaiah talks of that also. Then my task will be done.

"There is more, but these are the basic facts. Yahweh has spared my life, protected me in time of peril and danger, and has told me to be patient. In spite of my doubts, questions and failures, he will not let me go until my work is done. Now, I am on my way south, returning to the wilderness near the Salt Sea. There I will study, pray and wait, waiting until Yahweh calls me. Then, and only then, you and the entire world will know!

"Trust me, I would rather return to my family home, marry and raise a family. I would rather Yahweh leave me alone, but he will not. Jesus's mother Mary tells me I will suffer much, as her son will suffer much. That is not welcome news. However, I have been called. As I have spoken to you, I will speak again."

John bowed before the crowd; waiting for the reactions he knew would come. He could do no more. He had spoken as Yahweh had instructed. The rest was up to him! As soon as the Sabbath was over he would leave for his wilderness.

It was the middle of the day before the final prayers and dismissal were given. Overwhelmed by the many questions, John did his best to respond. A few stalked out, shaking their heads in disbelief. Most stayed, hopeful of finding some thread they could grasp and keep for the days ahead.

John was convincing to many. A few knew it! Yahweh had spoken through his prophet John! The Romans would not have the final word. Yahweh would set them free!

At last they left the synagogue, returning to Alexander's home. Before leaving, Jarah expressed his appreciation for John's presence and participation.

"Only time will tell, my friend. I believe you are sincere and are telling the truth. That gives me hope. However, we will have to wait and see. May Yahweh watch over you as you return to your home."

Yes, thought John, time will tell, Yahweh's time.

# CHAPTER 25

*. . . who has believed our message,
and to whom has the arm
of the Lord been revealed?*

Isaiah 53:1

Alexander and Clarice begged John to stay longer. There was much they wanted him to see. He had to visit Herod's amphitheater facing the Great Sea. It was an impressive structure, even though a pagan one.

Actually, they did not want him to leave! It was as simple as that. He had entered into their lives in a very meaningful way! Thinking of all the possibilities they overwhelmed him with suggestions. Why did he have to leave? Surely he could wait for Yahweh's call in Caesarea!

John understood. He knew their reluctance to see him go. He had brought a new and exciting dimension into their lives, something to give them hope. If he left, would that hope disappear with him? They simply wanted to be able to touch this prophet of Yahweh. In their minds, he was the assurance of the presence of Yahweh.

John did his best to comfort them. His departure would not take away their hope. He would be with them in spirit. Above all, they must not forget Yahweh's promises. Yahweh would be ever present. When he was ready he would set them free!

At the evening family gathering, after the sun was down,

they shared light refreshments. The Sabbath was over. No one was really hungry, but coming together was important. Besides John, one other visitor was present, the head of the synagogue, Jarah. Knowing John would be leaving soon, possibly tomorrow, he asked Alexander if he could come by.

They wanted to know more about John and his family. What happened to his father? Was he alive or dead? Where had they lived after leaving Jerusalem. Would he be willing to share his growing up with them? The big question, of course, was Yahweh! When did Yahweh speak first to John, calling him as a prophet?

John was honored by their interest and promised to do his best in filling in the gaps. Laughingly, he warned them this might take all night.

"After my mother died, my father was never the same. They had lived together so many years. She was only sixteen when they were married. It was a beautiful love affair, and they were very close all those years. My father's Division leader, Jonathan, out of respect for my father, tried his best to support his continuing service in the Temple, but it was impossible. He and the elders decided it was best for us to leave Jerusalem and live near the Salt Sea. The weather was milder and Jonathan had good friends in the village of Tobba. It was part of the Essene community, but not under such strict and rigid rules like Qumran."

"Yes," responded Jorah, "I have heard of Qumran. It is different! The men are most pietistic, some former priests of the Temple. I had a friend, a rabbi, who left Caesarea for Qumran. I suppose he is still there, writing or copying the Scrolls about the sons of Light. To me, he was a fanatic!"

John replied. "There is a degree of pietism, far beyond what we might desire, but they have a collection of Scrolls that are priceless.

"Anyway, on our way down to the Salt Sea, just before we reached the fork in the road, we were attacked by robbers. My father died of shock and I was wounded trying to resist, and almost died. I was carried to Tobba on a threshing sled.

"I don't know what I thought I could do in resistance. At the time I was only fourteen and had no weapon. It was a terrible disaster, and it took a long time for my wounds to heal. As you might imagine, I was devastated. My parents were dead and the friends I had known were back in Jerusalem.

I was certain Yahweh had deserted me. If I was to be a prophet of Yahweh, as my father had said at my naming, Yahweh wasn't helping, or so I thought!

"You asked about Yahweh speaking to me. He spoke first through his messenger Gabriel as my father was offering that Evening Sacrifice. He spoke through my father at my naming. Strange as it might sound, he spoke to me through an Egyptian seer. At an earlier age, when I was twelve, I had run away from the Temple, ending up in the lower city of Jerusalem. His men rescued me and brought me back. The night I was lost, cold and afraid, this Egyptian said he saw in me a holy person, and bowed down before me.

"However, at Tobba I decided to forget about Yahweh. He hadn't helped me when I was in trouble and I was not going to think about him. If he wanted me, he would have to make the first move! Wasn't that something, a fourteen, no, a fifteen year old, talking like that?

"Yet, the longer I stayed in Tobba, the more I was convinced I had to get away, live alone, prepare myself for Yahweh's call. When you think about it, no one can forget him! That was a most difficult time for me. I'm sure my age had much to do with that, but it was more than age. It was that deep down inner feeling of lostness. I needed a renewed hope!

The leader of Tobba, a man by the name of Tobiah, was of tremendous help. Once he sensed my dilemma and my determination, he not only introduced me to the leaders at Qumran, he obtained their permission for me to study the Scrolls, the words of both Moses and the prophets. This I did, until I knew them by heart. I was convinced this was Yahweh's way of speaking to me, calling to prepare me for what he wanted in the years to come.

"Along with my studies I learned to hunt deer. Some of the men of Tobba were deer hunters. They provided meat for their village and deerskins for the Scrolls of Qumran. Would you believe it! I was good at making bows and excellent arrows. On my first hunt, I killed a deer. That part I did not like, but I knew the importance of the Scrolls. They would hold, someday, Yahweh's word!"

It was Rufus' turn to interrupt.

"Did you really go deer hunting? I wish I could do that! Father, why can't I go with John? He says he is going back to where he lived. He could teach me to hunt deer. Please! At least let me visit him sometime. You have men taking cloth as far south as Hebron. That shouldn't be too far from Tobba."

Alexander smiled. "No, son, not this time. When you are older you might have a chance to make that visit, but not now. Let's hear the rest of John's story."

John, after asking for a drink of water, went on with his story.

"As I continued to read, and as I learned the skills of wilderness living, I made my plans to leave. I would go out on my own, waiting for Yahweh to speak. The villagers knew I would leave, but not when. Late one night I slipped out into Yahweh's wilderness.

"It was during that period Yahweh did speak directly to me, several times. No need to go into all the details, but he was preparing me for what would come. Also, it was Yahweh's suggestion I travel to Nazareth. There I met Jesus and his mother Mary. Joseph had died, but there were four other sons, half-brothers to Jesus. They had a sister, but she had married and was living in nearby Bethlehem. I thought that was very interesting, in that Jesus was born in Bethlehem. Of course this was a different town, a small village in the ancient territory of Zebulon. There was another girl who had lived with them for a while, but had moved south to live with her aunt and uncle in Sepphoris. Her parents had died when she was quite young. Mary and Joseph helped raise her. Mary thought of her as a daughter.

"It was a long journey, something I had never done before, but a meaningful visit. Yahweh was right. It was a trip I had to take. You could write a book about my adventures along the way, but those things are not that important. As I indicated at the synagogue, I did speak to one of the shepherd of Bethlehem on my way north.

"By the way, I've passed my nineteenth birthday. I feel as though I am getting old! Surely, Yahweh's call will come soon! I must return to my wilderness and wait. With all my heart I believe that will come soon. We still sit in darkness and bondage and I pray for deliverance. Be assured, my friends. He will come! For myself, I would like to stay longer, but I cannot!"

It was getting late, and all could see John was tired. It had been a full day! With a word of appreciation, Jarah excused himself and slipped out the door. One of Alexander's employees would escort him home.

John wished he could have been more persuasive. He knew Jarah had his doubts, yet wanted to believe. He was certain Jarah would soon know, with all doubts removed. He would be a strong believer!

John climbed the stairs to his room overlooking the Great Sea. In the quietness of the night he could hear the sounds of the waves breaking against the shore and the breakwater of the harbor. He thought of Josiah, telling about his father's accident and death, working with those heavy stones of Caesarea, as well as his own escape during a violent storm. He had been washed out to sea, escaping his imprisonment at Herod's hands. Caesarea was no place to live, not for those looking for the redemption of Israel. This was enemy territory!

With those thoughts running through his head, John fell asleep. Not even the raucous cries of the sea gulls could keep him awake! One thing was nice, very nice. The breeze blowing in off the ocean made sleeping a pleasure, a far cry from the heat of his wilderness.

The next morning the entire family was up. All wanted to see John before he left. His presence in their home had been a memorable one. They would miss him! After sharing grapes and dried ocean fish, along with some leftover bread, the women gave John a hug.

This time Dorcus was bold enough to kiss him, whispering she wished he would come back! Alexander shook his hand, sending him off with Rufus. He would escort John to the edge of the city and to the coastal road to Joppa.

"You will enjoy the coastal route, John. It is a part of the Plain of Sharon, a rather flat plain holding a variety of plant life. The flowers are beautiful at this time of the year. However, stay on the road. It will be safer! May Yahweh keep you in his care!" Alexander was concerned.

With all the family present, as well as the employees working in Alexander's shop, plus several servants, it was quite a sendoff. People passing by stopped to see what was happening. The merchant was a prominent resident of Caesarea and any special activity at his shop always attracted attention.

Rufus talked all the way to the edge of the city, to the southern gate. He kept repeating his wishes. Someday he would come south and find John. Then they could go hunting together!

"Rufus, I wish you could go with me, but that is not possible, not now. There is one thing you could do, learn to make bows and arrows. If you ever come south you would already know that much. That's not easy, but don't give up. You can do it! Surely, you can find someone in this large city capable of teaching you. Here is a gift, arrowheads for your first arrows."

With that, he picked out three stones from his pack, handing them over. With his encouragement he hoped Rufus would do what he suggested. He patted him on the back, waved goodbye and headed down the road. Joppa should be his next stop, if he stayed on the coastal road. The Plain of Sharon beckoned him on.

It was a nice day and the road was easy to follow. There was no questioning the route. There were plenty of travelers heading in the same direction. There were just as many heading toward Caesarea, and John had to avoid running into those he met. He wanted no more encounters with Roman soldiers. This was no time for hostile confrontations.

In the distance, on his left, the ground was rather flat. There were several swampy areas, small pools of standing water, and lots of sand. Yet, there was much fertile soil where grain was growing profusely. Not too far down the road, where the land was just a little higher, there were flowers, beautiful flowers, roses, lilies and crocus. He could see women harvesting the flowers, probably for the Caesarea markets.

As he walked along he remembered the Scrolls. There was one attributed to King Solomon, called the Song of Solomon. John remembered questioning that one, with its vivid description of lovers, especially the description of the young woman. When he first read it he couldn't help but think of Debra, but he knew there was something else. It had to do with Yahweh's love for Israel. He was confident of that. What really made him think of the Scroll was the sight of the flowers, one called the Rose of Sharon.

However, there was another reference, one from Isaiah! In it Isaiah suggests the desert will blossom like the crocus. It would see the majesty of Carmel and Sharon. Above that, the people would see the glory of the Lord, the majesty of Yahweh. That was the importance of it all! How did it read?

> *"Say to those who of a fearful heart, 'Be strong, fear not! Behold, your Yahweh will come with vengeance, With the recompense of Yahweh. He will come and save you!"*

Of course! Salvation belongs to Yahweh! It had always been

so, and it will be so again! He will come and save us! Hope in Yahweh! John's spirits were lifted again. Any sadness over leaving his Caesarea friends was being pushed aside. Yahweh was with him. He would take care of him. He would be with him, all the way!

Yet, he had to admit, the sadness did not go away easily. As John walked along, moving farther on into unknown territory, his thoughts were troubling. Now that he was alone again, he realized he had been given little time for any meaningful reflection on the events of recent days. He had been so very busy in Nazareth! Trying to deal with Jesus' responses and ideas, trying to relate his own pre-conceived ideas to what Jesus had said, he realized they were far apart on their thinking. That disturbed him.

At Megiddo he had wrestled with Josiah's concerns, with few moments for evaluating what he had experienced along the way. Then, in Caesarea, his accident, his interaction with the Jewish community, his speaking at the synagogue worship and the late night sharing of his own story, prevented sorting out personal feelings. He had met wonderful and friendly people, but now that was behind him! How did all that fit together? What good had been accomplished? When would he ever see clearly what Yahweh wanted, where Yahweh was leading him? It was another one of those times in his life when he was wrestling with his calling. There was a sense of uneasiness as he walked southward.

At a mid-afternoon rest stop on the outskirts of the coastal town of Apollonia, he sat in the shade of a few scrubby trees, still disturbed and troubled. He had stopped earlier when the sun was directly overhead, but that was very brief. He was not hungry and was in no mood for lingering along the way. With no familiar or friendly faces nearby, he was lonely. The world confronting him was not his world.

He had been told Apollonia was a pagan community, the town having been built in honor of the Greek sun god Apollo. They didn't worship Yahweh. They worshipped the sun! They didn't worship the Creator. They worshipped his creation. That was wrong!

Deep down, he wished such people would leave this land. Centuries before, the Philistines had occupied the coastal area and the descendents of Abraham had little success in driving them out. To John this was alien territory and he wanted to move on as rapidly as possible. As he was always prone to do, he looked up, watching the soaring eagles overhead. How he wished he could move like that, effortless and swiftly! How he wished he could leave the bad and the evil behind him, shutting his eyes to all that was wrong! He missed his family! He missed his friends!

An encounter with several young men and women turning into the coastal town didn't help. They were laughing and they laughed at John. His clothes stood out in contrast to theirs. One called him a hill-country peasant. As they moved off, the men were teasing and fondling the girls. In response, the girls lifted their skirts high and danced away, daring the men to catch them. Their immodest behavior disturbed John. It was indecent!

The birds didn't help either! To John, the sea gulls were both ugly and noisy. Unfamiliar with their habits, he had thrown out crumbs for the few songbirds perched in the scrubby trees. They had little chance as the sea gulls swooped in, fighting over the food. Not far away there were several ravens, adding their voices of protest, some trying to chase a nearby hawk from their territory.

For John it was time for some reassurance, some word of encouragement. Looking about him, he spotted a grove of trees some distance inland. It stood at the beginning of a gradual rise toward a higher range of hills. Moving in that direction he looked for an out-of-the-way spot. He wanted to hear from Yahweh, now!

The trees were farther away than anticipated. He walked a good hour before arriving at the place he had seen from the coastal road. By now it was late in the afternoon. On the way he met two shepherds moving their few sheep northward. Other than that the area seemed to be deserted. However, in the center of the grove of trees there was an old shelter, a ragged tent stretched over a pole held up with several wood braces. Underneath, there smoldered a small fire. There was no blaze, only a curl of smoke rising from under the shelter. No one was in sight.

John walked carefully and slowly around the grove. Each time around he moved closer in. After circling several times he concluded there was no person anywhere in the vicinity. Finally, he found what he wanted, the largest of the cedar trees, a short distance from the fire. Sitting down and resting his back against the tree, John closed his eyes and waited.

He did not have to wait long. Yahweh was speaking:

"John," Yahweh called. "Your life has not been an easy one. As my son said, it will never be an easy one. You will suffer, for my sake. He will suffer. I know you miss your friends in Tobba, and those friends you have met in your travels. You miss your Nazareth family. It was most difficult for you to leave them. Some you will never see again. However, be assured. You have touched the lives of many people. You have helped many people. You will do so again.

"But, John, you are mine! You belong to me. I love you, as I love my own son. I am with you and will ever be with you. Even in those times of great difficulty, in times of danger, even when you might believe I have deserted you, I will be present. You have been called to speak for me! There is a most important task I will ask of you and I know you will accept. Trust me, John! I am Yahweh, your Yahweh! I know your life has been difficult, but I am with you! Do not despair!"

When John opened his eyes he realized he was not alone. An old woman was standing nearby, watching. Once she saw that John's eyes were open, she spoke:

"Young man, I hope you have some food in that big pack of yours. It will soon be dark and I am hungry. I have been searching through those hills all day, with little to show for it. I did catch one small creature, a badger, but it will have to be skinned and cooked. Even the locusts have disappeared. Are you hungry?"

John was amused by the woman's concern for food. Surely, small as she was, she would not require much. He was glad he did have some food to share.

"This 'young man', to whom you are speaking, has a name. My name is John. I will be happy to share what I have with you. May I ask, what you are called?"

"My name is not that important, young John, but if you insist, my name is Naamah. You might not know it, but King Rehoboam's mother was named Naamah. It is a good name! Now, what do you have we can eat?"

John dug into his pack; found the bread given him that morning in Caesarea. Along with the bread, there were several figs, carefully packed in his small clay pot. He opened a soft pouch of leather containing pieces of dried meat. That, along with the water from his skin, provided a meal. With the food items spread out on a large piece of cloth, he had to stop Naamah's hand reaching greedily for the food.

"We do not eat until we have thanked Yahweh for these gifts of food! The eyes of all wait upon thee, O Lord, and you give us what we need, when you will. We thank you for this food and drink, the gifts of your blessing...."

With bowed head, John prayed, hoping Naamah would know why. After his "So be it" he was hardly prepared for her response.

"You are John! You are that John, called of Yahweh before you were born. I was present at your naming. Your father Zechariah and your mother Elizabeth said you would be called John! You would not be given your father's name. You didn't know it, but that upset a lot of people. Everyone was saying that after your miraculous birth, your mother, being far too old to have any more children, and your aged father not expected to live many more years, should preserve the family name. No one seemed to understand your being named John.

"But I know! Yahweh created you. Your birth and your life are miracles. He will not let you go! You will die for him!"

John could not believe what he was hearing, this unexpected witness from his past. What was she doing here, and why had she come? What did she have to do with him? How would she know anything at all about what would happen to him?

"Tell me, Naamah, why were you in Jerusalem when I was born? How did it happen you were present at my naming? Did my parents know you? Surely, you have no idea as to what will happen to me!"

"John, you ask too many questions!" Laughingly, she insisted they eat first. Then she would talk.

He was impressed. This small, shriveled-up old woman had quite an appetite. She consumed most of the food set out on the cloth. She ate all the figs. There was little left for him, only one strip of dried deer meat, and a small piece of bread. There was a little more in his pack, but he hesitated to bring it out. However, she seemed to be satisfied with the meal and John was more concerned to hear what she might reveal to him. It was time to talk!

"Naamah, where is your home? Do you live nearby? I assume this is your tent, so perhaps you are on a journey. Where are you going? Tell me, what do you know concerning what will happen to me?"

"John, be patient! My home, the place of my birth, is up there, in the hill country, the town of Gibeon. It has quite a history. Joshua came there and protected it, a large city at the time. That's where the battle with the Amorite kings took place, when the sun stood still. That gave Joshua time to win the battle and save the city. Yahweh was watching over his people, don't you think?"

Sure, John remembered the history found in the Scrolls of Qumran. How did this woman know that, and what did that have to do with his other questions.

"Yes, Naamah, Yahweh was watching over his people. I have read the Scrolls, but how does that relate to my birth and naming?"

"Gibeon is not too far from Jerusalem. My father made the journey many times, carrying oil, grain and skins to the market. At one time he trapped pigeons for the Temple sacrifices. He raised them, mostly pure white. The priests liked that!

"He visited the Temple many times, bringing the birds as well as coming to worship. My father was a very religious man! He knew your father Zechariah, and when the news was out about the baby's birth, a lot of people wanted to be present for the naming. He was getting pretty old, but he was there, and we went with him. You didn't know it, but you were a celebrity."

"But," asked John, "what about the rest, the thing you were saying about my death? How would you know anything about my present life, or my future? It makes no sense."

"That comes from what your father said that day. He said you would be a prophet; you would go before the Lord to prepare his way. You should know the rest, what Isaiah predicted. The Suffering Servant would suffer and die. He would be cut off from the land of the living. His enemies will destroy him, as well as those who are with him. You should know that! You, too, will suffer and die! It is in the stars, the clouds, and the wind sweeping across the land. No, our people don't know that, would not understand that, but I do. Yahweh has spoken. I see him in the flames of my fire, in the stars moving across the night sky, in the winds that come howling down from the north in those winter storms. I see him in the Temple Scrolls. They speak the truth!"

Naamah stood up as she was talking, almost screaming her final words, tears streaming down her face.

John could not believe what he was hearing.

"Do you mean to tell me, you have read the Scrolls, the Books of Moses, the prophets? Where did you learn to read? How were you, a woman, permitted to handle the Scrolls? I lived in and out of the Temple for several years, and no female was permitted that."

"John, you forget what I said about my father. He was a very religious man. He had many friends, both priests and Pharisees. He did a lot of favors for them and he persuaded those friends to let him borrow copies of the Scrolls at night, returning them in the early hours before dawn. He could read and he taught me to read.

"No one learned his secret and he was able to share with me the words, the prophetic words of Yahweh. No, I have not had that opportunity since his death, but I remember! It is in the Scrolls. It is in the fire, the clouds, the stars, and the wind, the cold winds! You will suffer and die!"

With John trying to grasp what she had been saying, what she had been shouting, she continued.

"There is one question for which I have no answer. Who is this Lord, this Suffering One, and when will he come? If I knew that I would know when you will die!"

With that Naamah sat down, wiped her eyes on her rough garment and bowed her head, waiting.

Finally, with John saying nothing in response, she looked up at him in anticipation and hope. John's eyes were staring into the little fire she had stirred up earlier. It was getting dark now and the shadows were flickering across his face, a face filled with wonder.

"You are right, woman. Yahweh has called me to serve him, to go before the one who is to come. He is the Messiah, the promised one. He is Yahweh's own son, but born of a woman. I have met her and I have met him!"

Now, it was Naamah's turn to stare, to catch her breath in wonder.

"John, who is this Messiah? Where is he now? When will we see and know him? Who is his mother? I cannot grasp all you are saying! Yahweh is Lord, not man!"

"Naamah, you speak of miracles, the miracle of my birth, the prediction made by Yahweh's messenger. Surely, you can believe what I am telling. The Messiah's name is Jesus. He lives with his mother Mary in Nazareth. His earthly father is dead, but before he died they had other children, four boys and one girl. I have just come from there. I tell you the truth!

"The rest I cannot answer, the time for the beginning of his ministry. Only Yahweh knows. It may be soon. It may be several years. I do not know. I do know this. Yahweh has instructed me to return south, to where I have been living, to wait for his call.

"I will live alone, in the wilderness, waiting. When Yahweh is ready Jesus will come and I will be there to tell you and all our people about him. I will prepare the way. Once that is done, my task will be finished. What happens after that? I do not know! That is in Yahweh's hands."

"John, my son, I am getting old. I have trouble with all you have told me. My story I know quite well. The rest disturbs me, excites me, and fills me with wonder, but that is enough. I am tired and I must sleep. I invite you to sleep here, near the fire. We will be safe. I do know this, Yahweh watches over his own!"

Naamah stopped talking, found her blanket, pulled it over her and, without another word, went to sleep. John was ready to do the same, but sleep did not come easily. He knew he would die, someday, but when? After what seemed to be a very long time, he slept, still wondering what lay ahead. Only Yahweh had the answer, and he wasn't speaking, not tonight!

# CHAPTER 26

*. . . I am utterly spent and crushed;
I groan because of the tumult of my heart . . .*
                                    Psalms 38:8

John awakened once. The fire had gone out and a light rain was falling. Trying not to disturb the woman Naamah, he moved under the shelter of the old tent. As before, he had difficulty getting to sleep. There were so many things running through his mind. Naamah's predictions were both puzzling and disturbing. He knew death would come someday, but why was she dwelling on that? Yahweh had assured him of his presence, direction and purpose. Yahweh would not let him go, not until the Messiah had come in power and glory! The rest would have to wait. Yahweh would see to that! He would have to be patient. Now, he needed to get back to sleep!

With daylight creeping into John's face, he yawned and sat up. It was cooler and rather damp. A steady, light rain was falling. Outside the tent area, the ground was really wet. Beyond the clearing, the grasses were tipped with droplets of water. The weather had changed drastically, unusual for this time of the year! Even the birds were silent.

Looking around, John realized Naamah had disappeared. She was nowhere in sight. He called her name, but there was no response. She was not in the grove of trees. He noticed she had added several pieces of wood to the small fire, but these were now hot coals. Stretched over the heat was a green stick frame holding the skinned badger. It would cook slowly, as long as the fire would last. She did have food for her next meal!

Not knowing when Naamah might return, John was determined to be on his way. The rain would be uncomfortable, but bearable. It was time to continue south. There was that town not too far down the coast, the town of Joppa. Perhaps he could sleep indoors!

Josiah had talked about this town. After being washed out to sea at Caesarea, he had made his way ashore just above of the harbor at Joppa. As he related his adventures to John, he described the town, located on a rocky rise that projected out into the Great Sea. The rock helped form a natural harbor that opened only on the north side. It was enough to protect ships from the stormy sea.

The old name of the town was Japho, Josiah told him, a name that meant "beauty," a name related to some ancient goddess. Josiah remembered it as a beautiful town, but also an old town. In the rebuilding of the Temple, cedar logs were floated down as far as Joppa, all the way from Lebanon, then hauled overland to Jerusalem. John would stop in Joppa.

Gathering up his blanket and dishes, ready to put these away in his pack, he found a surprise. Sitting on top of his pack was a coin, a silver coin, a shekel! Its size and weight were impressive. The inscriptions bore the imprint of King Herod. The design was a tripod holding a bowl. John was familiar with the coins of similar design, those exchanged for Temple coins, but those were smaller in size and made of bronze. This was a valuable coin! Obviously, Naamah had left the coin for John, but why? Not wanting to offend her, he pushed the coin down inside and under his blanket. Lifting his pack to his shoulders, he stepped out into the morning rain.

Realizing he had some distance to travel, he wasted little time in moving westward toward the Great Sea. He was not hungry. In fact, there was a hard knot in his stomach. It was an uneasy feeling. Also, he was thirsty, quite thirsty. He drank more than usual from his skin. It would have to be refilled, soon!

Shortly, he was back on the main road, moving rapidly. With the misty, rainy weather, he was sure there would be few travelers moving in either direction.

He was right. The main road was empty. He did have to stand aside once, waiting for a troop of horsemen to pass. At least there was no dust! They paid no attention to him and were soon out of sight. He had the road to himself. With nothing to distract him, he began to think of the best route home to his wilderness. Again, he had to rely on what he had been told by those who had traveled this way in the past. Knowing he would soon turn more to the east, he had two choices. Both would take him from Joppa through a smaller village, Lydda. From there he could go directly east toward Jerusalem, or travel more to the southeast through Bethlehem.

John wasn't quite sure why, but he still had no desire to enter Jerusalem. He was reluctant to seek out old friends. Perhaps the memories were too painful! He preferred Bethlehem. He would have good news for Shemuel and his mother Tamar. Perhaps Shemuel's uncle had already forwarded the price of their home in Samaria!

From Bethlehem, he could take the old donkey path directly toward the Salt Sea. That would save the longer walk near Hebron. From what he had been told, it was a steep and rugged trail, but John knew he could climb up or down with the best!

It was noon when he entered Joppa. By now his cloak was soaking wet. The rain had penetrated to his tunic and that, too, was quite damp. He needed some dry clothes. Stopping at the nearest shop, he asked directions to the nearest inn.

The shop owner chuckled.

"That's a good one. You want an inn? There are no inns in Joppa, young man. There is a barracks down by the dock, but you don't want that one. It is filthy! And, the sailors, if there are any ashore now, are filthy. They would cut your throat for that pack you're carrying. Take my advice and stay away.

"There is a man living south of the harbor, just on the edge of town. His name is Simon. Simon the Tanner we call him. That's his business. Thanks be to the gods! His business is farther south, where the wind blows the terrible smell away from the town. Anyway, Simon is a good man, always ready to help a stranger. If he can't put you up for the night, he will find someone who can. He can also find you some dry clothes. Looks as though you need something dry to wear. You must have been on the road a long time. You are wet! My dear mother would always fuss when I got wet. 'You will get sick and die if you aren't careful' . . . . . 'Get out of the rain!' she would say."

As John turned to leave, the man called after him.

"Tell Simon that I sent you, that old Reuben sent you. He will help you!"

John thanked him for his advice and followed his directions to the home of Simon the Tanner. He was wet, soaking wet. Also, he was beginning to feel most uncomfortable. The knot in his stomach would not go away. The breeze blowing off the Great Sea made it worse. He shivered with something new, a sudden chill. His face was flushed. His forehead was warm, too warm! It was a miserable feeling, something John had never experienced before. He was sick!

Beginning to stumble, he came to the house the shopkeeper had recommended, the home of the man called Simon. Knocking on the closed door, he waited. It seemed no one would ever answer, but, finally, the door was opened. Peering out through the cracked opening was a woman, obviously suspicious of this stranger at her door.

"What do you want? My husband Simon is not home yet and I don't know you! You are a stranger and I cannot let you in. If you want something from us, you will have to wait until he comes home. Now be on your way!"

With that, she started to close the door. She was not going to help him and John needed help, now! Already beginning to feel faint, he called out:

"The shopkeeper Reuben sent me here. He said Simon would help me. I am wet and have a chill! Could you help me?"

This time the door was opened wider. Simon's wife stepped outside, looking intently at John.

"Why didn't you say so in the first place, that Reuben sent you? He would never send anyone he did not trust. Whoever you are, come in and sit down. My, you do look sick! I'm not sure what I can do, but my husband will be home soon."

With her help, John entered the front courtyard, looking for a place to sit. There were two benches and a small table just inside. Above them were a trellis and a green vine. It would provide shade on a sunny day.

John could move no farther, almost collapsing before he reached the nearest bench. Sitting as still as he could, he leaned forward on the table, cradling his head on his arms. He did not know it, but he passed out, totally unaware of his surroundings.

When John opened his eyes, he found himself lying on a couch. Looking out an open archway he could see blue sky and the water of the Great Sea. The rain had stopped and the sun was out, but low in the western sky. It was late afternoon. He had been unconscious a long time.

He did feel a little better, although he had a bitter taste on his tongue. Someone had forced medicine into his mouth! From what he could tell, it tasted like that provided by Debra's mother. If that was it, it should be working! He felt lightheaded, but the hurt in his stomach had eased off.

Closing his eyes he was content to rest. He knew that was important. How many times had he told others the same? He would have to be patient. It would take time for healing. Confident of his recovery, he dozed off again.

Shortly before the afternoon sun disappeared into the sea, John heard steps coming up from below. He realized his couch was on the roof of the house. It was partially enclosed and covered. At the sound of steps John tried to sit up, but fell back, exhausted. It was too soon for that.

The man entering the roof space had to be Simon. John

caught the faint smell of hides. This man was a tanner! Not only that, he was a man, a big man, a large man, a tall man. He was big! He reminded John of the man Joseph, the one who trained donkeys and horses and camels on the Mount of Olives. Few men were that large.

Simon came right to the point.

"Sir, you are sick, sick with a fever! You are fortunate old Reuben sent you to my door. Yahweh was watching over you! I'm convinced he sent me home early, so that I could give you the medicine. Here, in Joppa, I've learned what to do when fevers come. In fact, I'm one of the few men in this area able to help with these coastal fevers. You will be better soon. You can depend on Simon . . . and Yahweh!"

Again, John tried to sit up, but was unable. He did find enough strength to voice his appreciation.

"I want to thank you, sir. You and your wife were most kind to take me in, a stranger. I also want to thank the shopkeeper Reuben. I don't know what I would have done, if he had not given me directions to your home! Yes, I am convinced Yahweh's hand was in this, too! He does watch over his own!"

John had to pause. Those few sentences sapped all his strength. He tried to take a deep breath, but with little success. His head was spinning! He felt sick! He felt the perspiration popping out on his forehead. He wanted to throw up, but could not.

Simon remained silent and waited. He knew John would feel better soon. His medicine was good medicine and this stranger was young. He would recover!

Several minutes went by before John could continue, but he was determined! He had to let Simon know Yahweh's hand was, indeed, in this matter, along with Simon's skills.

"My name is John, son of Zechariah. He was a priest and served many years in the Temple, almost up to the time of his death. Growing up in that area, near and in Jerusalem, I learned the true worship of Yahweh! He is good!

"Also, and you may not believe this, Yahweh has called me

and is preparing me for a special task. He is not ready for me to die! I'm certain he did send you home early. I'm convinced I was directed to your home and to you, because you did have what I needed, the proper medicine."

That was as far as he could go. He shivered. The chills had returned and this time he knew he would be sick, really sick!

Simon realized John's needs and lifted him to a sitting position. He placed a large clay pot between his legs and held his head. He wondered about Yahweh's hand in this stranger's life, but that would have to wait. The fever seemed to be worse than he first thought.

John thought his vomiting would never stop. He knew there was nothing left in his stomach, but he could not stop the retching which brought nothing up. Finally, it was over and Simon helped him lie down. Exhausted, he was content to shut out the present and sleep.

The night was one he would never forget, worse than the night he was carted from the Jericho road fork to Tobba. Several times he tried to vomit, with little results. Simon came and went, going up and down the stairs any number of times. John was sure he was not far from his side for any length of time. At some point he thought he heard Simon praying, asking for mercy for John. Was that for real, or was he dreaming? He was not sure.

Just before the first hint of dawn, John fell into a deep sleep. The vomiting was over and the fever seemed to be abating. Simon made sure he was properly covered with a light blanket and left him. As he saw it, the worst was over. He would let John sleep, undisturbed.

John was quite unaware of the passage of time. He slept through the whole day! When he finally opened his eyes, it was dark again. Thinking he had slept only a short time, he waited for the light of dawn to burst across the sea. Yet, the sunlight did not come as expected and that was puzzling. How could that be? When would the new day begin?

Struggling to clear his head, trying to make sense of the time, he attempted to sit up. It was not easy, but he made it. At least the nausea was gone and he actually felt hungry. It was more thirst than hunger, but he knew he was better, much better. Yet, he made no effort to stand. That, he believed, would not be wise. He would need help!

Help arrived as Simon came up the stairs, carrying a small lamp for light. Delighted to see John sitting up he grinned and laughed.

"Young John, you have proved the point. I am a good doctor! You are better, much better. I can see that! Simon only asks you to give him a good recommendation!

"But, I am joking. You know, I'm sure, as I know; Yahweh is the one to be recommended! He has been watching over you, day and night. We thank him for answering our prayers! Now we are to thank him for this tray of food my wife has fixed, just for you. I have brought you a cup of the best wine, as well as a bowl of the best broth, along with a loaf of freshly baked, unleavened bread. My wife, Serah, is noted for her fish broth, the best around! It is time for you to receive some nourishment, to regain your strength."

Placing the tray next to John, he waited. He wanted to make sure John would be able to feed himself.

John was embarrassed and hesitant. How could he tell Simon he did not drink wine, even, as Simon described it, "the best wine"? The broth was another matter. The tantalizing smell was overwhelming. He was ready to eat!

"Simon, my friend, I am most grateful for all you have done for me. I can hardly wait to devour this broth. The odor is wonderful and I'm sure it will be tasty. However, I do not drink wine. Could I have some water, instead?"

Taken back by John's reaction to the wine, Simon was silent for several minutes. How could he persuade this young man he needed the wine to help settle his stomach? It was only a small cup, more like medicine than strong drink, and Simon was confident John needed it.

"John, hear me out. Apparently you believe you should not drink wine, and I approve of your choice. I admire your decision. However, I want you to drink this! It will be good for your stomach and you need it. It will be like medicine, something to help you regain your strength. You said you are convinced Yahweh was watching over you, and I believe you.

"You have to remember Yahweh's creation included the fruit of the vine, providing it for good. Sure, misuse of wine is bad, but he makes possible the good. We would not have wine at all, except for Yahweh's hand in the matter."

With that he picked up the cup, thrust it into John's hand and, like a father dealing with his child, spoke forcefully, "Now drink this!"

Simon wasn't sure he had said the right thing, but he was certain the wine would benefit John. He had never had to explain before, but he knew he was right. The wine would help!

It was John's turn to pause, silent. Simon had a point. Yahweh was lord of all, the creator of all things. Misuse was not to be blamed on Yahweh. And Simon was to be trusted! He was convinced of that. He lifted the cup, closed his eyes, and drank. He shivered, not from any chill, but from the unexpected tasty flavor of the wine. He had to admit the taste was not that bad.

Again Simon laughed.

"That is good! You have obeyed the doctor's orders and you will soon be well. Can you handle that delicious broth by yourself, or do you need some help?"

With John's "yes" to handling the food, Simon turned to go down the steps.

"You may not realize it but you slept for a full day. Now it is night again, but not late. When you finish eating we will have time to talk. If that is too tiring, we will let you sleep and talk tomorrow. Another night's rest will do wonders!"

Left alone, John wasted little time. The bowl of broth and the unleavened bread soon disappeared, his hunger satisfied. That left only one question. Was he strong enough to stand and walk?

Looking about him, he saw that Simon had left a stout staff by the couch. How wise to think of that! He knew that sooner or later John would try to get up. Simon was both smart and caring!

Feeling better, he was ready to try. With the staff in hand he pulled himself up. His efforts brought perspiration to his forehead, but his stomach felt so much better. The wine had helped!

His next effort centered on walking, moving about. Leaning heavily on the staff, he shuffled slowly to the parapet on the western side, where it faced the sea. Darkness prevented him seeing the water, but he could hear the noise of the waves crashing against the breakwater. It was a sound distasteful to John, something difficult to explain. He realized he had grown up far from the Great Sea, and this was unfamiliar. Yet, it was more than that. He remembered the many references found in the Psalms, references to the fearful depths of the sea. At one place the psalmist had said: "Out of the depths I cry to thee, O Lord!", asking for deliverance. At this moment in his life, that was his need, deliverance! He desperately needed both direction and assurance for the days ahead. When would Yahweh get on with it, what he desired of him? Why did Yahweh let him go through all this?

Trying to close his ears to that constant, penetrating sound, John lifted up a silent prayer. "Yahweh, help me!"

As he closed his eyes and waited, he heard no voice. Instead, he saw a light, a brilliant light, a light focused on a Scroll. It was one of the Scrolls Tobiah had given him to read, a Scroll containing some of the Psalms. He was back in the library in Tobba!

> *Let the sea roar, and all that fills it;*
> *the world and those who dwell in it!*
> *Let the floods clap their hands;*
> *Let the hills sing for joy together before the Lord,*
> *for he comes to judge the earth.*

*He will judge the world with righteousness!*

It had to be! Yahweh had spoken! It was his word of assurance. The sea was part of Yahweh's world and he was in control. "John," he told himself, "let Yahweh do it his way and in his own time!"

Deep in thought he failed to hear Simon climbing the stairs, and was startled to hear his voice!

"Well, my young man, you are regaining your strength! I am relieved. There were times I had my doubts, wondering if you would pull through. I should have known better. Yahweh does work wonders. The medicine worked and our prayers have been answered! Now, do you feel up to going down the stairs? It will be a bit warmer there and my wife is anxious to see you. Ever since you arrived, she has been fretting over you, ashamed she did not let you in as soon as you knocked at our door."

"Sir, your wife should never feel ashamed. I was a stranger and she was right to be cautious. Yes, I think I can handle the stairs. I'll lean on the staff and ask you to be by my side. I'm sure we will do just fine."

Slowly, carefully, they moved down, pausing for a moment at each step. This was no time to hurry or invite a fall, and John wanted to avoid any more nausea. Upsetting his stomach was the last thing he needed.

Serah was waiting at the foot of the stairs. She reached out to John, and helped him toward one of the leather-covered couches. Simon the Tanner had furnished his home with the best! At the end of the couch was a small table and on it was a cup of goat's milk. Next to the cup were several sweet cakes.

"John, I hope you are up to some nourishment! If those sweet cakes are too much, I'll heat some more broth. Begin with the milk. It will be good for you and I believe you will like it."

She was doing her best to be of help. Simon had shared with her John's initial comments about himself and now she wanted to hear more. Could it be that this young man was truly chosen of Yahweh? Both of them, husband and wife, were faithful to their religion and this was important! Yahweh was their Lord and they wanted to be certain this one was being truthful. They were hopeful!

John thanked her and sipped the milk. He wanted to try that first, before getting to the cakes. He would take one thing at a time. The milk was good. He drank all of it and felt better. His stomach seemed to have settled down and the milk helped. After a bit he tried one of the small sweet cakes. It, too, went down well.

He was now ready to continue sharing his story with these gracious people. They deserved to hear what Yahweh was about to do! It was time to talk!

"I'm not sure how long I can talk this evening, but I will do my best. First of all I want to thank both of you, for what you have done for me. I'm confident you saved my life. You have taken me in, a complete stranger, cared for me, helped me through a most difficult time. For that I am most grateful!

"As to what I said yesterday . . . or the day before . . . I've lost track of time . . . I was telling Simon that Yahweh is not only good in watching out over us, but Yahweh has, indeed, called me to a special task. He will not let me go, or let me die until that work is done.

"Let me explain. I introduced myself to you, Simon, as John, son of a Temple priest named Zechariah. Living here, on the Great Sea, you probably never heard of him, but he served for many, many years in the Division of Abijah. Just about 20 years ago he was on duty, offering the Evening Sacrifice. While standing at the altar, a messenger of Yahweh came and spoke to him, telling him his wife Elizabeth would give birth to a baby boy. My father Zechariah didn't believe him and told him so. He reminded him old people couldn't have babies! He and my mother were quite elderly at the time, far beyond the age for having children.

"This messenger of Yahweh, Gabriel, insisted it would happen. Provoked by my father's refusal to believe him, he told him he would be speechless. He would not be able to talk again until I was born. Also, in sharing Yahweh's plan for my parents, he said I would be named John. It happened! It turned out just as predicted. All this is a matter of record and can be confirmed by many people, including Jonathan, the Division head.

"Since that time, both of my parents have died, but at my birth my father spoke of Yahweh's plans for me, plans which Gabriel had shared with him that night in the Temple. I would be a prophet of Yahweh, of the Most High Lord! Yahweh would send a Savior, his Messiah, his Anointed One and, when he was ready to appear, I would be the one to go before him, to prepare his way.

"There's much more to the story, but the most important part, and the most startling, centers on him, the Messiah. He would come, Yahweh's own son, born of woman, just as the prophet Isaiah predicted centuries ago. He has come! He is here, living far to the north. I have met him, talked with him.

"You see, this same Gabriel, Yahweh's messenger, went to a young woman of Nazareth, far away, up in the territory of Galilee, telling her she would be the mother of Yahweh's son. She accepted that, married a carpenter named Joseph, came with him to Bethlehem during Caesar's census, and gave birth to that son. It was not Joseph's son, but Yahweh's son! In keeping with Gabriel's instruction, they named him Jesus, which meant he would be our savior.

"In order to convince Mary, the child's mother, and Joseph, all this was true, Gabriel sent them to my parents' home, while I was still in my mother's womb. My mother and this Mary were cousins. It was a long journey, but a necessary one.

"They found Elizabeth, my mother, and Zechariah, my father, as promised. My father could not speak! It was true! Others can confirm that.

"Now, for several years, I have been living in the wilderness down near the Salt Sea, receiving messages from Yahweh himself. Several weeks ago he told me I should travel to Nazareth, and meet his son, Jesus. This I have done and I am now on the way back down to my wilderness home. There I must wait, waiting for the time Yahweh will send me out to declare his coming, the Messiah's coming. He will deliver us from our enemies! We will be free! Yahweh will save us!"

John stopped, his voice beginning to weaken. He could not go on.

It was just as well. Simon and Serah were looking at each other and staring at John. Simon's mouth was open, but there was no sound. Then he began to shake his head from side to side, as in disbelief. This was too much, too much to understand!

Serah sat quietly, hands folded tightly in her lap. Then Simon stood up, pacing back and forth. Going to a rear window facing the Great Sea, he stood for a long time, peering into the darkness.

Suddenly, turning to their guest, he began to question John.

"You are saying that Yahweh's promised Messiah has come, the one the prophet's talked about centuries ago? Is that right? You have seen him, talked with him? Is that right? Now, you are waiting for Yahweh to use you to tell our people about him? Is that right?"

"Yes, Simon, that is right. I know it is hard to believe, to accept. Everywhere I have gone, people have questioned me, doubted me, but not everyone. My story has touched the lives of a number of strangers I have met in my travels north. Recently I met a man living alone on the ruins of Megiddo. He was lonely, without any hope, doubting Yahweh at every turn. He now believes. His life has been changed, transformed. He now lives in hope, waiting for all this to happen, and it will happen! That is the one thing that gives meaning to my life.

"I cannot blame you if you think I am crazy, or out of my mind. Everything I have told you seems unbelievable. I know that. Yet, I know what I am saying is true! My life has been filled with miracles, Yahweh's miracles! One miracle was you, saving my life!"

"Young man, I hope you are right!"

Simon hardly knew what to say. He kept repeating himself.

"I hope you are right! . . . I hope you are right! . . . I hope you are right!"

Little more was said that evening. Simon helped John back up the stairs, seeing him settled down for the night. Making sure he was fine, he left him, wishing for him a good night's rest. Down below Serah was still sitting, staring into the distance, deep in thought. The one thing running through her mind was something very simple, but quite profound. Yahweh had sent a miracle into their lives! She did not understand it. She had no idea how it would work out. She wasn't sure she could believe what she had heard. She did know one thing. Their faith, always a vital part of their lives, had been given a new dimension, hope!

It was amazing! Looking out the open window facing the Great Sea, she gasped at the sight. The night sky was filled with stars, far brighter than she could ever remember. Suddenly, one of the brightest rose swiftly from the south, and disappeared far over the sea. Was it an omen, or a sign? In faith and, now, in hope, she was positive. It was a sign, a good sign!

When Simon came back down the stairs, he startled Serah with his reaction to what they had heard.

"This John is not crazy. He was sent to us for a purpose. I don't understand it. I can't see how I can believe it, but I am convinced. Yahweh's hand is in this.

"If ever our world needed a savior, it is now. We have to believe that John is right, that the Messiah has come, and will come to us!"

With that, telling Serah it was time to sleep, Simon closed his eyes, bowed his head and with heart-filled emotion, said,

"Yahweh, thank you!"

# CHAPTER 27

*. . . and the glory of the Lord shall be revealed . . .*

Isaiah 40:5

When John awoke, the only sound was the seawater breaking against the rocks. The house was quiet. Sitting up, he waited. As the sun was up, he assumed Simon was at his work. Serah should be in the house, but there was no response to his call; perhaps she had gone to the market. He would have to try the steps on his own.

Standing was easier this morning. He could move about with no dizziness. His fever was gone. Although still weak, he believed his recovery was assured. It would take time to regain his full strength, but each day would bring improvement. It was time to think about leaving. As always, he would miss new friends, and these two were special! They had been Yahweh's instruments in rescuing him. His life had been in their hands. He would never forget them!

Not only that, he sensed something unique about Simon and Serah. He couldn't put his finger on it, but he felt sure Yahweh would use them again. Their faith and trust in Yahweh was evident, quite strong! They would be a blessing to others.

He realized that the strict keepers of the Law would see things differently. Tanners were considered by some to be "unclean." Anyone working with tabooed animals was "unclean."

In most places they had to live outside the town. Apparently that was not the case in Joppa. Simon and Serah did live on the outskirts of the village, but, according to the shop owner, Simon was well respected.

Anyway, enough of that, John told himself. It was time to try the stairs. The staff helped give support as he went down, successfully! He was right. No one was in the house. Serah had disappeared. John moved through the large room where they had talked the night before, on through an open door to a rear courtyard. From this position he could look down on the waters of the Great Sea. For one who had grown up far from the sea, it was an awesome sight. To the west, as far as he could see, there was nothing but water, lots of water! Finding a vantage point, he was content to sit and watch. In the distance, almost out of sight, a small sailing vessel was approaching the Joppa harbor. It seemed to take forever, as it angled back and forth, catching the wind in its sail.

Fascinated by the boat's progress, John did not hear Serah until she spoke.

"Good morning, John! It is so good to see you up and out. I trust you slept well?"

Serah's question was an opportunity for John to express his gratitude again.

"Yes, Serah, I slept well! You have taken such good care of me. Your delicious food has renewed my strength and a good night's rest has been a blessing. Through you and Simon, Yahweh has provided all I needed in this sudden illness. I thank you!

"I do need to improve my hearing. In the wilderness, hearing the slightest sound was important, especially when we were hunting deer. Sitting here and watching that ship coming in, I did not hear you come out of the house."

"Deer hunting? What's this about deer hunting? Simon gets deer hides from time to time. Hunters bring them in to sell. Where in the world did you go deer hunting? You told us about living in that wilderness, but we didn't think it had anything to do with hunting for animals. You amaze me!"

"I'll be glad to share my experiences, if we have time before I leave. As I said last evening, I'm on my way back to my wilderness home. I feel I should not delay. As soon as I am strong enough to travel, I must go. My time is drawing near!"

Serah was perplexed. She had listened intently to everything this young stranger had said, but there was more. It was evident in his eyes, in the way he looked as he spoke. Here was a person transfixed by something far beyond her ability to comprehend. She shivered! Miracles were difficult to grasp. It was time to change the subject.

"Simon goes to work quite early. Sometimes he leaves home before daylight. He has to make sure everything is ready when his workers arrive. The tanning pit water is cold in the morning, and he insists on heating it for the first washing. Warm water gets rid of the dirt and dried blood. Also, it makes it much easier to remove the hair. That's the first thing he does each morning. He lights the fires.

"Also, today is the day to meet Tabitha. She lives on the other side of Joppa, but is seldom home. Everyday she is busy, looking out for people, those who need assistance. Food, clothing, medicine; whatever is needed, she tries to provide. If she doesn't have it, you can be sure she will find it."

Serah chuckled.

"The rich people of Joppa hate to see her coming! They know what she wants, money! Yet, they are willing to help her. With her around they don't have to deal with such problems. I hate to say it, but the rich don't care for the poor. Most could care less!

"Anyway, Tabitha will be checking on Simon's workers today, asking about their families. He tries to pay decent wages, but one can do only so much. She asks a lot of questions. She wants to know about any special needs. Do the children have enough clothes? Is there enough food for everyone? Is there any illness at home?"

"Serah, I would like to meet this lady," John responded. "She must be a good daughter of Abraham!"

"I'm not so sure about Abraham, but she is a faithful follower of Yahweh. She, like so many of us, looks forward to the redemption of Israel. Yahweh's promises mean a lot to all of us.

"I'm sure she would like to meet you, John. You have given us hope, far more than we would have ever expected. If what you are saying is true, we will soon see the dawn of the Day of the Lord! We pray you are right!"

"Serah, believe me! The time is drawing near. He will come, Yahweh's son! He will come! We will be delivered from our enemies. We will have freedom and peace. Yahweh will restore our nation. Israel will be great again. And, be assured, the wicked will be punished!

"However, for the moment, I need to regain my strength. I need some exercise. At least I could move about. Would you walk with me?"

"John, if you feel up to it, we could visit Simon at his work. I don't go often. The smell bothers me, something I've never been able to appreciate. I know, it's Simon's work that provides us with what we need, but I would rather leave that, the smell, with him. However, that's enough. Let's go! We can take our time and, if it is too much, we can always stop, rest, and turn back."

It was a difficult walk for John and he quickly realized his inability to travel any distance until he gained more strength. Serah was patient, suggesting they make frequent stops. Moving beyond the last few houses, there were any number of boulders, large limestone rocks, where they could sit and rest. It was a warm day, with only a light breeze coming off the water, and they had time to appreciate the beauty of Yahweh's creation. In the blue sky the sea gulls rose and dipped above the Great Sea. Serah had brought along some scraps of bread for the birds. She explained her joy in watching them dive for the pieces, squawking over the feast.

"I love to feed them! They move so effortlessly, so free, seemingly, with no care in the world. They, too, are Yahweh's creation. He provides for them, just as he provides for us. I like to help!"

At each stop Serah overwhelmed John with her questions. Her's were a woman's question, concerning his early years, as well as his life in the wilderness.

"Tell me, John, about your mother. You said your parents were elderly when you were born. How did your mother cope with a baby at her age?"

"Serah, she didn't do too well. It was impossible for her to nurse me. The only solution was a woman who had lost a child at birth. It was her milk that kept me alive and gave me strength. She was a real blessing for my mother.

"Also, it was most difficult for my mother to keep up with me. As I gained weight it was impossible for her to lift me to her lap. When I began to crawl, and then walk, I was really on my own. She could not handle such an active, get-into-everything child. It got so bad that my father began to take me with him to the Temple, whenever he was on duty.

"A lot of that I don't remember, but I was told, more than once, the Temple would never be the same! I was into everything! Yet, I know my mother loved me. She had wanted a child all her married life, and Yahweh finally granted her wish. I did recall hearing her say, from time to time, "Yahweh, why did you wait so long?" She wished, so very much, she could have enjoyed this young son!"

"She lived a number of years after my birth, but was in poor and declining health. After her death, my father went to pieces. His mind was never the same. That's why we moved away, down near the Salt Sea. His Division leader suggested we move, thinking the warmer climate and new surroundings might help. However, my father never had the opportunity to enjoy any of that. Just as our group neared the road heading east toward the village where we were to live, the wild ones, the robbers, attacked us.

"It was a terrible experience. My father collapsed and died. His heart gave out! Also, I was wounded as I tried to fight off the robbers. Really, it was horrible, especially for a child losing both his parents. I was angry with Yahweh for letting that happen. It was hard for me to accept our tragedy."

Serah, sensing the emotion in John's voice, reached out and took his hand.

"You poor boy! What an awful thing! No wonder you questioned Yahweh. We have done so in the past, and we were much older. Sure, our faith is strong, but when tragedies touch our lives, we have to ask 'why?' Why do things like that happen to good people, people who believe in Yahweh? Bad things are supposed to happen only to bad people!"

"But, Serah," John was quick to respond, "I learned that Yahweh works through all our experiences, and he will bring good out of the bad. Bad things can happen to all of us, no matter how good we are. Yet, Yahweh is always with us! We need to remember that.

"As it turned out, the people of the village of Tobba were wonderful. They nursed me back to health, gave me a home, helped me grow up. My main problem was Yahweh. I wanted to hear from him, but for months and years he was silent. It was during that time I was invited to go hunting with the men, hunting for deer. I'll tell you more later, perhaps this evening."

John stood up, ready to move on. He was looking forward to seeing Simon at his work. Back at Tobba he had little interest in the tanning of hides. He just didn't like the smell or the mess. He knew the process, but hoped he would never have to use those skills. However, now that he was older, he had far more appreciation for the results. The contents of the Scrolls were most important, vital to his understanding of Yahweh's purpose in human life. Simon was a tanner! John was sure he was a good one.

This time they had a longer walk before having to stop and rest. John knew he was getting stronger, doing better. Walking was helpful.

At the next stop, John continued his story.

"Finally, after several years, after I had moved out of the village and into the wilderness, Yahweh did speak to me, assuring me he would care for and direct me. I knew, somehow, such was necessary, that I get away, that I live alone. I was right! He has cared for me, watched over me, spoken to me. He has been with me all these years. He has assured me, more than once, that I did the right thing in leaving Tobba. Since that time he has spoken to me frequently. I know he is directing my life and, through people like you, Serah, preserving my life. He will always watch over me, until my task is done!"

Sereh was silent. Trying to sort out John's words, she threw more bread into the air, laughing at the immediate response of the sea gulls, their noise and movement. It was a sight she really enjoyed. Also, it helped clear her mind, a mind filled with wonder!

John was silent, too, his mind filled with memories of Tobba, and of the wilderness. At the same time, he realized there were a lot of unknowns just over the horizon. In spite of his assuring talk, he still realized a degree of anxiety. What will come next? When will Yahweh call me to my mission? Where do I go from here? When will I see my cousin, Jesus, again? He needed to be on his way, back to his wilderness. At least there, he would be in familiar territory, confident that Yahweh would be waiting, ready to have him take that next step.

From their vantage point, they couldn't see Simon's work place, but it was only a short walk to the nearby ridge and the ravine below. There it was, Simon's tanning operation. Actually, there was only one building. Adjacent to the building was a thatch shelter, providing shade from the heat of the sun. Several men were hard at work. Two were working with the skins placed in the warm water, making sure the leather was well soaked. John learned that Simon added salt and lime to that first water, a secret mix he had learned by trial and error.

Two others were scraping fat and hair from the skins taken from the first washing. The real softening process would involve other water pits containing a mixture of plant extracts, lime and oak bark. That produced the worst smell! Then, after treating the skins with a solution of desert pods from the acacia tree and sumac, the final scraping, carefully done, reduced the leather to the proper thickness. The dried, soft skins were stored and protected. Such would be used for clothing, caps, pouches, bags, shields, girdles and writings. Some would provide containers for oil, water or wine.

Sitting in the shade of the thatch shelter was Simon and the woman Tabitha. She was doing most of the talking, as Serah and John approached.

"Simon," she was saying, "you must let Manean leave early this afternoon. The merchant, Joel, has promised cloth for Manean's wife. Their baby needs new clothing. She has outgrown her birthing garments, and needs a dress. And don't cut his wages. He is one of your best workers."

There was more, with Simon nodding in agreement. He wanted to be through with Tabitha's list and get back to work. He did appreciate her concern for his people, but there was work to be done. A lot of her talking, as far as he was concerned, was not necessary. He was glad for the interruption!

"Welcome, John. You continue to improve. You must be better, walking all the way from Joppa. Welcome!

"John, I want you to meet Tabitha. She looks out for my workers, and their families. She means well, and does a lot of good. I'm sure Yahweh will bless her, even though she makes me lose money every time she comes."

That last was said with a smile and a laugh. He just wanted to tease her. However, John and Serah's arrival gave Simon what he wanted, a chance to change the subject. He did care for his workers, and Tabitha did talk a lot.

John shook hands with Tabitha.

"I have heard a lot of good things about you. Both Simon and Serah speak highly of you, of the many good things you do in caring for others. I'm grateful to Yahweh for using you in such a marvelous way. You are a blessing!"

"Don't believe everything you hear young man. These two

talk a lot, almost as much as I do," she chuckled. "But what about you? What are you doing for the good of Yahweh's people, just wandering around the land?"

Tabitha had a way of getting close, looking intently in a person's eyes. Some said she was staring, in an intimidating sort of way. She always approached situations, and, people like that, head-on.

This time it was different. As John held his gaze, and his smile, it was Tabitha who looked down and turned away. This young man "just wandering around the land" was, to say the least, disturbing. She kept trying to figure it out, size him up, to no avail.

Almost in a whisper, she asked, "Who are you?"

John laughed, but not in a critical way.

"Have you ever read Isaiah, the prophet, any of it?"

"Yes, I have! My own father taught me. He was one of the synagogue rulers when I was a child and he let me read the scriptures, both the Torah and the prophets. I'm quite proud of that. You men have nothing on me! Why do you ask?"

"Because I have been called, as the prophet said, to be the voice of Yahweh, preparing for the coming of the Messiah. Do you remember Yahweh's words spoken through his prophet Isaiah?

> *In the wilderness prepare the way of the Lord.*
> *Make straight in the desert a highway for our Yahweh.*
> *Every valley shall be lifted up,*
> *And every mountain and hill made low;*
> *The uneven ground shall become level,*
> *And the rough places a plain.*
> *And the glory of the Lord shall be revealed,*
> *And all flesh shall see it together,*
> *For the mouth of the Lord has spoken.*

"Who am I? I'm the son of a priest, now deceased, Zechariah. My mother, his wife, was Elizabeth. They never had children, not until they were too old to have children. Then, I was born, because Yahweh decided it. He sent his messenger, Gabriel, to my father in the Temple, while my father was offering the Evening Sacrifice and told him Elizabeth would bear a child they should call John.

"So, here I am, waiting for Yahweh to tell me what to do next. Does that help answer your question?"

For once, Tobitha was speechless. She wasn't prepared for what she had heard. Simon had said nothing about their guest, other than a young man, John, was visiting, recovering from a fever. She looked at Simon. Then she looked at Serah. Both added to her confusion, for both were nodding, and smiling.

Finally, Simon spoke.

"Tabitha, we felt the same way when we first heard John's story. We couldn't believe it. We didn't believe him! We were thinking that this young man's fever had made him delirious. We were sure Yahweh didn't work through young men like John. He would speak only through great, elder prophets. Boy, were we wrong!

"Now we believe! We are convinced that what John has told us is the word of Yahweh. If you don't believe us, and if you don't believe John, I would suggest you travel up to Jerusalem and see what they have to say. Does that make sense?"

"No, it doesn't make sense. None of what this young man is saying makes sense. But, I don't need to go all the way to Jerusalem, to believe, either. Do you take me for an idiot, someone who just pesters you, and all the people of Joppa, trying to impress everybody with her good deeds"?

"Every day, mind you, for years, I've prayed for our deliverance. If I've pestered anyone, it's Yahweh. Every day I've asked for a sign, something, anything, to show me he hears me. Now the sign has come! I believe you, and I believe John! I don't know why, and I don't know how, but I believe! I believe!"

Tabitha was beside herself, her voice rising with each word. She hugged Serah. She almost hugged Simon. She hugged John. Then she sat down, smiling.

"Tell me young man, how all this came about, how this will work out. Where is the Messiah? When will we see him? When will he set us free? Tell me what I need to hear!"

"It's a long story, Tabitha, but I'll try. First of all, I'm impressed, not by your response, but by Yahweh's way of touching your life, making sure he gets through our tendency to reject something so radically different from what we have known."

After Simon checked on his workers, sending Manean on his way to Joppa, he came back and sat down. John's story was much more important than processing animal skins.

For the next hour, John told the story of his life. Although he left out a lot of his personal adventures and relationships, he talked about his parents, the Egyptian, Mary and Joseph, Jesus and his brothers. He talked about Yahweh, how and where Yahweh had spoken to him. He also shared his own questions as to what was ahead, and what Jesus would accomplish.

With his repeated emphasis on freedom from their enemies, the return of Israel to its former greatness, and the punishment of all evildoers, Tabitha broke in and made a disturbing statement.

"Perhaps Yahweh isn't so interested in restoring Israel to is former greatness. From what I can understand about his plans, given though his prophets, he would want Israel to help all nations, whether enemies or not. Sure, the Romans are here, ruling over us, but our hearts and our minds are free. As I see it, Yahweh's big word is love, love for all people. Isn't that true, John?"

Now it was John's turn to pause, listen and wonder. Could it be this do-gooder was closer to the truth, closer to what Yahweh had in mind? He would have to think about that. However, he was tired. He had talked too long. He needed to get back to Joppa and rest.

"Tabitha, you may be right. We will have to wait and see."

With the sun sinking toward the water of the Great Sea, John and Serah started their long walk back. Tabitha had said her goodbyes, rushing off for another appointment with the owner of flocks of sheep and goats. He employed several families as helpers. She wanted to make sure they were being cared for properly, and she would! That was her calling, her Yahweh-given task.

Simon had to close down things for the night, making sure everything was in order. He had no desire to lose any of his valuable skins. His investments were important. He trusted his workers, but it was his responsibility to make the final check at the close of each day. Many days he arrived home after dark, but it was a familiar, well-worn path. Serah would be waiting, with a delicious supper.

Serah and John took their time on the return trip. Some one had left two large bunches of grapes at the door, a welcome addition to their food supply. Serah was positive about the giver, her neighbor Rachel. She and her husband were the owners of a large vineyard some distance inland, away from the wind and water of the Great Sea. Serah would thank her tomorrow. Insisting that John go up and rest, she began to prepare the evening meal

John was happy to excuse himself, climb the stairs and collapse on the upstairs couch. He was tired!

Closing his eyes, he tried to sleep, but sleep would not come. Instead, the voice came, softly but clearly.

"John! John! Listen to me. It is time for you to leave. I know you need to regain your strength and I will help you. You should sleep well tonight. Plan to rest tomorrow and tomorrow night. Be on your way the following morning. I know it will take time in getting back to the wildernees. Remember, there will be difficulties and dangers, yet I will be with you. I will prepare you for your mission. No matter what comes, trust in me. Do not despair. Do not give up hope. I will not let you go! My word will accomplish what I intend. Before it is all over you will understand, and accept my way. Tabitha is right. It will be the way of love!"

Sleep came as Yahweh's voice faded away. It had been both a comforting and a disturbing message, but John had to let it go. As Yahweh had said, it was time to rest.

# CHAPTER 28

*I will praise the Name of the Lord with a song;*
*I will magnify him with thanksgiving.*
                                    Psalm 69:30

John stirred at Simon's call. With little energy, still recovering from the fever, he would have been content to sleep through the night. The day's events, particularly the walking, had been rather tiring.

For Simon, the day's work was over and he was hungry, ready for the evening meal. It was almost dark now, but the full moon was rising in the east. There was sufficient light, enough to enable John to maneuver the stairs safely. Down below, Simon was waiting for Serah to finish final supper preparations. Outside in the courtyard was an earthenware pot set over the fire. A lentil stew gave off a savory odor. Next to the pot was a spit, holding the shoulder of a lamb. The hot, glowing coals sputtered under the drippings from the meat. That, too, gave out a tantalizing smell. Then, there was the oven, an essential part of every household. Serah had baked bread for the meal.

Simon, clothes changed, talked about the problems of handling animal skins. Most people would have little to do with tanners, but in Joppa he was accepted as a good neighbor and friend. His operation was far enough removed from the community and no one was offended by the odor. If he was tanning the hides of unclean animals, few seemed to care. His leather was top quality!

"It's quite a job, John, getting rid of the smell. At the close of each day I have to do a lot of washing. Just below my work place there is a small stream that comes down the valley of Charashim. I had my workers dig out a deep pool, a perfect place for bathing. My friend Reuben, the shopkeeper, buys the best soap for my needs. Some call it Fullers' soap. It must contain some oil, possibly olive oil. It not only cleanses well, but it has a nice fragrance."

He laughed.

"Serah is grateful. She says the cleansing soap makes me acceptable. The interesting thing about the stream and the valley of Charashim is the name. I've been told it had to do with descendents of David and Solomon, some of whom were craftsmen. I suppose you could call me that, a craftsman. Yahweh has enriched my life with the ability to produce the best leather. I have been blessed!"

While they were talking, they could hear Serah singing, softly, but clearly:

> *Hear my cry, O Lord, listen to my prayer;*
> *From the end of the earth I call to you,*
> *when my heart is faint.*

There was a short pause, and then she continued, joyfully.

> *So I will ever sing praises to your name*
> *as I fulfill my vows day after day.*

John knew the Psalm; one of David's songs. It touched him again as a reminder of his own wrestling with life. His life had been confronted with difficult questions. At times, many times, his heart had been faint. Yet, he knew Yahweh's powerful presence. He would keep all of them, Simon and Serah included, in his care. While he had rested on his couch

Yahweh had spoken of difficulties and dangers, but he assured John he would see him through! Even so, he could not help but wonder.

Also, her singing was a reminder of his years in the Temple, of the happier days there. The priests sang that Psalm frequently. Of course, the voices were all male, but the melody and the emotion were the same. Serah had a beautiful voice!

His thoughts were interrupted as she came in to announce it was time to come to the table. The evening meal was ready. Neither John nor Simon hesitated in following her into the courtyard. Tonight they would eat outdoors. Light from the cooking fires and the rising moon was enough. The weather was quite pleasant, with a warm breeze blowing off the Great Sea. They asked John to offer a table blessing, as well as a prayer of thanksgiving. All were aware of their blessings, including Tabitha's response to John. During the meal, Serah remembered John's promise regarding his deer hunting. Responding, he told them about the hunters of Tobba. He described the process of making weapons, arrows tipped with the leg bones of deer. He told of his first hunt and his first deer. He had little pleasure in killing, but he knew the value of the skins, once they were ready for the men at Qumran.

One additional note had to do with the arrows. A man he met at Megiddo had given him several flint arrowheads, something seldom found in the southern part of the country. If he ever reached Tobba again, he would give them to the hunters. Also, he would look more intently at the work of their tanners. Were their skins as good as Simon's?

After that, there was little conversation. Serah's cooking was, in John's words, superb. All were hungry and there was little left at the close of the meal. Once they were through, the men helped clean the table. Serah washed the bowls and spoons, putting them away in her storage cabinet Simon had built for her. Then she gathered up the leftovers and disappeared.

Simon explained. Serah was concerned for her neighbor, Rahab. She was a widow, with no one to help her. Serah and the other neighbors, including Tabitha, did what they could for a woman in need. It was the right thing to do!

As they prepared for bed, John shared his plans. If it were agreeable with them, he would like to stay one more night, leaving the following day. He believed his strength would be sufficient for the journey. He would take his time, resting along the way. He did need Simon's help concerning the route to follow.

"Bethlehem! I have friends there and would like to see them. From there, as I have been told, there is an old donkey path leading directly toward the Salt Sea. It would be the shortest way back to my wilderness. I believe the nearest town along that route is Lydda. What do you think?"

Both Serah and Simon protested the idea of John leaving. Yet, they realized his plans for obeying Yahweh came first. He must do what Yahweh wanted. Yahweh did move in mysterious ways, and John's departure was included. They would help him as much as possible. Hopefully, they would see him again.

"John, you need to go southeast, and Lydda is the first town of any size on that road. If you are tired, you might spend the night there. We have a friend for whom we are always concerned. He is paralyzed, bedridden. Sometimes he is depressed, wondering why Yahweh doesn't help him, cure him. He would appreciate a visit, and our greetings. His name is Aeneas. It would be a good stopping place for you."

It was late and all agreed it was time to sleep. The day had been filled with so many momentous things. So much had been said, Yahweh-centered things! With emotions of joy and thanksgiving filling hearts and minds, it would be a restful night. John wished for Simon and Serah pleasant dreams. With a word of thanksgiving for their hospitality, he climbed upstairs to his couch.

The last day of his visit was, for the most part, uneventful. Simon went to work quite early, but returned early in the afternoon. With the Sabbath beginning at sundown, it was time to finish all labor, clean up and rest. Serah would prepare the food, and finish the cooking before dark. Everything had to be ready before the seventh day of the week, the Sabbath. Tomorrow Simon and Serah would go to the local synagogue. John would not. He would be on his way, early. Sure, he knew the Sabbath rules about travel, but he was going home, following Yahweh's directions. Yahweh's commands stood high above any priest's commands.

Even before the sun was rising over the eastern hills, John gathered his belongings and picked up his pack. Lifting it to his shoulders, he was ready to travel. It seemed heavier this time, but he thought he could handle the load. It was time to say his farewells.

Serah, tears streaming down her face, gave John a lingering hug. She was unable to speak. Simon had difficulty, too. He patted John on the back, trying to say the right thing.

"Take care of yourself, my friend. We will pray Yahweh's blessings on you. And, remember, if you get sick again, you know where to come."

John smiled, hugged Serah, waved his hand and headed in the direction of Lydda. He did turn once, just before he topped the first rise in the road. Simon and Serah were still there, watching. This time they both waved as John disappeared down the slope. He was on his way again, headed for his wilderness.

For the first hour, the road provided easy walking. This was the southern part of the Plain of Sharon. However, as John continued eastward, he was aware of the rising elevation. It was not difficult, but the terrain was beginning to change. Although he could still see the Great Sea from the high points along the way, he was leaving the coastal plain. In the far distance he could see higher ridges ahead. To his left was a small stream of clear water. After his second hour of walking he stopped to rest by the stream. He refilled his water bag, drank and ate a piece of sweet bread Serah had provided for the journey. He knew he could be in Lydda by early afternoon, so was in no hurry.

Recovering from his illness, he knew the value of taking care of himself. He would not rush!

Once he stopped to watch several deer bound up the far slope to his right. They hesitated once, watching this intruder in their territory, then quickly disappeared in the trees. There were other animals to watch along the way. Several badgers popped up their heads from the rocky slopes, watching as John approached. They did not linger, once he came closer. Overhead, as always, the eagles soared effortless in the blue sky. There were few travelers on the road, this being the Sabbath. John could enjoy the many creatures of Yahweh's world with little interruption.

With the warm sun directly overhead, John stopped again. Sitting in the shade of several larger trees, he removed his pack. He placed it against one of the trees, leaned back and closed his eyes. He wasn't sleepy, but was ready for a brief rest.

Trying to think through his plans for his journey, he was startled to hear voices. Opening his eyes He was surprised to see two priests, two young priests. They had stopped and were talking to him.

"Sir, why are you here on the Sabbath? There are no houses nearby and the nearest village is beyond the limits of a Sabbath's walk. We think you have broken the Law. You have sinned!"

John thought for a moment, got up, chuckled, and responded.

"Sirs, I mean no disrespect, but I suppose I could ask you the same question. Yes, you are correct. The Law is very specific on the matter of travel on the Sabbath. However, let me ask this. When did this rule come into existence? Did it come from Moses? Or, better yet, did this come from Yahweh himself, and was given to Moses on the mountain?"

The face of the taller of the two young priests, obviously the leader, turned red. John could see that he was angry.

"How dare you make fun of our Law? I doubt if you know very much about Moses, or about our Yahweh. At the very beginning of our priesthood we were taught proper respect for the Law. We have no right to question what has been given us. If you have any respect for the Law, you should obey it!"

John could see this was going nowhere, and he did not want to start an argument. He would back away.

"Thank you for sharing your thoughts with me. You are right. The Law you have been taught speaks directly to the matter of work, and travel, on the Sabbath. My traveling doesn't measure up, does it? I have been properly reprimanded."

As the two young priests nodded to each other, proud of what they saw as a victory for their priesthood and the Law, John continued.

"I assume you are on your way to Jerusalem, and the Temple. Is that right?"

"Yes! We are on our way to take our turn with our Division. What would you know about Yahweh's Temple, and why do you ask?"

"If you would be so kind, I would ask you to carry a message to Jonathan, head of the Division of Abijah. Would you tell him you met a man named John, the son of Zechariah? He will understand. And, I can assure you, he will commend you for honoring my request."

In response, the priest nodded. He promised he would speak to Jonathan. If this stranger were correct, a good relationship to a Division head would be good. It certainly couldn't hurt his career! With a proper bow to John, they hurried on their way, commending each other for their defense of the Law.

It was time to move on. He had his own needs and plans, Yahweh directed. He had to laugh to himself. He had observed so many young priests as they did their best to climb the ecclesiastical ladder, obey every law. With age and experience they would learn what was important in their journey of life and service. Hopefully, they would be good servants of Yahweh.

As he hoisted his backpack and water skin, he moved slowly back onto the road toward Lydda. He took his time, having no desire to catch up with the two priests. Noticing the changing terrain as he walked, he remembered something of the history of the area. The road was a main one, going east toward to Jerusalem. At Lydda, there was a road crossing, the great caravan route between Gaza, Edom, Egypt and Arabia on the south, and Damascus to the north. As such, the area had been fought over many times. Egyptians, Philistines and Hebrews had been involved in that struggle. Now, the Romans were in charge.

He also remembered the story of Samson and the other judges, how Samson had failed in his calling to serve Yahweh faithfully. Samson had died at a Philistine temple in Gaza, the temple of Dagon. Many of the pagans died with him. At the end, Yahweh gave him strength!

In entering the town, he was surprised to see that it had no walls. Most cities in that area were walled. To be sure, most were in disrepair, but some still had their gates. Lydda was different. There were no walls. Apparently, there had never been any walls. Any powerful army could have marched right in, and probably had at some point in the past.

His main concern was to find the home of Aeneas, friend of Simon and Serah. He would honor their request. Also, he wanted to encourage the man in his illness. That was the least he could do. The sun would not be down for another four hours, so he had time for a proper visit before moving on.

The first man he asked gave him directions. Everyone knew Aeneas, the cripple! He was the concern of the whole town, a person everyone respected. His wit and his wisdom were known by all, as well as his bouts with depression. The local rabbi, from what the man on the street said, did what he could, but his skills were limited. So, all the friends and neighbors made a point of stopping by. Sometimes the children would visit, bringing their pets. One had a dog. Another had a young pet fox.

When John arrived at the house, several people were leaving, calling their "goodbyes" as they left the courtyard. They bowed to John and suggested he go on in. Aeneas was outside, resting.

Apparently, all who came by did not knock or call out. Aeneas was ready to welcome any and all visitors. Seeing John hesitate inside the gate, he welcomed him in a weak, but clear voice.

"You, sir, are a stranger, a traveling stranger. You are carrying a heavy load, so I know you have traveled far. See how intelligent I am! Am I not correct . . . . not the intelligence, but my conclusion? Come in! Come in!"

"Yes, Aeneas, you are correct. I have traveled far, and will go farther. However, my purpose in being here is to bring greetings from your friends in Joppa, Simon and Serah."

Aeneas' emotions spilled over. Tears filled his eyes. Simon and Serah were dear friends. After a long silence, he regained control of himself.

"Simon and I grew up together, in Joppa. We played together. We hunted together. We fished together. We had a small fishing boat, one we would take out on the Great Sea. Those days I remember so well. They were happy, enjoyable days. Then, we grew up! Both of use married, drifted apart. He and Serah had no children. My wife, Jemima and I had one child, a son. He is grown now, lives near Bethlehem.

"We probably would have had more contact in the married years, except for my illness. I awoke one morning and couldn't move. My legs were paralyzed. That summer, about a year ago, I had experienced a bad fever. However, it went away and I thought nothing more, until the day I could not use my legs. No one has been able to tell me why I'm paralyzed, or if I will ever walk again.

"My dear friends, Simon and Serah, pray for me every day. Prayers are offered weekly in their synagogue. Here, in Lydda, it is the same. Prayers are said every day, every Sabbath, and I believe that those prayers will be answered. Yahweh will send one to heal me! Would you be the one?"

John thought for a bit, trying to put into words what he should say to this man's hope. Paralyzed legs are not the same as a fever, or a stomach sickness. You can't take medicine for that. It would have to be a miracle, a Yahweh-given miracle!

That was the answer! He was a miracle! His cousin, Jesus, was a miracle! Yahweh does do miracles. Why not a miracle for Aeneas?

"Aeneas, Yahweh does answers prayers. He hears us when we pray. He listens and he answers! He provides miracles but he answers in his own time and way. I trust you believe that?"

"Yes! It has to be so, and I believe in miracles. Some stories I hear create doubt in my mind, but others are different. Yahweh does work in mysterious ways. I believe!"

The intensity of his thinking spilled over into his voice. With each additional word his speaking could be heard throughout the house. As John saw it, here was a man of deep faith, believing Yahweh would respond to his personal needs. He believed he would be healed!

John waited for Aeneas to finish; nodding in agreement to all the man was trying to share concerning his feelings, his beliefs. Finally, as Aeneas paused and lay back to rest, he had the opportunity to speak.

"Aeneas, my friend, let me tell you a story, a true story. It is the story of my life, a life filled with miracles. All these miracles are from Yahweh himself!"

John began to share the events of his birth, the prediction of his birth, and all the rest. He told about Yahweh calling him. He went beyond that to tell him about the promised Messiah, how he traveled to Galilee in order to meet him, talk with him, He gave him his present plans for returning to the desolate land near the Salt Sea. Yahweh was about to act!

"Aeneas, I have learned many things about life. I have been taught to take care of life, human life. I have medicines for healing some illnesses. Yahweh has used me to help any number of people I have met in my travels. However, the best I can do for you is to ask Yahweh's favor in your life. I do know some elders in our nation's history have placed hands of healing on some. I can and will do the same for you, asking Yahweh to heal you, to restore strength to your legs. However, the answers lie with, come from, Yahweh, and you can depend upon him! I know he will heal you, but in his own time and way. I believe he will heal you, but he will do so when he is ready."

Aeneas, by this time, had leaned back again. With eyes closed, and no visible response, John wasn't sure. Was Aeneas listening? Had he really heard all John had shared?

Finally, the tears! Aeneas' eyes were brimming over with tears. His shoulders were shaking. As best he could, he rocked back and forth! Even with out him speaking, John could see he was deeply moved. His emotions were getting the best of him.

It took him several minutes to regain his composure, but when he did he began to shout, to call out his wife's name:

"Jemima! Jemima! Come here, quickly. Here is a man with good news, very good news. He believes! He believes Yahweh will heal me!"

Jemima came, hurrying in, but John could sense her reaction. She was filled with doubt. She had heard her husband's expressed hope many times before, with nothing happening. How could it be any different today?

"Yes, my husband," she exclaimed. "I believe, too, but what makes today any different? What has this young man brought you that is new? Sir, I don't mean to doubt you, but even our rabbi has failed to bring us a miracle. What can you do?"

John tried again! He repeated for her the story of his life, all he had told Aeneas. As he shared his assurances of Yahweh's miracles in his life, her eyes opened wider and wider. He had her full attention! She, too, was moved!

"Young man, this is too much for me. I hear what are saying, but I want to know when! If you are so sure, tell me when. When will my Aeneas walk again?"

John had wanted so much to tell about the promises of Yahweh, his promises for all his people, how he would come and set them free. Aeneas' situation made that possible, but they weren't hearing. He could appreciate their personal concerns, but they really weren't listening. Israel's problems really didn't concern them that much. They wanted a miracle for themselves.

Again, John tried to make it clear. He did believe Aeneas would be healed, but he simply could not say when. That was in Yahweh's hands. He would pray for Aeneas. He would place his hands on Aeneas, but all would have to wait on Yahweh. Have faith! Believe!

Jemima thanked John, and went back inside. As far as she was concerned, nothing had changed. They would have to keep on praying, and hope for the best. Maybe, just maybe, Yahweh would act.

After she left the yard, John placed his hands on Aeneas, and prayed fervently for healing. He asked Yahweh to strengthen their faith, keep them faithful in believing. He concluded his prayer with a word of thanksgiving, thanking Yahweh for what he would do for Aeneas. He would be healed! He would walk again!

At the end of his prayer, he took Aeneas' hands in his, looked deep into his eyes, and said:

"Aeneas, Be patient, but do not give up hope. You will be healed! Believe me!"

With Aeneas' nod, tears filling his eyes again, John picked up his pack. With a final salute to the man lying helpless on his couch, he left, heading out of Lydda in the direction of Bethlehem. He would travel until it was dark.

Before leaving Lydda, John stopped a man coming in from the east. He, too, was traveling on the Sabbath, and John believed he would share information on the road ahead.

"Yes, I have come from Bethlehem. If you want to go in that direction, you must leave the main road to Jerusalem, just beyond that last house. Of course, the better road is the one to Jerusalem. From there you can go directly south, but I prefer this other route. You avoid a lot of traffic, and a lot of Roman soldiers. They pay no attention to Sabbath laws.

Pointing in that direction, he continued: "Your best place for tonight is the ancient town of Gezer. It will be dark by the time you arrive. It is mostly ruins, but there are plenty of caves near the broken down walls. Also, there are a number of water springs. There is an inn on the northern side of the valley, a place to get food, if you need it. I wish you well on your journey."

John thanked the man for his kindness, turned right at the last house on the road, heading for Gezer. He did remember something about the town. It had been a fortified Canaanite town, one that was never captured by the early Israelites. Later it was given to Solomon by an Egyptian king. His daughter was one of Solomon's wives. As he recalled, it became one of Solomon's border fortresses.

He had the road to himself. Few would travel before sundown. Although the terrain was changing, with more hills and valleys, the road to Gezer was very pleasant. He had time to think back to his Lydda visit with Simon and Serah's friend, Aeneas. He had to admit his disappointment in the way his story had been received. Their wrestling with Aeneas' plight overshadowed the promise of the coming Messiah. He could understand that, but, at the same time, the news of the coming of Yahweh's promised son was far greater. If the predictions of the great prophets were correct, his coming would bring miracles of all sorts, including the healing of the lame; not only that, they would be free people, free from the power of Rome. Israel, itself, would be great again!

Just as the sun was sinking in the west, John arrived in Gezer. With the ending of the Sabbath, a number of people were out, some apparently heading for Lydda. It would be a late arrival, but the weather was good and the moon would be rising soon. Few were going east. The landscape was different in that direction, much more rugged. That road, he was told, would go just south of Mt. Seir, a high mountain. That would be his route tomorrow. Tonight he would rest, sleeping in Gezer, or nearby.

As the man in Lydda had noted, there was an inn on the northern side of the valley. However, it was filled. A lot of travelers had been caught on the Sabbath. Most would not leave in the dark, but would stay over one more night. It was time to find an unoccupied cave on the hillside. He had water, and he had the bread Serah had baked. Somewhere in his pack was some dried meat. If he was too hungry he could heat water in his little pot, and soften the meat. It was enough.

Some of the caves were occupied. There were some permanent residents in the larger ones. However, he did find one higher up. It was clean and would serve his purpose well. Also, it was secure. Anyone approaching would be heard, easily. John felt secure in Yahweh's hands, but he had learned from experience. One had to be very careful in unfamiliar places.

After thanking Yahweh for a safe journey, for food, for friends, for all his blessings, he ate some bread, drank some water, and settled down for the night. The floor of the cave was fairly smooth, and his one blanket was enough. He was ready for sleep! Tomorrow night, he hoped, he would be in Bethlehem.

# CHAPTER 29

*. . . the Lord who girded me with strength,
and made my way safe . . .*
                                Psalm 18:32

It was difficult to predict the weather. When John awoke, it had changed. The morning was much cooler, windy, with a few drops of rain falling. The cave was dry, but if he wanted to travel, he would have to brave the elements. Moving out, he hurried down to the nearest spring, one of the warm springs. He washed his face, drank from his water skin, and headed south. He would have to travel half the day in that direction, before turning east toward Bethlehem. He did remember the instructions for avoiding the steeper road nearer Mt. Seir. Anyway, that would bring him back to the Jerusalem road. He was going to Bethlehem!

Although the Sabbath was past, there were not many travelers out. The weather, plus this out-of-the-way route, attracted few people. The man was right. The Jerusalem road was the favorite in this area of the Judean hills. John would have little trouble moving toward his destination. There would be few distractions.

It was almost noon before he entered another village. He had stopped once to rest, but with renewed strength there was no need to linger. Also, the low clouds were breaking up and the sun was trying to shine through. He wanted to take advantage of the better traveling conditions. The frequent rain showers had been light, but were not very pleasant for walking.

The village, Zorah, had a market, although limited in items for sale. There was olive oil, as well as grain for flour, but little else. One shop had dried meat. Another had several pieces of woven cloth, quite colorful. Today would be the day for baking, but here the villagers did not start such things early. Life moved along at a leisurely pace.

John did take time to wander through the market area, speaking to those selling and buying. Everyone seemed friendly, ready to discuss the weather, or the cost of food. There was no mention of taxes, or the Romans, or religion. He did learn there was a synagogue in a nearby town, just south of Zorah. One of the residents reminded him of their heritage, that of the tribe of Dan. However, over the years the population had changed. Many of those returning from Babylon had settled here. Sharing that information with John, he surmised some must have wanted the protection of a fortified city. After the kingdom of Solomon was divided, Rehaboam strengthened the town's walls.

The greater interest for the area and the town was Samson's father. He had been a resident of Zorah. Somewhere nearby was Samson's grave, but, as in other places, no one was certain as to the exact location. As John had learned in his travels, the residents of various towns and villages were proud of their forebears, well-known names in Israel's history. Zorah was no exception.

With Mt. Seir rising high above him to the north, and with Zorah being situated on a ridge, John asked for directions, the easiest route to Bethlehem. He did not want to do a lot of climbing up and down. The valleys, if they went in the right direction, would be ideal. However, no one gave him much encouragement. It would be a long and difficult walk. Most doubted he could reach Bethlehem by nightfall. One man suggested he would have to stop short of his destination, spending the night at a small town a few miles west of Bethlehem, He thought the name was Bether, a very old town, but of no real importance. He wasn't sure about a place to stay. Most likely there was no inn.

With that in mind, John was determined to be on his way. If he could find a good route, he was confident of reaching Bethlehem tonight. From Zorah he headed south, moving quickly down the town's ridge. Walking was quite pleasant for the next hour. John's returning strength enabled him to cover a lot of ground, but suddenly he reached an impasse. Just ahead was a higher ridge, one he did not want to climb. What to do?

Before long he heard the bleating of sheep, a lot of sheep. To his surprise, they were coming out of a grove of trees to the left side of the road. Perhaps that was the better, easier path!

Following the sheep were two shepherds, and they confirmed John's thinking.

"Sure, you do not have to climb that ridge. That would be foolish. Go through those trees and you will see where we have been traveling with our sheep. Yes, you can be in Bethlehem tonight. We left the area this morning, separating our sheep from our neighbor's sheep, our neighbor Joel. It is not a difficult journey if you follow our directions."

"Did you say 'Joel', the big shepherd from Bethlehem, the one who talks a lot?"

"He is the one! How do you know Joel, if you don't know your way around in these hills?"

"Oh, I met him some time ago. I'm just not familiar with this route. The last time I was in Bethlehem, I came up from Hebron."

That seemed to satisfy the shepherds. They waved and headed on west with their sheep. Feeding sheep was much important than talking with strangers. Too bad most people weren't smart enough to follow sheep. It would make traveling much easier!

John soon found out they were right. It was not a difficult trail to follow. A lot of sheep had traveled back and forth on this remote, off-the-road path. Striding along briskly, he was on his way. He would see his friends in Bethlehem before heading back home. He did have to skirt the high ridge, going some distance northward, but it was not long before he was headed east again, directly toward his destination.

Thankful to the two shepherds, and thankful for Yahweh's continued care, John arrived safely in Bethlehem just as the sun was setting over the western ridge. In a way, it was like coming back home. It was from this town he had set out on his journey north, ending his travels in Nazareth.

As he paused to catch his breath, his thoughts were flooded with a sense of amazement. He had lost track of time, but was impressed! Yahweh had led him along many paths, through many troubles. He had met many he now considered to be friends. They, too, had aided him in his travels.

He had met his cousin and his mother, Jesus and Mary. They had talked! They had talked concerning events to come. Above all, he had been able to share Yahweh's message of promise and hope with so many! Now, he was back, where Jesus was born! Yahweh had blessed him!

Yet, there was still a question, a disturbing question. It continued to haunt him, day in and day out; his message and the real purpose of Yahweh's son's coming. Tabitha had intensified the wrestling with his own heart and mind. Surely, judgment had to come upon all evil and all evildoers. The wicked would be put down, even destroyed. Justice would triumph! They would be free again, free from their oppressors, the Romans. Jesus would save them, restore them and free them! It had to be so.

What was it Tabitha had said? "Perhaps Yahweh wasn't that interested in restoring Israel to its former greatness." Then she added, if he remembered her exact words, "Yahweh's biggest word is love, love for all people, regardless." How could that be? Somewhere in the Psalms of David it was written:

> *The Lord loves those who hate evil;*
> *he preserves the lives of his saints;*
> *he delivers them from the hands of the wicked.*

It was a problem, a big problem.

Just then, the young man who had taken them to see the stable interrupted his thoughts. John remembered! His name was Nathaniel.

"John! You are back. We talk about you a lot, how you touched the lives of the people of Bethlehem. Where have you been?"

"Nathaniel, it's a long story. I have traveled far, all the way to Galilee. Now I am back, safely. It is so good to see you, to be here in Bethlehem once more. Have you seen Shemuel today? I want to visit him, he and his mother."

"Yes, he was in town this morning. Kemuel had to go into Jerusalem and Shemuel was keeping his shop. It's hard to know where you will find him these days. He stays so busy, helping the merchants, working as a stonemason and, now, building his own house. He and his mother will be moving in soon. Shall I tell him you were here?"

"No, no. I'm on my way to see them. I hope I will be spending the night. It's good to see you. Tell your friends I'll be back in town sometime tomorrow. I look forward to visiting with them."

John didn't linger. Hurriedly, he left the town and walked the high, long ridge to Tamar's house. Sure enough, Tamar was there, bent over her cooking, unaware of John's approach. She didn't look up until he called.

"Would it be possible for you to feed a stranger passing through? I'll be glad to pay!"

Tamar screamed with joy, running to embrace John.

"John! You are back. You are safely back! You have come back home!"

Tamar couldn't stop talking. With tears of joy running down her face, she exclaimed her welcome over and over. She hugged John, backed away to look at him, and then hugged him again. It was impossible for her to stand still. She had never been so excited!

In answer to John's: "Where is Shemuel," she paused, put

her hand to her mouth, and gasped!

"Shemuel! I forgot all about Shemuel. He is just over the ridge, working on our house."

With that, she started running down the path, calling to her son each step of the way.

"Shemuel! Shemuel! John is back! John is back! Hurry! John is back!"

The new house was not that far away, just down the ridge from their cave. Shemuel emerged from the shadows, running up the hill. Trying to brush off the stone dust as he ran, he was laughing in his welcome to his best friend.

"Well, it's about time! I thought you had forgotten us, completely!"

His embrace was just as warm as his mother's, only stronger. He was touched, moved. The one who had turned his life around had come back to see them!

That evening, after one of Tamar's good suppers, Tamar and Shemuel began to share their good news. They had heard from Shemuel's uncle! He had sent a messenger all the way down from Samaria, bringing the money for the house he had taken from them. It was more than enough, making it possible for them to build and furnish their new home!

Above the payment, more precious to them, was his attitude. He asked for their forgiveness, hoping they would return to Shiloh. However, if they wanted to stay in Bethlehem, he hoped they might visit!

"And, guess what!" Shemuel asked, "Who gets the credit for the change? You! His message was about you, John, how you had helped with his healing. Also, you were the one making him see the error of his ways. He couldn't say enough about you! We couldn't believe it! How did you do all that?"

"It wasn't that difficult. Your uncle was in great pain. His foot was swollen badly and he was willing to do whatever I asked. His wife, Martha, was most helpful. Once she knew I had a message from you two, she let me in. She knew her husband Ira was not a bad man. He had let his greed get the best of him and now regretted it. With her help, and with Yahweh's presence, things changed, for the better. When I was ready to leave, he assured me he would take care of you. I'm glad to see it. He did what he promised."

"Yes! He did!" responded Tamar. "He did what he promised you! We have been blessed, and we have you to thank!"

John changed the subject. He wanted to make sure things were going well with Shemuel and his mother.

"Tell me about your work, Shemuel. I understand the merchants have been good to you, giving you work in their shops. Then there is your stonework. You have been building additions for several families, including the construction of your own home. I'm told you have built up a good reputation as a stonemason!"

"John, I can't believe what has happened to us! I stay busy all the time. Between helping out in Bethlehem and erecting buildings, I have little time left for other things. I am unable to do much in helping Joel anymore, watching over his sheep. There is so little time!

"However, the main thing is our relationship with the community. We are accepted by all, most all. There are a few wealthy families still ignoring us, but that's because I am a laborer, a craftsman. I guess that's to be expected. Bethlehem is really no different than any other town. We can't complain."

"Shemuel, you mentioned Joel. Where is he now? I sure would like to see him again. Earlier today I met two shepherds traveling west with their sheep, over near the town of Zorah. They were most helpful in giving me directions for following an old sheep trail into Bethlehem. In talking with them, they mentioned Joel; separating their sheep from his earlier today. Where is Joel tonight?"

"I'm not sure, John. The last I heard, he was planning to move his sheep in a different direction, west of Jerusalem. The rains have been heavier there, and that was important. I doubt if he will be back for several days."

"That's too bad! Tell him I asked. I will have to leave tomorrow. It is time for me to get back to my wilderness home. I know, you want me to stay longer, but, honestly, I can't. I hope you understand."

Tamar was the first to respond.

"John, I'm not sure we understand. It is hard for us to appreciate what Yahweh has in store for you. Only you know that. We do understand this fact. You are special! You have become a part of our lives, and we will never forget you. You are like a son to me, and we would be honored to have you stay longer. We love you!"

Shemuel echoed his mother's feelings, what she had tried to say about John. He, too, would remember, ever grateful for what John had done for them.

"Tell us, John, what really comes next for you. Why do you have to leave so soon? You talked about Yahweh speaking to you. Couldn't he do that while you are here? You have just returned from a very long trip. Surely, you could wait a few more days!"

"Shemuel, it is hard to explain, but trust me, what I am saying. It is time for me to leave, to go back to my starting point. I believe Yahweh has made that clear. It will be most difficult to leave you, but I must!"

Again, John changed the subject. He wanted to know about the new house he would see in the morning. Finally, he reminded them he was tired after a long day of traveling. Also, he shared the story of his recent illness. He was not quite up to full strength. It was time for some much-needed rest.

The trip into Bethlehem gave John the opportunity to thank the town merchants for hiring Shemuel. Following an inspection of the new house, voicing approval of Shemuel's building skills, they walked into town together.

Shemuel gave him a full account of relationships established in Bethlehem. He had more than enough work. In fact, he could spend every day working for others. Kemuel had indicated his full trust in Shemuel. If anything happened to him, he wanted Shemuel to run the business for his family. He had that in writing, with the Kemuel family approval. The people of Bethlehem had learned to know and appreciate this young man. He was dependable and trustworthy!

As they entered the town square, and as the merchants recognized John, most of the selling stopped. A crowd gathered around John and Shemuel, welcoming John back. They were happy to see him!

Filled with questions, they didn't want John to leave. Asking about his travels, they were disappointed to learn he was just passing through. John, of course, told them very little about his visit north, or the reason for his immediate departure. He talked mainly about them, their work, and their families. He asked about Shemuel.

"I understand this young man has helped you out some. Has he worked out well?"

The last question was with a smile and a laugh. He knew the answer!

All the merchants tried to talk at the same time, strong in their praise. Shemuel was tops, and a good friend. They had John to thank for that!

By early afternoon, John was ready to be on his way. He had difficulty getting away from the townspeople. He had a harder time saying goodbye to Tamar and Shemuel. Yet, he had to leave, now!

He had asked about the old donkey trail to the wilderness below, but few could give him any details. Few had ever traveled that way. The long way around was better, and safer. The best he could learn was not encouraging. He was told that, in places, the path was steep, and dangerous. One should not be traveled down that way after dark! If he insisted, he should wait until morning!

Perhaps they were right, or were they simply hoping to delay his departure? It was past noon, so his daylight traveling time would be limited. At the same time, he knew he must be on his way. Waving goodbye, he headed east. From what he had been told, he would move more to the south before the day was out.

For the first hours, the walking was not too bad. He managed the steeper drops with not too much difficulty. The donkeys would have had little trouble, even carrying loads. However, the farther he traveled, the rougher the walking. It was steep, very steep. In a few places he stumbled, sliding some distance below. It was not the best way to get down the cliffs, and he had to wonder about this being a donkey trail. Had he missed a turn along the way?

However, there was no turning back now. With the shadows closing in, he had to go on. He needed to get to a safer spot for the night, hopefully a level spot. Finding that, he could rest and start out fresh in the morning. Sunlight would replace this approaching darkness. By now he could see little of what lay below. How far did he have to go, in order to reach the wilderness plateau?

Then, it happened. He fell! He fell and thought he would never stop. Burdened by his backpack, having nothing to grab onto, he kept tumbling down, faster and faster. Finally, his fall came to an abrupt end, but he was not aware of that. Everything went black. He had landed on his face, his forehead hitting a rock, a big rock. Darkness, there was nothing but darkness!

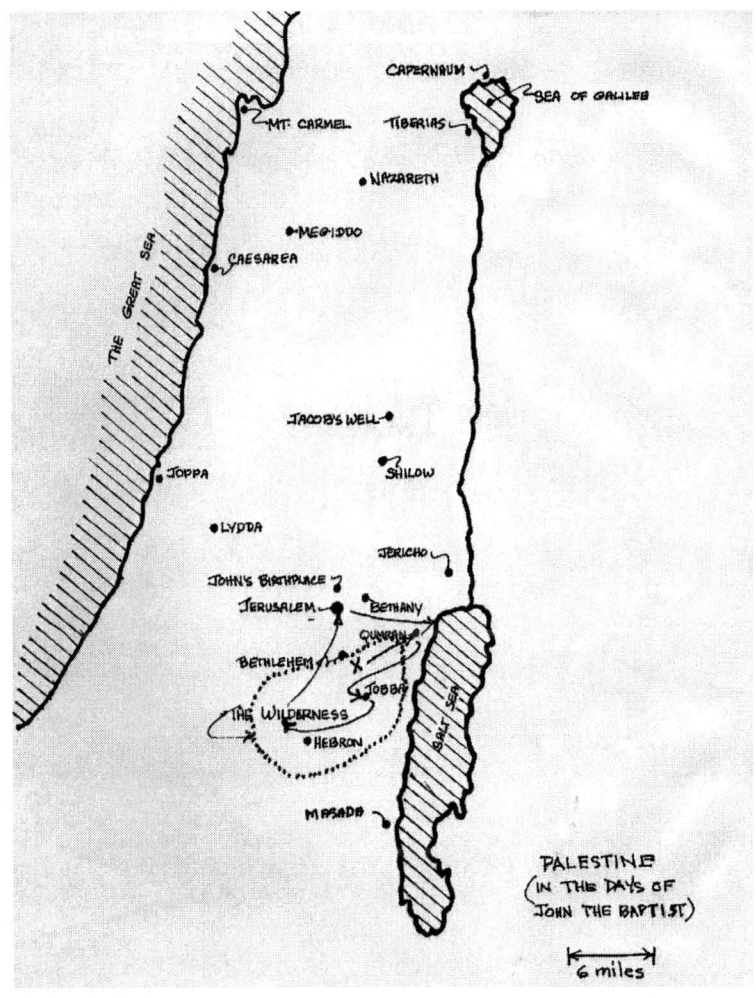

# CHAPTER 30

*. . . out of the depths I cry to thee, O Lord . . .*
*Psalm 130:1*

The darkness faded. There was light. It wasn't much at first, but the deep darkness was gone. Actually, it made little difference, whether it was light or dark. John did not move. He could not move! His fall had brought down a lot of loose stones, some quite large, with most of them holding him down. However, that was not the main reason for his immobility. He had no strength, having lost a lot of blood. He could not move!

Hours past, more darkness, then light again. This time something else was there. Someone was there, and there were more, more than just "one" someone. John heard voices, male voices. Unable to open his eyes, he strained to hear what those voices were saying. He wanted to speak, to cry out, but no sound came. He fainted!

The next time he was able to hear anything, those same voices were much louder, and angry. Suddenly, he realized they were talking about him, or about what belonged to him. They were fighting over his backpack, what was in his backpack. There were few valuables, only that one silver coin. It had value, a lot of value. There was his knife, his blanket, some other clothing, all worth very little. He remembered there was a little dried meat, some bread, his cooking pot and, yes, there were his stone arrow-heads. Why did he remember the arrowheads? He was sure they were worth nothing to those men.

From the tone of their voices, arguing voices, John knew they were not there to help him, but would probably kill him. He was sure these were the wild ones. They would divide up what was his and leave him to die. If they did not kill him, they would simply leave him to die. Which would it be? Amazing, that sort of reasoning seemed so logical.

With that running through his mind in a confused sort of way, John smiled to himself. There was Yahweh, and Yahweh would not let him die! Yahweh would save him! He didn't know how, or when, but Yahweh would save him.

He hurt! His pain was almost unbearable. He was near death, but Yahweh would not let him go! Would Yahweh let him die? Of course not!

Again, he lost consciousness, a blessing in the midst of tragedy; but he did not die! He was left to die, but he did not die.

The next darkness came, the darkness of another night, but all was silent. There were no voices. Forcing one eye open, open enough to look at his surroundings; John saw the glow of a dying fire somewhere above him. Apparently the men had built a fire and left it, just as they had left him. But, there was something else. Those loose stones were not holding him down. He was lying on his side, down in a narrow wadi. They had pushed him in, leaving him to die. His cloak was gone, stripped from his body. Only his loincloth was left, too bloody to be worth stealing. Again, he wanted to cry out for help, but could not. Anyway, what difference would that make? Hidden in that narrow draw, no one would ever hear him or find his body! Where was Yahweh? He could not speak, but his prayer, "Yahweh, help me!" was heard!

Time meant nothing to John, but just before dawn, it began to rain. For that time of the year, and for that part of Israel, it never rained. Such was impossible! Yet, it rained, and rained, and rained! By daylight the little, narrow wadi was filled with water. It became a flood, washing everything in its path, faster and faster, washing sticks, and rocks . . . and John!

It was a wonder he did not drown; there was so much water. Yet, he did not. A mass of sticks had been pushed under him by the strong force of the flood. They caught in his loincloth, holding him up. He did not drown. Even where the water plummeted over one or more waterfalls, he did not drown. The sticks held, continuing to hold him up.

With the darkness giving way to light, and the raging flood subsiding, John realized he was off the cliffs. He had to be somewhere in his beloved wilderness. He was alive, but where? With the water draining rapidly away, he was left stranded on a spit of sand.

However, was he any better off? He could not move. He had no strength. He could not call out. He was alone, and unless Yahweh produced a miracle, he would surely die! Then the darkness returned, the darkness of unconsciousness.

It was in the air, swirling in every direction. Yahweh's creatures could sense it. The deer came out and stood on the limestone outcroppings, something they seldom did during the day. The badgers popped up on isolated rocky crags. The foxes were on the move. The mice scurried from bush to protective bush. Overhead, the birds dipped and rose, noisy in their flight. An old lion had come down the wadi, looking for small animals that might have drowned in the flood. He sniffed the body lying on the sandy spit, then dashed away. There was restlessness in the wilderness! This day was different! One of Yahweh's own was down, hurt, alone!

In Qumran, that restlessness was evident in the daily routine. It had been shattered. Men working at their writing desks kept making mistakes. Pens were broken. There was a sense of impending danger. It was as though their cozy, secure, little world was falling apart. They stopped what they were doing, went outside to look anxiously at the sky. They, too, noticed the creatures, visible and restless. Far in the distance, high over the distant cliffs to the west, there were storm clouds, clouds moving to the west. That could not be! If there were ever any clouds like that at the right time of the year, they moved east, not west. It was an ominous sign!

Over in the village of Tobba it took a different form, a stranger passing through, wanting to sell a leather pouch filled with arrowheads. As the hunters of Tobba gathered about this rather unsavory character, entranced by the stone arrowheads, some of the other villagers approached the group, including Tobiah and his daughter Debra.

Suddenly, the air was split by her scream.

"The pack! The backpack that man is carrying is John's! I know it! That is John's! What have you done with him?"

Rushing forward, she did her best to grab the man, to wrestle the pack and the pouch from his hands. Hastily, the man backed away, ready to run. He was in trouble, with no good answers.

He had nowhere to turn. He could not run! He was surrounded! The village's hunters, skinning knives drawn, moved in, closer and closer. Terrified, he dropped to his knees, trying to make his excuses.

"We did him no harm. He was already dead. He had fallen, lost blood. There was no way to save him. We simply divided what we found. That is the truth!"

His words, voiced in terms of pleading, rose in intensity.

"Please, I beg you, let me go. You can have what is here, all of it. Just let me go!"

Tobiah stepped forward, shaken by what he had heard. His angry was evident, but his command was quite clear.

"Bind this man's arms behind him! Put a leash around his neck! If he makes any move to escape, treat him like a deer you might be skinning.

"Make him lead you to the spot where he says he found a man and a back pack. Let's see if he is telling the truth. Jakan, you will be in charge. Do what you have to do. If there is a body, and it is John's body, bring it and this man back. He will be turned over to the authorities in Jericho for punishment."

Then, turning to the others clustered around, he spoke, softly, with tears in his eyes.

"Most of you did not know that our dear friend John has been chosen for a special task by Yahweh himself. Yahweh made that clear a long time ago, long before he came to live with us. As far as we know that task is not done. John shared that with me before he left us for the wilderness. In fact, that is why he left. Out in the wilderness he would wait, waiting for Yahweh to call him. I believed him, and did my best to help him. It was not a test of the community, seeing if he could survive. We told you that, covering up his real purpose for leaving. However, I still believe what he told me is true. Yahweh will use John as was predicted.

"Jaken, you will not find him dead! Now, go! Time is important!"

Debra knew it was useless, but she tried to persuade her father to let her go with the men. His "No!" was most emphatic. She would have to wait.

The trip to the cliffs took longer than expected. It was rough going and their prisoner did not help. He was not accustomed to such strenuous exercise, and the forced march was taking its toll. It was the continual prodding of a skinning knife that kept him moving. He dared not stop. He knew it would be fatal to stop. These men were anxious and angry! Finally, they climbed over the last ridge, coming to the foot of the cliff. One of the hunters exclaimed:

"That's the end of the old donkey trail, coming down from Bethlehem. No one ever uses it any more. It is too dangerous."

There was no John, no evidence of John. The sticks from the robber's fire were there, but no sign of John. The thief did make one final admission. They had pushed the body into that wadi, and left it there. The hunters checked, running up and down, but the wadi had been scoured clean.

It was that clue which made them think of the possibilities. If this was the spot, and if his body had been pushed over into that narrow wadi, either John had been able to walk away, or he had been washed away in a sudden flood. It had rained! That much was clear. There had been a lot of rain. There was no trash, no debris in the wadi. John was not there! If the things this thief had told them were true, they would have to search below. Tobiah was right. Time was important, most important.

They had no time to retrace their steps to Tobba. Immediately, they followed the wadi, moving steadily downward. In a couple of places there was an abrupt drop, with some water still spilling over. It must have been some rain to do all that. All the usual trash had been washed away.

After several hours of walking and climbing and descending, they reached the flats, the uneven land near the Salt Sea. There they found him! John had pulled himself up to a sitting position, but made no response to their loud shouts of happy greeting. He sat, staring into the distance. It was as though he was in another world.

Quickly, they freed John from the matting of sticks, made a hammock sling and hurried into Qumran. The flood had deposited him at Qumran's back door. How fortunate! The hunters knew there were former priests there, men skilled in healing. It was the place to be! Yahweh had brought them, and John, to the right place! He was alive!

Two of the hunters took their prisoner into Jericho. This one, called Gestus, would be imprisoned there. His fate was in the hands of others, not the people of Tobba. The others hurried back to Tobba, carrying the news of their discovery. John had been found! He was alive, but injured. For the moment he was in the hands of those at Qumran. They had the better skills for healing. It would not be good to try to move him back to Tobba, not now. Tonight they would offer special prayers for their friend!

With that good news being shared by all the residents of

Tobba, Jakin took Tobiah aside and confessed his concern. John did not know them! He looked at them, but he did not know them!

"Tobiah, what does that mean? Was the trauma of his fall and treatment too much? Was it the blow on his head, the deep cut on his forehead? Will he recover from that? Surely, if what you say about Yahweh is true, he will be well again!"

"Jakin, I cannot thank you enough for bringing John back to us, alive. It is a miracle, that he is alive. I am confidant Yahweh was watching over him. I am also confident John will recover. That might take a long time. We just don't know. Tomorrow morning, early, I will go to Qumran. Perhaps he will be much improved.

"Can you imagine? He must have lost a lot of blood, and I'm guessing he has had nothing to eat for a long time. How long we don't know. I'm sending Nathan up to Bethlehem tomorrow. Perhaps he can learn something, whether John had visited there, and when he might have left. Surely we can find out when he left, coming down that old donkey trail. Be assured, Yahweh will continue to watch over him! We can only hope and pray, pray for this young man who means so much to all of us!

Later that evening, after the ritual bathing, after the prayers, Debra came to her father. It was evident, she had been weeping. In a weak, trembling, voice, she shared her need for his comfort and support.

"Father, I have a confession to make. I know I have done wrong. I have sinned! While John was living here, I fell in love with him. I wanted him to love me, and I did my best to make him love me. The night of his first hunt, after he and the hunters returned, I went to his quarters, trying to make him lie with me. He almost did, but nothing happened. We did talk, long into the night. It was then I realized he was different, that he was being called of Yahweh. As such, he would never respond to the love I wanted. He would never marry. He was Yahweh's!

"I'm not sure what would have happened, if he had stayed with us, but I knew he would not stay. That same night I came to that conclusion. He would leave us! I think I realized that before he did, and before he shared that with you.

"Father, I still love him, but not in the way most would think. After he slipped away that last night, I have wrestled with my feelings, and now I know he is, and will be, a special servant of Yahweh. I wanted you to know that. Also, I want to help restore him to health. He needs to come back here. We are his family! We are his friends!"

Debra dropped her head. Her shoulders shook. She was crying, again. What would her father think of her now? Would he let us stay and help, or would he drive her out of the village? She had committed a great sin! As the elder of the village, he had to do what was right, best for all.

The one thing she did not, would not share, was the events of that last night, the night John left. She knew what that would do to her father. She had said enough. The rest she would take to her grave. Forgiveness for that would have to come from Yahweh!

For several minutes Tobiah sat in silence. He looked down. He looked at Debra. He stared into the night. Then, standing up, he lifted his daughter up, embraced her, and wept with her.

"Debra, I have lived a long time. I have two fine children, a son and a daughter. I have watched you grow up, and I know much, far more than you might imagine. I knew you were in love with John. I watched you go through the development of that love. Some things, of course, I did not know, only suspected. At the time I did nothing, said nothing. I believed it was best for you to learn for yourself, what was best for you.

"You have learned! You understand what lies ahead for John. I can, to some degree, appreciate how you must feel. That has been most difficult for you! It will always be difficult for both men and women, when that sort of love is never fulfilled. I can understand that.

"I thank you for coming to me, talking to me, sharing your

feelings. That was not easy, and I appreciate that. We will not speak of this again. No one else will ever know! And, yes, you will help John. I have an idea that could make a big difference in his healing. We will have to wait and see the possibilities. However, the main thing is to bring him back here, Hopefully, he will respond to familiar surroundings. Now, let us get some sleep."

With one final embrace, Tobiah left his daughter and headed for his quarters. Neither he nor Debra would do much sleeping.

Tobiah was up early. Calling the villagers together for morning prayers, he asked Yahweh's blessings for John. He also prayed for guidance, that Yahweh would help them do what was best for John. The focal point for all of them was their friend, soon to be, again, a resident of Tobba. He was one of them! Then he hurried on his way. He wanted to see John himself! He would not be content with less. Accompanied by Jakin, they headed for Qumran.

Welcomed by the leader of the community, Kemuel, they were taken to see John. As they walked toward the infirmary, a separate building overlooking the back wadi, Kemuel warned them. John was better, physically. His cuts and bruises had been treated. Cleansing and bathing had done wonders. Beyond that, there was nothing. John did not know them, did not know his situation, his present situation. He made no response, other than smile. He did not speak, seemed unable to speak.

"On your first visit here, when you brought John to meet us, I said to him, 'If you are ever in need, or if we can help you in any way, we will be here.' Now, he is in need and we have been unable to do very much. Tobiah, I am distressed! John's recovery, beyond what we have been able to do, is in Yahweh's hands. We have been able to feed him a broth of the best lentils. He will regain his physical strength. We are confident of that! The rest is in Yahweh's hands."

"Kemuel, we thank you for your help, your immediate

response to John's critical needs. Jakin told you yesterday what we suspected. Apparently he had fallen, coming down the old donkey trail from Bethlehem, Found by a band of thieves, he was left for dead. In fact, they took his possessions and pushed him into a narrow wadi. It was only by Yahweh's intervention he was found. A sudden, out-of-season, rainstorm washed him all the way down to us and to you.

"Now, we will continue to ask Yahweh's help in John's full recovery. I am confident that will happen. He will recover!"

"How can you be so sure? We have seen other cases where nothing changed. We have seen men lose all touch with reality and never recover. What makes you think this will be different for this young man? Sure, we will continue to pray! We will do so every day. Do you know something more, some information we do not have? I do remember his father Zechariah, a well-known, faithful, respected priest. However, nothing was said about his son, other than his birth was a surprise. Both his parents were elderly when he was born."

Tobiah asked Kemuel to sit down before they went in to see John. Under the shade of a willow tree, Tobiah told him the full story, all he knew about this special individual. Yahweh's messenger, Gabriel, had predicted his birth. He would be, some day, a prophet of Yahweh. John would recover! How long that would take, was up to Yahweh. They, those living in Qumran and those living in Tobba, could only help, watching over their friend day by day.

Amazed by this new knowledge, Kemuel smiled. It was his first good news of the day. He, too, believed in the power of Yahweh. He knew it! John was, indeed, Yahweh's own!

Inside, John was propped up in bed. Looking straight ahead, he made no move to recognize his visitors, not until they spoke. Kemuel spoke first.

"John, your friends from Tobba are here, Tobiah and Jakin. They want to visit with you. One of these days you will be able to go back home with them. What do you think of that?"

John turned; looked at all three men, smiled, but said

nothing. He did respond, but there was absolutely no awareness of relationships. He was, indeed, in another world. The best and only response was just that, a smile.

Tobiah tried! He talked about Tobba. He talked about his friends there. He talked about the hunters.

"See! Jakin is here, the one who took you on your first hunt!"

Again, there was the smile, nothing more. John had not come home, not yet. Only time, and Yahweh's action, would change that. How long that would take was anyone's guess. They could only wait and do what they felt best in support. He would be fed, clothed, and loved! When the healers believed it appropriate, he would go home to Tobba.

# CHAPTER 31

*. . . for thou doest not give me up to Sheol,
or let thy godly one see the Pit . . .*
                                Psalm 16:10

He sat quietly, eyes narrowed against the afternoon sun. Yet, it didn't seem to matter, whether his eyes were open, narrowed, or closed. There was little reaction. Even the deep blue of the Salt Sea stirred no interest. Blue water, blue sky, white lacy clouds overhead, sea gulls, long-legged cranes, brown, rocky cliffs to the north, all were the evidences of Yahweh's beautiful creation. They meant nothing to John.

His recovery from the cuts and bruises of the fall and flood was complete, his physical strength restored. The priests of Qumran had given him the best of care. Now, well-fed, neatly dressed, beard trimmed meticulously, he was the picture of health, a handsome young man. Daily exercise was a requirement at Qumran and John followed those orders, but with no understanding. He worked side by side with the younger men, moving cut stones for a new building. He could lift with the strongest. Yet, there was no healing of heart or mind. He did not speak. He did not respond, other than a sometimes smile, never a big one.

For his friends, both at Qumran and at Tobba, John's condition was a constant heartache. Daily care, daily prayers, daily attempts in seeking some improvement, went nowhere.

They all failed! After six weeks at Qumran, it was decided to move John back to Tobba, to more familiar surroundings. It made no difference. Nothing changed.

As the days and weeks, and, yes, years went by, nothing changed. Most of the residents stopped coming by, weary with the failure of all their efforts. It seemed so useless, so hopeless. By now the healers of Qumran were convinced there would be no restoration of mind or spirit. The daily prayers were offered, but, for the most part, that, too, had become a matter of routine and habit. The words were said, but always with a sense of question and doubt. Yahweh's ears were closed to their calls for deliverance.

Tobiah and his family became John's family. They gave him their son's room. Son Joel had married and moved away, just east of Jericho. The restrictions of the pietistic life at Tobba were not for him.

Tobiah's wife, Huldah, made sure John had the best of foods. She would keep him strong and healthy! Tobiah cared for his physical needs, his bathing and dressing. He made sure John continued with his strenuous exercise. Building was always going on, that or repairs to existing buildings. Debra washed his clothes, walked with him, stayed by his side and talked to him, day after day. He was alone only when he was sleeping. During his waking hours someone was always near, always hopeful for a miracle.

Special days were important to these people of Tobba, anniversary days, birth dates, marriage dates, death dates. As it was with all the people of Israel, so it was with them. The records were important! They remembered!

John turned twenty-four, and they celebrated. Around an open fire they sang songs of hope. They brought gifts, small gifts, pretty gifts. They hugged John and wished him well, and, as they departed, they wept. John's smile was still the same, his eyes open, but not seeing.

After all had left, and the fire had died down to red coals, Tobiah came to escort John back to his room for the night, but Debra asked him to wait.

"Father, you said several years ago, when John was found, you had an idea that might make a difference in his healing. To my knowledge, you have never mentioned it again. What was it? John needs our help!"

""Yes, Debra, I did have an idea, but never put it to the test. In fact, I had forgotten about it. We were trying so many things, hoping Yahweh would act. Now, I'm not so sure my first idea would even work. It sounded good to me at the time. We would read to John, reading from the Scrolls he knew so well. I thought that might stimulate a response, but after all these months and years I'm doubtful.

Debra brought her hands up to the sides of her head. She hit her fist against her forehead. Her father's response was the answer!

"Why didn't I think of that? That could work. Remember how John was so intense when it came to those Scrolls? They are still in the library, are they not? Let me try, father. Let me try! I can at least do that, read to him."

Tobiah was thinking; Debra could read. She had been well educated by her father. Perhaps it would work. Nothing else had worked! Why not?

"Very well, Debra, go ahead, try it! Tomorrow morning take John to the library. We will have to clear more space, provide a place for both of you to sit. Perhaps, when the weather is good, you could sit outdoors, over there under the trellis. Who knows, it might work! We pray so! However, let me caution you. Don't be too disappointed if this fails. You know how long it has been since John came back to us. None of the healers have ever seen that happen, not after all these months and years. They say it is impossible!"

As her father walked with John to his room, Debra picked up a lamp and headed for the library. "Yahweh, help me to select the right scroll as a beginning!"

Excited over the prospects, Debra couldn't wait to finish the morning meal. Following the prayers and the bathing rituals, she led John to the library. Sitting him down, she reached for a Scroll and began to read.

It was from the Torah, the words of Moses. Much of it she did not understand, but she read, hour after hour. John gave no response. There was no reaction. She could have been reading anything, letters or tax records. There was no response.

This went on for days, but nothing changed. She sensed no awareness in John. She talked it over each evening with her father, thought about each night as she tried to sleep. She prayed about it, asking Yahweh's guidance. It was most discouraging. Several times, her father cautioned her. John's recovery was doubtful. He may never respond, even to the reading of his precious Scrolls.

Then, she changed her approach. She would forget about Moses, all those laws and rules and regulations. She would turn to the songs, the songs of David, some happy, some pleading, and some rejoicing.

Sitting next to John the next morning, she spoke slowly, distinctly. She leaned toward his right ear, and began to read:

> *Give ear to my words, O Lord; give heed to my groaning.*
> *Hearken to the sound of my cry, my King, my Yahweh,*
> *For to you I do pray.*
> *O Lord, you do hear my voice;*
> *In the morning, I prepare a sacrifice for you, and watch.*

As she continued through the words of the psalm, she kept her eyes on John's face, looking for, hoping for some response. She saw nothing!

Searching for another song of David, she picked one which spoke of rejoicing:

*I will give thanks to the Lord with my whole heart;*
*I will tell of all your wonderful deeds.*
*I will be glad and exult in you,*
*I will sing praise to your name, O Most High.*

This time, as she continued to read, she reached out to hold John's hand, and almost dropped the Scroll. Stifling a cry in her throat, she continued to read, again raising her voice. John had squeezed her hand! She did not stop as his grip became tighter. She had reached him! He was listening to the words of Yahweh!

Finishing that Psalm, she paused. What to do? Did she dare broadcast what had happened? Should she find her father and tell him? No, not yet. She had to be sure this was no accident, no odd coincidence, no involuntary reaction. She would continue.

What to read next? Searching through the Scrolls, she turned again to David. His songs were beautiful, and so meaningful. Surely, they would speak to John's heart!

*Preserve me, O Yahweh, for in you I take refuge.*
*I say to the Lord, 'You are my Lord;*
*I have no good apart from you.*

*Therefore my heart is glad, and my soul rejoices;*
*My body also dwells secure.*
*For you do not give me up to Sheol,*
*Or let your own see the Pit.*

She continued, watching intently for some additional, visible sign, and it came! Not only did he squeeze her hand, his eyes narrowed, as though he was thinking. He turned his head, and looked at her!

Almost afraid to go on, Debra put the Scroll back into its proper slot, reached over and hugged John. This time she could feel his reaction. He shivered, as though he had never been hugged before. She was getting through to him. It wasn't much, but a door was opening!

Debra couldn't help herself. She said it, loud and clear, something she had never vocalized:

"Yahweh! Thank you! Yahweh, thank you!"

This time, John turned to her, as though in wonderment. It was something he couldn't quite grasp, but he was reacting, not only to her voice, but to her words. She was getting through!

Almost overcome by the emotion of the moment, Debra stopped the reading. Taking John's hand she led him outside.

"John," she said. We don't want to overdo it. Let's go for a walk."

John said nothing, as though he heard nothing. Pulled by Debra, he walked by her side. She was looking for her father, but he was not to be found. Then, she remembered. He and Jakin were to take more skins over to Qumran this morning. They would not be back until afternoon. Her report to him would have to wait.

Not quite sure as to what to do next, she kept walking toward the west. As they walked she talked of what they were seeing, especially the plants and trees. Trying to find the words she hoped would reach through to John, continuing to move westward, she suddenly realized they had reached the place of practice, where she had taught John to shoot.

The memories of that day touched her, if not John. For a brief moment, with flushed face, she though of what might have been. However, she quickly put that aside. There were more important things to do, and perhaps the bow and arrows might help. She would seek Jakin's help.

Returning to the village, getting fresh drinking water for the two of them, she led John back to the library. This time she would read something different, something from one of the prophets, but which one? She did not realize it, had no way of knowing it, but, reaching to the top of the cabinet, she pulled out the first Scroll John had opened years before. It was the prophet Joel!

Reading first to herself, she had her doubts. This one began on such a gloomy note. Yet, she was entranced by the prophet's words of warning. Perusing the writing, she began to read aloud:

> *Sanctify a fast, call a solemn assembly.*
> *Gather all the elders and all the inhabitants of the*
> *land to the house of the Lord your Yahweh*
> *And cry to the Lord.*
> *Alas, for the day!*
> *For the Day of the Lord is near and as destruction*
> *from the Almighty it comes. Is not the food cut off*
> *before our eyes . . .*

Suddenly, she stopped. She had to stop! John jumped up, arms raised above his head. In a trembling, weak voice he spoke! "Yes! Yes! Yes!"

This time it was John shaking with emotion. He buried his face in his hands, sobbing. Then, dropping to the floor, he curled up in a fetal position, and fainted!

Debra screamed for help. Leaving John, dashing from the room, she found her mother and sent her to look for Japhia. He was getting old, but was the only one in the village with any medical skills. In the absence of her father, she didn't know what else to do.

Returning to the room with a wet cloth, she started washing John's face. In a few minutes Japhia hobbled in, wondering about all the commotion.

"What happened to John? Why is he curled up like that on the floor? Debra, what's going on?"

Debra did her best to explain, describing the events of the morning, carrying out her father's suggestion.

"Japhia, I think John is better. He heard me reading, and he responded. For the first time in all these years, he has spoken.

He must be better! Tell me, Japhia, what can we expect? Is he going to be all right? What is happening to John?"

"Debra, this I cannot explain. Those at Qumran could not explain John's problem. To them, as to us, it was a mystery. Only Yahweh knows the answers, but I do know this. John is breathing easy and I don't think he is in any danger. We can only watch him and wait. Hopefully, he will recover, fully. There is nothing else I, or anyone else, can do. We should take him back to his room. There he can rest comfortably."

Debra called for help, and they did what Japhia suggested. John was carried in and put on his bed. All left, except for Debra. She would not leave his side. Even after her father and Jakin returned from Qumran she would not leave.

"Father, you were right! Reading from the Scrolls was the answer. John did respond. He spoke! He spoke for the first time! When he wakes up he will be fine!"

"Debra, you can't be sure. Japhia doesn't know. How can you know? What makes you so sure?

"I can't explain it, but I know! He will be fine, as soon as he wakes up. I will not move from this room until he does!"

Tobiah could only shake his head. He knew his daughter, how stubborn she could be. Perhaps she is right. Regardless, we will have to wait.

"I'll have your mother bring you something to eat. You might be here a long time."

He left. There was no point in both of them sitting and waiting. Debra would have to learn the hard way. Yes, there had been a change, a dramatic change, but now John was not responding. It seemed to be a cruel setback.

It was a long night, but Debra would not move from the bedside. She did stand up from time to time. She had a basin of warm water and would wipe John's face. He resisted, but did not open his eyes. She prayed! Yahweh was besieged with her pleas.

In the midst of her praying, she almost laughed out loud. Here she was, Debra, the one who had so little to do with religious affairs, praying. A few years back she would have laughed. Back then, as she told John, she wanted to deal only with things she could see and touch! Now, here she was, praying, and praying, and praying!

The one window in the room was open to the east, and Debra was able to see the light of another dawn. The oil lamp had gone out, but the light of a new day was penetrating the shadows. Standing up, stretching her arms, she looked down at John. His eyes were open! With wrinkled brow, he was staring at the ceiling. Then, he turned, saw Debra and asked her.

"What are you doing here? You don't belong here. This is my room!"

Debra reached down, hugged John, sat back down and wept tears of joy. She was right! John had come back to them. He was well! Yahweh had answered her prayers, and the prayers of all the people!

"I don't understand," John responded. "This really isn't my room. Why am I here? The last thing I remember was falling, falling down a steep trail. Where am I? And what are you doing here, Debra? You are supposed to be in Tobba! How did you get here? I'm confused."

He set up, turned, put his feet on the floor, and stood up. It was confusing. It was a familiar room, one he had seen before. Although he did not remember when, it was the room he had occupied when he arrived in Tobba on a threshing sled. But, how did he get here? How did Debra fit into the picture? Why was she here?

"John, we know about you fall. You did have an accident, coming down from Bethlehem. We checked that out, a long time ago. You not only fell, hitting your head, badly; you were caught in a wadi that was filled with water from a sudden rainstorm. You were washed all the way down, off the cliffs, to the valley below, just outside the community of Qumran.

"At Qumran they healed your wounds, helped make you

well. Then you were brought back to us, here at Tobba. However, there was one problem we could not solve. You didn't know us. You didn't know anyone. You could not speak. You were alone, in your own little world, and we could not reach you!"

"Debra! I cannot believe that! How long did this go on? How long ago was that? I've lost all track of time. That must have been weeks ago!"

"Yes, John, not only weeks, but months, and years. That happened about four years ago!"

John, startled, looked at Debra, looked at himself, his cloths, felt his face, his beard.

"I am older, and, I have to assume you are older. Debra, you haven't changed that much, but I can see a difference in your face. There is sadness there. Why is that?"

"John, when you lived here with us, I was in love with you. You know that, and you know what happened with us, between us, something that should have never happened. You have to live with that and so do I.

"However, that is past. I know about you and Yahweh. You told me that a long time ago. You are his, called to do what he wants of you. That relationship comes first. I don't understand what that really means, but I do know you cannot belong to me. That makes me sad. I will love you and, as long as you are here, care for you. Believe me! We will be good friends, I hope. I will help you as much as I can."

It was the most difficult speech Debra had ever made, more difficult than telling her father about her relationship with John, and her feelings about John. Yet, it was one she had to make. Her heart was broken, but she felt relieved. A burden had been lifted from her shoulders! Her voice was strained, her face washed with tears, but John had come home to Tobba and to his family. Yahweh had heard her, listened to her. Yahweh had answered her!

Catching her breath, trying to hide her emotions, she took John's hand and led him out the door.

"I'm hungry! Let's go find something to eat."

# CHAPTER 32

> ... make a joyful noise to the Lord all the earth;
> sing the glory of his Name.
> Psalm 66:1

That night, all the residents of Tobba gathered in the villa courtyard. It was filled to overflowing. They would have invited the residents of Qumran, but knew they would not come. Their lives were in Qumran. They would leave only in death. Even then, their bodies would be buried there. John would visit them in a day or so, thanking them for their help in restoring him to health.

He would also thank them for the Scrolls, their dedicated work of copying the words of Yahweh, Moses and the prophets. There were other writings, but these held little interest for John. Through Debra's reading from the scriptural Scrolls, Yahweh had touched his life again, restored his life!

It was a night of celebration. John had come back to them! Given the place of honor, he received all that came, young and old. It was an amazing event, with John remembering most of the names. Although the stone arrowheads had come to the hunters in a most unusual way, they thanked him for remembering their needs for the hunt. The arrowheads were the key to finding John alive. These would be treasured, used over and over again. They wanted to talk about future hunts, but tonight was not the time. Yet, they did remind him to look up. The full moon rising over the Salt Sea was perfect for hunting, outshining the many torches set around the courtyard. John laughed with them, thanking them for the reminder. Perhaps they could go hunting again.

There was one difference, however, a sense of wonderment and awe among the adults present. These were Yahweh's people, dedicated to him, not only in ritual, but also in daily living. Religion was a way of life, the only way. However, they were now faced with something far above their spiritual experiences.

Anyone called of Yahweh had to be special and, from what Tobiah had told them, John was special! He was more, far more, than a young stranger who had come to be a part of their lives. He was, or would be, Yahweh's servant. Some envisioned him as a future *Mashiach*, one to be anointed as prophet. How does one approach a person called of Yahweh?

John did his best to put all at ease, recounting his many mistakes as a resident of Tobba. His first efforts at sowing seed and sewing garments were disasters! He had trouble making flour and baking bread. Daily household tasks had been difficult for him to learn. They should remember how he failed so miserably in handling the bow and arrow? They were the special ones, not John!

With that give and take, they enjoyed the evening. Finally, most forgot John's unique position where Yahweh was concerned. After all, he was one of them, a child, a brother, a neighbor, a friend come back home! John belonged to them, a full-fledged resident of Tobba. For the present, regardless of the future, he had come back home! Yahweh was far above the heavens, but, as Debra had said, John they could see and touch.

It was no wonder there was little sleep that night. Even after the torches gave out, the full moon discouraged any thought of retiring. With the children asleep, the adults continued to share stories and raise questions. They wanted to know about John's travels, his wilderness adventures, where he had been, what he had done.

In response, John gave them an abridged account.

"I couldn't begin to describe to you all the places I have been, those I met along the way, all that happened to me, but let me share one story about a place far to the north."

He told them the story of Megiddo, how he found the place with the help of a Roman centurion. He told them about Megiddo's one resident, Josiah. He told them about the tunnel to the water supply. Above all, he told them about Josiah's sense of hopelessness. Israel was no more! Kings Solomon's fortress was in ruins. Israel was in bondage. Israel needed a deliverer, a Savior. With that as background, he reminded them of Yahweh's promises. A Savior would come. They would be free! There would be peace, again. Those faithful to Yahweh would rejoice!

As the moon moved into the western sky, nodding heads made it quite clear. It was time to call a halt. The morning would come far too soon.

John continued to sleep in the son's room. He was family! Under other circumstances that would have proven awkward. Debra's room was just across a narrow courtyard. Now, it was different. Although both he and Debra would never forget what had happened, or what might have been, their relationship was different.

Yet, there was for Debra an emptiness she knew would never be filled. She could not have what she would have given her life to have, John! She had fallen in love, willing to give herself fully to him. How could she deal with that, never letting John know how she felt deep inside? She had to come to grips with the conflict between her mind and her heart. Her mind told her the affair was over, even though her heart was broken!

With everyone else asleep, Debra and John sat side by side on a bench in the connecting courtyard. They would talk until almost dawn. John sensed Debra's dilemma, her desperate need for answers, and he needed to respond, for himself, as well as for her.

"John, tell me about this Yahweh thing. I remember some of what you said to me the night of your first hunt, the night I tried to seduce you."

The last was said with a smile, almost an embarrassing smile. It was still difficult to bring to mind those special moments in her life.

"Tell me more. You shared some of that before I left you, and my father told us that before you were born, Yahweh's messenger spoke to your father with a prediction. You would grow up to be one of Yahweh's prophets. You would prepare the way for the Lord. You would, someday, announce the coming of a Savior. What does that mean? How do you do that? Who is this Savior, who will come? Our elders speak of a Messiah to be anointed. Is that the same as a Savior? I don't understand all this religious talk."

"Debra, it is difficult to understand, and I don't have all the answers. I wish I did. It would make life much easier, for everyone, especially for me.

"First of all, I don't understand why this last tragedy happened to me, why I fell and why it took so long to recover. I suppose Yahweh was not ready for me, and still isn't. Perhaps Yahweh thought I was in too much of a hurry to get back to the wilderness. Who knows? I don't.

"As to the main part of the story, it involves me and another man, my cousin. He was born a few months after I was born. He has an earthly mother whose name is Mary. They now live up in Galilee, in the town of Nazareth. I say an earthly mother, because he is Yahweh's son. His name is Jesus, a name which means Savior."

Debra sat up straight, eyes wide open, a startled look of bewilderment on her face, as John began his story of Yahweh's promise to his people. He would deliver his own from bondage. Roman rule would be a thing of the past. He would fulfill that promise, made centuries ago, through his own son. They would be free again! Then, they would be a light to all nations, whatever that meant. Yahweh's messenger, Gabriel, had predicted both his birth and the birth of his cousin, Jesus.

John did his best in sharing what he knew, and believed. He wanted her, above anyone else, to understand, and believe. She deserved nothing less! He did love her, not as a lover, but as the closest and dearest of friends. Their lives had been joined physically, and now they must be joined spiritually. Yahweh would use them both! He was hopeful of that.

It was almost dawn when the two parted, going to their separate rooms. Debra was still shaking her head in wonder, almost disbelief. John's story was incredible, difficult to understand. The more disturbing factor was an awesome reminder of Yahweh's presence. He, the Almighty, had come to their little village of Tobba. He had become reality, a present reality. He had not only touched their lives, but he would direct their lives. Where and when he would lead them was a great mystery, but he was not through with them, not yet. The word Debra wrestled with as she lay down, seeking sleep, was "fear." She shivered with the thought. It was, indeed, frightening!

Tobiah let them sleep, the whole community. Even the younger children had stayed up far beyond their bedtime. He would not call them at the usual, early hour. John had recovered, cause for celebration. As far as Tobiah could tell, his healing, his restoration was complete. There was work to be done, but prayers and the ritual baths could wait. Once all were up, they would gather again, in thanksgiving.

It turned out to be a beautiful day and, for all the residents, a lazy day. Once the prayers were offered and the rituals completed, Tobiah required only the most essential tasks, caring for the animals and preparing for the evening meal. The curing and tanning of skins could wait another day. It was fortunate the grapes for the winery could wait another day. Bread had been baked the day before. The hunters would not be going out until the following month.

John did not return to Qumran until after the next Sabbath. He, too, was content to rest, gradually working his way through the village, visiting with all the residents. Each family deserved attention and words of appreciation. All had offered prayers to Yahweh on his behalf. All had been attentive to his needs during his illness. Many of the men had made the trip to Qumran, bringing gifts while he was still there.

On the first day of the following week, he walked to Qumran, alone. This time he wanted to focus on them, the residents of the community, without any distractions. Also, if Kemuel approved, he would spend the night. He wanted to visit the scriptorium again, watch the scribes at their work, and thank them for their writings. The Scrolls had become an integral part of his own life and he wanted to express his thanks. They were doing Yahweh's work!

He had to step aside once, between Tobba and Qumran. A body of horseman forced him out of their way. At first he thought they were Roman soldiers, but they were not. They belonged to Herod, apparently heading for his fortress at Masada. As they slowed their pace for a moment, he heard their curses, cursing Jews who acted so pious. They would have run him down if he had not stepped behind a large boulder.

Kemuel welcomed him warmly. He and the other residents had heard about John's miraculous recovery. Yahweh had blessed them! In response to John's words of gratitude, those gathering for the evening meal simply bowed their heads in acknowledgement. To do more would have been an act of pride. Tonight they shared a grain broth, unleavened bread and a small cup of sour wine. It was not for pleasure, but for cleansing. John was grateful the cups were small. Wine, even bitter, was not for him. Actually, the community was renowned for its wine, the sweetest of wines, but that was for export, much in demand.

Qumran was noted for its wine. Their wine was an excellent source of income for the community.

The meal was served and shared in silence. Following the prayers, no one spoke. At the conclusion of the meal, each one carried his bowl, cup and spoon to the adjoining room. Others would scour and wash the utensils in hot water. These people knew the essentials of good health.

Typical of all the villages, job assignments were made. Every member of the community was expected to do his share. There were farmers, vinedressers, cooks and bakers. There were keepers of the wine vats and presses. There were the potters and the makers of ink and pens. There were the caretakers of the beehives. Honey was one delicacy all were permitted to enjoy.

Separate from all the rest, were the scribes. Bent over their desks in the scriptorium, they wrote on leather, copying the scriptures as well as recording the communities' writings of teachings and beliefs. Much of that dealt with both history and prophesies concerning the "Sons of Light," in contrast to the "Sons of Darkness."

Belial was the Prince of Darkness, standing in opposition to the Teacher of Righteousness. There would be a Holy War, and evil would be defeated. There would be not one, but two messiahs, one a priest and one a royal king. Their victories would bring to an end the Age of Wickedness. Peace would prevail, with Yahweh's kingdom set up here, on earth. False teachings and disregard for Mosaic laws would be no more!

The thoughts and teachings of the elders of Qumran, as well as those in the nearby communities, were preserved in the Scrolls. Concerned for the future of the nation of Israel, these Scrolls would be treasured and shared. For them, these were the proper and holy thoughts of Yahweh!

Following the meal, John sat at length with Kemuel, answering his questions about himself and the promised Messiah. He did his best to help Kemuel accept his thoughts on Yahweh's revealed plans and promises. He told about the miracle of Yahweh's son, as well as his own role, as he understood it.

Kemuel was not convinced. He heard John out, but gave no indication of acceptance. In response, he talked more of conflict and war, the Holy War. Good would clash with evil in a terrible encounter. Eventually, the "Sons of Light" would prevail, but he could give no specifics. The leader of light was yet unknown, but, at the proper time, would be revealed. In the meantime, they would have to be patient, continuing to prepare their writings for those who would come after them.

Jerusalem had gone over to the side of evil and would be destroyed. Most of the priests and, certainly, the High Priest, had gone over to the side of the forces of evil, the Romans. King Herod had pacified and pleased them in the rebuilding of the Temple, but Herod was evil. He had murdered members of his own family, including a wife and a mother-in-law. Strict adherence to the Mosaic code had been forgotten, ignored. They, too, would be punished. Only the true sons of Yahweh would prevail!

He went on to talk of preparations. When the time was right, they would fight! The wilderness would run with blood! The Scrolls, their work would be hidden from the evil ones. No one must find them not until their new leader, their *Mashiach*, would arise and bring them to victory. He used the Hebrew word for Messiah, but with a special meaning. He would be the one anointed with holy oil, destined to be a warrior, called to lead them in the Holy War.

Surprised by the intensity of Kemuel's voice, John listened quietly. A silent prayer to Yahweh, asked for guidance, a way to help his Qumran friends see the proper message, the revealing light of Yahweh's son. What more could he do?

There was one point of contact, one common ground, the need to protect and hide the Scrolls. At least they were in agreement on that.

"Kemuel, you are so right! The Scrolls must be stored away, carefully. This must be done, before it is too late. Do not neglect that responsibility. I would ask you, again, to read Yahweh's words, carefully, then prepare for the safety of the Scrolls!"

Kemuel, once he had finished talking, kept his promise. He went with John to the scriptorium, asking those at their desks to welcome their visitor. Would they be so kind as to let this special man of Yahweh watch what they were doing?

John wasn't sure. The scribes gave no indication of their thoughts. They continued to bend over their work, no words spoken. Kemuel assured John they were willing. If they had been unwilling, they would have simply walked out. John could stay as long as he desired.

It was intriguing, fascinating, the way these men handled ink and pen. Swiftly, but carefully, the letters were applied. Their writing was beautiful. John had seen none finer. Every letter, every word, was a work of art. Even in the darkness of the night, smoke rising from the oil lamps, the writing was done. One scribe was copying the words of Isaiah. Another was working on the Scroll containing a commentary on the writings of Habbakuk. Looking over the shoulders of the writers, John could make out many of the words, words he had read and memorized.

How could they write so beautifully, so adroitly? Some had been at their desks for many years. Gnarled, ink-stained fingers had difficulty in sharpening and dipping pens in the cups of ink. For some the movements were swift and smooth, but for others the writing was slow and labored. Yet, the results were the same, works of art! These men were dedicated, intensely faithful to their calling.

He lost track of time, but the position of the rising moon let him know it was late. Although the scribes gave no indication of being tired, he was. It was time to find his assigned place for sleeping. Tomorrow he would return home to Tobba. As he moved out of the building, he shuddered, disturbed by what he had seen and heard. The words and thoughts of Kemuel were unsettling. How could these people come to their own conclusions, not in keeping with the promises and purposes of Yahweh? More important, how would this play out in the days and years to come? How would Jesus see this, when he came? Surely, he would not approve.

It came as no surprise. Lying in the darkness of his private cell, he heard the voice of Yahweh. The first thing that came to mind was the time. It had been so long!

"John, it is time for you to return to your wilderness. Your mission is not yet, and, as I have said before, you must learn patience. However, you must be fully prepared for what is to come. Know that I was watching over you all along the way, when you fell and while you were unaware of your surroundings or your friends. That, too, was a part of my plan for you. You must understand that.

"You are right concerning Kemuel and his followers. They do see things differently. Yet, they are good people. Their efforts must be preserved before troubles come; and they will come! There shall be death and destruction, darkness and despair. Evil men will want to destroy all that is good. Kemuel is right concerning the terrible events that lie ahead. He is wrong concerning the Messiah. He is my son, and his kingdom will have no end, not an earthly kingdom, but one joining heaven and earth. The words are forgiveness and love, not hate or conflict. This, too, you must learn!

"Also, you have to know! Before it is all over, you will suffer and my son will suffer. However, your present way is clear. Return to Tobba. Go through the Scrolls again. They must be burned into your heart and mind, those that are my words. You do not yet fully understand what you are to do, what my son is to do, and what he will accomplish. It is all there. Find it! I know, it would be much easier for me to tell you, but I will not. Your own discoveries will mean more to you. My words are forever, and they are there, in the Scrolls.

"John, my beloved, there is one more thing. When I give the word, you are to make one more trip to Jerusalem. Find Jonathan and speak with him, no one else. One other will recognize you, and warn you. Listen carefully!

"Above all, Jonathan will be able to share with you the

current situation, the unrest and the coming dangers. That, too, will help guide you for what lies ahead. Trust me, for I am with you!"

John was both pleased and puzzled. Yahweh had spoken, again. His assurances were most gratifying, but what was missing? What was he to find in the Scrolls, something he had missed? Tomorrow he would return to Tobba and, hopefully, find out.

As he closed his eyes, the last thing he remembered was the library setting, where both he and Debra had read Yahweh's awesome words. What was there he needed to learn? He couldn't think. He slept!

# CHAPTER 33

*You are my servant, I have chosen you
and not cast you off*

Isaiah 41:9

The trip back to Tobba was uneventful, but there was little time for casual visits now. Tobiah had everyone busy at his or her assigned tasks. With the coming of the harvest it was time for diligence on everyone's part. Even the children were busy, cleaning out the almost empty granary. The new crop would be aired in the walled yard, protected from the farm oxen and donkeys. When properly dried, the sheaves would be stacked inside, waiting the later winnowing. The final storage would be in the large pottery jars lining the walls. There was work for all.

John found Tobiah coming in from the fuller's fields where the newly woven cloth had been treated, washed with lye and treaded by foot. Later, bleached in the sun, the cloth would be smoothed, dried and pressed. Tailors would do the cutting and sewing. Loincloths, tunics, under garments and dresses were always in demand. At Tobba, they had learned one additional and popular step, dying the cloth into a few rich colors. Their speciality was blue! As with some of their other endeavors, the cloth of Tobba found a ready market in the distant towns and villages.

John felt somewhat guilty in not joining in some phase of

the village work, but he knew he must follow Yahweh's instructions. He told Tobiah he would be in the library, reading and studying the Scrolls. From what Yahweh had indicated, it was time!

This time, and he couldn't explain why, he pulled out the scroll concerning the story of Daniel. He did remember something of Daniel, a young man taken to live in the court of the conquering king, Nebuchadnezzar, king of Babylon. He had been told that story when he was a small child. Both his father and mother wanted him to know that Yahweh was Lord of all and that Yahweh would keep him safe, always protecting his faithful ones.

It was a fascinating story for a young boy, the story of firey furnaces and hungry lions. However his attention was drawn now to the evils of Nebuchadnezzar's son, Belshazzar. One of his worst sins was drinking from the captured Temple vessels of gold and silver. This was truly an abomination to the Lord. That's when the hand and the handwriting appeared on the wall of the banquet hall: "MENE, MENE, TEKEL, and PARSIN.... Yahweh has numbered the days of your kingdom ... you have been weighed in the balance and found wanting ... your kingdom will be divided!"

What a story! Yahweh will come, shattering the pagan kingdoms of the world. Peace will come, as Yahweh's son comes. Yahweh's kingdom will be restored! Was that what Yahweh meant when he suggested studying the Scrolls again?

Sitting in the deepening shadows of the afternoon sun, John had to shake his head. There was more, something more and something different. It had to be! He had trouble ridding himself of a feeling of doubt and frustration. He realized his search was just beginning. His study and seeking had to be elsewhere, perhaps in the Psalms or in the great prophet Isaiah. He doubted he would find the right answers at this point in the Mosaic Law. He had poured over the stories of Yahweh's beginnings in Genesis. He had tried to remember the many laws in Leviticus, but was positive such would be of little help.

Lighting an oil lamp, he pulled out the largest scroll of all, Isaiah. Although he had read through this before, he wanted to retrace his steps. There he had found his calling, "a voice crying in the wilderness." He remembered, also, Isaiah's vision in the Temple, seeing the Lord Yahweh, high and lifted up, sitting on his throne. He remembered his final word in that awesome event: "Go!"

Yet, there had to be a deeper richness relating to what lay ahead. It had to do with Yahweh's purpose in sending his own son into the conflicts of human life. John knew his own thoughts centered on freedom, freedom from those pagan Romans. Israel would be free! Israel would be brought back to a right relationship with Yahweh, cleansed of all evil, all unrighteousess. We must be washed clean! Yahweh's rule, under the presence and power of the son, would be restored! Israel's enemies would be punished, destroyed!

As he unrolled the scroll, his eyes were drawn to Isaiah's oracle against Babylon. That certainly fit his own ideas concerning the enemies of Yahweh. They would be destroyed! Then, there were other passages of similar nature, Yahweh's anger against evil.

However, Isaiah wrote of joy and peace, and of love. There were those very positive words of encouragement:

> *Behold, Yahweh is my salvation. I will trust and will not be afraid.*

> *The people who walked in darkness have seen a great light; those who dwelt in a land of deep darkness, on them light shines. You have blessed the nation, increased its joy.*

Just below that was something about a special child. That had to be Isaiah's leap forward to Yahweh's son:

> *For to us a child is born, to us a son is given; and the government will be upon his shoulder, and his name*

> *will be called Wonderful Counselor, Mighty Lord,*
> *Everlasting Father, Prince of Peace. Of the increase of*
> *his government and of peace there shall be no end.*

Sure, there was that ongoing struggle with the bad. It had to go, be destroyed, but there was an outreach to all those Yahweh created. Isaiah was declaring that Israel would be a "light to the nations!"

> *I will give you as a light to the nations,*
> *that my Salvation may reach to the ends*
> *of the earth!*

John stopped to reflect on something he had heard somewhere in the recent past, Someone else suggesting a different word, different from John's approach of combating evil, of restoring Israel's fortunes. Where was it, who was it? Whose words had disturbed him, stirred him to rethink his position?

Deep in thought, John did not hear the opening of the library door. It was Debra. This time she couldn't resist. She leaned over John's shoulder, laughed, hugged and kissed him.

"I know, I shouldn't do that, but I had to. It is so good to have you back! Now, if Yahweh would just let you alone, I could have you back, for myself."

John sensed her laughter was strained. She was still wrestling with her emotions, her passionate desires. And, he had to admit; it was not easy for him. Her nearness stirred desires difficult to control. Why did this beautiful girl disturb him so?

In response, he stood up, held her close for a moment, and then sat her down on the stool next to his.

"Debra, you know what I think of you. I do love you, but we cannot do what we want. Please! Try to understand. We both need to be strong, do what Yahweh wants, not what we want."

Tears spilled from her eyes, but Debra nodded, trying her

best to produce a smile.

"You are right, but I don't like it, not one bit!"

That exchange made John remember. It was a girl, a woman, talking about love. It was Tabitha! How did she say it?

> "Perhaps Yahweh isn't so interested in restoring
> Israel to it's former greatness.
> From what I can understand about his plans,
> given through his prophets, he would want Israel
> to help all nations, whether enemies or not.
> Sure, the Romans are here, ruling over us, but
> our hearts and our minds are free.
> As I see it, Yahweh's big word is love,
> love for all people."

John jumped up and, surprising her, gave Debra a hug, a big hug!

"Thank you for coming in. You helped me remember what I couldn't remember. I do have a lot to learn."

That made no sense to Debra. She shook her head and started back out. At the door she turned and, with a quisical look, announced supper. It was time to eat, bathe and pray. Too much work, too much study was not helpful, and John was making no sense.

Making sense, or not, John gave most of his waking hours to the Scrolls. Reluctantly, he began to make sense of what he believed to be his mission. He must speak Yahweh's word, demanding repentence, yet prepare the way for the one coming with Yahweh's word of love and concern. The big question! How to put these two extremes together?

He knew he had much to learn, lessons which would fill his life in the months to come. Would he be permitted years to come?

Again, on a night following the routine of the day, John slipped away. The harvest was in. The barley grain was safely stored in the clay jars. The supply of deer meat had been dried and preserved. A sufficient number of skins had been put in the hands of the scribes of Qumran. All was quiet and peaceful. It was time to go! With no forewarning at all, John slipped away to his wilderness. There he would wait, waiting for Yahweh's call.

This time there was no well-filled backpack, no bow and no arrows. There was a blanket, a bowl, a spoon, and a knife. Tucked in with those items, there was a water skin, a loaf of unleavend bread and a few strips of dried meat. Clothes? He was wearing them, a loincloth and a linen tunic. Beyond that, Yahweh would provide.

# CHAPTER 34

*. . . an abomination has been committed in
Israel and in Jerusalem . . .*
                              Malachi 2:11

The morning sun penetrating the cave's opening awakened him. Most mornings, he would have been up and out before daylight. Usually his search for food began quite early. It was good to watch the sun burst over the distant ridge.

This morning was different. He knew this was the day for his departure, and he faced it with some reluctance. His daily routine was precisely that, routine. He knew what to expect each day, each week, even each month. That was comfortable, reassuring. Although he had decisions to make, where to walk or run, what to seek, those were his choices. This was his world, his home!

How many years had it been since he slipped away from his friends in Tobba? He knew, but had difficulty accepting the fact. It had been eight years, come next month, eight years from that harvest time he remembered so well. It didn't seem possible, but it was true!

Some distance down the valley, there was a small stream where John had cleared out the rocks and the brush. With a lot of hard labor, he had scooped out a basin for bathing. The cool, cleansing water was refreshing. He missed that on those days he traveled too far to return before dark. However, the darkness was no hindrance. He enjoyed the adventure. With Yahweh's care, as well as his ability to cope with new situations, he could always find a place to sleep.

This morning, looking into the smooth face of the still water, he laughed to himself. Was this the face of the son of Zechariah? It couldn't be! Bushy eyebrows, long hair, heavy black beard, clothes made of skins, nothing looked like the John others would recognize. His skin was dark and wrinkled, his arms covered with hair. His dark brown, deep-set eyes matched the depths of the pool into which he was staring. Yes, the years had changed him. He was older and, hopefully, wiser.

It must be so, for Yahweh had said so. At least, he said it was time to go. John must leave. His next stop would be Jerusalem. Yahweh had made that clear, years before. Now, only a few nights ago, he had repeated the message. He was to find Jonathan, speak to him, and no one else. After that, he would know what he was to do next. Tumultuous times lay ahead. More important, his cousin Jesus would come south, meet him at the river Jordan.

He felt sure Jonathan would never guess his identity. He would be seen as a wandering hermit of the desert, forbidden to enter the inner courts of the Temple. Any priest would have drawn back, declaring him unclean.

Jonathan would have changed too, but John believed he could identify him. It would be good to see him again! How many years had they been separated?

He felt some reluctance in making contact with Jonathan. It had nothing to do with appearances, but with the political situation. Several times he had come close to travelers wandering through. Listening to their conversations as they sat around an open fire, John was disturbed. Several uprisings against the Romans had been crushed, violently. He sensed unrest in the air, and the other ruling authorities had not helped. The Herods, beginning with King Herod, had gone over to the Romans. Brutal in their rule over Abraham's descendants, ominous clouds were rising over the horizon. How did Jonathan fit into that?

Jerusalem must be in an uproar, faced with so many changes in the power structures. That included the Temple and the priesthood. Before John and his father had moved away, the ruling governor, Quirinius, had appointed a new High Priest, Annas. From all indications, he had been a pawn of the governor, more interested in power than prayer. The house of Annas, the Sadducee, had replaced the house of Boethus.

Some eight years later, Valerius Gratus deposed Annas, replacing him with Ishmael, son of Phabi. With Annas and others competing for power, the High Priesthood changed hands again and again. In short order, Ishmael was followed by Eleazar, son of Annas, then Simon, son of Camithus, then Joseph Caiaphas, son-in-law of Annas. Caiaphas was no improvement. The house of Annas continued to hold onto its power. John had heard that news many times over, listening to passing travelers. The signs were not good!

John removed his clothing of skins, trimmed his beard, but not his hair. He bathed, walked about until his body was dry, then returned to the cave. On a ledge there was a piece of dry bread, which he had baked the week before. It didn't have much flavor, only some salt he had extracted from the water of the Salt Sea. Earlier, he had gleaned barley stalks left on the edge of a small farm far to the west. Crushing the grains between two smooth rocks, these had been mixed with milk from a wild goat. She really wasn't wild because John had tamed her. He had found her near death. A lion had killed the mother and the kid had run away to hide. She would come when John called, providing companionship, as well as milk.

John was proud of his oven, which he had erected years before. Carefully selecting small flat stones, he fitted them together with patience and skill. Shemuel would have been pleased with the results. It worked fine for what little baking he attempted.

Also, in a cup John had carved out of a dry piece of wood, was a bit of honey. The bees had resented the robbery, but John escaped with only a few stings. It was worth the effort. From time to time, John would find edible pods and greens. These were some of the food items John appreciated, gifts from Yahweh. Along with all the rest, there were the locusts. They were not his favorite, but they were nourishing.

Yahweh's care over the last, wilderness-lived years had been marvelous. He had learned to cope with and appreciate his amazing creation. He could sit for hours, watching. He watched the movement of life, from the smallest ant to the large deer at their favorite water hole. At the entrance to his home, the cave, a spider would weave its nightly web and wait for insects. He never disturbed her. Always, both near and far, the birds filled the sky with their beauty. Long legged cranes stalked along the water's shore, while high soaring eagles caught the winds far above. This was Yahweh's creation, rich and bountiful.

In the midst of all that, Yahweh talked! How many times had he spoken to John! In the quietness of the night he would speak, words of warning, but words of encouragement. His son was still in Nazareth, waiting. Mary was older, but in good health, trying to hold an active family together. Jesus' brothers were helping with the work of the carpenter shop, but were getting restless. They knew Jesus would be leaving, but they did not know when. They had no idea of what was to come. Only Mary had some sense of the future, a disturbing awareness of troubles and conflicts ahead.

Over the years John had learned his lessons well, not only the appreciation of Yahweh's created world, but also patience. The passing years were reminders that time was in Yahweh's hands. He would wait! As he waited he went through the Scrolls, over and over again. Yahweh made sure of that. He had a beautiful way of bringing them to John, clearly visible to his mind's eye. He also had an uncanny way of having John focus on what Yahweh wanted him to see, and remember. He had to admit, Yahweh was a good instructor, the best!

John hardly knew what to take with him, but he ended up taking only his knife and pouch. In the pouch were a few silver coins collected over the years. Several he had found along the road running north of Masada. Riders of horses were careless. Bouncing along, coins would spill to the ground.

He did make one change. Years before he had set aside his woven tunic. Knowing what was expected of him, he wanted to make sure he had a civilized piece of clothing. It was clean and would attract far less attention than a garment of skins. The garment was a little tight now, but comfortable. It would have to do. Once he was back, if he came back, he could change, again.

Moving northward, he followed the valleys cut into the rising hills. Avoiding the worst of the cliffs he worked his way to the north. Finally, he came to the ancient road just west of Tekoa, one of the outposts of long ago. The valley was south and east of Bethlehem, a fairly easy route into the Kidron valley and up the ridge to Jerusalem. With long, deliberate strides, John moved rapidly. By late afternoon he entered the western gate, the Dung Gate.

Most of the people were going in the opposite direction, heading out of the city, going home. The shops were closing and the Evening Sacrifice was just beginning. Apparently, for whatever reason, the priests were late getting started, and those leaving the city wanted to get out before dark. The Evening Sacrifice was not that important to them. For most it was dull routine!

Moving along with the smaller crowd approaching the Temple Mount, John looked for some familiar faces. There were none. It was not the turn of the Division of Abijah. These priest at the Temple were strangers, many much younger men. He would have to look elsewhere. He did remember where Jonathan lived, but he was hesitant. He wanted to see Jonathan, alone. His wife would have difficulty keeping his visit a secret.

Turning away, moving toward the steps, joining those going in the same direction, John was startled to see a familiar back. Yes, it had to be Jonathan. There was no mistaking that broad, humped shoulder. Jonathan was a tall man, standing above most others. It was Jonathan!

As he moved slowly down the steps, John approached him on his right side, and spoke, in a quiet, low voice:

"Could I help you, sir? You seem to have difficulty coming down."

Jonathan whirled around, ready to shout the name "John!" but did not. John placed his finger on his lips, and whispered:

"We must talk, just the two of us. Where can we go?"

Jonathan responded as John had indicated, leading him to a secluded area at the eastern edge of the Temple Mount. There, he entered a room, a place John had never seen before. It was a secret room, know only to Division leaders and High Priests. It was perfect for small meetings and for those seeking the sanctuary of Yahweh's Temple. Strangers would be brought in blindfolded.

Inside, Jonathan hugged John, and wept. It had been so long, and there had been no news over the passing years. Jonathan had heard about Zechariah's death, but little more. Tobiah had sent a messenger early on assuring him that John was in good hands. After that, there was nothing. With all the demands and difficulties of the Temple, as well as the political turmoil, no other contacts had been made. There were good intentions, but no actions.

They sat quietly for the longest time, eyes rimmed with tears. It was an emotional moment for both. Memories flooded in. There was so much to recall. Finally, with voice choking, Jonathan began to ask questions. First and foremost were the questions which had been raised long before. What was happening with the prophecies of long ago? Where was Yahweh in all this? Why are you here? What comes next?

John responded, trying his best to cover the passing years, his life at Tobba, his wilderness adventures, his journey north to Nazareth, and his visit with his cousin. Jonathan did remember John asking about his mother's cousin, her visit to his home.

John then retraced his steps south, telling about Megiddo, Caesarea, Joppa, Bethlehem, and his fall. He talked about his friends in Tobba and the men at Qumran.

Then, he began to talk about Yahweh, how Yahweh had spoken to him many times, how Yahweh had watched over him, protected him, directed him. As he talked, he revealed what Yahweh had done in sending his own son. The Messiah had come; now ready to be revealed to Yahweh's people.

Trying to keep it simple, trying to keep Jonathan's mind focused, John spoke slowly, but clearly. His miraculous birth was a part of Yahweh's plan. He had been promised by Gabriel, conceived, born, reared, and prepared for this one purpose, to be the forerunner of Yahweh's promised Messiah! Now, the time had come. Very soon the Messiah would be revealed to the entire world!

For the moment he was here, coming to Jerusalem, at Yahweh's request. He was to find Jonathan, speak only with him. Yahweh had made that quite clear. What Jonathan could share concerning the problems of both politics and religion, would help John in taking his next step. At the right time, he would meet his cousin, Jesus, at the Jordan River. There it would begin, the revealing of Yahweh's plan for his people.

Jonathan had difficulty taking in what he was hearing. He remembered Zechariah's encounter with Yahweh's messenger, Gabriel. He recalled Zechariah's words at John's naming. Yet, with the passage of years, he wondered. Does Yahweh operate like that? He had never come like that before. Sure, there was the promise made long ago, but Yahweh had given no word to any of his Pharisees or priests, certainly not to the High Priest.

No prophet had come forth to declare the Day of the Lord! How could this be?

Finally, his mind filled with too many questions, Jonathan made a suggestion.

"Let's put that aside for the moment. I cannot take all that in, not yet. As to Yahweh's suggestion that you come here, let me speak a word of warning. We are facing trouble, big trouble. We have before us a rising wave of unrest. Men are rallying around an intense desire for freedom. Weapons are being purchased and hidden. Some clashes have occurred and men have died violent deaths. Some have been captured and tortured. The Roman authorities are ready to crush any sort of rebellion.

"Even our religious life is suspect. We are being accused of fostering this unrest. It takes every ploy available for our High Priest to insure them there is nothing to their suspicions. Even though the High Priesthood is more political than anything else, appointed by the governors, the Romans don't trust anyone. If Pontius Pilate had his way, there would be no High Priest appointed. He would like to do away with the Temple worship, get his hands on the Temple treasury.

"I have to confess, Caiaphas and his followers are trying to throw suspicion on communities like Qumran and Tobba. They think those people are so warped in their religious pietism, they pose a threat. You know that's not so, and I know that is not so, but our rulers have their doubts. They could very easily go to the extreme of destroying those villages. If they did that, they would kill or make slaves of all the inhabitants. The situation is not good. It is like a tinder box, ready to explode in flames.

"As for your Messiah, I do not know. Sure, your birth was a miracle. No one can deny that. You say this same Gabriel spoke to a young woman of Nazareth, asking her to be the mother of Yahweh's son? How can that be? How did her husband handle that? Surely, he must have been the father!"

"Jonathan, believe me! Search the scriptures, the words of the prophets, especially Isaiah. Do so with an open mind. You must believe! Yes, there is danger, great danger. There is far too much evil! Even the High Priest, from what I have heard, will not stand up for the people. Joseph Caiaphas is a pawn in Roman hands, more concerned with his own fortune. When have you heard, 'Thus says the Lord of hosts,' admonishing our nation?

"Jonathan, that is the message you and all the people will soon hear, just what I have been telling you. The Messiah, Yahweh's son, this son of Mary, is ready to come forth. Then you will have to believe!"

"John, I just don't know. I just do not know. I want to believe you, but at this point I have my doubts. If all you are telling me is true, why doesn't Yahweh do something about our problems, now?

"I will do this, I will pray to Yahweh, asking him to help me see what is true. I promise I will do that."

John realized he could go no further. The rest was in Yahweh's hands. He did know the dangers, which were before him, dangers that could engulf his wilderness world. From his visit with Jonathan, he could see the way to go. Qumran would be his next stop. There he would do his best to bring them to protective action. It might mean they would have to flee for their lives.

It was growing late, and would soon be morning. Their visit had to end. However, there was one more question, Eljah.

"Jonathan, tell me about Eljah. How is he? Is he becoming one of your better priests? How is his health?

"Eljah has done well. He doesn't talk much about the past, but, from time to time, he asks if I have had any word from you. He misses you, terribly so. At one time he asked for leave. He wanted to go north, all the way to Galilee, in order to find your cousin. He would have gone, but his father died, and he had additional responsibilities. He never made that journey.

"May I tell him I have seen you? He would want to know. He did receive some news of you several years ago from a priest from Hebron, a young priest named Ishvi. Also, two other priests came to me, rather hesitant to bring your greetings. They had met you traveling on the Sabbath. I wanted to laugh as they described their admonitions to you for breaking the Law. It was good to hear!"

"Jonathan, please give Eljah a message from me. Tell him I can never thank him enough for what he did for me. Tell him I miss him, too. As to what I have told you about the Messiah, you decide what you want to share. I leave that up to you."

They embraced, asked Yahweh's blessings on each other and slipped quietly out the room. Just before the first light of a new day, Jonathan went home to a distraught wife, wondering where he had been.

John moved hurriedly off the Temple Mount, ready to head east. He would be out of the walled city before full light.

Concentrating on his thoughts concerning the best and quickest route out of Jerusalem, he had an unexpected collision. It was with a Roman soldier. Both fell, and as they struggled to get up, the man tugged at his short sword, ready to defend himself. Then, he stopped, shaking his head in disbelief.

"I know you! You are the young man who gave me directions to Tiberius. Yes, even though we are older, I remember you. I never forget a face. What in the world are you doing here in Jerusalem? More important, what are you doing out at this time of the night? Don't you know you could be arrested?"

It was the Centurion!

John, caught by the surprise of the encounter, wondered how he might respond. How much could he share with this representative of Caesar? Would it be wise to tell him anything?

As he brushed off his clothes, he decided to be honest with his response. They had discussed that years before, in the sharing of information. One must not be deceitful!

"Yes, I am the one you met far to the north, up in the territory of Galilee. Did you make it to Tiberius that evening?"

"Yes, indeed! You were most helpful. Did you find your way to the coastal road, beyond Megiddo?"

"That was quite an adventure, but I found Megiddo, and I traveled the southern road to Caesarea, and beyond. You see, I have lived several years near the Salt Sea, in one of the small villages in that area. People there helped raise me after my father's death.

"Young man, I'm curious. That's the area of those people some call Essenes. From what I've been told they stay to themselves, never travel far, do a lot of ritual bathing. Their religion is quite unusual, to say the least. I would hardly think you would fit into that.

"Also, you have just come off the Temple Mount, a place those Essenes say is not doing what their god expects. He is called Yahweh, is he not? You told me that when we first met. Tell me! Why are you here, and at this early hour?"

John knew he had to satisfy the Centurion's curiosity. This was no time to play games. Also, time was a factor. He had to be on his way, and soon.

"You want the truth, and you deserve that. I came to Jerusalem to see an old friend. He is old, a friend of my father. My father served as a priest in the Temple, serving under this friend who was my father's Division head. That was years ago.

"And, yes, I lived in a village with those you call Essenes. They do have their own ideas about Yahweh, but they are good, sincere people. They have their concerns about the future. They fear you, the Romans. They also fear those who are priests here in Jerusalem, those they believe are not true to Yahweh's teachings. I'm sure you can understand that. There is so much unrest these days, all around us.

"My purpose in this visit was to get the feel of that unrest from one who was like a father to me long ago. He would tell me the truth!

"And what did he tell you? Would you be willing to share that with me? I have a responsibility to the man in charge, Pontius Pilate, the one who depends upon my ability to keep the peace."

"Sir, I am disturbed. He believes that trouble lies ahead. There are those, not my religious people, mind you; there are those who would fight you. However, they are not my friends living near the

Salt Sea, even though the High Priest, and others of influence, suggest that. They want you to deal harshly with Essenes, not with the Temple hierarchy. Do you hear what I am saying?"

Now it was the Centurion's to consider his answer. He knew precisely what John was trying to say, and he knew what was being considered as Rome's response to the rising unrest.

"Young man, what is your name? I want to speak directly, and honestly!"

I'm not sure that's important, but my name is John."

"Very well! That's good! John, you need to warn your friends they are in danger. What you have said about those religious leaders is true. They want to stay on our good side, avoid trouble and keep on with what they have been doing for many years. The way I see it, they are self-centered and selfish. You might not agree with that, but that's the way we see it.

"I would suggest you pass that warning on to your people. I'm not sure what they might do, other than move away; try to hide, either out in the wilderness; perhaps travel north or east, into other territories.

"Please take this advice seriously. I'm risking my life and my career just telling you this. I do so only because you have been honest with me, and I must be honest with you. Also, and I cannot put my finger on it; you are different. There is something different about you, as though you are a person with a special mission. I can only think it has something to do with your Yahweh. Could that be possible?"

John smiled and reached out his hand in appreciation.

"You, too, are special, and I thank you for it. Yes, it has something to do with my Yahweh. Some day, just perhaps, you will understand. Go well, my friend! With your permission I will be on my way to the Salt Sea."

The Centurion lifted his right hand in a salute, smiled and turned away, heading toward the Roman quarters.

John turned eastward. He was returning to his wilderness home, but would make one stop, Qumran. They must be warned of things to come. Surely, this time Kemuel would listen and respond.

# CHAPTER 35

> ... in danger from robbers,
> danger from my own people, danger from
> Gentiles, danger in the city, danger in the
> wilderness ....
>
> II Corinthians 11:26

John greeted the day some distance down the Kidron valley. He wasted no time in moving along the brook, in the direction of the Salt Sea. Turning south, away from the Jericho road, he strode immediately into the wilderness of Judah. He knew he would meet few travelers. This was desolate territory, but John felt he had no choice. He wanted to be in Qumran today.

Over the years the Kidron brook had cut deeper and deeper into the limestone hills, washing the silt onto the valley floor below. Deep, narrow, winding gorges left little room for a useable roadbed. This was dangerous territory, where the wild ones lived and roamed. Even the Roman troops stayed away. The main road to Jericho was safer.

It would have been prudent to stick to the ridges, but John was in no mood to worry about the possibilities. He had a mission and a message. He felt he must be in Qumran as soon as possible, and he was confident he could handle the dangers. Both Jonathan and the Centurion had confirmed his suspicions. It was time to deal with more serious dangers.

Stopping briefly after the first hour of walking, he spotted a sturdy staff someone had dropped at the edge of the water. He wondered why it had been overlooked. If needed, it should serve him well. Most men would have had difficulty in lifting it, and perhaps that's why it had been discarded. John could swing it and twirl it with ease. Pausing for water, he tested his weapon until he was satisfied.

Ready for any confrontation, he did not have long to wait. At one of the sharp turns of the gorge, three men attacked him. They, too, were carrying heavy sticks. One was carrying a knife. John stopped and backed up. Certain of success, the three rushed forward; a big mistake! As they raised their weapons, John spun around, swinging his heavy staff in an eye-level circle. They never knew what hit them. Farther down the way, two more men jumped up from where they had been hiding, running in the opposite direction.

Turning his attention to the three lying on the ground, John took the sticks and knife, threw them far up the side of the cliff. As to their wounds, John believed they would recover. One had a broken arm. Before he could regain consciousness, John found enough material, including the man's rope belt, to set the arm. It would have to do. He regretted his actions, but had little sympathy for the thieves. Evil must be punished! He wanted to turn them over to the authorities, but none were near. He could not be burdened with that responsibility. He must move on!

Remembering that encounter years earlier on the Jericho road, he was thankful for Yahweh's presence and protection. This time the ending was quite different!

Reaching the Salt Sea, he moved up the shore of the lake. As the sun moved westward, past its zenith in the cloudless sky, John turned away from the water, finally reaching his destination. Most travelers would not have arrived until late in the afternoon. For John the journey had not been that difficult. Wilderness life had sharpened physical skills and stamina.

Hurrying onto the grounds of the Qumran community he went

searching for Kemuel. He was not to be found. One of the residents reminded John of the time and significance of the day.

"You must be a stranger to our community. Kemuel is not to be disturbed. At our noon meal, our leader led the community in devotions. He is now at prayer in his own quarters. You need to know that today is a special day in Kemuel's life, an anniversary. Fifteen years ago he was chosen leader of the Qumran community. Each year on this day, Kemuel prays at length, asking for a sign, some reassurance that he has been faithful to his responsibilities. You will have to wait.

"All of us try each year to assure him of our support and gratitude, that he is a firm, caring and dedicated man. We know he is Yahweh's chosen. Yet, after he thanks us, he still spends hours in prayer. He is a holy man, Yahweh's chosen!"

John did not identify himself. Hungry after his long night in Jerusalem, his hurried journey back to Qumran, as well as his encounter with the robbers, John went looking for food. In the community kitchen, he found a responsive friend. He was doing the final cleaning of the kitchen vessels.

"I remember you. You have changed, but you are John, from Tobba. You've been here more than once, but that was long ago. We haven't seen you in years. My name is Matthias. How can I help you?"

"Right now, I'm hungry. I left Jerusalem before dawn, and have had nothing to eat. Do you have any bread, Matthias, or anything left over from your last meal?"

"We do have bread, plenty of that. Other than that, there's not much else. There are some grapes from the vineyard, if you would eat those."

John assured him that would be fine. He sat down at one of the tables and thanked Yahweh for his gifts. The bread and grapes were devoured quickly, something he had not enjoyed in years.

Waiting for Kemuel to appear, his thoughts were interrupted by the man in the kitchen, Matthias.

"When you were here some years ago, you and our leader, Kemuel, sat here and talked a long time. Working in the kitchen at that time, I couldn't help but hear what you were saying. You talked about your calling, and you spoke of a Messiah who would appear. You said he was here, now, waiting for Yahweh's directing word. As Yahweh's own son, he would bring us freedom and peace. He would save us from our enemies, from evil. I have not been able to forget that, even after all these years. You would not have known it, but you gave me hope. Is that why you are here? Has he come?"

"Matthias, the time is at hand. Very shortly I will meet him. Very soon the world will know. They will see and hear him. Yes, That is why I am here, to share that, again, with your leader.

"At the same time, there will be conflict, especially for all of you. Your communities are in danger, great danger. I hope Kemuel will listen to me this time. You must be kept safe. The Scrolls must be kept safe. At least Kemuel sees that. He spoke of hiding your writings the last time I was here.

"But, why do you ask? I think there is more here than your curiosity. Why do you speak of giving you hope? What are your real concerns, Matthias?"

Matthias was silent for a time, not quite sure how he might answer John. He had to put into words what had been in his heart and mind over the years, his longing for something more than his life at Qumran.

"I mean no disrespect to our beloved Kemuel. He is a good man, a great leader. He has been able to hold us together, we who come from many different backgrounds. We respect what he has accomplished here. Yet, for me, and I think for some others, we hope for something more.

"As I listened to you back then, I couldn't help but be touched, not only by your words, but by your passion. I could sense the promise of Yahweh's redeeming purpose being worked out in you. I need that, John. Others living here need that! I want to go with you, follow you, help you. I want to see him, this promised Messiah!"

"Matthias, it would be wrong for me to ask you, or any others, to leave. I would not do that to your leader. You will have to make that choice. However, let me assure any and all, you would be welcome. Your support and your companionship would be most helpful. All these years I have been alone. With you, with whoever might join us, we could be a great witness and help to him, the Messiah."

As a final thought, before leaving the room, John smiled and added, "It would be nice to have someone to talk to, in addition to Yahweh."

Seated outdoors, waiting on a bench placed under an arbor of green, John heard Kemuel's voice of greeting.

"Welcome back, my friend. We have missed you. How many years has it been? Look at you! My, how you have grown, changed. I would hardly recognize you. What a handsome beard!"

John stood up, embraced him and ignored the compliments.

"Kemuel, it has been a long time, and there have been some important changes. Do you remember what we talked about years ago, my telling you about the promised Messiah?

"Not only has he come, but we will be meeting soon, somewhere near the Jordan River. Yahweh is about to act, as he promised long ago. We must be prepared!"

"John, I do not understand you. Yes, I heard what you said before, but I feel nothing has changed, even after all those years. I've received no sign. There has been no fulfilling of our prophecies concerning darkness and light. We still wait for the two Messiahs, the Priest and the royal King. When they come, the Age of Wickedness will be over. No, we will have to be patient. We must wait. We will continue with our writings, just as we have done, lo these many years. Ours is a holy calling and our *Mashiach* will come to us. Without that and without him, our lives and our work are worthless!

"Kemuel, I hear what you are saying. I understand and appreciate what you are doing here in Qumran. You and your people have been faithful to your duties. I commend you for that, for your devotion to Yahweh.

"At the same time, I beg you to consider seriously what I am telling you. The word of Yahweh came to my father almost thirty years ago. His messenger, Gabriel, made it quite clear, that the time was near and that I, when Yahweh was ready, would tell all his people about his son.

"That same messenger, Gabriel, went to that young virgin of Nazareth, and she accepted Yahweh's word. She would bear Yahweh's son! She has done so. He is now an adult, about my age. I have met him, talked with him. Now, he is coming soon, very soon.

"You say you stake your life on what you believe. I stake mine on what I know and believe! Please, hear me out, listen to what I am saying."

Kemuel, deeply disturbed by John's response, continued to shake his head. It could not be! If John was right and he was wrong, his whole life had been wasted. It could not be!

"I'm sorry you made this trip, just to repeat what you said some years back. John, nothing has changed. We can only wait, and pray. We pray Yahweh will give us his sign. I know he will do so, when he is ready."

Realizing he could not modify Kemuel's fixed thoughts and conclusions, John changed the subject. Perhaps he could persuade Kemuel to make some preparation for the dangers ahead. The writings must be preserved!

"The last time I was here, we talked about the writings, the Scrolls. You agreed they must be protected. Now is the time to do just that. We must hide them, soon!

"I left Jerusalem early this morning, after spending hours with one of the older Division leaders in the Temple. His name is Jonathan. He and his Division were on duty the night Gabriel spoke to my father. Yahweh suggested I seek him out. Jonathan would share with me the present political climate. He did so, and it is not good.

"You are right concerning the religious leadership in our

nation. They are vassals of Rome. Also, in order to remain in favor with the governor, Pontius Pilate, they are beginning to point their fingers at people like you. They are implying you are causing the unrest that has ended in attempts of rebellion.

I'm afraid that has been accepted by Rome and you are in the greatest of danger. That suspicion was confirmed by one of their own, a Centurion, willing to warn me. They will not hesitate to destroy you and all your people. They would pillage and burn. They would burn all your writings, your Scrolls. The fine work of many years would be lost.

"Behind your village there are many caves. The lower ones are used from time to time by wandering animals and by shepherds. No one climbs up to the higher caves. If you have enough tall clay jars, we could fill them with your Scrolls, hide them up there."

Kemuel, weary with so much conversation he did not want to accept, finally nodded his head. The Scrolls must be protected, regardless of their disagreements. He, too, had heard the stories, the rumors. He did know they were in danger. He also knew they would stand little chance in resisting the Romans. Fight they would, but they had no weapons of war.

"John, you are right concerning the Scrolls. We must do what you say, hide them, and soon. I had never thought of the caves on the other side of the wadi, but our writings should be safe there. We can only trust Yahweh to watch over them.

"As to the jars, we have plenty. Our winery is filled with empty ones, waiting for the next crop of grapes. We have agents selling our best wine each year, which provides us with some income. This year those vessels will be used for a better purpose!"

John breathed a sigh of relief. At least he had convinced Kemuel to take that step, protecting what to John was priceless. He would help! In fact, he wanted to be in charge, making sure they would succeed.

Kemuel reminded John he had other duties for the day. He would work out the details concerning the Scrolls, later. John would be welcome to stay for the evening meal and devotions.

"Kemuel, may I make a suggestion? You do have many responsibilities. If it is agreeable to you, I will be happy to see to this matter of the Scrolls. If you recall, a number of these are in the library in Tobba. Don't you think these should be included?

Again, Kemuel nodded. He would be grateful to John for his assistance.

"When you return with the Scrolls from Tobba, we will give you any help you need. The clay jars will be clean and ready. I would suggest we do this at night. Travelers pass this way during the day. No one outside our community must know what we are doing."

Kemuel walked away, heading for the scriptorium. He would begin to prepare them for what was to come. John returned to the dining area, looking for Matthias. Finding him getting food ready for the evening meal, John shared with him some of the details of his conversation with Kemuel.

"I am leaving now, headed for Tobba. We will return with the Scrolls, putting them with those here, the ones Kemuel is willing to hide. Once they are safely put away I will return to my wilderness home, waiting for Yahweh's call."

"May we join you, then," Matthias asked. "I know there are a few others who will want to follow you. If you will, give us directions so that we will be able to find you. You will be our Teacher, our Rabboni."

"Matthias, I'm not worthy of that title. I am not the great Master, only a servant of Yahweh. However, I will welcome you to my wilderness home, you and whoever might come. Together we will serve our Lord. I will give you directions when I return. It may be tomorrow, or the day following, but I will be back. Tell Kemuel, if he asks about me, I thank him for the invitation for supper, but I must be on my way. Time is important!"

Almost before Matthias could return to his duties, John was out the door, heading once more toward Tobba. Would it be his last time?

# CHAPTER 36

*. . . the Lord watch between you and me,
when we are absent one from the other . . .*
                              Genesis 31:49

Mered stopped and stared. He couldn't be sure, but the man striding down the east road toward Tobba had to be someone he knew. The beard didn't help, but the man's posture and bearing were familiar. Where had he seen this stranger before?

Of course! It had to be! It was John! Rushing forward, Mered raised his hand high, the salute of a friend. Then, laughing for joy, he grabbed him, wrestled him to the ground. Over and over they rolled, until they could move no more. Between the wrestling and the laughing, they had to catch their breath. When they both sat up, they could do nothing more than look at each other. It was a happy reunion.

"John, why don't you tell someone when you are leaving, and where you are going? We have worried about you, talked about you, wondering if you were ever coming back. How many years has it been?

"Just look at you! You have grown! I bet you're proud of that beard. You look just like one of those rabbis."

John had no idea this would be his welcome back to Tobba. It was funny, but it was just what he needed, something to make him laugh, and something he had almost forgotten.

"Mered, it's good to see you again! You, too, have grown up. Honestly, I have truly missed you. I still remember our first adventure together. You had to teach me to find the right wood, how to make bows and arrows.

"Not only that, you were willing to deal with a young boy struggling to find himself, trying to adjust to a new home, a new life. You, and everyone else here in Tobba, helped. I'll never forget you!

"But, tell me about yourself, your family. Have you married? Any young woman would be fortunate to have a husband like you."

"No, John, not yet. I haven't found the right one. My parents keep pushing me, but, at the same time, they need my help at home. They are not well and I should care for them. At one time I thought I wanted to take Debra as my wife, but I don't think she will ever marry. Anyway, I am still working on my own house, as well as going with the hunters. I'm an excellent hunter now, if I do say so! I still have time to take on a family. That can wait.

"Now, tell me what you've been up to these last years. Why have you come back? How long will you stay this time? What comes next? What about your special calling from Yahweh? Where will that take you?"

"You sure do ask a lot of questions," John chuckled.

"Give me a little time, and I'll see if I can fill you in on my adventures. First of all, I've been living out in that desolate, barren area west of here. There is a remote, isolated valley over there. My home for the past eight years has been a cave, a large, dry, nice one. Down the valley there is a pretty little stream, plenty of good water. I even dug out a bathing pool for myself. I have no complaints. Yahweh's world out there is safe and peaceful.

"I'm sure you remember what Tobiah said when that man came, wanting to sell arrowheads, that I had been set apart to do what Yahweh wanted. He told me about that later, when I had recovered.

"That's exactly what Yahweh desired, my living alone, listening to what he had to say, preparing me for my mission. Out there he watched over me, cared for me, provided for all my needs. Of course, Tobiah, as well as many others here, including you, taught me how to survive in the wilderness. Survive I did!

"I know, eight years is a long time, but Yahweh acts when he wants it. I had to learn that. I had to learn patience, waiting for him to make the next move. I had to go over in my mind, again and again, Yahweh's words as recorded in the Qumran Scrolls.

I'm not bragging, but I can quote any part of what I have read. Of course, I didn't actually have the Scrolls in my hands, but Yahweh would bring them up in my mind's eye, one by one. It was amazing!

"With that accomplished, he sent me to Jerusalem to talk with our old Division leader, Jonathan. From there I hurried down to Qumran to talk with their leader, Kemuel. I left him just a short time ago, hurrying to see Tobiah, and all of you. I have a message, one I will share with everyone when you come together this evening."

Mered wanted to ask more, but hesitated. Hopefully, John would shed light on those things the people of Tobba had pondered over these past years.

"Very well, let's go find Tobiah. He should be at the villa, waiting for the evening meal. Tonight we are adding deer meat to the menu, a deer I killed!"

By the time they reached the old villa in the center of the town, they were surrounded. The men, once they realized it was John, punched his shoulder, pulled on his beard, and tousled his hair. Their joy was unrestrained! Children, although the young ones had no idea who they were greeting, danced round and round. The women, old and young, came forward one by one, embracing him. Some, including Debra, hugged and kissed him. This was a community celebrating a favorite son's homecoming.

When all had come forward and with most of the adults beginning to ask questions, Tobiah held up his arms for attention.

"This is a happy day for all of us. John, we thank Yahweh for your safe return. I'm sure you realize how much we love you, and we want to hear whatever you can share with us. However, we need to make sure everyone is present. Some are still away at their tasks.

"I suggest we gather in the dining area, following the evening meal. At that time we will continue our celebration, hopeful you will tell us what has been happening in your life. Is that possible?"

"Yes, that is possible. Your suggestion is a good one. I have a story and a message you need to hear. It is important, very important!"

Many still wanted to talk and ask questions. John did the best he could, without divulging the full story. He understood their emotions, as well as their feelings for him.

Finally, he begged for a break. Asking for a drink of water, he found a shaded seat and table just outside the villa's library. Tobiah did his best to protect him, asking those still pushing up close to let John have some rest. He would talk later!

As the crowd drifted slowly away, Tobiah reached across the table, grasping John's hand. He, too, was overjoyed with John's return.

"Thank you for coming back. We have missed you! I'm sure you will not stay long, and I think I know the reason. Am I right in believing your time is almost here?"

"Yes, Tobiah, the time is almost upon us. Momentous events lie ahead, as well as some disturbing dangers. The political climate is not good, certainly not good for you living here, not good for those in Qumran and the surrounding villages. You need to know that, but I don't want to upset your people. You will have to decide what you want them to know.

"The dangers, as I learned from the Division leader, Jonathan, come from the religious leaders. They keep trying to stay on the good side of the Romans, blaming people like you and the others living in nearby villages, including Qumran, for the unrest and the rebellions that have taken place. You know that's not so, but that doesn't help. They are saying that your pietistic way of life, as well as your demands for keeping the Mosaic Law, encourages men to resist Roman law. If the Romans come, they will not hesitate to burn and pillage. Many people would die!

"In fact, surprisingly enough, a Roman soldier, a Centurion, echoed that warning. I had met him years before, up in the territory of Galilee, had helped him with some travel directions. I bumped into him just after leaving Jonathan, and he, too, confirmed the rumors. Rome is ready to wipe out any uprising or unrest. The situation is not good, Tobiah.

"I've shared that with Kemuel in Qumran. He doesn't believe me in what I have tried to tell him concerning Yahweh's plans, but, at least, he has agreed to one thing. We want to preserve, hide the Scrolls, those stored here and those kept at Qumran. We are going to hide them in the caves back of Qumran, high up on the cliffs. We will put them into clean wine jars, taking them up to the caves at night. We want no one seeing what we are doing."

"Why, John, why worry about the Scrolls? Our people are more important than the writings. If we are in danger, we need protection for ourselves!"

"That's true, so very true, but we don't know how that will play out. You have to protect your own, as best you can. Yet, the Scrolls must survive, too. They are the records of Yahweh's presence in the lives of his people, as well as the prophecies of what lies ahead, what I will be involved in very soon. This has to do with the Messiah, Yahweh's son. Most of these writings are Yahweh's own words, holy words! I'll try to explain that tonight."

"John, I'll have to accept your word on that, the hiding of the Scrolls. How can we help you?"

"We must act soon, hopefully tomorrow. We need enough jars, and a cart to carry them to Qumran. I would suggest we move them tomorrow evening, after dark. We will have to travel quietly, but quickly. I will come back here when that is done, when we have hidden all the writings, but not for long. I'll explain that tonight."

"Very well. I will find Jakin; explain to him the matter of the Scrolls. His men will be the best ones to handle the heavy jars. With their baskets and ropes the job will be done!"

As Tobiah hurried off to find Jakin, John opened the door to the library. They were still there, the Scrolls. These were the precious writings John had read over and over, the ones memorized, burned into his heart and mind. These were the ones Yahweh had brought up before him, many times over.

Sitting down, he reached for the Psalms of David, knowing these were words of beauty and encouragement. However, just as he began to unroll the Scroll, the door opened. It was Debra. Slipping in quietly, she said nothing. Coming over to John, she knelt down and put her head in his lap. Hesitantly, John began to stroke her hair. He knew she was crying, sobbing. Her tears spilled across his hands.

"What is it Debra? Are these tears of joy, or tears of sorrow? I hope you know I'm happy to see you again. I've missed you! You have been at the very center of my life in so many ways. You helped restore me to health. I love you, and I'm sure you understand what I mean when I say that. Please, dry your tears. Let these hours be joyful ones."

It took some time, but finally Debra lifted her head, and smiled.

"John, you are so right. You were always right. I missed you, too, terribly so. And, I have to admit, some of that had to do with that physical longing which doesn't want to go away.

"Sure, I know that's over, and we won't mention it again. My tears have more to do with what lies ahead for you. When you leave here, and that will be soon, I will never see you again! I have this frightening feeling I will not live to see you again."

Her response brought some terrible images to John's mind. Debra might be right. If the towns were in danger, Debra would be in danger. How could he save her, protect her? That would have to be in Yahweh's hands.

The hour was late and they heard the call to the evening meal. It was time to go. Debra turned, pressed her body against John's, looked long into his dark eyes. With her right hand she pulled his head down, kissed him as she had done the first time, when she had taught him to use the bow and arrow. Choking on her tears, she left, closing the door behind her.

The meal was a festive one. Everyone was in a happy mood. John was back! Tobiah had called for quiet, for the thanksgiving prayer and blessing, but once that was over, everyone wanted to talk at once.

It was impossible, but most wanted to sit next to or close to John. He was home again. The meal was a lengthy one, but finally over. After the dishes were cleared, Tobiah called for silence.

His welcoming speech was spoken with warmth and emotion. John was special to him. Over the years there had developed a close bond between the two. There was a lot of interrupting applause, but he was finally through. At the end he reminded the villagers of John's role as one called of Yahweh. It was time to hear from him!

As John stood up, he raised his arms toward heaven and blessed them, asking that Yahweh would watch over all, when they would be apart, away from each other, a blessing spoken long before at Mizpah. Then he sat down and began to speak of his Yahweh-given mission. Slowly, carefully, he told his story, from Gabriel's promise to his father, all the way to the present moment, omitting much of the details of his travels. For the important story of Yahweh's call, little of the other was important.

When he began to speak of Gabriel's coming to Nazareth, his call to young Mary, the birth of the son of Yahweh, there was not a sound from the people gathered before John. Even the children were silent. This unbelievable story was one they had never heard before.

Some shook their heads in disbelief. Most eyes were opened wide in amazement. How could this be? Yahweh was not man, could not be man. Yahweh was Lord, high and lifted up!

Finally, there was a turning point for some, Isaiah's prediction of the birth of a son, a son born to a young woman, a virgin. Yahweh was Lord of all, able to do what he desired and chose. It just might be true.

John ended with his calling. He would meet this son of Mary at the Jordan River. He could not promise the day, but it would be soon. In the meantime, he and many of the men of Tobba would be busy protecting the Scrolls of Qumran. John did not speak of the dangers ahead, only of the need to find a good, safe storage place for those precious recorded words of Yahweh. Jakin and his hunters would be called upon to do the work.

The hour was late, and the many yawns indicated there would be very little talk the rest of the evening. They thanked John and headed for their beds. Awed by John's disclosure concerning the coming Messiah, they wanted to hear more, but that would have to wait until tomorrow. Their dreams would be visions of hope. Their entire lives had been centered on Yahweh's promises, and now John had brought them to a focal point, for some a crossroad. How did he say it? "The Messiah had come!"

# CHAPTER 37

*Make me to know your ways, O Lord;*
*teach me your paths. Lead me in your truth,*
*and teach me . . .*

Psalm 25:4

While the men of Tobba were packing their gear for the trip to Qumran, others were collecting wine jars. A number had been stored in the old barracks and could be spared. Wine making was not a priority with the people of Tobba. Qumran made much more.

John was busy in a different way, besieged with the villager's questions. Whenever a large group gathered, he did his best to explain Yahweh's plan for his people. The Messiah would bring freedom and peace. He would restore Israel. Enemies would be defeated. Yahweh, again, would be Lord of all! Some came out of curiosity. Others came, enthralled by the hope of fulfillment. They would participate in the coming of a new age. Above all, they wanted to see Yahweh's son with their own eyes.

Two men stood in the background, waiting for the others to leave. Their intent was made clear, once they were able to share their thoughts with John. They would follow him! One, called Jeuel, had brought his brother Suah. Suah was a resident of Jericho and had come to Tobba for a visit. Both saw in John the fulfillment of their hopes for life. As with Matthias, living at Qumran, John made it clear he would welcome them; he would tell them where he would be staying. However, their decisions must be their own. He would not entice them away from their homes. He also reminded them, life would not be easy in the wilderness.

Late in the afternoon, as the shadows of night began to spread across the water, the village, the rocks and trees, a small band of Tobba's residents moved eastward. Two oxen were pulling one of the largest carts the town possessed. Clay jars filled with the Scrolls had been tied securely with the hunter's ropes. None of the jars would be broken.

Led by Tobiah and Jakin, they moved as quietly as possible. If they heard anyone approaching on the road, they knew what to do. They would turn toward the cliffs and find a hiding place.

This time, Tobiah gave Debra permission to accompany the men. She would not be permitted to enter Qumran, but would keep the records; numbering jars, contents and hiding places. Her skills in writing would serve them well! She had already made a listing of those Scrolls which had been stored in the library at Tobba, the Scrolls John had read so many times. Each jar had been numbered, the Scrolls listed. Cave locations would come later.

Arriving at Qumran, John, Tobiah and Jakin found Kemuel. Surrounded by the writers, the copiers of the Scrolls, the remaining empty jars were filled with Qumran's Scrolls. Here again, records were kept, this time by those who worked in the scriptorium. Once they arrived at the foot of the cliffs, Debra would complete the process. The caves would be numbered.

Kemuel, once the work of storing the writings in the jars was complete, demanded a moment of silence. Lifting his voice in thanksgiving and petition, he asked Yahweh's favor on what they were about to do. These treasures were being committed into Yahweh's hands. Confident of their Lord's approval, Kemuel gave the order. It was time to go! The work must be completed before the rising of tomorrow's sun.

Once they arrived at the foot of the cliffs, John pointed out the caves to be used. Higher than most of the others, the openings were quite small, somewhat inaccessible, but ideal for their purpose.

Without hesitation, the hunters of Tobba worked their way up the face of the clay and rock. With ropes slung across their shoulders, they moved slowly, but steadily, upward. Arriving at the first cave, ropes were lowered down to those below. With clay jar placed in each basket, the men above lifted their fragile cargo to the cave entrance. Others carried the jars as deep as they could into the cave. It was a slow process, but extreme care was vital. The jars must not be broken!

Once that cave was filled, the men moved on to the next one, working their way across the face of the cliff. Actually, they did not fill the caves. They wanted to use the back, darker, depths of each cave, minimizing the possibilities of discovery. These were treasures, deserving the best protection.

Down below, Debra continued to write, making sure the final records would be accurate. These would be turned over to Kemuel. He alone would be able to identify the hiding places of his Scrolls. All records, if necessary, would be passed down from generation to generation.

It was a long night, but the work went well with no real problems. One rope had broken, but four ropes secured each basket. They took no chances! With the jars safely hidden, the men above made their way down to the valley floor. Careful not to disturb or scratch the surface of the cliff, they left little evidence of their climbing. The Scrolls were safe! It was time to go home.

As they were gathering their gear for the return trip to Tobba, Kemuel pulled John aside.

"We have taken your advice. Our precious Scrolls have been hidden. They are safe. No one else knows what we have done. Now, I have to ask you. What comes next? When will we be able to bring these treasured words of Moses and the prophets out for reading and study?

"If we are attacked, the Scrolls will still be there, waiting for the end of all hostilities. We, or those who come after us, will be able to find and use them again. However, if we do not survive, if all the records of the hidings are lost, what then?"

"Kemuel, if you are asking what I know of the future, I have to say I don't know. Only Yahweh knows that, and only time will tell. I do know this; the Scrolls are safe and they will, someday, be a blessing to future generations. Yahweh has assured me of that. We must have faith. Yahweh will be triumphant!

"You have done the right thing, and remember this, your work here is important, most important. If you insist on staying here, in spite of my warnings, get on with your work. Have your writers continue with what they are doing."

Kemuel thanked John, left him standing and went to his quarters to pray. He needed Yahweh's assurances, over and above what John had said.

Before leaving Qumran, John had the opportunity to speak privately with Matthias.

"Here are the directions, a map. I have marked it with the locations of Qumran, Tobba and the route you will follow. Guard it carefully.

"Wait one week before you come. I may be staying in Tobba a few days, but I will be waiting for you and for those who might come with you.

"Bring little with you, only the clothes you are wearing, something for sleeping and eating, nothing more. Beyond that, Yahweh will provide."


The journey back to Tobba was slow. They arrived just as the sun came up. All agreed, the size and color of the rising orb signaled a hot day! It would be difficult to find a cool resting place. Hopefully, they could sleep some, before the heat became unbearable.

Satisfied with the work done, John thanked everyone, suggesting they try to get some rest early. He, Tobiah and Debra headed for their rooms in the main house.

Rest did not come easy for John. It had been an exciting and tense-filled night. Concerned for the successful completion of what he knew to be essential, he tossed and turned, rethinking each step in their planning and action. Would those words of Yahweh be preserved for generations to come? He had to trust Yahweh, just as he had told Kemuel. The Scrolls were safe!

Finally, closing his eyes, he tried to envision his next move. He knew he must return to his valley, his wilderness home. From all indications, he would not be alone this time. Several men had expressed a strong desire to follow him. This was something entirely new. He had never considered being a leader of disciples, but it could be good. He had been disturbed by a woman's prediction made years earlier that he would die. If Yahweh permitted that, others would have to carry on in his place. The message, Yahweh's message, must be shared! He wasn't concerned about his own death. That was in Yahweh's hands. His life had one purpose, preparing the way of the Lord, Yahweh's son!

Later that day he went looking for Tobiah. His intent was to share his plans with the village elder. This time he would not slip away unannounced. He would be returning to his wilderness home before the beginning of the Sabbath. He would sleep in Tobba tonight and tomorrow night. The next evening he would leave, traveling at night. With a full moon rising, it would not be difficult.

By now the breezes had shifted, blowing in from the west. It should be a pleasant night. The evening meal was over and most of the men had already settled down for the night. The ones who had worked with the Scrolls were tired. John found Tobiah and Debra sitting outside the villa's gate, under one of the taller palm trees. Tobias's wife had gone visiting, checking on a sick neighbor.

"Tobiah, Debra, I'm glad I found you together. I want to thank you both for what you did last night. Your help will never be forgotten!"

This time it was Tobiah jumping up, embracing John. Debra didn't move. She knew her emotions would bring her to tears if she dared move. She also knew John's intent in seeking them out now. He was ready to depart, and she may never see him again. She could do nothing but smile. If anyone knew and understood John, it was Debra.

Tobiah's words were brief, and to the point. Totally unaware of his daughter's thoughts, he responded to the events of the previous night.

"John, you amaze me! How did you get Kemuel to agree to hide the Scrolls? I know it was most difficult for him.

"My other question has to do with the Scrolls. Are they really that important, those we have hidden? From what I know, there are plenty of those same Scrolls kept in Jerusalem as well as in other places."

"You must remember, Tobiah, what the Scrolls mean to Kemuel, and to those writers of Qumran. They would do anything to preserve their writings. Once I convinced him of the dangers of possible destruction, the rest was easy. It is done, and all are to be commended."

"Concerning the value of the Scrolls. You have to think back, far back, to the time Yahweh called our forefather Abraham. These writings are the records of those ancient days, Yahweh watching over, caring for his people. Also, these are the records of the promises of Yahweh. He will come. He will send his own son to deliver us.

"Then there are the writings and the commentaries of your own people. For you, these are priceless. I, and others, may not agree with all these documents include, but they are your thoughts, your convictions. You, too, are Yahweh's people!"

Tobiah could only nod his head in agreement, again amazed at John's ability to say the right things. John was right. Kemuel saw that and now Tobiah saw that. These documents were treasures, and should be, must be, preserved.

"I had almost forgotten about the Scroll's amazing value,

how they helped restore you to health. It was Debra's reading from the Scrolls, which opened the door to your mind, waking you up again to our world. Isn't that so, Debra?"

"Father, I could have given you both those answers. Yes, we have done the right thing. The Scrolls are safe, writings that have meant so much to so many people.

"My concern now is John. What comes next for him? John, when are you leaving? Is it tonight or tomorrow night?"

Before Tobiah could protest his daughter's boldness, John answered her questions. He couldn't help but smile at her wisdom.

"My dear friends, it is almost time to do what the Scriptures say: 'prepare the way of the Lord.' It means I will be leaving again. I will sleep here tonight, tomorrow night, and then leave the next evening. The moon will be up late, but will be helpful for traveling.

"Tobiah, I would like to stay. I would prefer living here in Tobba. If I had my choice, I would like to marry your daughter Debra, give you grandchildren. Debra knows that, and I assume you are aware of her desires. However, all that is behind us. It cannot be so. I will have to leave you.

"I trust I will see you again. I hope so, but that is in Yahweh's hands. Be assured, I will never forget you!"

Debra and her father were silent. No words would come. Finally, as John stood up to go to his room, Tobiah embraced him once again and moved through the gate without a backward glance.

John turned to Debra, pulled her to her feet and put his arms around her. Then, lifting her head, he looked into her eyes, smiled, and kissed her. With a softly spoken: "I love you," he left her standing, alone, by the old palm tree.

# CHAPTER 38

*I am the voice of one crying in the wilderness.*
                                    John 1:23

John was awakened by the sound of voices. Stepping out into the morning sun, he was surprised to see, not two or three men, but ten. He recognized Matthias, Jeuel and Suah. The others were strangers, or had he seen them before? He couldn't remember.

"Matthias," he called, "who are these other men? Are they from Qumran?"

"Good morning to you, John. I think we surprised you! Yes, my friends Jonathan and Thaddaeus are from Qumran. Both have lived there several years. They are farmers, two of a large number of workers growing food for the community. Although they lived in Qumran, they seldom entered into our religious affairs. Kemuel was hesitant about taking them in, but he needed their help. We depended upon their skills in growing crops and caring for the vineyard.

"The others are from Jericho, friends of Jonathan and Thaddaeus. They, too, are farmers. Although they were not residents of Qumran, they helped with the crops when needed. Two of the five grew up in a small village just north of Jericho. There was another one from the territory of Galilee, one I do not know too well. He insisted on going back north, before coming here. He wanted to tell his friends about you, what you have been telling me.

"The word has been getting around, the message you have spoken in both Qumran and Tobba. All these men want to follow you! It could well be others will come.

"Let me introduce them. John, I want you to meet Judah, Bartimaeus, Simeon, Rehum and David."

John's smile was a broad one, as he greeted them, one by one.

"Welcome to my wilderness world; not really mine, but Yahweh's beautiful world. However, I must ask you, all of you, why you have come to join me, to stay with me. Why have you come?"

Matthias spoke first.

"Each man must speak for himself, and they will, once they get to know you. However, permit me to bring their answers together. After leaving Qumran, we met in Jeuel's home in Tobba, spent the night there. The next night, last night, we left after it was dark, following your directions.

"While in Tobba, not knowing the ones from Jericho, I asked them the same question. I wanted to know: 'Why have you come?' The answers were the same. All of us know there is something missing in our lives. There is no sign of hope in what we do day by day. Sure, all of us know what we were taught as children. Yahweh is Lord of all, but that is not enough. Nothing changes. All the washing, the praying, the rituals of both Qumran and Tobba do not stir us or excite us. In Jericho there is far too much wickedness. Life must be more than that.

"Now you have come with a message of hope, and the promise of a Messiah, saying the time is near, very near. He will come to us, to all of us. He will set us free, free from all that is wrong and bad."

That was as far as Matthias could go. He believed he had expressed their thoughts well. All nodded their heads in agreement. He also knew it would take time for the others to speak what was in their hearts. John would have to take it from there.

"Thank you, Matthias, and thank all of you for your willingness to join me. You must understand this is a new experience for me, being a teacher, a leader for others. With Yahweh's help I will do my best.

"Now, let me remind you again, life here is not easy. We do not have the comforts of village homes. We must hunt for our food. Our shelter is here, in this cave. Here we will sleep and eat. Yet, we are blessed in so many ways. Yahweh provides! I trust you come accepting a new way of life.

"Also, we must be ready to move at a moment's notice. When my cousin comes, we will leave our home here, join him at the Jordan River. Do you understand?"

With the nodding of heads, John led them down to the nearby stream, and to the pool he had fashioned years before. Almost without thinking, he baptized them! As they stood around him in the waist deep water, he cupped his hands filled with water, and poured it over their heads, one by one.

"I wash you, I baptize you, with water, cleansing you of your sins. Repent, for now you belong to Yahweh. His kingdom has come!"

Everyone smiled, embraced, shouting his response.

"Praise to Yahweh our Lord!"

"His kingdom has come!"

"We have been washed, cleansed!"

Rejoicing, John led them back to the mouth of the cave. There they shared bread and honey.

As the days went by, John's greatest task was to share the Scriptures with his ten disciples. There was so much to give; so much they needed to learn. None of the men had any understanding of the words of the prophets. They did have a smattering of knowledge relating to the long history of Yahweh's people, but little more. John taught them! Each morning they would gather under the shade of the trees lining the stream. After bathing, and while their bodies were drying in the morning air, John spoke the prophetic words of Isaiah, Jeremiah, Micah and others. These men must know and understand Yahweh's plan and purpose.

Just as important was the need to know these men. Each one had a story to tell. Each one was different. Yet, there was a common thread of hope and desire. All were looking for the fulfillment of Yahweh's kingdom.

Relationships, close relationships, relationships of trust, take time, as John found out. These were simple men. All their lives they had been told what to do, where they could live, with no concern for what they wanted in life. Now, he had to earn their trust, their respect.

With the passage of time, John brought them into his circle of friendship, one by one. By his actions, as well as by his words, he gained their respect. They soon learned; here was a man of sincerity and honesty. Here was one skilled in the ways of the wilderness. His knowledge was astounding. Above all, he would not ask any of them to do something he was not willing to do. He taught by example. It was only right; John was, indeed, their leader. They not only respected him, they came to love him!

Out of those developing relationships, John uncovered skills in the others. Thaddaeus and Matthias were excellent cooks. They could take whatever was on hand and provide a good meal. Rehum and David knew where to find the best plants, leaves and pods. Simeon, Suah and Judah were the hunters. Setting traps for small animals and birds, they kept the group supplied with meat. The other three ended up being the 'housekeepers,' Fresh water was needed every day. Skins had to be cured, a good wood supply had to be on hand for the fire, and the cave had to be kept clean. Palm and willow branches were excellent for making softer beds.

This wilderness community had come together. They were

family! John could now teach, inspire and prepare these men for what was to come.

Finally, it came, Yahweh's call. In the darkness before dawn, John was awakened.

"John! John! Take your disciples with you. Take the Wilderness Road toward Jericho, but do not stop or enter Tobba, or Qumran. East of Jericho you will come to the Jordan River. Stop when you come to the great bend opposite Bethany across the Jordan. There you will begin to preach and teach. At the proper time my son will come and find you. Prepare his way well, my chosen one. Call those who come to hear you, call them to repentance, and call them to follow him! When the sun rises you should be ready to depart."

Although it was still dark and all the others were still sleeping, John could not close his eyes again. The time had come, the time set years before in Yahweh's Temple! The holy messenger Gabriel had declared it to his father, Zechariah, "he will go before him in the spirit and power of Elijah," It was time to depart.

Slipping quietly out of the cave, John made his way to the top of the ridge behind the cave. There he knelt down and prostrated himself on the ground. Facing eastward, he could see a faint glimmer of light, the hint of a new day. It was his time to respond, and to speak humbly.

"My father you have brought me to this moment. You have raised me up, called me to do your will. You know I am not worthy of your trust. In so many ways I have fallen into wrong. I have sinned! I have done evil in your sight. Yet, you have not abandoned me, you have not driven me away from your presence.

"Now, I ask you to cleanse me anew. Wipe away my sins. Give me strength, O Lord, to be found faithful. Let me not stumble or fail to speak your word of truth. Teach me, lead me, use me, and hold me!"

John's final words were spoken as he stood up. Erect, he lifted his arms to the sky, a plea for Yahweh's power and presence. Finally, bowing his head, he came down from the crest of the hill, and walked into the pool below. In the cool, fresh flowing stream, he poured water over his own head and spoke, to himself: "You, John, son of Zechariah, have been forgiven of your sins. Now, it is time to go and do Yahweh's will!"

Under the morning sun, John and his disciples watched the people bathing in the Jordan. Some, who lived nearby, were washing their garments, blankets, bags and baskets. Others were crossing the river, some headed for Bethany, while others, coming toward them, headed for Jericho or Jerusalem. It was a busy spot, even this early in the day.

Just above the bend in the river there were a few merchants, sellers of oil, grain, dates, grapes, even cloth. Setting up small shelters, they were trying to attract those traveling through.

By early afternoon the number of people had increased. Several groups were headed toward Jericho and the road up to Jerusalem. Traveling together for safety, they wanted to be in Jerusalem for the Harvest Festival.

More than a few paused to look up at John and the men with him. Standing on the first rise above the river, John was drawing a lot of attention. Dressed in his wilderness garment of skins, his long hair blowing in the light breeze, leaning on his heavy staff, he was an imposing figure. They wanted to know! "Who is this?"

Others found the sight to be quite humorous. No one, other than hermits, dressed like that. "Who is this?"

John knew it was time to speak! Yahweh's voice must be heard, now! His first words were electrifying, stopping everyone in their tracks.

"Repent! Repent! Repent! Yahweh's kingdom is at hand! Come and be cleansed, baptized! Only repentance will save you. All of you have sinned. Yahweh's judgment is coming upon you. Unless you repent of your sins, you will not escape the wrath that is to come."

As John continued to speak in booming tones, hands cupped around his mouth, the crowd was hushed. His voice penetrated every ear on both sides of the Jordan. Even the merchants stopped calling out to potential customers. They, too, were listening.

With so many beginning to come closer, some began to question John.

"If what you say is right, what shall we do?"

"Repent of your sins! Be cleansed of your sins. Come to the river and be cleansed, baptized! Come!"

As John continue to speak, calling, pointing his finger with a sweeping motion, he started down the steep slope. By the time he reached the water's edge, a large crowd was pushing in behind him. As he moved farther into the flowing stream, he was faced with more people than he could have imagined. How could he possibly baptize so many?

Calling to his disciples, he gathered them about him, instructing them.

"Ask each one, 'Do you repent of your sins?' When they say 'Yes,' pour water over their heads, or, if the water is deep enough, immerse them, saying 'I baptize you with water in the Name of Yahweh!' You are my disciples and I need your help, now!"

By the time the sun was beginning to drop behind the higher hills to the west, the crowd had thinned out. John and his disciples were elated, but weary. How many had they baptized?

As they moved out of the water, Matthias asked John a question.

"You have said nothing about him, the promised Messiah. From what you have said, and told us, he is coming. He should meet us here, very soon."

"Matthias, you are right, but we must be patient. What we did today will get the attention of the leaders in Jerusalem. I want them to come and hear what I have to say before Jesus comes. They will come; you can depend on it. Some will come tomorrow. We will rest; spend the night in that grove of trees over there.

Waiting for them at the trees were two men, strangers. They had come from the northern territories, looking for John. They had heard! One was a fisherman. The other was a tradesman. The fisherman was called Andrew, the other's name was Judah. They were ready to be baptized of John, ready to follow John!

Sitting around the open fire, John welcomed the two men, introduced them to the other ten. Now, there were twelve, twelve men looking for the fulfillment of Yahweh's kingdom!

A number of those heading toward Jerusalem had shared some items of food, grapes, figs and bread. Full water skins were sufficient for the group. With the darkening shadows moving across the water, John had them pause for a prayer of thanksgiving. Then, after sharing the gifts of food, John talked. Speaking at length, he repeated and shared with the larger group his calling, his mission. He was not their Messiah, only the one preparing the way for the One who was to come. Once John's task was done, all would be free to follow Jesus!

Matthias spoke for the group, responding to John's speech.

"You are our teacher, and we will follow you! Surely, you will be one of his leaders in the restored kingdom. The Messiah will be ours, too, but we will stay with you!"

John knew it would be hard to explain, and the hour was late. In due time they would understand.

He found a comfortable spot and suggested they all rest. Tomorrow would be a busy day!

# CHAPTER 39

*... and they were baptized by him in the river
Jordan, confessing their sins.*

Matthew 3:6

By the time the sun had burned off the mist drifting over the river Jordan, the banks were lined with people. The word had reached Bethany across the Jordan, Jericho and Jerusalem. A new prophet had arisen!

Could it be that the great Elijah had returned? No matter, here was one calling Yahweh's people to repentance, baptizing them in the river.

Today's larger crowd almost overwhelmed John and his disciples. Even with the twelve helping, it was a daunting task. They were coming from the area around the Jordan, from many towns and villages of Judea and from Jerusalem. They wanted to see and hear this imposing figure; one that obviously had no ties to the religious hierarchy. He was from the desert, the wilderness!

With so many present, John knew it was time to take the next step. Beginning with his strong call for repentance and baptism, he moved back into the water with his followers. Then as he continued his cry for repentance, he began to speak of his cousin.

"'I baptize you with water for repentance, but he who comes after me is mightier than I, whose sandals I am not worthy to carry; he will baptize you with the Holy Spirit and with fire!

"His winnowing fork is in his hand, and he will clear his threshing floor and gather his wheat into the granary; but the chaff he will burn with unquenchable fire!"

The crowd was stunned by John's words. Of whom is he speaking? Who would be a mightier figure? Would it be another prophet and when would he appear? The crowd pushed closer, waiting for John's next words. His warning of burning chaff, of unquenchable fire, was frightening. If repentance and baptism were needed, it was time to respond.

The cries could be heard on every hand, asking for John's cleansing by water.

"I confess! I confess my sins. Baptize me, now!"

Those words were repeated over and over as those in the water pushed forward.

Suddenly, there was a hush that spread over the crowd. Some began to draw back into shallow water. John turned and looked up. Standing on the same spot where John and his disciples had stood, were priests and Levites from Jerusalem, dressed in all their regalia. The High Priest had heard and wanted some answers.

One of the priests called out, "Who are you? Are you the Messiah?"

"No! I am not the Messiah!"

Another shouted, "What then? Are you Elijah?

John answered, "I am not!"

"Are you the prophet?"

Again John said, "No!"

Putting their heads together, the priests and Levites tried to come up with another question. They were getting nowhere.

"Who are you? Let us have an answer for those who sent us. What do you say about yourself?"

John almost laughed, and he would have if it had not been such a serious matter. How blind they were, these priests and Levites! They didn't even know the Scriptures! He finally tried once more.

"I am the voice of one crying in the wilderness; make straight the way of the Lord, just as the prophet Isaiah said."

Perplexed by John's response, they tried another approach.

"Then why are you baptizing, if you are neither the Messiah, nor Elijah, nor the prophet?"

John answered them once more, "I baptize you with water, but among you stands one whom you do not know, even he who comes after me, the thongs of whose sandal I am not worthy to untie!"

Then, pointing an accusing finger at those sent from Jerusalem, John shouted so that all would hear, "You brood of vipers! Who warned you to flee from the wrath to come? Bear fruit that befits repentance, and do not presume to say to yourselves, 'We have Abraham as our father,' for I tell you Yahweh is able from these stones to raise up children to Abraham.

"Even now the axe is laid to the root of the trees; every tree therefore that does not bear good fruit is cut down and thrown into the fire!"

With that, he turned his back on his inquisitors, calling again to the waiting crowd. "Repent! Repent! Come, be washed clean. I baptize you with water. Come!"

Some of those in the crowd, having heard the priests and Levites, began to ask their own questions.

"What then should we do?"

It was the same question someone had asked the day before, but this time John gave another answer.

"He who has two coats, let him share with him who has none; and he who has food let him do the same."

Among those who came to be baptized were some hated tax collectors. The crowd tried to shout them down, but John held up his hands for silence.

The tax collectors asked, "Teacher, what shall we do?"

John responded, "Collect no more than is appointed you. Be fair in your collecting."

To a group of soldiers asking the same question, John made it quite clear as he said, "Rob no one by violence, or by false accusation. Be content with your wages. You should protect your people, not harm them."

John and his followers thought they were tired the day before, but at the close of this second day, they were exhausted. Heading for their grove of trees, they were ready to sleep. No one had the energy to fix supper. They would be content to share a few grapes and figs, nothing more.

To their surprise, they found a small fire burning. Sitting over it, on a circle of river rocks was a large pot of lentil soup. On a larger flat rock were small loaves of bread, next to a jar of honey. There were a sufficient number of small bowls, one for each man. Standing in the background shadows were several women. They, too, had been baptized that day. Now they were expressing their thanks and joy by preparing supper.

John invited them to share the food, but they would not. They simply bowed in gratitude and disappeared. Yes, Yahweh did provide!

There was another surprise, a rather large tent erected in the very center of the grove of trees. At first they were sure such a shelter was wasted effort, but it rained just as they were settling down for the night. Someone had a better sense of the weather. Protected from the light shower they were soon asleep, all but John.

Lying awake in the darkness, he tried to picture Jesus' arrival. He knew he would come soon, perhaps tomorrow. How would it go? What was he expected to say? He wasn't sure, but it would have to wait. He was too tired to think.

The crowd was just as large the third day. Other priests and

Levites were there and you could sense their disapproval. They said very little, but John knew their thoughts. The High Priest would get a very negative report on this upstart baptizer!

Then, just as John was starting into the water, he looked up and saw him! There he was, watching and smiling. Catching John's eye, he raised his hand in greeting.

Overcome by Jesus' sudden appearance, John cried out, pointing his finger at his cousin.

"Behold the Lamb of Yahweh, who takes away the sin of the world! This is he of whom I said, ' after me comes a man who ranks before me, for he was before me.' At first I did not know him, but for this I came baptizing with water, so that he might be revealed to Israel."

Jesus moved quickly into the water, came to John and hugged him.

"It is good to see you again. We have missed you. Just look at you, your beard, and your hair. You look like a prophet! How are you, John?"

"Your father was right. He told me you would be here, that I should come right away. It has been a long time, but now we are together again."

"Yes, my dear cousin, we are together again, and there is something you must do for me, baptize me!"

"I can't do that! You don't need baptizing with water for repentance. No, I won't do it."

"John, look at me. Let it be so, now. It is only right. Do it, now! Baptize me!"

What else could he do? Yahweh's own son had commanded it and he must obey. This time, as they stood in deeper water, he immersed his cousin in the flowing stream. As he brought him back up, he said it for all to hear, "You have been baptized in Yahweh's Name! You are the Messiah, our Messiah!"

No one could have ever imagined what came next. There was a brilliant flash of light and a voice, a strong, penetrating voice at the top of the rising light.

*This is my beloved son, with whom I am pleased!*

As the light and voice faded away, John saw a bird, a dove, flying slowly downward, lighting on Jesus' shoulder. John knew, beyond all doubt, it was the Spirit of Yahweh. John's work was done!

His disciples, watching the meeting of the two men, stood riveted where they were. They had not been able to hear the interchange between John and Jesus, but they had watched the baptism, John baptizing his cousin. It made no sense. Was he really the promised Messiah?

The people engrossed in their own desire for baptism, wondered. Was this truly the Lamb of Yahweh? It must be right for John had said so and John spoke the truth. What should they do, follow John or the one he baptized?

Standing above the scene in the waters of the Jordan, the priests and Levites continued to shake their heads in disapproval. To them, John was a charlatan, a hoax, and that other character could not be the Messiah. Ridiculous! Impossible! They had wasted their time in coming.

With the crowd pressing around him, John moved toward the shore. He wanted to talk more with his cousin. He needed his thoughts on what would happen next. Yahweh had told him long before, his work would be done once Jesus came. He wanted confirmation of that from Jesus, but he couldn't find him. He had disappeared.

Disappointed, he left his disciples in the water, telling them to continue baptizing. He would see them later at the shelter in the grove.

It was a strange feeling. Where would he go from here? What was Jesus expecting of him? Now was the time to act. Together they would carry out Yahweh's plan for freedom and peace. He had no idea just how they would go about it, but they had to do something. Jesus had come to deliver them from bondage! Evil must be eradicated! Surely Yahweh would speak, and soon!

That night there was nothing, no voice. Yahweh was silent. None of his disciples had seen Jesus leave. They had no idea where he had gone. They did have one bit of news told them by a group from Jerusalem. King Herod had done something the people knew was wrong, and many were discussing it. They had confessed their sins. They had repented, but kings don't do that when they sin.

"Tell me," asked John, "What has he done this time? He thinks he is a king, but is not, really. He is only a petty ruler appointed by the Roman emperor. He is not one of us, not a son of Abraham. Anyway, Yahweh's son will be our king! However, tell me what you heard about Herod. What were they saying?"

"Herod has a half-brother named Philip. He is only a tetrarch, living up in Galilee, but he had a very pretty wife. We are told Herod took that wife, Herodias, away from Philip. She and her daughter Salome are now living with him. Philip is furious, but there is nothing he can do. Herod is too powerful."

John thought for a long time before responding. He shook his head, saddened by their report.

"If what you tell me is true, our so-called king has committed adultery. That is wrong! Someone should tell him so!"

"But John, who will do that? No one would listen to us. None of his family will speak up. Philip might be angry, but he has no power."

"I will speak up. I must! If I call Yahweh's people to repent, I can call Herod to repent, and I will. Tomorrow, while I wait for Jesus to return, I will preach. I will denounce evil, all evil, Herod's evil. Now I am weary, wondering what will come next. I pray that Yahweh will give us a peaceful night."

# CHAPTER 40

*Come O blessed of my Father, inherit the kingdom
prepared for you from the foundation of the world.*
                              Matthew 25:34

Where was Jesus? In the excitement and confusion of yesterday's awesome events, Jesus had simply disappeared. He was not to be found and no one had any clue as to his whereabouts. It was a mystery.

Although the crowd was smaller, there were a few newcomers seeking baptism. A number had walked all the way from Samaria and Galilee. The word had spread like wildfire, even to the northern territories. John had spoken of the Messiah, had identified the Messiah and had baptized him. If this man Jesus was the Promised One, they wanted to see him and hear what he had to say.

So, they were there to be baptized, wanting to see Jesus. Perhaps there would be more spectaculars today, another burst of light.

Early that morning, John had gathered his disciples around him. He needed to talk, share his thoughts. He was facing a new challenge in his life and the path ahead was difficult to see.

"I want you to know how much you have meant to me. I

have come to love you as brothers. My life has been enriched by your presence. Now, I must leave you. My work is done!"

Over their protests, he insisted they hear him out. He had to point them away from himself and to the Messiah. They would find in him the one they were really seeking.

"Yahweh told me years ago, I would be the forerunner of his son, the Messiah. I have done what I was called to do. He has come and the work of redemption will be on his shoulders. Like you, I wonder where he is, now. What will he do next? I don't know. Perhaps he will return to us today. I hope so. You can be sure you will see him again!

"When he does come, follow him, not me. He will lead you into all truth and into the wonderful work of the Kingdom. You came to me because of him, because of what I had said of him. He will be the fulfillment of your dreams and hopes. Trust me! He will come and use you to do what Yahweh has planned for our world, for our people.

"In the meantime, let us continue with our work here. As we baptize, I will be speaking to those who have come. Perhaps Herod will hear what I have to say about him. That will be dangerous. I know that, but I must speak! As long as we can, let us be faithful to our calling."

All twelve stood around John in a small circle, disturbed by what they had heard. Surely their leader, their rabbi, would not desert them. Yet, at the same time, catching the sense of what he was saying, they knew! He would leave them.

One by one they approached him, knelt before him, placing his hands on their heads. Then, with eyes filled with tears they embraced him. All were silent. No words would come!

With fewer people to be baptized, John made his way to a higher spot overlooking the river. Raising his arms for attention, he began to speak.

"People of Yahweh, hear me well. The Messiah has come. He was here yesterday and will return soon. I have baptized you with water, but he will baptize you with the fire of the Holy Spirit. You must hear and follow him. He will redeem Israel. He will set you free. He will bring peace to our land. He, not I, will lead you.

"You have come, repenting of your sins, seeking baptism, and that is proper. All sinners must repent, all sinners, those in high places as well as those in low positions. We have a so-called king named Herod. He rules over us, but he, like you and me, is a sinner. He has done a terrible thing. He has committed adultery, taking his brother's wife. He has sinned! He, too, must repent. Yahweh demands it of him.

"I do not know why our priests, our High Priest, have not condemned Herod. If they do not, they have failed to speak for Yahweh. They are a brood of vipers, also sinners. Surely, Yahweh will strike them down unless they, too, repent!"

As John continued to speak, several men moved back from the river, mounted their horses and rode hurriedly away. They had a message to deliver to their king. The prophet had stepped across the line. Preaching about Yahweh was one thing; to condemn the king was treason!

The day passed, but there was no sign of Jesus. For John there was no word from Yahweh. Puzzled, he retired to the grove of trees early. The crowd had departed. John was sure they would not return. He had spoken out against their ruler and their religious leaders. It would be foolish, dangerous for them to come back again. As John fell asleep, he had no answers. His head ached and his heart was heavy, but there was no relief. He had done his best. The rest was up to Yahweh.

Before dawn, John and his disciples were awakened by a large band of soldiers. Kicking and pushing the disciples aside they bound John with ropes and tied him across a horse. Quickly, they rode away with their prisoner. There was no question in

John's mind. These were Herod's men, taking him to Herod's fortress and to his prison. He was sure Herod would not let him go!

The pain was excruciating! With no regard for his comfort, the soldiers had lashed John tightly to the back of the horse. His arms and legs were going numb. He could scarcely breathe. The dust kicked up by the horses' hooves was choking him. He passed out.

He was awakened once, choking on the smell of smoke. The soldiers had stopped to rest and water their horses. In the distance John could see flames rising above the horizon. In his position he could not tell, but he shuttered with the thought. It could mean only one thing. Villages were being destroyed and people were dying! Was he dreaming, or was this the feared tragedy he had predicted? Again, for John, there, there was darkness, oblivion for both body and soul!

When John awoke, he could hardly move. He was cold! His throat was dry, very dry. Every bone in his body ached. Almost as bad was the darkness. There was a little light somewhere in the distance, but it wasn't much help. As best he could tell, he was sitting on a rough stone floor, his back against a wall of stone. He was in Herod's fortress prison.

He had no idea of time. Was it night or day? His beloved wilderness was shut off from his sight. The beautiful blue sky was no longer there for him to enjoy. The warmth of the sun had been cut off. His world of open valleys and rugged hills had vanished. The animals, the deer, the birds, the eagles floating high above were gone. There was only cold and darkness!

The space was small, but John could move about, a few steps in each direction. On one side there was a door, a small iron door. There were chains attached to the wall, but John had not been put in chains. Apparently, the soldiers had simply thrown him into his small space.

Standing up, taking a few steps was helpful. John moved arms and legs as best he could. Regaining some strength, he felt better. The cuts and bruises should heal, if he lived that long. He had no illusions concerning his future.

Hours passed, but there were no sounds heard outside his cell. All was quiet. The darkness enveloped everything. He could see somewhat better now, as his eyes adjusted to the dark. He had always been able to see well at night.

Peering through the door, he could see a passageway going off to his right. There was a small glimmer of light in that direction, most likely a torch fastened to a wall.

As more time went by, John decided to bring things to a head. He would try to get some attention, no matter the consequences. He cleared his throat and began to shout.

"Herod, you are an evil man! You have sinned! You have broken Yahweh's Law. He condemns you and will cast you into outer darkness. Do you hear me? You are an evil man!"

Silence! There was no response. An hour went by, and no one came. John tried again, repeating his words of condemnation, scathing words that no one else would have dared utter.

Another hour went by. It was then he heard some noise in the distance, and light. Someone was coming down the stone passageway. Peering out through the door John saw four guards. He laughed. Four guards! Was he that dangerous?

However, as they came closer, opening the door, he knew the reason for four guards. There stood Herod himself. It had to be Herod. No one else would have dressed so finely.

"So you say I am a sinner," Herod chuckled. "Aren't we all sinners? Are you not a sinner? Tell me, who will do anything about our sinning? You spoke harshly about me at the Jordan, you called me bad names, but what happened? Your Yahweh did nothing to protect you. Now you are my prisoner. It seems to me your sins are worse than mine. I am still king and you are no longer free."

John listened, looking intently into Herod's eyes without

flinching. He would not be intimidated. Yahweh would have the last word, regardless, and he said so.

"Yes, we are all sinners. I am probably the worst. I should have proclaimed Yahweh's word to you and to all others much sooner and more forceful. I repeat what I have finally said. You have sinned! You have ignored Yahweh's Law."

The guards were appalled! No one had ever spoken to King Herod like that. Anyone else daring to do so would have been executed on the spot. Herod only laughed.

"I like that! You have done what no one has done. You speak your mind. I like that. Tell me what you think about this Yahweh you say makes laws for us to obey. Sure, I know your people worship him, but tell me why you worship him.

"But, not now. I am tired of this discussion, and this filthy place. We will talk later, when I have nothing else to do. You can entertain me. Guards, go to the kitchen. Find some food and drink for this prophet. When it is ready, take him up the corridor to the first guard station. There is a table there where he can eat. We must take care of our guest!"

Herod laughed again, turned and walked away. The guards locked the door and hurried after him. They had never seen anything so perplexing, but who were they to question their master!

Herod's orders were obeyed, and quickly. Before long, the door was opened and two guards led John up the corridor. At the guard's station there was food and drink. The meat was pheasant, the bread unleavened. There was an abundance of figs and grapes, also some nuts. The drink was wine, but there was also a flask of water.

John could fast, refuse Herod's hospitality, or else sit down and eat. He decided to eat. He was hungry. Taking his time, he tried to engage the guards in conversation.

"My name is John. What are your names? Where were you born? I was born just outside of Jerusalem. My father was a priest in the Temple. Have you ever been to the Temple?"

The guards looked at each other, not knowing how they

should react. Finally, the older one smiled, answering John's question.

"Yes, I have been to the Temple. I was born in Jerusalem, grew up there. I never knew your father because we didn't go to the Temple very much. We were more concerned with making a living for our large family. That's why I'm here as one of the king's men. He takes care of his soldiers and guards.

"My friend here is too young to be a guard, or a soldier, but he is learning."

"And your names?" John asked.

"It really doesn't matter, but my name is Simon and his is Jonathan."

"That's interesting. My father had a Division leader named Jonathan. He still holds that position in the Temple. You have a good name."

The young guard blushed and turned away. They shouldn't be talking with the prisoners!

John finished his meal and the dishes were taken away. The guards took him back to his stone cell. He was alone, again. The lighted torch disappeared with the guards and John was left in darkness. He had forgotten to ask about the hour, where the sun was in the sky. Was it day or was it night? He would ask next time someone came.

As the hours went by, John had time to reflect on the past several days. He had approached the River Jordan with great expectations. He and Jesus would meet and declare Yahweh's intent and plan. They, together, would call upon the people to repent and join forces for action. He envisioned a march on Jerusalem, confronting the religious leaders. It did not happen. Jesus had disappeared! His own work was done. Now, from all he could tell, he faced either death or slavery.

With all the uncertainties surrounding him, John called upon the name of Yahweh; "I ask you to help me, hear my prayer!"

There was silence. Yahweh was silent, even though John

knew he had been heard. Why? There had to be a reason, but he would have to wait. There was nothing to do, but wait, and sleep. Propping himself up in a corner he tried to sleep, but with little success. Finally, he slid down and went to sleep curled up on the floor. Later, when he did wake up, he found himself covered with a blanket. Someone had taken pity on him! He wondered whom he might thank.

Several days went by. John was fed on a regular schedule, learning the time of day. It wasn't easy to keep track, but the guards helped. He asked the guards if Herod permitted any one to visit his fortress. Would it be possible for some of his disciples to come see him? Surely, that would not create a threat to their king. Most shook their heads, but the older guard, Simon, said he might get a chance to ask, depending on the king's mood. One never knew!

Weeks went by and John was shaken by doubts he had never experienced before. Here he was, locked up in a hilltop prison, and nothing, from all he could tell, or learn from his guards, had changed. Surely, the guards would have heard of any momentous events. They were not that isolated from the outside world. The Messiah, Jesus, had come, but nothing was different. Why? What was his cousin doing to change things? Yahweh had raised John up to proclaim the coming of Yahweh's son, but was all that in vain? Had he spent his life, wasted his life on a false dream? His doubts were gnawing deeper and deeper. He could not sleep. He paced the limited space of his stone enclosure. He called for Yahweh, but there was only silence.

A few days later Herod surprised him with another visit. John was eating at the guard's station when he suddenly appeared.

"I understand you would like to see your friends. I'm not sure where we will find them, but I will send one of my men. Most likely they have all run away. Yahweh worshippers do that, you know."

"Sir, I don't think so. They can be found, most likely near Qumran. If you will permit that I will give your man their names."

"Fine, but tell me, what has your Yahweh done for you these past weeks? Tell me about him. What sort of power does he have?"

John knew he had to be careful with his answers. He did not want to anger Herod, but he had to answer truthfully. Hopefully, he could touch this ruler. It might be his only chance.

"Sir, this world we live in was created by Yahweh. We believe that. Also, we believe he created people, like you and me. I'm sure you know our history is a long one, how far back we are not sure.

"In this creation he gave us certain rules to live by, telling us how to get along with one another. Some are chosen to rule, like yourself. We believe rulers should take care of their people, protect them from any enemy, and make sure they obey Yahweh's laws.

"Long ago, almost at the very beginning, there were those who disregarded Yahweh's laws, doing what was wrong and bad. We call that sin. Such has continued. Today our land is ruled for the most part by the Romans. We believe that is wrong. We should be free. What do you think?"

Herod had to agree on one thing, the Romans. He hated them, too. However, Herod was a realist. The Romans were too powerful.

"Tell me, John, why doesn't your Yahweh drive out the Romans? If he is so powerful he ought to be able to do that."

"Sir, Yahweh works in his own way, and I can't answer your question. Yet, he has sent his own son into the world. He is the Anointed One, the Messiah. He will set us free!"

Herod roared with laughter. This was too much, the very idea of a Messiah. John had lost his mind! Yet, for a brief moment, Herod stopped laughing, peering into the distance. He had heard there was a new prophet. People were flocking to hear him. His name was Jesus!

Surprised by his sudden, lengthy silence, the guards glanced at each other with raised eyebrows. Their king was acting strangely. They would have been more surprised if they had been able to grasp his thoughts. Deeply inside, Herod shivered. There was a hard knot in his stomach. Surely, this desert so-called prophet was a babbling idiot. There was no Yahweh-appointed Messiah. There was no Yahweh, only the gods of fate, and Herod controlled his own fate!

Abruptly, Herod stood up, ready to leave. As he started up the corridor he turned back.

"Your friends, only three of your friends, may come. Tell my man their names."


Early one morning, the steel door was thrown open and John was escorted to the guard's station. Standing there was Matthias, Jonathan and Thaddaeus, all from Qumran. Rushing forward with tears in his eyes, John embraced them. They, too, were weeping for joy. John was alive!

"Tell me about yourselves. How are you? What have you been doing? Where have you been?"

Matthias was the first to speak, his voice cracking with emotion.

"The Romans came, burning, pillaging and killing. Many men were taken away. Several smaller villages were attacked, including Tobba. Apparently some of the men, the hunters, fought back, but were struck down. Others fled into the western wilderness. We could not find any others alive."

What about Tobiah and his family? What about Debra, his daughter?"

"We don't know, John. Their bodies were not found, even though we searched through the burned buildings. We searched the area as best we could."

John couldn't stop asking questions. As he talked, overcome with emotion, he wept.

They did their best to give John the answers he wanted. They were well, but had gone back to Jericho. That was now their home, having no other place to go. Qumran had been attacked and pillaged. Most of the men had been taken away. Kemuel had died in the fighting, trying to defend his people.

They had heard stories about Jesus, that he was far up in Galilee, but could give no details. Andrew and some others had gone with him.

John knew Herod would not permit a long visit. He had to know what Jesus was doing, why nothing had changed.

"Matthias, Jonathan, Thaddaeus, I want you to go directly to Galilee and find Jesus. Tell him you have seen me and ask him this question, 'Are you the one who was to come, promised by your father Yahweh, or will we have to wait for another?' Then come back here with his answer. I have to know! I have to know why all this destruction of our people has not been avenged. Evil has the upper hand, and my heart is broken. Surely, Yahweh will act, and soon!"

John was right. The guards pushed his friends out, but promised they would let them visit again. Herod had given his approval.

Two more weeks went by, with John wrestling with his doubts. Almost in despair, he waited. The days and nights went by dreadfully slow. He had difficulty sleeping, thinking of his many friends who had lived alongside the Salt Sea. They had never been a threat to anyone!

Finally, they returned. They came with Jesus' answer, to John a disturbing answer.

Matthias was, again, the spokesman for the group.

"Yes, we saw Jesus, talked with him. Strangely enough, he said he knew where you were, in Herod's prison. Then he said, 'Tell John what you hear and see: the blind receive their sight and the lame walk, lepers are cleansed and the deaf hear, and the dead are raised up, and the poor have good news preached to them. My father is working through me,'

"John, those were his very words. We didn't understand all he said, but we did see what he was doing. He was performing miracles, the like of which no one had ever seen before. Sending us back to you, he had one final word. 'In the kingdom of Yahweh, John is the greatest. He has done all things well.'

They had no time for more. The three were pushed out. John could only stand and stare. What did Jesus mean?

That night John went over Jesus' words again and again. Where were the changes? What about the Romans? When would Yahweh's people be set free? What did miracles have to do with the Messiah's coming to earth? In John's mind, one thing was certain. Jesus was the one! Only Yahweh could do what his own disciples had seen. Yet, what would come out of that?

Moving back and forth in his small cell, John wrestled with questions and doubts flooding in upon him. His whole life, from that Yahweh-promised conception, had been led, moved, pushed by the divine hand. He had been chosen to do great things, prepare the way for the restoration of Israel, the saving of his people. Sure, he had his moments of weakness. He had even questioned Yahweh's place and purpose in his life, but he had done what he had been told to do. He had been faithful!

Now it had come to this! Cut off from his beautiful world, his wilderness, separated from his friends, there was no glimmer of light, no hope for tomorrow.

"Yahweh! I am cut off from the land of the living. I have been thrown into darkness! I live in the pit of Sheol! Let me hear, or let me die!"


His answer came in the middle of the night, the voice of Yahweh.

"John, John, my son is right. Of all men, you are the greatest. You have finished your mission. You have done well! I know this has demanded your all, your life, but you have fulfilled my promises from of old. In my eternal kingdom, you will live in joy forever.

"Now, understand what my son is doing. The one word you have wrestled with, looked for, is the word love. As we love you, we love all people, our total creation, from the very beginning to the present. We love your enemies, those who abuse you. You have shared and shown that love to many people, in many places. That will bear good fruit in years to come. Because of you, many others will share that same love.

"My own son will give his life in love. You will not see that, but it will be done. The world will learn and be changed forever. Your life has not been lived in vain! You have helped bring in the dawn of a new day, a day that will reach into all eternity for the whole world. Rest in peace!"

Yahweh had said it, loud and clear. His work was not in vain, and Yahweh was right. The word was love; love for him and for all people. Evil could not be eradicated by force, but by love. Evil would have its own reward. Yahweh's word would stand forever. Herod would have to face that. Yahweh would be triumphant. He would have the final word. Somehow, somewhere, the light would shine, the light of Yahweh's redeeming love.

John slept well that night, the first time in many nights. All during the following day he thought of the people who had touched his life, supporting him along the way. He had been blessed. No matter what came, he could look back on many precious memories.

The next day was a peaceful one. He did miss the beauty of the sky, a sky sometimes speckled with white patches of clouds. How many times had he watched the movement of Yahweh's heavens and the soaring eagles lifted on the wind! He missed the freedom they enjoyed as they floated silently high overhead. How many times had he wished he could soar like that, totally and completely free from the turmoil at hand! Isaiah had said something about that, and he tried to remember.

Finally the day came to an end and his guards summoned him to his small table set in the passageway. Tonight his keepers were pleasant and he enjoyed the food. Finally, back in his cell, he settled down for the night.

Sometime later, and he wasn't sure how long he had slept, he was awakened by the sound of heavy sandals. Two guards, giving no explanation, pulled him out into the dimly lighted passageway. Behind them stood a man he did not recognize. In his hand he held something John had seen before, an executioner's axe.

Aware of what was happening, John felt pity for the younger of the two guards. He was trembling, violently. He, too, knew what was taking place. As they forced him down, John spoke to both men:

"Let me lie on my back, and do not be afraid. It will be over, very soon. My Yahweh is calling me home!"

Now, he remembered what Isaiah had said. Those ancient words were now his!

> *Those who wait for the Lord will renew their strength.*
> *They shall mount up with wings like eagles!"*
> *They will run and not be weary.*
> *They shall walk and not faint!*

He was going home!

What was it the old woman had predicted, back there in the grove of trees near the coastal road?

"You will die!"

With a quizzical expression on his face, that was John's last thought. 'Naamah was right!'

# EPILOGUE

It was spring. The day was cloudy; the sky overcast. There was little traffic along the road running parallel to the Dead Sea. There was a war going on, the Palestinian War of 1947.

On the side of the road away from the water there was a wide but shallow wadi. Two Bedouin shepherd boys, were walking along the sandy bottom, looking for their goats. Goats were valuable and they dared not go home without them. Climbing around and up the sides of the steep, rather forbidding, cliffs rising high above the wadi, they stumbled into a cave. To their surprise they found a number of tall jars, some stone and some clay. Several tops had fallen off and were broken.

Curious about their discovery, they pulled out several linen-wrapped rolls of leather. With no idea as to what these were, they took their find to a nearby market. Although the leather was quite old, they could perhaps have sandals made, and sell the rest.

Scrolls! Before long the world knew better. The discoveries made that spring would not end up as sandals, but as confirmation of God's (or should we say Yahweh's) word of promise. How was it said long ago?

*The Word of the Lord shall stand forever!*

Two thousand years earlier, under the cover of darkness, a small band of men had scaled those same cliffs, placing in that cave, and others, the Scrolls, Yahweh's words of promise, confident those writings would survive.

In the ancient city of Jerusalem there is a building, built around those treasured documents hidden centuries before.

Those Scrolls stand as a tribute to those who prepared them and those who hid them. They hold high the everlasting Word and point to the one who answered Yahweh's call, something the prophet Isaiah had predicted even earlier:

> *In the wilderness prepare the way of the Lord,*
> *Make straight in the desert a highway for our*
> *God.*

The Herods of the world are all but forgotten. One who faced the wrong and evil, who served his Lord to the end, will never be forgotten . . .

> . . . *the voice of one crying in the wilderness.*

His word, too, will stand forever!

BVG